Worlds Collide

Sunset Rising, Book Two

By

S.M. McEachern

Published by Clownfish Publishing

Summary:
The continuing story of Sunny O'Donnell and Jack Kenner and their quest to free the Pit.

Young Adult (16+) Science Fiction/Dystopian

Cover Art and Design: Nathália Suellen
Edited by: Joann Dominik, Red Adept Editing
Proofreader: Christina Galvez

Special thanks to Dr. Adam Johan Bergren, National Institute of Nanotechnology

Author's website: smmceachern.com

ISBN: 978-0-9917330-6-4

Let freedom reign.
The sun never set on so glorious a human achievement.

- Nelson Mandela
July 18, 1918 to December 5, 2013

Sunset Rising Series
by S.M.McEachern

The ease and imagery of S.M. McEachern's writing style is so captivating you are truly sucked into the story ... This book has it all: love story, good vs evil, drama, suspense - definitely a book you can't put down!

– Midwest Book Review

Worlds Collide blew me away! I was enthralled throughout the entire narrative: the plot twists, the characters, the suspense and conspiracy, it was all captivating and superb!

– Sparrow's Reading Corner

New World Order was a thrilling read! It was a great way to end a series and I'm looking forward to see what future stories from the Pit may hold.

– Juniper Grove Reading Blog

Worlds Collide is the second book of the *Sunset Rising* trilogy, and picks up exactly where the first book left off.

For reviews, series updates, and satellite stories on the series, please visit the author's website:

smmceachern.com

CHAPTER ONE

I watched speechlessly as a man ran toward us at full speed. Dressed in dirty, tattered clothing too big for his skeletal frame, he pointed wildly behind him. Jack moved protectively in front of me, but the man ran past, screaming at us to run, too.

Something was coming.

The distant hum of machines became louder, drowning out the sound of my pounding heart. I clutched Jack's arm just as the first bike came flying out from the trees, following the same path the man had taken just seconds before. The person sitting astride the vehicle brought it to a screeching halt when he saw us. A second bike came out of the woods and skidded to a stop behind the first. They wore the uniforms of Dome soldiers, with guns strapped to their thighs and rifles slung across their backs.

In one single moment, all my hopes for freeing the Pit came crashing down. The bourge were already out here.

The discovery shouldn't have taken me by surprise, but it did. Even though I knew what a liar President Holt was, it never occurred to me that he could be lying about the condition of the Earth. All his talk of drones coming back with only radioactive material sounded true. And why shouldn't it? We had been taught since birth that the Dome was the only sanctuary on a badly crippled planet. But now I fully understood the lengths the Holt regime went to in order to ensure the obedience of its people.

Fear, disappointment, and the urge to run all vied for my undivided attention. I wouldn't run without Jack—we were in this together. And the odds of me making it very far while blinded by the sun were slim at best. That left fear and disappointment for me to grapple with.

More bikes roared toward us and one came flying off a ledge high above our heads. Another followed, but that driver fell off his vehicle and hit the ground with a thud. His bike flew farther, its wheels still spinning as it skidded into the trees. He picked himself up, brushing away the dirt and leaves with a joyful "whoop!"

One of the soldiers glared at him. "You idiot," he said. "It better not be broken or you'll be paying for it with your own credits." He turned his angry glower on us, but his frown quickly dissipated when he saw Jack. "For chrissake, is that you, Kenner?" He dismounted his vehicle and walked up to Jack, his hand outstretched.

"Or should I be calling you *Mr.* Kenner now that you're part of the presidential family?"

With the admission of Jack's identity, the rest of the group snapped to attention. Shock and confusion quickly took center stage as I saw the genuine smile the man gave Jack and the respect the group now showed him. Didn't they know we were traitors on the run from President Holt?

Jack had been slightly crouched in a defensive position, but as the man walked toward him, he straightened, and squared his shoulders. "What the hell are you doing out here, Alex?" he asked, accepting his handshake. "I haven't seen you in at least a year."

"When they offered me this gig, I jumped at it. I couldn't believe we were able to leave the Dome. I've been out here in the clean, fresh air ever since," Alex said. "What are you doing out here? Oh wait, I bet you're Dirk's replacement. You two always were the best tech guys."

Still clutching Jack's arm, I felt him stiffen for just a moment before he easily lied. "You guessed it. What happened to Dirk anyway? Did he go back inside?"

"He drove his bike off the side of a mountain. You know, as smart as that guy thought he was, he couldn't follow simple instructions."

"Yeah, I know. I wonder why they picked *him* to come out," Jack said. I wasn't sure what surprised me more; the jealous edge in his tone or his ability to show no fear.

"I think the president had a different job in mind for

you," Alex said, conspiratorially. "Speaking of which, aren't you supposed to be on your honeymoon?"

Alex glanced in my direction and I stepped behind Jack a little farther, vainly trying to make myself small and inconspicuous. I wished I had Jack's confidence. My heart was pounding so hard I was sure every man there could hear it.

"You know Holt doesn't believe in time off. He ordered me back to work right after the wedding."

Alex was still staring at me but laughed when Jack did. My anxiety at being trapped in the forest with four armed bourge grew. It was obvious they thought Jack was still the presidential heir, so he was safe. But I was an urchin and they could do whatever they wanted to me.

"I see you brought a playmate with you," Alex observed. "I didn't think the Kenners were into that."

"*That* was too bold," Jack said in a hard voice. "I know we were college buddies, Alex, but that doesn't give you liberties. You'll speak to me with respect."

Alex quickly looked away from me and stood up straighter in front of Jack. "My apologies, sir. It won't happen again."

I turned my face toward the ground to hide my look of shock. Out here, Jack wasn't a criminal. He had authority and I knew with certainty it was the only thing keeping us alive right now.

"How far is the base from here?" Jack's tone was all business.

"Southwest a few miles. By the way, where's all your gear?"

He shrugged. "I was trying to cross a river and lost it."

"Hopefully an urchin doesn't get hold of it, especially if there are weapons in your pack. This is the range. One of us could have shot you."

"The range?"

"Yeah—the shooting range. We send the troublemakers here." Alex patted the pistol strapped to his thigh. "Hunting a moving target is an excellent way to hone your skills."

An image of the terrified man who had just run past flashed through my head. Alex was smirking at me and I realized my mouth was hanging open, disgust written all over my face.

"Don't worry, sweetheart—we only send the men here. We have other ways of disciplining the women," he assured me. He unclipped a communicator from his belt. "This is Captain Mills to base, do you read?"

"Go ahead Captain Mills."

"Inform General Powell we have Captain Kenner and will be bringing him back to camp. ETA is fifteen minutes."

"Yes sir."

Alex returned the communicator to his belt, straddled his bike and motioned for Jack to get on the back. "Hop on. The urchin can go with one of them."

"I'll take her," a soldier volunteered.

I expected Jack to come up with an excuse for why

we couldn't go with them, so I was blindsided when he strode confidently toward Alex.

"Go," he ordered, with barely a backward glance in my direction.

For a split second I was stunned by how easily he slipped back into the role of heir. But I knew our lives depended on both of us convincing these men we were meant to be there. The soldier moved forward on the seat, making room for me at the back.

As I approached the bike, he motioned toward the rifle slung over my shoulder. "Why don't you let me take that for you? Don't want it going off if we hit a bump." I gave him the rifle and he slung it across his chest. I straddled the seat, doing my best not to make contact with the man. "Now you be sure to hang on tight."

He revved the engine a few times as we waited for Jack and Alex to take the lead. As the bike jerked forward, I had no choice but to clutch my driver. We picked up speed, bounding over rough terrain and snaking our way around rocks and trees. With every bump, my back screamed in pain. To make matters worse, as we broke out of the woods I was forced to close my eyes against the brilliant sun. Then we were flying through the air and my driver yelled, "Woohoo!" I forced my eyes open and saw the ground coming up at us fast. We hit hard and the bike careened from side to side as my driver struggled to get control. Ignoring the searing pain in my side, I clung to him more tightly and braced for impact, but he righted the bike and increased his speed. I relaxed my hold on him.

Just when I thought I couldn't take the constant bouncing and jolting, the ground suddenly became smooth. It looked manmade. Steeling myself against the glare of the sun, I raised my head to see where we were going. Not far ahead were buildings—lots of them—and other vehicles shared the road. It was a town, just like out of the movies.

My driver slowed down and brought the vehicle to a halt alongside the curb. Resting the bike on its stand, he dismounted, walked to Jack, and gave him my rifle.

Thankfully, the shadow of a building gave me a little respite from the full glare of the sun. Half blind and not sure what I was supposed to do, I got off the bike and stood on trembling legs.

"General Powell, sir," Jack said in a clear voice. "I see the rumors of your illness have been greatly exaggerated."

Peering through narrowed eyes, I watched Jack greet a short, older man wearing a well-decorated military uniform.

"It's all a ruse, Jack. That's just a cover story so no one in the Dome would miss me while I'm out here," General Powell said, clasping his hand around Jack's. "I'm surprised to see you, though."

"You know my father-in-law. It took a bit of convincing, but he knew I was the best tech guy for the job."

Powell nodded in agreement. "It's true. You are. In

fact, I tried to convince Damien to send you out last year instead of Dirk, but your engagement to his daughter put a wrench in that. Speaking of Leisel, I can't imagine she was happy letting you come out here, given Damien's no-return policy."

Squinting up at the sky, Jack ran a hand through his hair. His confident demeanor faltered for a split second. I held my breath, wondering if anyone else had noticed. Then his mouth curved into a self-assured smile.

"That policy doesn't apply to *me*, General." There was a note of challenge in his tone, but he softened it with his next words. "I mean, if you can't trust the next president to keep state secrets, who can you trust?"

General Powell narrowed his eyes, but otherwise his face remained emotionless. "Forgive me. I forgot who I was speaking to." The men regarded each other for a moment. Powell was the first to look away, his gaze coming to rest on me. "I see you brought company with you."

Jack barely cast a glance my way. "You don't expect me to do my own housekeeping while I'm out here, do you?"

The general broke into a hearty laugh. "Housekeeping! Is that what they're calling it these days?" He gave Jack a friendly slap on the shoulder. "She needs to get tagged." He motioned toward me.

I had just gotten my heart rate under control when the group turned to look at me. Immediately, I turned my eyes toward the ground like every good urchin should in the company of the bourge.

"Tagged?" he asked.

The general nodded. "The president's rule. And it applies to everyone."

Jack shrugged. "No problem here. What is it? Some kind of birth control?"

"No," he shook his head. "Just control. Damien wanted to keep Culling them, but I said we needed them here to help build the city and do the farming. So I came up with the tagging system to convince him it was safe to let them come out. We installed subterranean electrical fences around their enclosures, farms, the range and anywhere else we put them to work, and a tag right behind the jugular, so if they try to cross the fence, poof. Dead. We've only had a few casualties in the urchin corrals, more in the range."

"Wow, that's ingenious. And you came up with that all by yourself?" Jack asked. I heard the hint of sarcasm in his voice but noticed the general had not.

"I admit Dirk was the brain child behind that one," Powell said sheepishly. He redirected his gaze to Alex. "Assign someone to take her to Doc."

"I'll take her myself," Jack said.

"Taking an urchin to get tagged is a little below your station," Powell said.

"Take her," Alex ordered the soldier who drove me here.

As the soldier walked past me, he beckoned for me to follow. I didn't want to get tagged, and I really didn't want to be separated from Jack, especially in my current state of half-blindness. I cast a covert glance at Jack, hoping for some kind of sign that I should stay—maybe even an excuse for why I couldn't go—but his focus remained on the general.

I turned and followed my assigned escort, forcing my trembling legs to move one foot in front of the other. Luckily the buildings were close together, so I could stay mostly in the shadows. If I kept my eyes on the ground with my hair falling around my face, I was able to keep them open. Unfortunately it meant that my curtain of hair prevented me from getting a good look at the city—a discovery my mind hadn't had time to process yet. Even more shocking was the news that the urchins weren't Culled—they were sent out here instead. *My mother could still be alive!*

Despite the maelstrom of emotions coursing through me, I managed to keep pace with my escort. We walked in silence for about ten minutes before he led me into a building. Here the light was much dimmer and it didn't take long for my strained eyes to adjust to the more comfortable setting. Directly in front of us was a large desk and to the right several chairs lined the walls. A young, delicate-looking man sat behind the desk. He stood at attention when we entered.

"Got an urchin that needs to be tagged," my escort barked.

"She's young."

"Yeah. Jack Kenner brought her out with him."

Delicate Man looked confused. "You mean the heir?"

"That would be the one," the soldier proudly confirmed. "She's a priority."

"Of course. I'll tell Doc." Delicate Man rushed away and returned a few minutes later. "He'll see you now." He gestured for me to go with him. My escort took a step to walk with me, but Delicate Man held up his hand to stop him. "Doc wants to see her alone."

The soldier looked disappointed, but he stepped back and took a seat.

I was led into a smaller room where curtains had been drawn and the lights were even dimmer. A man wearing a lab coat sat on a stool looking into a microscope. His thinning dark hair was streaked with grey and the overhead light glinted off a bald spot on the crown of his head. "Give her a gown," he said without looking up.

Delicate Man did as he was told and left.

I wondered if he expected me to undress and put the gown on. No one had given me instructions, and I wasn't comfortable being naked in front of this man. I put the gown on over my clothes.

"Is that your idea of joke?" he asked, looking up from his machine.

I gasped when I saw his black eyes.

Doc was from the Pit.

Chapter Two

"No." The word squeaked out of me. I realized that was the first word I had spoken since the soldiers had found us. I cleared my throat. "No," I said in a clearer, stronger voice.

"There's a screen behind me if your modesty requires it." He returned his attention to the microscope.

My modesty did require it, so I walked to the back of the room and stepped behind the screen. I stripped off my clothes and tried to put on the gown, but it didn't have any buttons or zippers to keep it closed. Not sure of which way I was expected to wear it, I decided to put the open side at the back. I held the back of the gown together with my hand as I came out from behind the curtain.

"How old are you?" he asked.

"Almost eighteen."

"So, you're seventeen. Are you sterilized?" I shook

my head. "So there's a chance you could be pregnant."

"No!" I said, offended by the thought. My outburst made Doc look up from his microscope. He gave me a thoughtful look. I bit my lip. That was stupid of me.

"I wonder how you can be so sure."

"I drink the special teas," I lied. We had our own ways of birth control in the Pit. One way was to drink an herbal tea to suppress ovulation. If that failed or wasn't available, there were "doctors" in the Pit to help end the unwanted pregnancy, which was preferable to sterilization.

"How long have you been sexually active?"

"Um…about…a few weeks."

"Were there any significant findings from your examination?"

That question gave me pause. What examination? Should I have had one? He raised his eyebrows, looking at me expectantly. I straightened up.

"No."

"You're favoring your left side. Why?" He got up from his chair and walked toward me. Instinctively, I shielded my bruised back with my arm. Gently, he turned me around and opened the back of my gown.

"How did you get that?"

"I made my owner angry and he punched me." I felt guilty just saying it. Jack would never hurt me.

"You're lying," he said to my surprise. He pushed the gown off my shoulders and examined me. "The pattern of the bruise radiates outwards from the center of a small impact and the chafing on top of your shoulders tells me you've been wearing something heavy. My guess is that you've been wearing a bulletproof vest and someone has been using you for target practice."

I looked at him with wide-eyed shock. "How do you know that?"

As soon as the words escaped my mouth, I wanted to call them back. I had just admitted he was right.

"Because I used to see this kind of injury all the time in the Dome. There's a hazing ritual at the beginning of every school year at the Academy that has seniors hunting freshmen in the hangar. The morons wear bulletproof vests thinking that will save them. Sometimes it does, sometimes it doesn't. Anyway, you'll live. I can give you some pain medication if you want."

I shook my head, too stunned to speak. Would he tell General Powell or someone else in a position of authority?

"So that's two lies you've told me. Why?" he asked.

His directness caught me off guard. For one thing, I wasn't sure which two lies he had clued in to, and for another, I didn't have a good-enough lie ready to cover up the ones I had already told. The silence stretched and he gave me a reproachful look.

"Your skin is already turning pink, see?" he said. He held up one of my arms for inspection. "It's called a sunburn. Why didn't you use the lotion they gave you in your survival pack?"

"We lost our survival packs back at the river," I said,

repeating Jack's lie. It was a relief not to have to think of a new one myself.

Doc went to the door and opened it slightly. "Jeffrey," he called. Delicate Man appeared at the door. "This young lady needs a survival pack."

I tried to appear uninterested that he just ordered a soldier to do his bidding. I had to try even harder when Jeffrey did as he was told. Were things different out here for our kind? If they were, then why was I here to be tagged? Why were troublemakers sent to the range to be hunted?

Doc walked across the room to a cabinet. I took the opportunity to straighten my gown and pull the back shut again.

"Like everyone else from the Pit, you're malnourished. There will be special vitamins in your pack that you need to take every day." He took a few items out of the cabinet and arranged them on a silver tray.

"What's that?" I asked nervously, backing away as he walked toward me. I didn't want to be tagged.

"Birth control." He wiped my arm and plunged the needle in. It stung. "Come back in three months for another shot."

"I thought birth control was illegal."

"It is inside the Dome, but we don't need to worry about polluting the water out here." He pulled the needle out. "I don't agree with much of what President Holt has to say, but I do approve of not mixing the bloodlines. There are far too many bourge in the world already."

He tied a tourniquet tightly around my arm and stuck me with another needle. I watched my blood drain into a vial.

"What's that for?"

The right side of his mouth curved into a knowing smile. "Looks like I have my secrets, too." He pulled the needle out. A drop of blood welled up and spilled onto my skin. He pressed a cotton swab against it and taped it into place. "You can get dressed now."

He hadn't tagged me, unless I missed it. But General Powell had said the tag was placed behind the jugular and Doc hadn't touched my neck. I decided it was in my best interest not to bring it to his attention and quietly went behind the screen to change back into my clothes. When I came out, Doc was sitting at his microscope again. Keeping my head down, I quickly walked past him and headed for the door.

"I almost forgot," he said, halting my escape. My heart sank. He remembered after all. He opened a drawer in his desk and took something out. "I'm not going to tag you," he said as he walked toward me, "but at least act like I did. Before you go through a door or a gate, wait until someone presses a button and tells you it's clear." He affixed a bandage to my neck in the place the tag would have been inserted.

He baffled me. Not just because he didn't tag me, but also because he was a doctor, an urchin and had authority.

"Why?"

"You mean why didn't I tag you?" he asked. My question was more complicated than that, but I would be happy to have even that one mystery solved. I nodded. "Tagging my own kind doesn't sit well with me, but when I have soldiers in the room threatening to kill those spared from the Cull if I don't, I have no choice. But every so often one gets sent to me without a military escort—or perhaps a soldier turns his head at that crucial moment—and I'm allowed a small victory."

I studied Doc for a moment, taking in his quiet, serious demeanor. There was no doubt his loyalties were with the Pit, but he was still an enigma.

"What happens if I forget? What if I cross a barrier and someone finds out I'm not tagged? Won't you get in trouble?"

Doc shrugged. "It's happened a few times. I've told the general that some tags turn out to be duds and I need to replace them."

"Thank you." I wanted to say so much to him, to ask him so many more questions, but those were the only two words that came to me.

"You're welcome, Miss…?" He raised his eyebrows in question.

"O'Donnell. Sunny O'Donnell."

"Sunny O'Donnell," he repeated. "I'll remember. And thank you. You've been very helpful," he said as he held up the vial of my blood. I wasn't sure what he meant. I wasn't sure I wanted to know, either.

He returned to his microscope and I took this as

a sign of dismissal. I walked out into the other room where Jeffrey was waiting for me. There was a backpack on the desk in front of him. He opened it and took out two items.

"Put the sunscreen on before you go back outside," he said, handing me a tube. I squeezed the lotion into my hand and rubbed it on my arms. "On your face too. Especially your nose." When I was done, he handed me a pair of dark glasses. "They're made especially for urchins. They'll help you see outside." He zipped up the pack and pushed it across the desk toward me. I took it. "You're tagged now. If you wander across a barrier, you'll die. If your tag ever starts vibrating, it means you're close to a barrier and you should back up."

I nodded, not sure if I should actually speak to him. No matter how different things appeared to be, I was pretty sure the protocols we followed in the Dome were expected out here too. An urchin simply didn't speak in the presence of the bourge unless given permission.

"Let's go," said the soldier who brought me here.

Before I went back outside, I heeded Jeffrey's advice and put on the glasses. It was like someone put a shade over the blinding glare of the sun, enabling me to open my eyes wide and take in my surroundings. The smooth man-made road we drove into the city on ran down the center of two rows of buildings, all built closely together. Some buildings were only one or two levels high, while others were taller and reached four levels high. They looked almost exactly like the ones I saw in movies, except these structures all had the same gray, molded, plastic look that only came from replicated materials.

The street wasn't as busy as the Pit after the *bong bongs* rang, but I was still surprised by just how many bourge there were out here. An open-topped military vehicle with the word "Jeep" written on the back drove past carrying four soldiers, all heavily armed. Why were they all carrying weapons? Who were they defending themselves against?

My escort led me back to where Jack was deep in conversation with General Powell and Alex. He saluted the officers. "Sirs. She's tagged." Then he sharply turned on his heel and left.

Another soldier had joined the group—a female. The first female I had seen out here. She looked from me to Jack suspiciously. I couldn't see her face very well because she was wearing a military cap. She was shorter than me and I stood up even taller under her scrutiny. There were times I appreciated my height.

"Well, it's already five o'clock—quitting time. Alex, find some accommodations for Jack. I meant to ask you, Jack, why are you out here wearing civvies?"

"Don't tell Damien, but I was hoping for a little vacation before I made my way here. You know, enjoy some sunshine and fresh air," he said, casting a glance at me. Everyone snickered, except the woman. "Unfortunately, I lost everything when my backpack floated downriver."

General Powell gave Jack a thoughtful look. Although Jack maintained a cool expression, his hand moved to rest casually on the handle of his rifle.

"In just a few hours, you lost your survival pack?" Alex laughed, oblivious to the tension. "Dirk lasted a year out here before he broke his damn neck. I give *you* a week."

"Laugh all you want, Alex, but as I recall it was you who almost flunked out of survival training at the Academy. I made straight As. I don't need a pack," Jack said.

"Excuse me," the woman said, looking at Alex. "Even I remember saving your butt a few times."

"Alright, alright," Alex said, holding his hands up in defeat. "Sorry I brought it up."

"Alex, you better get Jack squared away," the general interrupted. He turned to Jack. "And I'll get a security detail on you ASAP. I'm surprised Damien sent you out here without an entourage. Or did you lose them in the river too?"

For a split second, I saw a wary look on Jack's face before he regained his self-confident air. Even I was in awe of the power lurking behind those blue eyes. "That isn't necessary, General. I can take care of myself."

"I'm sure you can. Nevertheless, you are the heir and we need to make sure you're safe. I'll see you tonight at dinner." Powell gave him a curt nod and left.

"Come on, I'll find you a place to live," Alex said.

"Bye, Hayley," Jack said.

Hayley smiled brightly. "I'll see you tonight too." Her smile faded into a sneer when she looked at me.

Jack and Alex began walking down the street and I followed.

"Wow, looks like Hayley still has a thing for you," Alex said.

I couldn't help but wonder if Hayley was the high school girlfriend Jack had told me about.

"No she doesn't."

"You didn't see how she was looking at you? What are you, blind?"

"Well, I'm married now."

"Yeah, and happily I see," Alex said, casting a backward glance at me.

"Would it surprise you to know that Leisel practically picked her out for me?"

I almost shook my head at his comment, but caught myself. It really wasn't the time to be a smartass.

"Okay, that's just too much information. Whatever you and Leisel have going on, keep it to yourself," Alex said in dramatic disgust. "I asked Hayley out a couple of times, but she's not interested."

"Is Hayley the only female officer out here?"

"What do you mean *out here*? Hayley is the only female officer period." Alex laughed. "Powell tried to assign her to a secretarial position and you should have heard her! It didn't take him long to give in to her demands."

"She'll never change," Jack said affectionately. A pang of jealousy hit me and I swallowed it, pushing it down to join all the other emotions vying for my attention.

"So what's your cover story while you're out here?"

"What do you mean?" Jack countered warily.

"You know, so no one misses you in the Dome," Alex said. When Jack didn't respond, he continued. "A lot of us out here are *officially* living inside a new environment in the Dome that exposes us to low levels of radiation to see how well the human body can tolerate it. And as you already know, Powell's been quarantined in his bedroom with a mystery disease for the past two years. So what story did they give you?"

"Pffft. Leisel and I are locked away on an extended honeymoon, busy making the next heir."

"Nice," Alex chuckled. "So you don't expect to be out here long."

"Just as long as it takes to get the job done."

Alex opened a door to a building and we went inside. A long counter ran the width of the room, and a few men stood behind it.

"Can I help you?" one of them asked.

"This is Captain Kenner. He'll need accommodations, uniform, clothing—everything," Alex told him.

"Captain *Jack* Kenner? The presidential heir?" the clerk stammered. Jack nodded, a self-assured smile playing around his mouth. "Right away, sir." The man saluted before he hurried away to fill the order.

"So how does it feel to be so important?" Alex asked.

"I don't know. I'm still getting used to it," Jack replied. I almost laughed.

The clerk returned and stepped out from behind the counter to stand in front of Jack. "Sir, here is the address. The key will open the door, but you'll need to reprogram with your own code." Then he held out a pair of sunglasses. "I thought you could use these. The sun is bright after a lifetime in the Dome."

Jack accepted them with an appreciative smile. "Thanks."

"Now, with your permission, I'll need to measure you for your uniform."

Jack held his arms away from his sides as if he had done it a million times. The man passed a scanner over him and made a few calculations. Jack dropped his arms and motioned toward me. "She'll need clothes too."

The clerk looked me up and down. "Too tall for a small, too skinny for a medium. I'll see what I can find. I'll put a rush on having your uniforms replicated. Someone will deliver them within the hour and stock your refrigerator before the end of the day."

"I'll need my fatigues before dinner."

"Yes sir."

We all left the building and as soon as we were back outside Jack donned his sunglasses. Alex asked to see the address and Jack passed it to him.

"Yeah, I thought they would put you by Powell. The

presidential compound isn't finished yet. But maybe you'll get to see the house they're building for you and Leisel before you go back in the Dome. It's right next door to the president's mansion—the mansion you'll get to live in one day."

"Yeah, that would be great. I'll take some pictures to bring back to Leisel."

Alex led us away from the main drag of the city and down a street lined with houses. We were the only people here, save for the occasional military vehicle driving past. The windows of the dwellings were bare and I was able to look into the empty rooms. It was eerily quiet after the bustle of town.

The two men continued their banter, not paying any attention to their surroundings. I had never seen Jack so at ease with anyone before. But then again, the only place I ever really knew him was in the Pit.

As we walked, I noticed that the houses were getting bigger and spaced farther apart. Trees were strategically planted in front yards and bright flowers bloomed along paved pathways. Alex eventually stopped in front of one of the bigger homes.

"This street is where all the high-ranking officers and future presidents get to live. General Powell's place is over there." He pointed to a house across the street.

"Where do you live?"

"In the shacks with all the other captains, right where you would be if you weren't the heir."

"You mean you live on the party side of the base. You probably have more fun there."

"Oh, I don't know about that," Alex said, flicking a glance at me.

"Well, I better get showered if I'm going to meet Powell for dinner on time," Jack said.

"Do you want me to stop by and walk to the mess with you?" Alex offered.

"Sure," Jack agreed with a smile. "See you then."

CHAPTER THREE

Jack took out the code the clerk had given him and unlocked the door to the house. He reprogrammed it with his own code and then held the door open for me. As soon as I heard the door shut, I turned to look at him. In one stride he was in front of me, examining my neck.

"Are you okay? What did they do? Did they hurt you? Until we get the tag out, don't leave my side. The fences—"

"He didn't tag me." I perched my sunglasses on top of my head.

His face went blank. "You're not tagged?" he asked, confused. I shook my head and he sighed with relief. "How did you get out of it?"

"You're not going to believe this, but Doc is from the Pit. And he's a lot older than thirty-five."

"That was good luck—and we need it." He walked to

the window and looked through the sheer curtains.

"Did you hear me? The *doctor* is from the Pit!"

He shrugged. "Anyone in the Pit who scores as a genius on the IQ test is absorbed into the scientific community."

"Really? And they don't have to be Culled at thirty-five?"

He turned away from the window to look at me. "Right now, we have bigger issues than where the doctor comes from. The promised security detail is here."

"Does everyone in the president's family have guards?"

"Yes." Jack rubbed the back of his neck and returned his gaze to the world outside the window. I went and stood beside him, peering through the sheer curtain at the arriving soldiers. There were two—one assumed a position in the front of the house while the other one walked around back. "I had no idea Holt was already out here. All the dinners and meetings I've had with that man! The conferences with the other families! How did he keep *this* a secret?"

He was almost yelling, his voice laced with panic. It scared me to think Jack might lose it. He was the one that always held me together.

"We need to take a deep breath and try to think clearly."

He continued as if I had never spoken. "You know, I actually believed there was a project that had soldiers testing radiation levels. I thought it was all part of the plan to reintroduce people to a post-nuclear Earth."

"Jack!" I said sharply to get his attention. "We need

to figure out what to do."

He gave me an apologetic look and pulled me against him. I could feel the tension in his body—it echoed my own—yet the warm contact felt reassuring. It was the closest I had felt to being safe all day. I leaned my head on his shoulder.

"I think I do have a plan," he said. "If I can get the communication system working, we won't need to find a way back in. I should be able to get a message to the Alliance and they can fight their way out. But it means I need to stay here and keep up the pretense."

I lifted my head from his shoulder to look at him. Had he lost his mind? "We can't stay here. They'll kill us as soon as they find out we're wanted."

"It's a risk," he agreed. "And mine to take. You're out of here."

"Excuse me?" I said, pushing away from him. "I'm not going anywhere."

"It doesn't take both of us to send a message."

"So are you suggesting I just leave? Walk out the front door, wave goodbye to your security, and keep on going?"

"No! I mean yes." He stepped away from me and rubbed the heels of his hands against his eyes. "I don't know, but I'll figure it out."

I had never seen Jack this upset or confused. Only moments ago he had seemed so calm and collected in the company of the bourge.

"Jack, you know I can't leave. I came out here with the heir and they'll notice if I suddenly go missing." Picking up his hand, I laced my fingers through his. "Besides, you and I are a team. I don't want us to split up. We're in this together."

He directed his intense blue eyes at mine. "The second I get that message through, we're both out of here."

I nodded.

He pulled me back against him. "But, you know what it means to stay, right?"

"That we might be caught and executed?"

"And?"

"And? What?"

"We're not equals like we were in the Pit." I wanted to tell him we weren't equals in the Pit either. Jack was a bourge; I was not. "Do you know how to be a, um, mistress?"

I pushed back a little to look at him. "I have no idea."

"I'm not too sure myself. My family is against that practice. I can only go by what I've seen at social functions."

"We got through the wedding together, right? We'll play our parts now the same as we did then."

A knock came at the door, startling us.

"Who is it?" Jack called out.

"Supply. I have the clothes you ordered."

Jack left me and opened the door. A young soldier stood holding a large suitcase in either hand. He crossed the threshold into the living room, heaving with the exertion of carrying the enormous luggage. With great care so as not to drop them, he placed the suitcases on the floor.

"Will there be anything else?"

"That's it. Thanks." Jack dismissed him. The soldier saluted and left.

Jack closed the door and double-checked the lock.

"We're going to have to get through dinner," he said, coming to stand in front of me.

"I know. Don't worry about me."

He raised his hand and tucked my hair behind my ear, concentrating more on the task than on me. "You better get showered and dressed. We'll have to go soon."

I didn't want to leave him to go have a shower. He was too upset.

"Are you going to be okay?"

At my question, he looked me in the eyes. I saw the worry hidden there before he pasted a smile on his face.

"I'm fine. It's just going to be a stressful night for both of us." He pulled me in for a quick kiss. "We need to get ready."

"Any idea where the shower might be?" I asked, looking around the house. There were two hallways to choose from or I could climb the stairs to the second level.

"I don't know."

The house was enormous. A fireplace dominated the main room and behind it we were surprised to find a kitchen. Not like the big kitchens where Summer and I worked. These were smaller, family-sized kitchens, like in the movies.

"Look at this place," Jack said appreciatively.

I gave him a sidelong glance. "Don't get any ideas about me doing the cooking. I don't know how."

We continued to explore the main level until we found a bedroom that was bigger than the two-room dwelling I grew up in. The bed was so large I was sure it could fit an entire family. Adjacent to this room we found the bath, well stocked with fluffy towels, soap and shampoo.

"I could get used to living here," Jack said.

I felt intimidated by all the luxury and space—like a stranger who didn't belong.

"For such a big house, I'm surprised there's only one bedroom," I said.

Jack raised his eyebrows. "We need more than one?"

The heat of a blush crept across my cheeks. We had almost made love on our last morning in the Pit, and planned to go back and finish what we started, but we never dreamed the events of that day would lead us outside of the Dome.

I smiled. "No, we don't."

He returned my smile, but the strain showing in his face prevented it from reaching his eyes. It worried me. I held my hand out to him and he took it.

"We've come this far, Jack. We'll get through this too."

He nodded. "Go get your shower."

The shower was a lot like the one in Leisel's apartment, so I turned it on and stripped off my dirty clothes. At the sight of myself in the mirror, I almost laughed. The skin exposed to the sun had turned bright pink, leaving behind the outline of my t-shirt. I turned sideways to see the bruise on my back. It was several different shades of purple and black.

I stepped into the spray and nearly screamed when the hot water hit my pink skin. Jumping out of the hot stream, I grabbed the faucet with both hands and turned it toward the cold setting. The cooler water felt better, but within seconds I was shivering. I finished my shower as quickly as I could and gently dabbed my sensitive skin dry.

Wrapping the big towel around myself, I left the bathroom in search of clean clothes. Jack was in the bedroom investigating a vent.

"What are you doing?" I asked.

"Looking for cameras or listening devices. I never even thought of it when we first came in. I haven't found anything."

He had brought the suitcases into the room. I rummaged through the survival pack for something that might help my sunburn and found a lotion for skin irritations. I looked up to see him staring at me wide-eyed.

"What happened to you? Is that from radiation?"

"Doc told me it's a sunburn," I said. I went over and looked at his arms. They were pink as well. "You have one, too."

"I do not."

"Take off your shirt." He pulled it over his head,

revealing an outline of his t-shirt. I touched the pink skin on his upper arm.

"Ow!" he exclaimed. "What did you do?"

"Nothing. I just touched you. It stings because it's a burn. Haven't you noticed everyone out here has darker skin?"

"Are you wearing anything under that towel?"

"You can think of *that* at a time like this?"

He tried to look down the top. "It's never really far from my mind."

Maybe I should have chastised him, but I liked it when Jack flirted with me, and I was relieved that he was in a better mood.

I opened the tube of lotion and massaged some into his arm. "How does that feel?"

"Okay," he said, never taking his eyes off me. "What is it?"

"I don't know. Some kind of lotion."

"So you're testing it on me? Nice. I'm going to shower it off before my skin disintegrates." He kissed the top of my head before he disappeared into the bathroom. At least he seemed in better spirits, even though he was still jumpy.

I sat down on the bed and put the lotion on my own stinging skin. It didn't seem to help.

My suitcase was sitting open on the floor. It was full of short dresses, lingerie, and other clothing I would never wear. I was beginning to lose hope there was anything useful in the case when I came across short pants and t-shirts. There was even a pair of laced work boots.

While I was getting dressed, I heard Jack turn on the shower and scream. Wincing, I silently apologized to him. I should've warned him.

As I brushed my hair, I explored the rest of the house. Climbing the open staircase to the second floor, I discovered three more bedrooms and another bathroom. The place was huge. From the top of the stairs, I had a full view of the living room and kitchen below. It was a beautiful home, but what I liked most was all of the windows and the view beyond. I had to keep reminding myself that the mountains, blue sky and white clouds weren't just a vision on a television screen.

As I came back downstairs, Jack emerged from the bedroom, clean-shaven. He wore a white t-shirt, combat pants, and boots. There was a time when seeing Jack dressed like that would have frightened me; but now all I noticed was how the t-shirt accentuated the muscles of his upper arms and how his snug pants were belted against his flat stomach.

He looked up at me as I descended the stairs. "What are you wearing?"

"The only decent clothes I could find in the suitcase."

"There must be a dress in there." He returned to the bedroom and I followed him.

"Yeah, but I'm not wearing them," I said, just as he produced three.

"You're expected to wear a dress. Pick one."

I rolled my eyes and chose the one with the most fabric. He left the room, giving me privacy to change. The dress wasn't tacky like the green one I had been forced to wear at his bachelor party. This was just a dress.

"Pink's a good color on you, Mrs. Kenner," Jack said brightly when I emerged from the bedroom. He was strapping a pistol around his thigh. "It sets off your fiery hair." He winked at me. I wondered if he was just trying to make me feel better.

"You have a gun," I said enviously.

"Yeah. I wasn't sure they were going to issue me one. Glad they did. I'm feeling a little more in control." He tossed a small bag at me and I caught it. "I found that in the suitcase. You better put some on."

The bag contained makeup. I had no idea how to use the stuff. The only two times I had ever worn it were for the bachelor party and the wedding, and I wasn't the one who applied it.

"Um…I don't know how."

Jack gave me a blank look. "Isn't that an instinct with women?"

"No, Jack. It's *not* instinct."

"My mom put it on everyday, and my girlfriend in…" Jack's voice trailed off. "Leisel wore a ton of it," he said instead. "I'll try to put it on you."

"*You* know how to apply makeup?"

"I said I could try." He steered me into a chair, picked

up the makeup bag, and took a few things out. He swiped some pinkish-red powder onto a big brush and came at me with it.

"I don't want to look weird, Jack."

He swept the brush across one cheek and then the other. Taking a step back, he studied me, and then repeated the process. "Hey, I let you color my hair with a piece of coal. I looked ridiculous."

"How do you know you looked ridiculous? There are no mirrors in the Pit."

He put the brush away and looked through the case for something else. "By the look on your face whenever you finished." He raised both his eyebrows, challenging me to deny it. I couldn't. He came at me with something that looked like a pencil.

"What's that?" I tried to push my head away from the sharp-looking object, but the back of the chair stopped me.

"I think it's eyeliner."

"You *think*?" How did I ever sit still for Leisel? He was about to make contact with the pencil on my eyelid and I instinctively turned away. "Maybe I should try it myself."

"If you want, but I thought I was doing a good job."

"I'm sure you were."

I took the makeup bag from him and went back into the bathroom. The blush he applied was on a little thick so I wiped some off. I wasn't sure how to use the eyeliner, so I just dabbed some mascara on my lashes and lipstick on my lips. It would have to be good enough.

When I returned to the room, Jack said, "You look pretty, Mrs. Kenner."

"I'm not sure I want to look pretty, Mr. Kenner," I admitted.

"I'm not sure I want you to either. Don't stray far from me tonight. And if anyone lays a hand on you, scream and I'll be there."

It sounded like a good plan in theory, but I wasn't sure how it would actually play out if it came to pass.

"You trained me well in the Pit, Jack. I can look after myself."

"No you can't, Sunny. You're not that good."

I stopped in my tracks and stared at him, wide-eyed. "*What*?"

"I didn't mean it that way," he said quickly. "I meant every soldier out here has had *years* of training. Trust me, our sessions in the Pit don't compare."

I looked at him feeling a little deflated. Up until now, I was fairly confident that I could take care of myself if a situation arose. "When push came to shove with my supervisor, I won."

"She wasn't trained, so it was an even fight."

I hadn't thought of it that way...and now I was beginning to see the bigger picture, too. "Why did you agree to teach everyone in the Pit to fight if we don't stand a chance against a trained army?"

"Because they don't really need to know how to fight."

"Excuse me? How are we supposed to win a war if we can't fight?"

"Training is more than just learning how to fight. It builds camaraderie and confidence. Think about it—there are thousands of desperate, angry people in the Pit and if they can pull together and focus that energy, they'll vastly outnumber the Dome's army."

"So you're saying desperation is our best weapon?"

"It's a powerful one."

I hoped he was right. "I feel like I've been duped. You should've told me I sucked."

Jack laughed softly. "You don't suck." He closed the gap between us with a few steps and gave me a hug. "Our sessions gave you the confidence to take on your supervisor, right? I don't want you to lose that confidence. I just want you to recognize your limitations so you don't get yourself into trouble." His words were meant to soothe, and yet I still felt useless.

A knock sounded at the door and he thrust me away from him.

"That's Alex," he said nervously. "Are you ready to go?"

I took a deep breath, hoping it would calm the nervous flutters in my stomach, but it only reminded me I hadn't eaten in over a day. "As ready as I'll ever be," I said.

He went to answer the door but stopped halfway and came back. He took both my hands in his. "I'm not comfortable about tonight for a lot of reasons. No matter how I have to act, remember I'm on your side."

I gave him a reassuring smile. "We're a team. I trust you."

Taking a deep breath, he dropped my hands and answered the door. "Alex," Jack said brightly.

"Now you're looking more like the Kenner I've always known. Ready to go?" Alex asked.

"All set. Come on," he said over his shoulder to me.

Reluctantly, I left the small shred of safety the house provided and stepped out onto the front porch. I tried to recall everything Wynd had taught me at the bachelor party about serving the bourge. It was the only experience I'd had with bourge dinners and I had managed to get through that night.

I tried to convince myself tonight would be easier.

Chapter Four

Jack's security detail fell in behind us as we began our trek into town. The temperature had cooled considerably, although it was still warm. The light breeze blowing against my skin felt foreign. Goosebumps grew wherever it touched me. I hurried to catch up with Jack.

"Leisel's not in a rush to come out here," he said to Alex. "She's happy with all the comforts she has in the Dome. There's no one here to do her hair and nails."

"There won't be for at least another year," Alex said.

The two men talked amicably until we reached the main street. In stark contrast to the quiet residential area we had just left, people strolled along the sidewalks, most heading in the direction of a building with a makeshift sign that said "All Ranks (temporary)." Alex headed there too.

"We only have the one mess right now. The officer's quarters are still under construction."

It was noisy and standing room only. The tables were full of soldiers, all drinking and eating. A young man rushed toward us when he noticed Jack at the door.

"Captain Kenner, sir," he said. "General Powell is waiting for you outside, in the back. This way, please."

The man led us across the boisterous room and through a door into the backyard. It was much quieter here, with soft music piped in over a speaker system. A long table was set up under a canopy with a few people seated around it. I assumed this was the temporary officer's mess.

General Powell sat at the head of the table. "There you are, Jack." He motioned for Jack to take the empty seat next to him.

Hayley was the occupant of the other seat next to Jack's. Her military cap was gone and I could see that she was pretty. Her brown hair fell in soft curls around her shoulders, a feminine quality that seemed out of place with the woman Alex and Jack had described. I noticed she was wearing makeup, flawlessly. Maybe it was instinct for the women of the Dome.

Her face lit up as Jack took the seat next to her and she scooted just a little closer to him. Those jealous feelings I thought I had buried came back to taunt me. I pushed them away. Now was not the time.

For a moment I just stood there with no idea of where

to go or what to do. The two soldiers that made up Jack's security team discreetly stayed behind him, away from the table but still close enough to protect him if it was required. There was a woman wearing dark glasses just like mine, standing in a corner by herself. I assumed she was another mistress and I took my place beside her. No one corrected me, so I figured I had done the right thing.

"It's my first time. Can you help me?" I whispered.

She nodded almost imperceptibly. It was obvious she was doing her best to be quiet and blend into the background. I did the same.

"Jack needs a drink," Powell announced to no one in particular.

The woman beside me cleared her throat, catching my attention. She motioned toward the mess and started walking in that direction. Now I understood. Powell's order was meant for me. I followed her. We were almost to the door when Powell's voice boomed again.

"Gaia, did I tell you to move?"

She gave me a strained, apologetic look and went back to the corner. I was on my own.

I entered the building and saw a long bar where soldiers were ordering drinks. It was busy, but I managed to squeeze in. The men behind the bar were filling glasses with a frothy beverage.

"Who are you here for, darlin'?" the bartender asked me.

"Mr. Kenner."

"What would he like to drink?"

I had no idea, so I pointed to one of the frothy drinks. He left to get me one.

The man sitting next to me at the bar eyeballed me. "Captain Kenner has nice taste in urchins." He leaned back to take a look at my behind. If he touched me, would Jack hear me scream? I doubted it.

"Here you go," the bartender said.

Relieved to get out of there, I returned to the table outside and placed the drink in front of Jack.

"When did you start drinking beer?" Alex asked.

I almost did a head slap. I had no idea what Jack liked to drink.

"Recently," Jack replied. There was a large piece of paper covering the table between Jack and the general. It looked like a map. Although my curiosity was aroused, I knew I couldn't just stand there and join the conversation. I returned to the corner I shared with Gaia. Jack pointed to something on the map. "So what's all this empty space over here?"

"That's where the old city was, before the bombs. Back then people used steel frames to construct skyscrapers. They're all rusting through now, and the buildings are crumbling. It's not a safe area," Powell said. He directed Jack's attention to another area of the map. "We'll continue to expand northwest and skirt around the old city. Over here is all farmland. We've already brought livestock out of the Dome—cows, sheep, chickens and pigs—and they're reproducing nicely. Alex can give you a tour if you want."

"Yeah, I'd like that. Thanks. How many residences have you built so far?"

"About two thousand, which isn't bad considering we've only been out here for a little over a year and a half. Getting the infrastructure in place took most of that time. You know—roads, sewage pipes, cables and the like. Trenches had to be dug and the pipes and cables laid underground, although the urchins do the grunt work. Each house is equipped with solar power, but we need a backup power source for the long winter months. We started constructing a dam here." Powell pointed at the map. "So we should have hydropower by the time Holt opens the doors."

Jack was looking at the general intently. "Two thousand homes in not quite two years, so it's going to take… what, another two or three years to complete?" Jack asked.

"No, it won't take that long." Powell shook his head and took a sip of his beer. "The infrastructure is complete so it's just a matter of building another few thousand homes. There are condos under construction that will house a lot of folks too, especially the elderly. The only thing slowing us down are the replicators. If we could find a way to speed them up, we'd have it finished in about a year."

"Only another few thousand homes?" Jack asked thoughtfully. He narrowed his eyes slightly. "So Damien intends to go through with his plan for the Pit."

General Powell snapped his head up and glared

at Jack. "Can I have a word with you?" His tone was threatening. Powell pushed back his chair roughly and stood. "Gaia," he ordered.

At his command, Gaia picked up his drink and followed him. I scrambled to copy her, afraid of missing a word that might be exchanged between them. The two men moved to a smaller table where they could talk privately. Gaia set the drink in front of the general, and I did the same for Jack.

"I would think by now, Jack, you would know better than to blurt state secrets in front of everyone."

Gaia retreated from the table and I moved to stand next to her, still within hearing.

Jack leaned back in his seat and took a sip of his beer. Although it seemed like a casual movement, I was pretty sure he was calculating his next words. "The city has progressed enough for people to realize that not everyone in the Dome will be living here. I figured it would be common knowledge by now."

"Well, it's not. If anyone else has done the math, they haven't mentioned it to me." Powell took a healthy swig of his beer and set it back on the table. "So have things heated up in the Dome? Any rumblings about war?" There was a momentary look of confusion on Jack's face that Powell didn't miss. "Communications have been down for...well, come to think of it they went out around the time of your wedding. Anyway, I have no idea how that day turned out."

"My wedding day?" Jack said thoughtfully. "It started a riot in the Pit." There was a note of understanding in his voice. Casually, he leaned forward, gripping his beer glass with both hands. "Promising the urchins a feast and then just giving them bread worked like a charm."

"As Damien knew it would," Powell confirmed.

The jolt that went through me was like a slap in the face. *President Holt had deliberately taunted the Pit into a revolt*? I was getting a bad feeling about this.

Jack shrugged. "It seems like he's taking the long way around. He's the president, so he can do whatever he wants. Why bother going through the trouble of starting a war?"

"Because he needs the Families to be in agreement about shutting off the ventilation system. If not, he risks a mutiny."

I bit the inside of my cheeks to keep the look of horror off my face, drawing blood with the effort. Crystal's song came back to haunt me: *"...the Pit they want to blow."* I looked out of the corner on of my eye to see how Gaia was reacting, but she remained unmoved.

"Personally, I don't think he'll ever get them all to agree. But that's just my opinion," Jack said.

Powell huffed a curt laugh. "You should know by now your father-in-law doesn't do anything off the cuff. He's been reducing the urchins' rations and making their lives miserable for years. How much more are they going to take before they fight back? The Pit is a time bomb waiting to go off." He took a sip of his beer. "He's also reducing rations in the Dome and blaming it on the rising population in the Pit."

Jack leaned forward, resting his elbows on the table. "And that part of his plan is working—everyone in the Dome is getting nervous that the food supply is running out, and they're demanding to know if it's safe to come outside yet. Damien used the wedding for a few grandstanding speeches."

Powell laughed heartily. "He probably had everyone feeling ashamed of themselves for asking!"

Jack smiled and nodded.

"With their rations reduced and nowhere to go, how do you think the Dome will react when the ungrateful urchins reward their hospitality with an uprising?"

"And if the Pit starts the war, the Families will have no choice but to agree to a defensive strike. They won't argue when the president shuts off the ventilation system."

"Exactly. He's uniting the Dome," Powell said. "Kind of ironic when you think about it. The urchins have been digging out that mine for three hundred years, not even knowing they were digging their own grave."

Gaia tapped me on the ribs with her elbow and I turned to look at her. She was still staring at the ground and I realized I wasn't. I was openly staring at the men with that look of horror I was trying so hard not to make. Relaxing my face into a blank expression, I bowed my head and covertly watched them through my dark glasses.

Jack's knuckles turned white as they gripped his glass of beer, but he managed to keep a self-assured smile. "Sometimes I forget what a genius Damien is. Maybe he really will succeed in getting his master race."

Powell looked at him in surprise. "*You* know about that? And you're okay with it?"

Jack shrugged. "Why wouldn't I be?"

The general paused, his eyes straying toward the grip Jack had on his glass. Jack picked up his beer and took a drink.

"Because the Kenners have always been big supporters of the Pit," Powell said. "I recall it was your sterilization program that saved the urchins from an earlier Cull age. I'm kind of surprised you're on board with Damien's plans."

Jack was responsible for the sterilization program? The person I had placed my trust in to help free the Pit—the man I was falling in love with—was responsible for sterilizing us? Despite the warm evening air, I began to shiver. Gaia gave my side another subtle tap with her elbow, bringing me back to the present. I realized I was staring at the men again.

Jack's mouth turned downward as he considered Powell's words. "He's the president. He has my loyalty."

Powell raised his eyebrows. "My apologies if you thought I was questioning it." Jack flicked his hand as if it to brush away the thought. "I brought it up because you're the heir. You must have your own agenda for when the presidency passes to you."

"I think it's a bit early in my career to have an agenda. I just started my training."

Powell nodded. "And you must be doing exceedingly well for Damien to send you out here. This city is one secret he's extremely protective of." The general paused, twirling his glass on the table. "I hope you feel you can trust me as a confidante, Jack. I'd like to offer my services as your advisor while you're working out that agenda."

Jack smiled widely. "I appreciate that, General."

The door to the mess burst open, momentarily filling the backyard with the beat of rock and roll and the noise of drunken singing. The bartender announced that the food was ready.

"Well, let's eat. I'm starving," Powell declared, pushing his chair back. "And keep in mind that at least out here, it's not common knowledge. Until war is imminent, there's no telling how people are going to react."

Both men rose and headed back to the main table. Gaia walked toward the door to the mess and I trailed behind her. I was still in shock over what I had just heard. Although Crystal had warned us in her song, the thought of everyone in the Pit being killed was too unconscionable to believe, yet I had heard the general with my own ears.

I had also heard him say Jack was responsible for the sterilization program. My Jack. The man I had placed my trust in.

My whole world was falling apart and Gaia didn't seem to be remotely affected. As soon as the door clicked shut behind us, I turned on her.

"Didn't you hear him?" I demanded over the noise in the room.

"Yep."

She turned away from me and headed toward the bar.

"Wait! It doesn't *bother* you?"

"Of course it *bothers* me." She stopped and turned around with an impatient expression. "Look, he's been talking to Colonel Anderson about this for months and they're doing everything they can to talk the president out of it."

"So that's it?" I asked dumbly. "You're going to put all your faith in Powell trying to change Holt's mind?"

"That's all we have."

"We can fight back. How many others from the Pit are out here? If there are enough of us —"

"We can… what? Build an army?" Gaia raised her eyebrows, pausing for my answer.

I nodded. That was exactly what I was thinking.

"You're new out here, so let me enlighten you. We all have this little thing in our neck that instantly kills us if we walk in the wrong direction. All of the women are penned inside a corral that's surrounded by both a wire fence and an electrical one designed to set off our tags. All of the men are penned inside a separate corral that is—you guessed it—surrounded by fences. The range is surrounded. The farms are surrounded. There are so many fences buried out here that we don't know where to step. Now that you have the lay of the land, let's get back to your plan of putting an army together. We're all tagged and we have no weapons. And just in case you missed it, there are soldiers everywhere carrying firearms at all times."

"You and I aren't penned in an enclosure," I pointed out. "We can do something."

A look of understanding came across her features. "Oh, I'm sorry. I didn't realize you meant we should put together an army of mistresses. That's great. I bet we win." She turned and headed for the bar.

Half of me was seething with anger that she could be so accepting of what was going on; the other half of me saw her point. Still, if everyone in the Pit had her attitude, we never would have been able to create the Alliance. I drew a deep, cleansing breath and followed her to the bar.

The bartender noticed us standing there and went through a door to the kitchen. He came back with a tray of food in either hand and passed one to Gaia and one to me. Just like the last time I served at a bourge dinner, the plate was heaped with food. There was a piece of grilled meat and long, skinny vegetables—potatoes?—cooked to a golden brown. The agonizingly delicious smell of Jack's dinner hit my nose, and my mouth watered.

"Tell the general the rest of the meals will be right out."

In silence, we returned to the table outside with the trays. Despite the chaos going on in my mind, the smell of food was making my empty stomach growl. As I placed the plate in front of Jack, we made eye contact for only a split second. So much passed between us during that brief moment. I could tell he was uncomfortable. We were both now wiser about the war. And I was now wiser about his role as the heir.

I returned to my corner and tried to blend into the background. I was shaking with the injustice of it all. I knew the crime they were planning and I had no way of stopping it. My eyes strayed to the pistol strapped to the general's leg, and irrationally I wondered if I could find any solace in grabbing it and putting it to his head. Although killing him might help vent some of the anger eating away at me, every bourge at the table would pull out his own gun and shoot me. Dead, I was of no use to the Pit.

A young man arrived with a three-shelf cart stacked with plates of hot, steaming food and he served everyone else at the table. The diners dug into their meal with gusto and shouted out their compliments to the chef. Reflexively I swallowed, the empty gesture making my stomach growl loudly. I noticed Jack wasn't having any trouble eating his meal, although his beer was almost untouched. He carried on easy conversation with his dinner companions, joking with them in the way that only good friends could.

"I seem to recall your brother was always a better fighter than you, Jack," Powell slurred.

"I'll admit Ted's better than I am—but I'm the second best the school has ever produced."

Hayley turned a shocked expression on him. "You could never take me."

"That's because I always let you win."

A chorus of *ooooohhhh* rose up around the table and some of the officers elbowed each other. Jack not only fit in with these people; they revered him. He hadn't looked at me even once since dinner began and I was glad. Even though I was used to serving the bourge, I found it humiliating to be a slave in front of Jack, especially while the Dome's finest celebrated his arrival. Maybe he was right after all—we had been equals in the Pit.

"Well, I have to say I enjoyed the prize," Hayley said suggestively.

The table went wild with laughter.

"Jack," she said, "you're barely touching your beer. Didn't she know you hate it? Would you prefer wine? Or an after-dinner scotch?"

"No thank you, Hayley. I'm not used to this heat and I'm finding the alcohol a little too dehydrating."

"Girl!" Hayley said, looking at me. "Your master needs water."

Could this night get any better? The heat of my shame manifested itself in my cheeks at being ordered around by Jack's girlfriend. I resisted the urge to stomp my way into the building. An attitude like that would get me punished.

"Another beer?" the bartender asked me.

"Just water, please."

The bartender handed me a tall glass of water with ice and a slice of some kind of fruit in it. I went back outside and put the drink in front of Jack. This time, I didn't bother to make eye contact with him. I just kept my head down and returned to my corner, trying to blot out the merriment of the people gathered around the table.

After what seemed an eternity, General Powell slammed an empty beer glass on the table, drawing everyone's attention. "Well, I'm going to call it a night."

He stood on unsteady legs and Gaia went to his aid. They walked to the door of the mess and two soldiers fell in behind them.

Jack pushed away from the table. "I better get going too. I start my new job tomorrow."

"I'll walk back with you," Alex said.

"Me too," Hayley said.

Jack cast a glance in my direction and I knew to follow. As I fell in behind them, his security team fell in behind me.

After we had made our way through the crowded bar and back out onto the street, Hayley wrapped her well-toned arm around Jack's elbow. He carried on witty conversation with her and she laughed at everything he said. He didn't seem to mind that I was right behind him. Maybe what I thought no longer mattered.

As we arrived at the house, the trio stopped and continued to talk. I desperately wondered if they would ever leave. Not that I wanted to go into the house and be alone with Jack, but my feelings were overwhelming. What I really wanted to do was run, although I didn't know where.

"Listen guys, I'm tired," Jack finally said.

"I'll teach you how to drive the bike tomorrow," Alex called.

"Good night, Jack," Hayley said.

He waved.

CHAPTER FIVE

Jack unlocked the door and we went into our temporary home. It was big, unfamiliar and painfully quiet after the raucous noise of the mess. Closing my eyes, I pressed a thumb and finger against the building pressure behind them. My head was beginning to ache, although I wasn't sure if it was from hunger or information overload.

His hand gently wrapped around my arm and I resisted the urge to yank away from his touch. I was angry, but I was conscious of the fact that we promised each other before setting out for dinner that we were just playing our roles. It was necessary for our survival. I wasn't a stranger to being a slave. I was born one. Yet being Jack's slave had been humiliating. He was my partner, my almost-lover and my friend. It made hearing his role in the sterilization program that much harder to take. I thought I knew him, but he was still a stranger.

He turned me around to face him, his expression sad and apologetic. "Sunny…I'm sorry."

I could tell he was struggling and a part of me was grateful that he might be feeling some remorse. "The sterilization program?"

My voice broke around the lump in my throat. For once I was glad my emotions had stolen my ability to speak. I didn't want to talk. I just wanted to shut down.

"I was a little kid when my parents campaigned for that program," Jack said, his voice cracking with emotion. "They pushed it through as an alternative to lowering the age of the Cull. They saved thousands in the Pit from being rounded up and killed."

I opened my mouth to speak, challenging that lump, but my tears decided it was a good time to show up. I jerked my arm out of his grasp and started toward the bedroom.

"Don't walk away from me."

I stopped and turned to look at him. "Was that an order, *sir*?"

We glared at each other from across the room. Jack was the first to look away. "No, it wasn't," he said. He rubbed a hand across his eyes.

I continued to glare at him. "Is that why you were acting so jumpy earlier tonight? You were afraid I'd find out what you're *really* like?"

"I'll admit it was one of the reasons."

My eyes widened in shock at his honesty.

"Don't look so surprised, Sunny. I was the presidential heir! You think I didn't do anything to earn that title?" He stared at me, waiting for my reply.

I didn't have one. Maybe because at some point during our association I had convinced myself that the presidential heir I had seen on TV so many times didn't actually exist. That man was just an image and not the same person I had lived with in the Pit.

"I told you before we left the Dome, you changed me," he said, breaking the silence that had grown between us. "I had my eyes opened during my time down there."

I shook my head in disbelief. "Why didn't you tell me about the sterilization program? Why didn't you tell me the truth?"

"Jesus, Sunny, I was in the Pit surrounded by thousands of people who hated me. You really think it was the best time for me to come clean?"

I dug my nails into my palm. "You could have been honest with *me,* Jack!"

"So you could tell your boyfriend?!"

"Reyes? You're bringing *him* into this?!"

Jack balled his hands into fists and looked wildly around the room. I'd never seen him so angry. Wondering if he was looking for something to punch, I took a step away from him. He caught my movement and glared at me again. I returned his stare, refusing to back down.

He closed his eyes and his hands relaxed. "Reyes wanted me out of the Pit and he really didn't care how I went."

"What's that supposed to mean?"

"Everyday in the mines, he tried to provoke me into a fight. When I didn't take the bait, he tried to convince everyone I was some kind of traitor working for the bourge so they'd want to kill me. I'll give him credit—he never once said who I was. But that was for your protection."

I was speechless for a moment. Not because I didn't believe Jack—it sounded exactly like something Reyes would do—but because I wondered why Jack kept it from me. "Why didn't you tell me?"

"Because I thought you were in love with the guy."

"I told you I wasn't."

"You told me on our last day in the Pit."

He was right. I covered my face with my hands in a vain attempt to shut myself off from reality. Too much had happened and I couldn't make sense of it anymore. "When did everything get so screwed up?"

"It's always been screwed up. We just got caught in the middle of it."

Angrily, I rubbed the tears from eyes. "You still should've told me about Reyes."

"Remember the day I got into a fight with the guards?"

I nodded. How could I forget? It was the night I had to sit up with him because he might have had a concussion—the night we really talked to each other for the first time. It resulted in the formation of the Alliance.

"That was the day I hit a breaking point. Reyes and his friends were taunting me, the guards were getting in on the act, and then some poor kid stepped in the middle. I just...*lost it.* When I started swinging at the guards, I didn't care if I lived or died. I *needed* it to stop."

Why didn't I know about that? Had I even bothered to ask what his life was like in the mines? The truth was that I was too wrapped up in my own misery to even consider what he was going through. I was too worried about Summer and blamed him for not helping her enough. I was worried about my dad and held Jack responsible for his arrest, too. I didn't care what he was going through. I only cared if he could help or not.

Suddenly, I didn't like myself very much.

"I'm sorry, Jack. I should've known."

His shoulders slumped and I saw the fight leave him. "Unless Reyes told you, there's no way you could have."

My mind flashed back to that day in the Pit—the day the guards had dragged my father away and Reyes had cornered me about our future together. He had been adamant that we had to get rid of Jack. I thought I had made my position clear to him that it wasn't going to happen. But I knew what Reyes was like. I should've anticipated that he would try to find a way to get what he wanted.

The sound of my stomach growling suddenly filled the room and I quickly placed a hand over my abdomen to muffle the sound. The awkward noise drew a grin from Jack and the tension between us eased.

"You haven't eaten in a long time," he said. "The fridge should be stocked by now."

I shook my head. "I'm not that hungry." Why did I just say that? My head was booming and my stomach was cramping. I knew food would make me feel better, yet a stubborn sense of pride prevented me from admitting it. Watching him eat a king's meal while I stood on the sidelines drooling made me feel more than a little pathetic.

He held out his hand to me, his expression rueful. "Come on. It's my turn to serve you."

How did he *know*? With a heavy sigh and a roll of my eyes, I ignored my irrational grudge and took his hand. He led me into the kitchen and pulled out a stool for me.

"Have you ever had eggs?" he asked, rummaging through the refrigerator.

I nodded. "In your apartment before the wedding, remember?"

"Oh yeah." He pulled a few items out and placed them beside the stove. "Well, I think mine will be better."

While he hunted through cupboards and collected items, I sat at the counter and watched him. He seemed to know his way around the kitchen—another fact I hadn't known about him. Did they have private kitchens in the Dome?

"Where did you learn to cook?" I asked.

"During college. The first time we pulled an all-nighter studying for an exam, we woke up the cook and asked him to make us something to eat to keep us going.

Instead, he showed us how to use the stove and told us never to wake him up in the middle of the night again. He's lucky we never started a fire."

What a privileged life he had led to be able to wake up a cook and demand food. The image was a stark contrast to the Jack Kenner I had come to know in the Pit.

He poured a glass of milk and set it in front of me. I took a sip, conscious of the fact that he only poured one glass. "Aren't you having any?"

He shook his head. "I'm full—" I saw the barest hint of a blush creep up his face. "I'm not hungry right now."

He took the frying pan off the stove just as the toast popped up. I tried to remember the last time I ate. It must have been a few days ago. No wonder Jack was able to eat his dinner, despite our predicament.

He set a plate full of eggs, toast and slices of some kind of a red fruit or vegetable in front of me. It smelled delicious. "Thank you."

He sat down on the stool next to me. "You're welcome."

All he had was toast, and I'm sure he only had it to save me from eating alone. I didn't care. I was so hungry I wanted to dispense with the cutlery, open my mouth and empty the food straight into my stomach. Instead, I forced myself to pick up my fork. It took every bit of my willpower to not shovel the food in. When all my eggs and toast were consumed, I eyed the red things. My stomach felt ready to burst, but I didn't want to leave a scrap behind.

"That's tomato. It's really good," Jack said.

Picking up a slice with my fork, I bit into it. It was juicy, kind of sweet with a hint of a bitter taste. I put the other half back on my plate.

"You don't like it?"

"I'm just really full, I think. Thank you. It was delicious."

"But you didn't eat very much. I'll make more eggs." He stood up.

"Please Jack," I said, stopping him. "I'm fine."

"Do you feel better?"

I nodded.

He sat back down. "Then we should talk."

Although the food was taking care of my aching head and stomach, my emotions were still in turmoil. I put my elbows on the counter and rested my face in my hands, hiding my eyes. Talking wasn't going to change anything. "Will it do any good?"

He swiveled on his stool to face me. "I'd at least like the chance to explain about the sterilization program."

I turned my head to look at him. Though I wasn't sure I wanted to learn anything more about Jack the heir, I knew I had to. "I'm listening."

He took a deep breath. "Like I said earlier, my parents advocated that program fifteen years ago when Holt wanted to lower the age of the Cull to thirty. If Holt had been successful, it would've meant rounding up everyone between the ages of thirty and thirty-five and exterminating them. My parents presented the sterilization program as a way of curbing the rising population in the Pit. They managed to convince most of the influential families, which forced Holt to adopt the program." Jack paused to look at me to see how I was taking the information.

"Go on."

"I went to work for the Holt government when I became engaged to Leisel. I had no choice—I was the president-in-training. One of the first projects I was given to manage was the sterilization program, probably because it was my family who pushed it on Holt. In the beginning, sterilization was done by surgery, but in the past few years a compound had been developed for chemical sterilization." He paused, taking a deep breath. "I supported it because it's less invasive and I was told the problems cited with it were minor. I didn't know the extent of the problems until I met Raine's wife, Flo. I had no idea before I met her. I swear."

"But you knew there were problems, so why didn't you try to find out what they were?"

"Because women had died during surgery, but no one ever died from getting the injection."

The regret on Jack's face convinced me he was telling the truth, but it wasn't his sincerity I questioned. What rubbed me the wrong way was why the bourge never included themselves in their own policies. It was only the Pit subjected to population control. Even though we all knew we were bound by the terms of the treaty, it still caused a lot of resentment.

Wearily, I propped an elbow on the counter and rested

my head in my hand. I decided some thoughts were better kept to myself. There had been enough arguing between us and nothing good was going to come from debating the point.

"Then your decision was a fair one," I said. "Is there anything else I should know?"

Jack shifted uncomfortably and turned his stool back to face the counter. "Sunny, I grew up in the Dome. I worked for the president for almost a full year. I pretended to love his daughter. I think it's safe to say I did a lot of things you might construe as… questionable. So if we decide to stay here and keep up the pretense, I can't guarantee there won't be a repeat of tonight."

I raised my eyebrows. "What do you mean if we decide to stay here? What choice do we have?"

"We can run."

I sat up straight and searched his face. "You mean abandon the Pit? Let them all die?" I shook my head. There was no way I would agree to that.

"No!" He looked shocked by my suggestion. "I mean try to get away from here and find a different way into the Pit."

"You said it was a fortress."

He nodded. "It is. And we'll also have to contend with armed soldiers patrolling the area while we're trying to find a way inside."

I studied Jack for a moment, trying to gauge what he wanted to do. Yet his expression was expectant, waiting for my answer. "Earlier, you said our best option to save the Pit was by staying here, so why are you changing your mind now?"

He leaned an elbow on the counter and rubbed a hand across his eyes. "Because if tonight was any indication, staying here might rip you and me apart. We're a team, Sunny. No one from the Pit trusts me, so they aren't going to listen to anything I have to say. And you can't free them alone because you—frankly—don't have the technical skills. We need each other to do this."

Even though everything he said was true, his words hit me like a cold blast. They reduced our relationship to a business partnership.

An unhappy feeling crept over me and I fought to keep it at bay. I felt bad enough without adding sadness to the mix. Things had been so much easier between us in the Pit and I just wanted to have that again. I wanted to forget about what I heard, forget about seeing him with his friends…with Hayley.

Then I remembered things weren't easy for him in the Pit.

Feelings were beginning to cause a lot of confusion, distracting me from what was really important: freeing the Pit before Holt annihilated everyone. Life was complicated enough without the added worry of our relationship.

I turned to face him. "If staying is the best chance we have, then we stay. And I agree—we're better off strictly as partners." I held out my hand to him to shake on it.

Instead of accepting my offered hand, he held up his

own as if to ward it off. "Whoa! I never said *that*. And what exactly do you mean?"

"I mean that if there was some kind of...*relationship*... starting between us, maybe it's not a good idea." I looked at him to see his reaction.

"*If* there was a—" he repeated, then stopped. He stared at me for a moment. "I thought there *was* something between us."

It was hard to think while his blue eyes looked so intently into mine. "But after tonight..."

He held my gaze for what seemed like an eternity before he gave me a tight smile. "Oh."

He stood and took my plate to the sink.

The air crackled with tension, momentarily paralyzing me. I tried to steal a glance at his face, but he was at the sink with his back turned to me.

I got up from the stool and gathered the dishes he'd used to prepare the meal. "After what you said, I thought this is what you wanted too."

"I'm not sure what I said to give you that impression." He filled the sink with hot water and detergent, even though I was pretty sure I was looking at a dishwasher.

I found a towel in a drawer. "That you have the skills and I don't, and *that's* why we need each other."

He rinsed a dish and put it on the drain board, taking the opportunity to lean closer to me. "I'm sorry I said it. It came out wrong."

"No, it wasn't wrong. It just made me think that this

will be a lot less complicated if we're..." I thought about my next words. "Free to play our roles."

He stopped washing the frying pan and turned his full attention on me. "*Free* to play our roles?"

"Look at us! We just found out what Holt has in store for the Pit and instead of figuring out a plan, we're caught up in all this emotional...*stuff*."

For a moment, he didn't say anything. Just stared at me with a thoughtful expression that was guarded enough not to give me a clue about what he was thinking. Feeling uncomfortable, I took the frying pan out of his hand and dried it to keep myself busy.

"You're right," he finally said. He rinsed his cloth and started wiping the counter.

I shivered from the sudden chill in the room. "You're mad at me."

He stopped what he was doing to look at me. "No, I'm not mad *at you*. I'm just frustrated." He threw the cloth into the sink. "Our situation isn't going to get any better by staying here, but we need to stay in order to help the Pit. So if doing away with any...*romance* that was starting between us is going to keep us together, then I agree."

"I think it's for the best, Jack. We need to concentrate on what's important." He put away the dishes and I hung my towel to dry. It was hard to ignore the tension between us, but we needed to get over it. "Have you thought of a plan yet?"

He shrugged. "I don't exactly know how things work out here, but my initial plan is to fix the comms and get a message to the Alliance and my family."

"Sounds easy." I took a couple of glasses out of the cupboard, filled them with water, and handed him one. "Can I ask you a question about something?"

"Why not? Since we're being so honest with each other." The sarcasm was unmistakable. It told me there had been enough truths spoken for one night.

"Never mind."

He sighed, exasperated. "Ask the question, Sunny."

I hesitated, but since it wasn't a personal question, I decided it was a safe topic. "Do you think General Powell is right? Will Holt be able to convince the Families to kill everyone in the Pit?"

He sipped his water before he answered. "It's possible. The survival instinct kicks in when you're starving to death. The Pit has already reached that point, and if Holt keeps cutting back rations in the Dome, they'll soon be just as desperate."

"Why, Jack? Why does he want us all dead?"

"Holt is obsessive about not letting the bloodlines get mixed."

"I remember Crystal said that once, too. What exactly does it mean?"

"The Holt regime doesn't want urchins and bourge to make babies together, so a law was made against interracial marriages. It's one of the laws we broke." He gave me a weak smile and leaned against the counter. "Officially the law exists for population control, even though it doesn't make sense since it would be better to have a bigger gene pool. The real reason behind it is that the Holt regime doesn't want the two bloodlines mixed. I overheard Holt discussing some kind of master race with Malcolm West. I didn't catch the entire conversation, but now that I know he's building this city, I'm starting to put it all together and Powell pretty much confirmed it. Holt's plan is to repopulate the Earth with his master race, which only includes people from the Dome."

"And no one from the Pit," I added.

Jack gave me a direct look. "You and I will stop him. We won't let him get away with it."

"I hope we can."

"We should get some rest. I don't know about you, but I'm exhausted. And we have a long day ahead of us tomorrow."

I was exhausted too, but I wasn't sure I could sleep. We were living among the very people who would kill us if they found out we were wanted for treason.

Halfway through the living room I stopped, not sure where to go.

"What's wrong?" he asked.

"Um… there's only one room down here. Now that we've decided no romantic-stuff, maybe I should take the sofa. Or sleep upstairs."

"You and I stick together." He put his hands on the back of my shoulders and steered me toward the room. "If a maid finds out we're not sharing a room, she'll talk. Or if they do come for us, at least we can try and escape out the bedroom window *together.* Separated, we're vulnerable."

I noticed that even though the lights weren't on, Jack didn't have any trouble navigating his way to the bedroom. Even without sunlight, the house was still brighter than the Pit.

"We have a maid?" I asked, as he nudged me into the room.

"That's how it works in the Dome. I'm not sure about out here." He shut the door and engaged the lock while I closed the curtains. He turned on a lamp even though I didn't think we needed one.

While Jack was taking his turn in the bathroom, I searched the suitcase for something to wear to bed. All of the pajamas in the case were nothing more than provocative scraps of silk. I chose a pair of shorts and a t-shirt.

I was brushing my hair when he came back into the room. He was wearing pajama bottoms slung low around his bare hips and nothing else except the outline of his sunburn.

He looked mildly surprised at the way I was dressed. "Just making sure you're ready for work in the morning?"

"It was either this," I said, pointing to my outfit, "or this." I held up a slinky nightie.

"Good choice." He walked past me and flopped down on the bed. "Ow. Does your skin hurt?"

I nodded. It felt tight and sting-y. "Don't you have a

top to go with those bottoms?"

"Guy pajamas don't come with tops." He gave me a look that said I should know that. "I usually don't wear anything. The bottoms are for you."

"Thanks," I said, a little too appreciatively.

I approached the bed feeling awkward. I knew it was stupid. Jack and I had been sharing a bed for quite a while now. But after everything we said tonight, sleeping together just got complicated. Stiffly, I lay down, cringing as the sheet scraped against my tender skin. I looked over at Jack. The gulf of empty space between us could've accommodated a small family. "I've never seen a bed this big."

He had a smirk on his face. "Sunny, this isn't the first time we've shared a bed, and we both know it's not me who has a problem staying on my own side." He turned off the lamp.

"I'll stay over here," I said with more confidence than I had.

Rolling onto my side, I gripped the mattress and threw my leg over the edge in an attempt to anchor myself. Even though I was sure I wouldn't sleep, I wanted to be prepared, just in case.

Chapter Six

With a start I woke, sensing something different. Disoriented, I looked around the room. It was dimly lit in a foreign way—as if someone turned half a light on. In the Pit, the lights were either on or off. There was no in-between. A sliver of yellow filtered through the slit in the curtains and fell across the bed. I put my hand into the stream of light. It was warm.

After a night spent clinging to the side of the mattress, my muscles were stiff. Slowly I stretched out my limbs and felt Jack beside me. At least I had stayed on my side.

Quietly, I rolled off the bed and padded to the window to look outside. The top of the sun was barely visible above the mountains, but already its fingers were reaching out and stealing the darkness from night. It was already too bright to tolerate and I reached for my sunglasses on the bedside table. Jack was awake, his blue eyes quietly regarding me.

"Want to see your first sunrise?" I asked.

He left the bed and came to stand behind me and I pulled the curtains open wider. In the backyard a bird was singing, heralding the arrival of a new day. I searched the trees for the creature but couldn't see it. Then it flew to another tree, flashing its red wings. Another bird joined it and together they chirped, their throats pulsating.

Jack's arms circled my waist. "Amazing," he whispered against my ear.

I relaxed into him, resting my head against the side of his. As the rising sun caressed my face, the warmth of his bare chest gently pressed against me. It probably wasn't a good idea considering our no-romance agreement. But it was the single most beautiful moment of my entire existence and I was loath to give it up. I put my hands over his, holding him there.

I'm not sure how long we stood together at the window, but our fragile bond was broken when a guard stood up and stretched. We hadn't noticed him leaning against the back of the house. Jack dropped his arms and stepped away from me. I shivered from the cool air that rushed in to take the place of his body heat.

"We better get ready for work. You can have the bathroom first."

Work. The thought made my stomach knot. I should've thought to ask Gaia about work life out here. But I had been too overwhelmed by the news of what

Holt had planned for everyone in the Pit to be concerned with my own predicament.

I shut the bathroom door and turned on the tap to let the water run tepid. Before I met Jack, I never would've wasted water like this. It had become a guilty pleasure for me. Then I thought of the river we saw before we came to this city and my guilt eased. Out here there was an endless supply.

I scrubbed my face, cleaned my teeth and brushed my hair into a ponytail. Securing the elastic was more problematic since I found it impossible to stop my hands from shaking. Biting the inside of my cheeks, I gave my reflection a hard look, willing myself to calm down. There was no way I could get through today if I allowed my fears to take over. I reminded myself that I had posed as Leisel at her wedding. I had walked down the aisle in front of the entire Dome, pretending to be someone important, knowing I could be killed at any moment. I made it through that ordeal. Today was no different.

With greater determination, I smoothed my hair back and forced my fingers to perform the familiar task. This time I was successful. I gave my reflection an encouraging smile, took a deep breath and went in search of Jack.

"Have you ever had coffee?" he asked as I entered the kitchen.

"No. But I remember serving it at your bachelor party."

He picked up a steaming mug and handed it to me. I took a sip. It was hot and bitter. I pasted a smile on my face and made an "mmmm" sound. He gave me a satisfied grin and sipped his own beverage. I didn't really like it, but he looked so happy to share it with me.

He had toast and cut-up fruit already prepared and we sat down together at the table. Although my stomach was a fluttering mass of nerves, I forced myself to eat a slice of toast.

"Nervous?" he asked.

I shook my head. "I'm okay."

"Really?" He reached under the table and grabbed my leg. I hadn't realized I was swinging it back and forth. I uncrossed my legs and put both feet firmly on the floor. "I'm nervous too."

The fact that he admitted that seemed a little surprising. Jack oozed self-confidence, although I was beginning to wonder how much of that belonged to his persona as heir.

"But you know how to fight. I suck, remember?"

He smiled broadly and shook his head. "I never said you sucked." He leaned forward and took one of my shaking hands in his. I felt the tension in his grip. "We've done a pretty good job of hiding in plain sight up until now. We can do it a little longer, right?"

I nodded.

The sound of a vehicle pulling up in front of the house interrupted our conversation. We looked out the window. A shiny black car was parked in front of the house. An armed soldier exited the driver's seat and walked around to the back passenger door to lean against it.

Jack snorted. "Great."

"What?"

"It's an escort to take me to work. Powell's really laying it on thick."

"You mean we're late?" I felt the familiar tightening in my chest at the thought of reporting late for work. The bourge didn't tolerate that.

"It's okay. You're with me—the next president," Jack said. I regarded him apprehensively. How was that going to save me from a beating? "As far as they know, I'm the most powerful person next to Holt. No one is going to question me."

"Well, we still better hurry up."

Rushing into the bedroom, I donned a pair of socks and my work boots and slathered my exposed skin with sun block. Jack was sipping a second coffee when I came back into the kitchen. He wasn't even trying to get ready.

"Hurry up or you're going to get us in trouble," I said.

"Let them wait." He poured another steaming cup and handed it to me. "I'll get ready, and you try to relax."

When Jack left the kitchen, I poured the coffee down the drain and peeked out the window again. The soldier leaning against the car was chatting easily to one of Jack's security guards. There was another black car parked in front of the general's house. The driver of that car was leaning against his vehicle too, and I assumed he was waiting for Powell.

An open-top jeep joined the parked cars on the road, and shortly after its arrival, Powell and Gaia emerged. The general got into the black car and Gaia went to the open-top jeep. The black car pulled away from the curb and headed in the direction of town. The jeep remained. I wondered if they were waiting for me.

"See anything out there?" Jack asked as he came into the kitchen.

"The general just left," I said, turning to look at him. He was dressed in combat clothes again today, the pistol strapped to his thigh.

"Believe me, I wish you had one too," he said, noticing my eyes on the weapon. "You're not tagged, so if you need to run, do it."

I nodded. "If we get separated, we should meet at the slag heap."

"Do you remember how to get back there?"

"I think so."

"Slag heap it is." He took a deep breath as he put on his military cap. "Ready to go?"

I nodded, but the trembling of my hands gave me away. Straightening my fingers, I swiped sweaty palms against my back pockets.

I followed him to the door. As his hand gripped the knob, he paused and turned to regard me for a moment.

I thought I saw the barest hint of confusion cross his features before he put on his sunglasses.

"If anything happens… the slag heap," he said.

"I'll meet you there," I promised.

He pulled open the door and our privacy vanished. His security guard snapped to attention, but Jack didn't even acknowledge the man. He just walked past, heading toward the shiny black vehicle as if he had done it a thousand times. His guard fell in step right behind him.

I pulled the door shut behind me as I stepped out onto the front porch. A warm breeze tickled my skin. I wasn't sure I would ever get used to the sensation. Standing on the steps, I watched the driver open the car door for Jack and he slipped into the backseat. His head turned in my direction before the door was shut. The car pulled away and I watched it go until it was out of sight. Fear and loneliness mixed, leaving me feeling abandoned. It was an irrational feeling and I pushed it away.

Across the street, the driver of the jeep was looking at me, pointing toward the back seat. Steadying my nerves, I walked over to the vehicle and got in beside Gaia. I smiled. She acknowledged me with vague interest. I wondered if she was still upset about our conversation last night.

The jeep lurched forward and sped in the opposite direction from town. We drove through the neighborhood, passing plain houses surrounded by white picket fences. There was an eeriness to the desolate neighborhood as the houses stood empty, patiently waiting for their bourge families to claim them.

Abruptly the smooth pavement we were driving on ended and the road turned into rutted tracks in the earth. The houses were replaced with trees, which grew thicker as we drove. Eventually, the jeep broke out of the forest into a huge clearing and took a sharp left turn. Ahead of us I saw two large compounds. Each compound had four long buildings enclosed inside a tall wire fence. The front gates were wide open to allow vehicles in and out. We drove into the compound closest to us.

There were no flower gardens or green lawns in the urchin corral. Just muddy paths that ran between the rows of long, narrow buildings with pitched roofs. It was busy inside the fence. Sunglass-clad women were running in different directions, some carrying baskets of laundry, others rushing to join queues to get on large, open-backed trucks.

Our driver exited the jeep. There was a woman directing others, ensuring they were getting into the proper queues. He motioned for her to come over. "Got another one for you, Hazel," he said, as the woman approached.

Gaia and I got out. Despite her obvious contempt for me, I was glad she was there so I didn't feel so alone.

"Thank you, sir. I'll make sure she's put to work right away," Hazel said. She ducked her head, bowing to the man. Our driver didn't even pay attention to her. He just climbed back behind the wheel and drove off. As soon as he was gone, Hazel's manner changed. "So who do you belong to, princess?"

One second she was the epitome of respect and the next she was looking at me as if I were something she detested. "Excuse me?"

"You don't make your bed here at night," she said, flicking a thumb at the buildings behind her. "So who're you sleeping with?"

I openly stared at Hazel, confused. "Aren't you from the Pit?"

Gaia snorted. "There are no bourge supervisors out here so they have to pick from the urchin pool."

Hazel huffed indignantly. "I'll have you know I *earned* my place of authority. I don't get by on my back like you and this one."

The shock of her insult registered on my face and Gaia laughed. "There're a ton of urchin lords out here."

"Urchin lords?" I echoed.

"Urchins that turn bourge because they're given a little power," she sneered at Hazel, "over *their own kind*."

Hazel returned her sneer and then ignored her. "I asked you a question. Who's your master?"

Hazel crossed her arms, waiting for my answer. The way she acted, she could've easily passed for a bourge if it wasn't for the dark glasses and the way she was dressed. Was she so high on her position of assumed authority she didn't realize that she was still a slave? All she had to do was take a look around at where she was living—in a pen behind a huge fence with a chip in her throat that could kill her if she ever tried to leave.

"Jack Kenner," I said. She gave me an exasperated look and started tapping her foot. A truck loaded with women pulled out of the gates and caught my attention. An empty truck drove in to take its place and a new queue was formed. "Where are they going?" I asked, motioning toward the line.

"Farm workers," Gaia said.

My spirits brightened. My mother always loved reading about nature. If she was out here, she would try to be picked for work on a farm.

"Helloooo." Hazel waved a hand in front of my face.

"Can I work on the farm today?" I asked Hazel.

"Why would you want to work on a farm?" Gaia asked.

"My mom was Culled last spring and I'm hoping she made it out here. If she did, she'd want to be on a farm."

"I am going to take disciplinary action if you don't answer my question," Hazel said.

I wondered what disciplinary action an urchin could give another urchin. "I already answered you."

She threw her hands up in the air. "That's it, I'm reporting you."

"Why?" I asked in confusion.

I looked to Gaia for help, but she just crossed her arms over her chest and pointedly stared at Hazel. "I know *nothing*," she said.

I had no idea what was going on, but one thing was painfully obvious—these two women did not like each other.

"The heir isn't out here," Hazel said as if it were common knowledge. "I don't know why you're lying, but if you want to work on the farm, be my guest princess. I am going to report you."

I wasn't sure what it meant to be reported. In the Pit, if a worker displeased her supervisor, she was beaten. But I was anxious to see if my mother was here and decided it was worth the trouble of being reported. Hazel walked away in disgust.

"What's her problem?" I asked.

"I don't know. Whore-envy?" Gaia shrugged. "Nobody likes a mistress, especially an urchin lord."

Her comment reminded me of how Summer and Crystal were treated by everyone in the Pit. They hadn't been liked or trusted, either. I had to remember that my own kind might see me as a traitor.

"What do you do here?" I asked.

"Depends on what needs to be done, but it's always one of the easier jobs of the day. One of the perks of being owned by an old, pompous, disgusting drunk," she said. "You better get on the truck before it leaves without you. Good luck finding your mom."

"Thanks."

I hopped on the truck just before it pulled away. A few of the women gave me a curious look, but they didn't speak to me. The truck turned around and drove back out through the gate.

We were driven away from the corral, passing several large buildings spaced far apart. I could see animals grazing on green grass and fields of tall plants with people working between the rows.

Eventually the truck turned into the driveway of one of the farms and came to a stop alongside a tiny building. A lone soldier standing guard at the entrance stuck his arm into a small shed and then waved us through. We didn't go much farther before the truck stopped and let everyone off. Most people seemed to know where they were going, but I didn't. I wandered around, looking for someone in charge.

"You're new here!" a girl exclaimed.

She couldn't have been more than fourteen. I thought only those Culled were out here, but now I wondered if the homeless were sent here, too. The idea made me think of my father. Should I dare to hope they sent out prisoners they no longer had a use for?

"Yes I am," I said.

She linked her arm through mine and began to lead me toward a man who was shouting out orders.

"My name is Abby. My real name is Abrille, which is my family's old way of saying April—the month I was born."

"I'm Sunny."

"You were named for your fiery hair. It looks just like a sunset," Abby said with a smile.

That took me by surprise. Did she know my name was Sunset or was she just making a comparison? Jack and I had been counting on the fact that no one out here knew we were traitors. If word got around, it wouldn't take long for them to arrest us.

"Have you been out here long?" I asked casually.

"I just came outside this morning, silly. But I try to come out every morning."

"No, I didn't mean outside the corral, I meant outside the Dome."

"I've lived my entire life inside the Dome," she said. I shook my head. This conversation was going in a circle. She cupped her hands around her mouth and yelled, "Ben!" The man she was leading me toward looked in our direction. "We have a new one."

He walked toward us with a pronounced limp. "Hi," he said, shaking my hand.

"I'm Sunny."

"Lord knows we can use the extra help today. We're putting in a new field. Ploughed it out yesterday, but the magic soil has to be mixed in today. You can grab a tractor if you know how to use one or a rake if you don't."

"Looks like I'll be using a rake."

"That's the spirit! Not many volunteer for that. Can you take her… um… sorry, I forget who you are."

"It would be my pleasure, Ben." Abby linked her arm back through mine and pulled in the direction of the field. "That's hard work you just volunteered to do."

"I like the exercise," I said.

"Okay, you asked for it!" She laughed and broke into a run.

For a moment I watched her run ahead, a little perplexed by her behavior. I sprinted to catch up with her.

"That's one of the great things about being out here," Abby exclaimed. "Wide open spaces and lots of air!" She threw her arms wide and turned around in a circle laughing. "I wish my family was here. It's paradise! Maybe next time I come out, I'll bring them with me."

I was beginning to wonder if she was a few trousers short of a full load. "It is pretty spectacular."

"You've probably never put in a full day's work under the sun, so I'll just let you know you're in for a real treat."

At the mention of a full day's work, I thought of Summer. If only she was out here to work with me today. I tried not to think too much about what she might be doing right now. It made my heart too heavy. I needed to think about finding a way to free her instead.

"That's the field," she said, pointing at a huge area of land scarred by machines. "It doesn't look like much now, but one day it's going to be sprouting with life and we're helping to make those plants. We're like gods!"

I looked at Abby with an indulgent smile. As Summer would say, she was a wackadoodle. But I liked her and no longer thought she posed a threat to my identity.

She led me to a supply area, where rakes and other tools were kept. Small tractors were parked side by side.

"What job are you going to do today?" I asked.

"Oh, I'm not going to work. I only came for the food. I'll see you later, Sunny." She walked away.

I raised my hand, about to call after her, worried that she was going to get herself into trouble. She couldn't just wander around aimlessly and not get beaten for her laziness. But then I remembered it was urchin lords out here supervising our work. No one from the Pit would be cruel enough to hurt a sweet girl like Abby. I dropped my hand and watched her go.

I eyed the rakes, noticing they came in different sizes. Was there some kind of criteria for which size I should use? Picking one up, I tested its weight. It seemed okay.

"You should take a tractor before they're all gone. Makes for an easier day," said a woman. "First time I've seen you here."

"I'm Sunny," I said, extending my hand to her. "I just came out of the Dome yesterday."

"I'm Opal," she said, accepting my handshake. "If you don't mind me saying so, you're awfully young to be out here."

"Someone brought me with him."

She tilted her head slightly. "Do you mind me asking who?"

There was no point in hiding who I was here with. If word of the heir's arrival hadn't already gotten around, it would soon. "Jack Kenner."

"The heir?" she asked in disbelief. I nodded. She

looked alarmed. "So, is the president coming out soon?"

"I don't think so."

She put a hand on her chest and breathed out. "That's a relief. I'm not saying things are *good* under General Powell, but I am saying they could be a lot worse."

Looking around the farm, I nodded. "It's definitely not the Pit."

"No, it's not," she agreed. "I'll see you later, Sunny."

"My mom was Culled last spring," I said before she could leave. It got her attention and she turned back at me. "I'm hoping she made it out here alive."

"What's her name?" Opal asked.

"Lilly O'Donnell."

She thought about it for a moment. "Sounds kind of familiar…I don't know. One thing's for sure, she doesn't work on this farm."

My shoulders slumped at her answer, but I tried to shake off the disappointment. At least her name sounded familiar, which was encouraging. And there were lots of other farms out here. She could be at any one of them.

"Thanks anyway. I'll keep looking." I returned my attention to the rakes.

Opal hesitated and then walked back toward me. "I don't mind showing you how to use the tractor. We take shifts so no one ends up raking all day."

I smiled, truly grateful she had decided to take me on as an apprentice. "Thanks. I'd really appreciate that."

For the next fifteen minutes, Opal gave me a crash course on how to operate the small tractor. She told me they could be equipped with different tools, but today it was fitted with a shovel so we could scoop magic soil and deposit it on the field. From there, it would be raked out to cover the field. When I asked what magic soil was, she said she had no idea. It was Doc's concoction that worked with his magic seeds. The wheat we planted today would be ready to harvest in four weeks.

The tractor wasn't as easy as Opal made it look. Driving was difficult enough, but coordinating driving and operating the shovel at the same time was complicated. She did her best to get me started, but other farm workers were trying to get into her empty tractor and she had to leave.

As I tried to coordinate my hands and feet, a man stepped in front of the tractor and pointed toward the field. "If you can't drive it, get out and give it to someone who can."

Before I could react, I caught sight of Opal's tractor bearing down on him. He jumped, turned and ran. She chased him right back onto the field and then pulled up alongside of me. "Don't let anybody bully you. At some point, they had to learn too."

After several more failed attempts to the sarcastic cheers of the other workers, I actually managed to get a small shovelful. Triumphantly, I drove out onto the field and dumped it. Although several people scrambled to get out of my way, I didn't actually run over anyone so I considered it a success. Returning to the mound, I scooped an even bigger shovelful and returned to the field to dump it. Opal gave me a thumbs up.

After only a few trips, a horn sounded. The tractors came to a rest and the rakers walked off the field. It was lunchtime already. I had spent the entire morning just learning how to use the tractor and hadn't accomplished much. In the Pit, I would've been in a lot of trouble for wasting so much time. But here, no one seemed to care. In fact, there weren't many guards at all.

I parked the tractor and walked with the others to where tables were set up under a stand of trees. Platters of food—real food, not scraps or leftovers—lined the entire length of the tables. I picked up something big and red and stared at it.

"That's an apple," the person next to me said. "It's delicious."

I put one on my plate and then loaded it with other delectable-looking treats. There was no one here to ration it. People just helped themselves to whatever they wanted. I could almost imagine that this was a real farm instead of a labor camp. When my plate was full, I went looking for a place to sit.

"Come and join us, Sunny," Opal called. She was sitting under a tree with two other women.

"You're so young! What brings you out here?" one of the women asked.

"Jack Kenner brought her with him," Opal announced.

She looked satisfied by their shocked expressions.

One woman recovered quickly from the news, her initial look of shock transforming into a sneer. "And you're sitting with us?"

I hesitated, no longer sure if I should sit with them, but Opal still had an inviting smile.

"Jack Kenner is out here? Why?" the other one asked, a note of fear in her voice.

I sat down. "He's replacing the tech guy, Dirk," I said. Crossing my legs, I set my plate on my lap and extended my hand to the woman. "I'm Sunny."

"Ruby," she replied absentmindedly, shaking my hand. "Are you sure that's the only reason he's out here? I mean, somebody as important as Jack Kenner might be here to get things ready for the president."

"He told me there's a problem with the computers and he's here to fix it," I lied. The other woman was still looking at me with contempt. I tried to look sad for her benefit. "I never really wanted to be chosen for that kind of...*work*. My mom taught me how to color my hair black and wear loose clothes so no one would pick me. But I guess I'm lucky I got to come out with him. Never thought I'd feel the breeze on my face or see blue sky in my lifetime."

"Neither did any of us," Ruby said. "And we didn't come out here on the arm of a good-looking man—we all thought we were going to be Culled. I still kiss the ground every morning when I wake up."

"She does," Opal laughed.

"As if you don't," the other woman said. She gave me a tight smile. "I'm Violet." She extended her hand to me and I shook it.

"Sunny's looking for her mom—she's hoping she escaped the Cull. What did you say her name was?" Opal asked.

"Lilly O'Donnell." I looked at the other two ladies, hoping to see some recognition on their faces.

Violet shook her head. "Sorry. Doesn't sound familiar. Did she come out with our group?" she asked Opal.

"I'm pretty sure I know all the women from our group. When was she Culled?" Opal asked.

"A few months ago."

"She would be new then," Ruby said. "We don't know all the new women yet. How did you like driving the tractor this morning?"

"It was actually kind of fun," I said. "It took me a long time to get the hang of it though. I'm surprised I didn't get into trouble. But then again, there aren't many guards around to crack the whip."

"It's not like the Pit," Opal said. "Guards are really only used to oversee crews working outside of the fence."

"So what's to stop us from running away?" I asked.

"Uh, that thing in our neck," Violet said, pointing to her own throat.

"Besides, who knows what's *out there,*" Ruby said,

sweeping a hand toward the mountains. "They had to put a wire fence around the corrals to keep the animals out. The bears are huge and they like the smell of food."

My eyes strayed to the mountains and for the first time since leaving the Dome, I wondered what was out there. Jack and I had seen animal tracks in the woods, so obviously there were creatures living on Earth. Were they friendly animals? Or man-eaters?

"How are things in the Pit?" Opal asked.

They all looked at me expectantly. I wasn't prepared for the question. Should I be honest? I guess I could be… to a point. "Not good. There's been fighting between the Pit and the Dome."

Violet made a dismissive sound. "There's always been bad blood between the Pit and the Dome."

"No. I mean there was actual fighting. There was a battle."

The shock that registered on their faces quickly turned to one of disbelief. "You're lying," Violet said.

"Why would I lie about that?" I asked in confusion. "Crystal—Malcolm West's mistress—overheard President Holt say he planned to get rid of everyone in the Pit. He wants to kill us all. She exposed his plan through a song she wrote."

"What?" Opal exclaimed in disbelief. "There's no way the president would kill everyone in the Pit. It's too monstrous, even for him."

Ruby shook her head in denial. "The president has no reason to kill everyone in the Pit. Limited resources aren't an issue anymore. There's plenty of food and water."

"They executed Crystal. On television." My voice caught and tears stung my eyes. The memory ran uncensored through my head before I could even think to stop it. My stomach clenched with nausea. "They made us all watch. It sparked a bloody riot."

Ruby put one hand over her mouth and touched my arm with her other one.

"If that's true—" Opal started to say, but Violet cut her off.

"Sssshhh, here comes the crazy one."

Following Violet's gaze, I saw Abby coming toward us carefully carrying a glass of water. Pushing my fingers up under my glasses, I rubbed the tears away before they had a chance to spill.

Abby stopped beside me and carefully lowered the glass toward my hand. "Here's some water, Sunset."

In a state of mild shock, I accepted the offered glass from her. Did she actually know my name or was she coincidentally making reference to my hair again?

"Thank you," I said.

Abby looked at the other ladies. "She's new. She doesn't know about all the free water." Then she turned back to me. Hands clasped in front of her, Abby wore a motherly expression as she explained, "You can take it whenever you like. No one is going to get mad."

Violet snickered, but covered her rudeness with a cough.

Opal glared at Violet, her mouth drawn in a tight line. "That's very nice of you, Abby."

"Oh, it's my pleasure. You guys can take care of her now. I'm going to go home. My family might be worried."

"You do that, Abby. I'm sure they miss you a lot," Opal said softly. Oblivious, Abby skipped away. As soon as she was gone, Opal smacked Violet's leg. "I can't believe you would laugh at that poor girl."

"What happened to her?" I asked. My interest in Abby was definitely piqued.

"She hasn't been out here long—a few days maybe? Someone told me she lost her entire family. I'm not sure if it was a blessing or a torture to let her come out here instead of Culling her. She's still in denial, the poor little thing," Opal said.

It was impossible to hide my look of surprise. "She's only been out here a few days?"

Opal gasped, putting a hand over her mouth. "Oh my God! You're telling the truth about the battle in the Pit. I bet that's when her family died."

Understanding began to dawn on me. I looked back at Abby and watched her pick up some apples and stuff them in her pockets. She looked around to see if anyone had observed her stealing the food. Satisfied that she had not been seen, she patted her bulky pockets, happy with her secret.

Ben walked by and shooed us all back to work. I

didn't want to leave our conversation hanging in mid-air, but as each woman stood I knew it was at an end. In silence, we stacked our empty plates on the table and returned to work.

Someone had already claimed the tractor I had been driving. A protest hovered on my lips, but then I remembered Opal told me we took shifts so no one ended up raking all day. I found a rake and got to work.

The sun beamed down on the open field. If not for the constant breeze cooling my damp skin, it would've felt like the laundry room all over again. Abby was right—working outside in the clean fresh air really was a treat.

My heart went out to Abby. This entire war was an injustice. The terms of the treaty were clear: when the world was finally safe to inhabit, we would go free. We had paid our dues. We owed the bourge nothing more.

The bruise on my left side protested at the strain of raking. It had looked easy enough when I was driving the tractor, but now that I was actually doing the work, I understood why they took shifts. My hands were starting to hurt too.

"I have an extra pair of gloves if you want them."

I looked up to find Violet holding out the gloves. I smiled at her, happy that her scornful attitude was gone.

"Thanks. Why does it smell so bad?" I asked, poking at the soil.

"There's a natural fertilizer mixed in with it."

"What's that?"

"Animal dung. Although it doesn't stink too badly this time, so it's not chicken. It's probably cow or horse," she said.

"That explains it." Enviously, I watched the people driving the tractors. "I wonder why they don't have machines to do the spreading too."

"They told us the replicators are all tied up producing materials to build the city. They only invested in basic farm equipment. One day there'll be machines to do all this."

"And that will be the day they don't need us anymore."

Violet regarded me for a moment. "I pray you're wrong." She put her head down and went back to work.

Leaning my rake against my shoulder, I put on the gloves and used the opportunity to scan the field. Only a few soldiers stood guard along the perimeter. If it weren't for the tagging system, we could easily overpower them. I looked at Violet, who was now putting distance between us. Persuading this group to rebel against the bourge was going to be infinitely more difficult than it had been motivating the Pit. Out here they had something to live for. Hope. Not the kind of hope that was stretched thin across generations, but one that was almost within their grasp. They just thought they had to work a little bit more to get it. Somehow I had to make them realize their future was a false hope.

The real problem was the tagging system. If we could get that shut down, maybe everyone would take up arms to help free the Pit. Jack might be able to do it. He was good with computers.

As my thoughts strayed to Jack, a heavy feeling grew in my chest. I tried to shake it off. There was no point in longing for something that could no longer be. In the Pit we were equals. Out here, we were not. A relationship between us was never going to work. It was just getting in the way of keeping a clear head and staying focused.

I wondered what he was doing right now. Had he found a way back into the Dome? Or fixed the comms and sent a message? What if he *had* sent a message—would he be caught? For all I knew, he could be in custody right now...or worse.

My heart pounded at the thought.

Suddenly I had an urge to be with him, to see for myself that he was okay. Looking around, I tried to figure out what time it was. But this wasn't the Pit—there were no clocks hanging on walls. I had no idea how long it was until quitting time.

I tore into my raking with vigor, as if working faster might make the day end sooner. It didn't—but at least the physical activity helped keep my anxiety in check until the horn sounded.

I returned my rake to the shed and climbed into the back of a waiting truck. Violet surprised me when she sat next to me.

"If what you told me is true..." She gripped one of

my hands in hers. "I have family in the Pit. My son and granddaughter."

I gripped her hand tighter in response. "We all have family and friends in the Pit."

The truck left the farm and bounced down the dirt road to the urchin corral. As I looked down at our linked hands, it occurred to me that I didn't need to try to unite these people with the Pit. They already were.

Chapter Seven

Relief flooded through me when we pulled into the corral and I saw Jack standing there. I wondered why there were so many soldiers surrounding him. As I watched from the back of the truck, the soldiers flanking Jack questioned my supervisor. The woman appeared to be pleading with them, although he wasn't paying much attention to the drama. He was more interested in the arrival of our truck. He scanned faces until he came upon mine. His tense expression relaxed and he strode toward me.

As soon as I hopped off the truck he grabbed me by the arm and practically threw me on the back of a bike. His security detail caught up to him as he slid onto the seat in front of me.

He jabbed a finger at them. "Do *not* follow me."

The men looked at each other in confusion as Jack revved the engine. He sent a spray of dirt up as the bike roared out of the gate. I cast a backward glance at the corral. The soldiers were pacing nervously.

Jack steered the bike out onto a dirt road and across an open field. Within minutes we were in the woods. He dodged around rocks, trees and low-hanging branches. I wondered how long he had spent learning to ride the bike today and whether he had worked on the comms at all. He kept driving like a maniac for a long time before he pulled to a stop. He kicked at the stand and let the bike come to a rest before he climbed off. I did too.

"I almost lost it when the jeep showed up with only Gaia in the back, and that was *hours* ago, Sunny," he said. "Why were you the only one not where she was supposed to be and—oh my *God, what* is that *smell*?" He put a hand over his nose.

I sniffed. "It's me. I've been raking fertilizer all afternoon."

"What?" he asked blankly.

"Poop. They use it as fertilizer in the *magic* soil. I'm told it was probably horse or cow poop, but it wasn't chicken because apparently that really stinks."

The corners of his mouth twitched upward. "Why were you doing that?"

"Because they ploughed out a new field and it needed to be spread."

His expression turned droll. "No, I mean why didn't you go with Gaia today?"

"I didn't know I was supposed to."

"Didn't you tell your supervisor you were out here with me?"

"Yes, but she didn't believe me. Besides, I wanted to go to the farm so I could look for my mom."

He relaxed his stance. "Okay, that explains a lot. It's starting to make sense now."

"Are you going to let me in on it? Because I have no idea what you're talking about."

"Your supervisor told me no one of your description had come through today, which scared the hell out of me. A seventeen-year-old redhead is hard to miss out here. That's why I called in a search party. I was ready to rip the place apart."

"Why would she lie?"

"She was afraid of getting in trouble. You should have stayed with Gaia—we need to be careful out here, Sunny."

"I don't know the rules of being a concubine, Jack. I've never been one before and there's no one here to teach me," I said defensively. "And I told everyone that Mr. Kenner likes me to have a fit body and wouldn't mind me coming home smelling like poop."

"I'm not mad. I would've wanted to find my mom too." The tension faded away from his stance. "And for future reference, Mr. Kenner does mind you coming home smelling like poop."

I chuckled. "He's going to have to get used to it, because I'm hoping to try a different farm tomorrow if they'll let me." He wrinkled his nose. "Is that why there were so many soldiers at the corral? You were going to send a search party to look for me?" The thought made me happy.

"Yes," he said, as if it was obvious. "Speaking of search party, my security might come looking for me. Technically, they aren't supposed to leave my side."

"So why did they?"

Jack shrugged. "When I give them a command like that, they have two choices; ignore me and suffer whatever consequences I dish out, or obey me and suffer whatever consequences Powell dishes out. Leisel used to play with her guards like that all the time. Anyway, they might reconsider their choice and come looking, so we better hurry up."

"Why? What are we doing?"

"I want to teach you to shoot and how to drive the bike. It could come in handy if you need to make a fast getaway."

"I learned how to drive a tractor today," I said proudly.

"And that's great if you ever need a slow getaway." I laughed. "Now pay attention."

He took out his pistol and went through all the parts with me, where the safety was and how to manipulate it, how to change the magazine, and then how to fit it with a silencer. Next, he stood behind me, put the gun in my hands and showed me how to aim.

"Whoa," he said, waving at the air. I craned my neck to shoot him a wry look, but had to laugh when I saw his eyes were watering. I hadn't realized I smelled that bad.

"We're going to aim for that dead log on the ground."

His hands guided mine around the cold barrel of the gun, positioning my finger on the trigger. We pulled together, the gun fired, part of the log shattered. The shock of the gun firing reverberated up my arms.

"Now you try it," he said, dropping his hands.

I went through an entire magazine and hit the log only twice. Jack reloaded and I went through another, this time successfully hitting my mark five times, but by the end of the second magazine my arms felt weak.

"Good," Jack said. "You're getting the hang of it. We'll come back tomorrow and try it again. Now, on to the bike before my security tracks us down."

He took the back seat of the bike, motioning for me to get on the front. Once I was seated, he leaned around me and tapped the front panel. Our cheeks made contact, which probably wasn't a good idea, but his smoothly shaved skin felt warm and soft. I didn't pull away. "It's both solar- and gas-operated. It can run at a faster speed using gas, but it makes a lot of noise. You can still get decent speed using solar, and it's quiet. We'll use solar right now." He showed me how to set it to solar and start the bike. "Now, throttle and clutch," he said, easing the bike forward. "Try it."

I did exactly what he did and the bike lurched forward, throwing me back against him, and then stalled. Jack quickly put both feet on the ground to steady the vehicle. It took a different kind of coordination than driving the tractor.

"Try it again," he said. I did, with the same result. "Again," he repeated. I tried again and failed.

"It's not working for me," I said in frustration.

He covered my hands with his. "Thottle, clutch," he said, guiding my hands to make the movements. "When you have a little speed, we'll shift."

I took a deep breath and tried it again. Throttle. Clutch. The bike jumped but moved forward this time.

"Let go of the clutch and give it more throttle," he instructed. I did and the bike moved faster. "You need to switch gears, so clutch again." I did as he told me and then felt his foot kick mine—that's where the shift was located. "Ease off the clutch and it give it more throttle," he instructed.

"I'm doing it!"

I gave it more throttle and the bike went faster. The wind blew my hair away from my face and into Jack's. The faster I went, the more thrilling the ride was.

"Slow down, and bring it to a stop," Jack instructed.

I slowed, and I almost dropped the bike when it came to a stop, but Jack planted both his feet on either side.

"Whoops," I said.

"That's why I wanted you to stop—so you would see what happens when the bike isn't in motion. Okay, take me for another ride."

"This is fun!"

He smiled broadly. "I know."

"You've been doing this all day, haven't you?"

"Not all day. We'll talk it about it later. Ready?"

More than ready. This time when I engaged the bike it only hesitated a little before it took off. I shifted gears and went faster. Ahead of us was a hill and I increased our speed. But as we crested the top, I saw something on the path. Startled, I pulled the bike sharply to one side. The front wheel jerked out of control and I held onto the handles tight. I saw the rock sticking out of the ground but couldn't avoid it.

It didn't register that I was thrown from the bike until I found myself on the ground. It all happened so fast. I looked around for Jack and saw him pushing himself up from the ground. I sat up as he walked toward me.

"Are you okay?" he asked.

My already-bruised side was in pain, but nothing else. "Yeah. Are you?"

"What happened?" he asked, ignoring my question. He pulled me up.

"I thought I saw something on the road."

I searched the area to see where it was. That's when I saw them.

People, standing among the trees, staring at us.

Chapter Eight

Momentarily paralyzed, I stood as stock-still as they were. I counted at least eight.

"Sunny?" Jack's voice penetrated my brain. He waved a hand in front of my face. "Hello?"

"There are people here," I whispered.

"What?"

"Sssshhh," I said, even though I was pretty sure they could hear us. "There are people in the trees, watching us."

Jack's eyes widened at the news and he snapped around to scan the trees. "I don't see anyone."

"They're right in front of you."

"Did you get too much sun today?" he asked, without bothering to whisper.

Unmoving, I scrutinized the group standing in the forest. A couple of them were small, and it struck me they might be children. Tentatively, I moved one step toward them.

"Hello," I said.

Moving only their eyes, they exchanged worried glances.

"There's no one there," Jack said impatiently. To prove it, he strode purposefully toward the trees.

They bolted.

Startled, Jack backed up a few steps and almost fell over me.

"Get on the bike!" he ordered, picking it up off the ground.

I jumped on right behind him just as he switched it to gas and revved the engine to life. With a jolt, the bike lurched forward and I wrapped my arms around his waist to keep from being thrown off. He didn't slow down until we reached town.

We wound our way past the farms and urchin corrals and eventually parked in front of the house we shared. A security guard was at the front door. At our arrival, he unhooked his communicator and spoke into it.

Jack dismounted the bike first. He looked up and down the street.

"They didn't follow us," I said.

"What the hell were they?"

"People," I said. "They spooked me at first too, but now that I've had time to calm down, I don't think they meant us any harm."

"You can't be sure about that."

We walked through the front gate and up to the door. The security guard said nothing to Jack as we went into the house, but I noticed he unhooked his communicator.

I closed the door behind us. "There were eight of them. If they wanted to attack us, they had the advantage."

"Eight?" Jack asked in surprise. "How do you know that?"

"Are you telling me you couldn't see them?"

He walked to the window and peeked outside. "Not until they moved. Did you get a good look at them?"

"Yeah. They looked like they were painted or something. There were markings all over their skin and clothes, and they all had the same long hairstyle. I couldn't tell if it was braided or twisted, but it wasn't loose."

Jack narrowed his eyes and drew his brows together. "You saw them in that kind of detail?"

"Yes. They were right in front of us."

"Were they armed?"

"I don't think so. A couple of them looked like kids."

"Really?"

I nodded.

"Well, I don't think they followed us," he said, although I could tell by the way he kept glancing out of the window that he wasn't convinced. I moved to stand next to him.

"They didn't follow us."

"You should go have your shower now."

"What?"

He shot me a crooked smile. "No offense, but you really stink."

I looked at him wryly. "Wouldn't want to offend your

sensitive nose," I said, but he wasn't really listening. I headed for the bathroom.

Despite slathering my body with sunscreen, my skin had turned an even darker shade of pink, and it was slightly sore to the touch. I set the shower to a cooler temperature and washed away the day's dirt.

I couldn't get my mind off the people I had seen in the forest. Where had they come from? The obvious assumption was that they came from the Dome. Maybe they were escapees from years ago. But even as the thought crossed my mind, I dismissed it.

One of my favorite things to do with Summer was watch movies in the common room. There wasn't a movie we didn't like, because we really didn't watch them for the story. They were a window into the past and showed us what the world was like before the bombs obliterated it. And what a world it must've been with blue sky, sunshine and people in every color, shape and size you could think of. I always wondered why everyone in the Dome looked so much alike when history showed us that we hadn't always.

Although the people in the forest were all dressed alike, physically they were different. Their skin ranged in color from pale to khaki to dark brown. I looked at my own skin, now pink from the sun, and thought of everyone from the Dome I'd seen out here. The sun had made their skin darker, but it still wasn't as dark as the two I saw in the woods.

Their eyes were different too. At least four of them had Asian eyes. I had never seen anyone in the Dome with eyes like that—only in the movies.

But if they weren't from the Dome, where were they from? A shiver ran down my spine and I suddenly didn't want to be alone. I dressed quickly and went in search of Jack. I found him in the kitchen.

"Hungry?" he asked, without turning around. My lunch had been more than a full day's ration by Pit standards, but I would never turn down food.

"A little. Can I help?"

Jack took out eggs and some kind of meat from the refrigerator. "This is the only thing I know how to cook."

I was about to say I didn't know how to cook anything when someone knocked on the door. Jack's head snapped up in the direction of the sound, then back at me. He gave me an apologetic look. "That's probably Powell. I was hoping we wouldn't have to do this tonight. Last night was hard enough." He left to answer the door, squeezing my shoulder on his way past. I stayed in the kitchen. "General Powell, what a surprise." Jack's voice drifted into the kitchen.

"He's here," Powell yelled to someone. "I told them you just went for a joy ride and you'd be back."

"Please, come in."

"I can come in for a drink." I heard him stumble across the threshold and the door closed.

"What can I get you?" Jack asked politely.

"Oh, whatever you have stocked in your cupboard. I know it changes from week to week. And a little something to eat too, if you don't mind. I left the mess before they served dinner."

"Sunny," Jack called. I emerged from the kitchen just as Powell was settling his plump frame onto the sofa. "Some food and drink for the general and me."

I nodded silently, knowing better than to speak in front of the bourge, and returned to the kitchen. Eyeing the refrigerator, I tried to think what I could possibly make. The only work I had ever done in a kitchen was peel vegetables. I checked the refrigerator and found some carrots. Perfect. I knew how to prepare those.

I peeled the carrots, took out two plates and arranged the vegetables on each, and then realized it looked like a sparse meal by bourge standards. They were used to having heaps of food. I sized up the bowl of eggs Jack took out of the refrigerator. I watched him make them yesterday and it hadn't looked that difficult. I approached the stove with more confidence than I felt.

I found the frying pan exactly where I remembered he put it. The stove was a little more difficult to figure out. All I could do was turn knobs until I noticed an element turning bright red. I put the frying pan on it. Next, I turned my attention to the eggs. I cracked their shells on the side of a bowl and their contents slipped out. It wasn't difficult at all. Once I had all the eggs in the bowl, I stirred them with a fork. I didn't remember him adding anything else, so I poured the eggs into the pan. They sizzled and crackled, making a lot more noise than I remembered. A burning smell filled the kitchen. Quickly, I grabbed the pan off the stove and almost dropped it when I seared two fingers on the handle.

I bit back a cry and stuck my burning fingers under cold water. As soon as the pain subsided, I went back to cooking the eggs, but my fingers started stinging again. I found a cloth and made a cold compress.

The pan was cooler now, so I stirred the eggs around in an attempt to make them look fluffy like Jack's. But mine were a dark brown on the bottom and still kind of slimy on top. I divided them between the two plates, arranging them in an effort to hide as much of the brown as I could. At least the plates looked full. On to making drinks.

I hunted through the cupboards until I found a bottle marked *Scotch*. I recalled Hayley said Jack likes scotch. I took out two glasses and filled them.

With the food and drink ready, I took them out to the living room. I was kind of proud of myself for pulling it off. It hadn't been that hard at all.

Both men looked up at me as I entered the room. I set the plates down on the small table between them, although with the cold compress still wrapped around my fingers it proved a little difficult. One plate landed with a clunk. I shot Jack an apologetic look and was surprised to see an expression of mirth on his face.

I wondered what I had done wrong. I returned to the kitchen for the drinks.

"Carrots and...are those eggs?" Powell asked just as I came back into the living room.

"I think so," Jack replied.

I set the glasses on the table, one in front of Jack, the other in front of the general.

"And..." Powell picked up his drink and sniffed it. "Scotch?" He raised his eyebrows at me.

"Yes, sir."

"That will be all, Sunny," Jack said. I went back into the kitchen, but stayed close to the door to eavesdrop. "My apologies. She hasn't been out here long enough to have been trained in the kitchen."

"My point exactly, Jack. She shouldn't have been on the farm. If she had gone with Gaia she would've started her training today."

"I'll make sure she goes tomorrow."

"I want you to know that the supervisor in question has been dealt with appropriately," he said, his words slightly slurred. "By now all the urchins in the corral know exactly who your girl is and they'll treat her a little nicer."

"I appreciate that," Jack said. "I did want to ask you about another incident from today. I came across some people in the forest —" Jack began, but Powell interrupted him.

"You *saw* those little heathen buggers?" Powell asked incredulously. "You must have a keen eye, Jack, because those heathens blend in with the earth. You could be standing right next to one and you'd never know it."

"Heathens?"

"Jesus Christ, you saw them—running around the forest dressed in animal skins and all painted up. They're nothing like the God-fearing civilized people we are, Jack. They're *heathens*!"

"So *you* can see them?" asked Jack.

"I haven't personally seen them out here, although a few of my men have. The only ones I ever saw were in the Dome. The ones we captured."

"Yeah, the ones we captured," Jack repeated. "I was hoping I'd get to see them in the Dome, but...what happened to them?"

"The same thing that happens to anyone who outgrows his value. For chrissake Jack, the Dome isn't a goddamn hotel."

"Of course. I just meant it would've been nice to see one up close. Anyway, you were saying?"

"What was I saying? Oh yeah. We've been capturing the buggers over the past eighty years, running tests on them for radiation, disease, anything that could tell us the state of the environment. And we've interrogated them. All the captives tell the same story—the mountain gives them protection from the bad people." Powell laughed and I heard him slap something. "Apparently our mountain has the reputation of being alive or haunted or some damn thing so the *bad people* stay away.

Do you believe that?" Powell laughed so hard he fell into a fit of coughing.

"There are more people?" Jack exclaimed. "Are you telling me the earth's population survived the holocaust?"

"Jesus, Jack, Damien doesn't tell you much, does he?" I heard the general pick up his scotch and swallow.

"I haven't been in the family that long. I'm sure he was going to tell me eventually. Why else would he have sent me out here?"

"Well, considering the UAVs never came back the first time we sent them out, it was lucky for us the heathens made their home around our mountain. Otherwise, we might still be living inside the Dome afraid to come out." The general set his glass down with a thump. "About eighty years ago, we sent the first mission outside the Dome to collect samples. That's when they found a couple of heathens nosing around our garbage. They were the first ones we brought in for questioning. From the information they've given us, we've surmised the earth's population was pretty well devastated from the holocaust, but not completely wiped out. Population has increased over the past three hundred years and people are beginning to form small societies. The heathens tell us there are two warlords—one in the north and one in the south. They're rivals and like to cause each other trouble."

"Is that why you've turned this city into a military base camp?"

"We need to be ready for anything that comes our way. Although, I say bring on the bad guys. Wait until they get a load of us!" Powell chuckled. "The only advanced technology left on earth exists inside that Dome and we own it."

"Are you sure we're the only ones with advanced technology? Its seems to me if people survived the holocaust, maybe technology did too."

"It's possible, but doubtful. We interrogated a lot of heathens and they all told the same story." There was a pause in the conversation. "Think about it, Jack. We have all the power. One day you'll be the president of the goddamn world." Someone took a drink and I assumed it was Powell since he slurped it.

"I never thought of that," Jack said thoughtfully. "So have you made contact with them since you've been out here?"

Powell snorted in disgust. "Yeah. The buggers stole some of our livestock the first winter. Came at a real bad time because some kind of influenza was ripping through the camp. We lost a lot of good men that winter." There was a short pause before he continued. "We didn't have any houses then—just the shacks. I put together a task force to deal with them because there was no way I was going to let them get away with it. But the buggers are masters of camouflage, and it took weeks to find them. Anyway, they claimed it wasn't theft because they left behind a bag of dried weeds—said it was a trade!"

"How did you deal with them?"

"Harshly," Powell said in a firm voice. "The first time it was a couple of cows, the next time it will be a piece of technology. Right now we're superior, and we want to stay that way."

"Absolutely," Jack agreed. "We can't have heathens running around with our technology. I mean, what would the world come to?"

"I knew we'd see eye to eye. You're my kind of man, Jack," Powell said in a heavily slurred voice. "I think you'll make a damn fine president one day."

"Thank you, General. I appreciate your support."

I heard an empty glass hit the table. "Well, I best be getting home. Gaia's probably wondering where I am."

"I'm sure she's distraught. Thanks for stopping by, general."

I heard him walk Powell to the door.

"Remember what we talked about—no more giving your security the slip. I know your wife likes to mess with her guards, but out here riding around the countryside by yourself isn't safe. Have a good night, Jack."

"Good night."

I heard the door close and breathed a sigh of relief.

Chapter Nine

Jack was still standing at the door, hand on the knob, when I ventured into the living room. I cleared my throat and he looked up at me. A smile spread across his face.

"How did you manage to burn eggs and yet not quite cook them?" He walked toward me and unwrapped my compress. "And you burned your fingers too. No blisters though."

"What can I say? I wasn't trained in the kitchen."

"So you were listening."

"I heard everything," I agreed. "By the way, what's a UAV?"

"An unmanned aerial vehicle." He shrugged. "A drone."

Jack looked as tired and haggard as I felt. He put both hands up to his face and covered his eyes for a moment before he dragged them away.

"I don't believe those people are heathens, Jack, any more than I believe they're dangerous."

"One thing's for sure—they're not as dangerous as we are. I mean it's incredible to find out that humans not only survived the holocaust, but they're beginning to rebuild civilization. Three hundred years of struggling to survive and the Dome's on a collision course to wipe it all out."

"We'll find a way to stop him."

"I don't know how!" he snapped.

His flash of anger stunned me.

"I'm sorry, I didn't mean—"

"Don't you get it? This isn't just about freeing the Pit anymore! We can't let that man loose on this world. The whole reason Holt wants to kill everyone in the Pit is to repopulate the earth with his *master race*. So do you really think he's going to tolerate the chance that bloodlines might get mixed with people considered *heathens*? Or anyone else on the planet?" It was obvious he didn't expect me to reply because aside from taking a breath, he kept right on going. "Holt has nuclear warheads, tanks, helicopters, automatic weapons and the ability to replicate them all."

He stared at me as if demanding an answer. I didn't have one. If President Holt really was insane enough to kill everyone in the Pit, then it was reasonable to believe he wouldn't stop there. And what could we do about it? We were just two people against an entire army.

Jack rubbed the heels of his hands against his closed eyes. I was beginning to fear he was about to lose it. The thought was a little scary since I considered myself the weaker of the two of us. I needed him to keep it together.

Sitting down on the sofa, I pointed to the floor in front of me. "Sit here."

He drew his eyebrows together. "Why?"

"Just sit."

He gave me a dubious look, but did as I asked. When he was positioned in front of me, I dug my fingers into the tense muscles of his shoulders, working my way up his neck, then back down again. I remembered how much it calmed him in the Pit. After a few minutes of assaulting his muscles, I felt them begin to relax. Oddly, I felt my own anxiety ease with his.

He picked up his scotch from the table and took a sip.

"I didn't know you liked to drink."

"There wasn't any scotch in the Pit."

Leaning against him, I took the drink out of his hand and sniffed it. Gagging, I passed it back. "I liked it better when you worked out to relieve stress."

He set the drink back on the table. "Maybe we should."

"Should what?"

"Work out. Train. Anything to work off some of this anger." Jack stood and held his hand out to me. I took it and he pulled me up. We moved the low table out of the way. "Remember how to do the warm-up?" He backed up a few steps to give us more space and began with T'ai Chi.

Watching his slow deliberate movements, I copied them. "It wasn't that long ago."

"Still, I'll go easy on you. I wouldn't want to overwork you after you raked poop all day."

"Not to mention cooking and serving you all night," I said with a smile.

He stood straight, raised a leg, and stepped back, then crouched bringing his arms back. I followed.

"Cooking? Is that what you call it?"

"Okay, maybe the pan was a little too hot." My burned fingers had stopped stinging, although the skin felt leathery.

Slowly he brought his leg forward, still bent at the knee, and unfurled it into a high kick. I followed, feeling the stretch of my sore muscles. I began to relax.

Jack's expression sobered. "I'm sorry for the way things have to be out here."

"It's not your fault." I stretched my leg forward, balanced, and then brought it back to stand upright. "Can I ask you a personal question?"

"You know you can."

Even though I wasn't sure I was going to like the answer, I wanted to know anyway. "Is Hayley the girlfriend you talked about?"

Jack's face broke into a grin as he went into another crouch and circled one leg behind him, slowly passing one hand over the other and sweeping it in an upward movement. His muscles rippled with the control of his movements.

"You wouldn't happen to be jealous, would you, Mrs. Kenner?"

I shook my head. "No. Just curious." Even I could hear the lie in my voice.

"No, she's not. Well, I guess I should be honest about her too, in case she corners me and wants to talk. We might have had...relations."

"Might have or did?" I managed to keep a blank expression as jealousy reared up again.

"There's a hazing ritual for high school freshmen at the Academy. We go into the hangar wearing bulletproof vests, split into two teams, and hunt each other," Jack explained. I bit my lips to keep from smiling. Doc told me about the ritual. Morons I remembered he called them. "Hayley was on my team and she cornered me behind a tank and...started making out with me."

"And you didn't turn her down."

His cheeks flushed red and I knew it wasn't because of the exercise. "I was sixteen. Of course I didn't turn her down." He shook his head as if it were wrong to think otherwise. "Not that we went all the way or anything."

"She seems to still care for you." I eyed him to see his reaction.

He shrugged. "She only liked me then because I was the top student in combat training and the one to beat. She only likes me now because she thinks I'm the heir." He turned to face me. "All warmed up?"

"I guess so."

"That doesn't sound enthusiastic. Come on." He flicked his hand at me, grazing my arm. "Show me no mercy."

"I'll try, but I suck at this, remember?" I put up my dukes. He laughed at my pathetic attempt.

"Tell you what," he said, walking around, shutting off the lights. "I'll give you the advantage."

The twilight of the setting sun poured in through the windows. I rolled my eyes in a droll expression. If he couldn't see, he really was blind.

I studied him for a moment, pondering which way I should come at him. I stepped toward him and started to throw my left fist at him but followed through with my right instead. He grabbed my right fist and twisted my arm, making me bend forward to ease the pain it inflicted. He let me go.

"So you want to play rough?" I said, rubbing my arm.

"No mercy."

I decided to fake a roundhouse kick to his side and as I saw his arm begin to block my kick, I dropped my foot to the floor and leaned forward on it to deliver a punch to his face. Always ready, he snatched my hand before it could make contact and in one swift movement, he spun me around and pinned my arm behind me, right against my bruise.

My body arched reflexively against the sudden pain and I snapped my head backward, slamming into something.

"My nose!" He stumbled away from me, cupping a hand over his face. "I think you broke it."

The pain in my side was throbbing. "I'm sorry," I choked out. "I didn't mean it."

A bit of blood oozed out from between his fingers. Ignoring my own pain, I ran to the kitchen for a cloth.

"Let me see." I peeled his hand away from his nose. Using the cloth, I mopped up the blood.

"Be careful, it hurts."

"Stop being a baby."

"Easy for you to say. You don't have a broken nose."

"Your nose isn't broken. Sit down and put your head back." I guided him to the sofa and gently pushed his head back against the rest. He winced when I applied a bit of pressure.

"What happened? Did I hurt you?" he asked.

I shrugged. "The bruise on my side is still a little tender."

As I leaned over him, a few strands of my hair fell forward onto his cheek. His hand came up and smoothed them back behind my ear, his blue eyes never leaving my face.

"I forgot about your injury. Sorry." He dropped his hand away from my hair, trailing his fingers down my arm. Goosebumps sprang up and my breath caught at his touch. I cleared my throat in an effort to conceal it.

"So tomorrow… I guess we have to start saving the world?" I asked dramatically.

"Mmmhmm. Do you have a plan?"

I looked at him in surprise. "No. I was hoping you had one."

"I do."

"Are you going to share it?" I lifted the cloth and

examined his nose for blood. A thin rivulet escaped. I replaced it.

"Last night Powell said the comms went out around the time of the wedding, so I think—and I'm guessing here—that Holt shut down communications from inside."

"Why would he do that?"

"Because once I escaped, I became a wild card. He knows I'm capable of tapping into the system."

"But you told me you tapped into the system before, when you were looking for the codes to the warheads. You didn't find out about this city then."

"There's one place I haven't looked because I don't have access—Holt's personal computer. It's located in his suites and I would have to get past security to access it."

"If it's under guard, why would he need to shut it down?"

He raised his brows in question. "Just in case I could get past his security? Or maybe he's just being overly cautious. As I said, I'm guessing."

His fingertips returned to their exploration of my arm. Breathing was becoming difficult. I was beginning to rethink the no-romance policy. "What's your plan, then?"

"Even though I'm pretty sure I know why comms are down, I'll keep searching in case I'm wrong. The city is linked with the Dome through a fiber optic cable system buried underground. I sent out an order today to have the cable dug up and checked from end to end for any breaks. The cable's enclosed in an armored casing, so I doubt we'll find anything."

"If it's linked to the Dome, then wouldn't there be miles and miles of cable?"

Jack nodded.

"That's going to take forever."

"Exactly. It's a stall tactic. I need to look like I'm doing something to fix the problem." His fingers trailed back up my arm and along my neck, pushing my curtain of hair behind my shoulder. "In the meantime, I can find out how to turn off the tagging system and you spread the word for them to be prepared for when that happens. At least we can try to free everyone out here."

I needed him to stop sending shivers down my back or the no-romance policy was going right out the window.

"Bring your head up," I instructed. He sat up straight, bringing his head so close I felt the tickle of his breath on my neck. I steeled myself against the thrill it sent through me. "I think it's stopped." I stood up, putting a little distance between us.

"My turn to play nursemaid. Let's see your side."

"It's fine. It's just a little tender."

"Come on in the bathroom. I can't see out here."

Taking my hand, he stood and dragged me with him. I went reluctantly, feeling a little awkward about him caring for me. He turned on the bathroom light and we both had to shut our eyes against the glare. Then he was tugging at my t-shirt, pulling it up to see my bruise. I leaned against the vanity as he squatted to get a better look. I felt ridiculous.

"That's bad, Sunny. Maybe you broke a rib."

"No, I didn't. A broken rib hurts way worse than this."

He cast a glance at my reflection in the mirror. "Do I want to know how you know that?"

I shook my head.

He went back to his examination. "Did Doc look at it?"

"Yeah. He said it was nothing to worry about."

Jack traced an outline of the bruise with the tip of his finger and my back arched in response. As I watched his reflection in the mirror, he leaned his head closer to my back. I wasn't sure which registered first—seeing him kiss me or feeling his lips on my bare skin. My ragged inhale was audible in the quiet bathroom.

Jack's eyes flashed to my reflection. "Did that hurt?"

I shook my head, not trusting my voice. It took all of my concentration just to breathe. I needed to break this up or I knew where we were headed—to the bedroom.

He stood and wrapped his arms around my waist, easing me back against his chest. His eyes never left my reflection.

"I know we agreed we're better off as strictly partners, but…I missed you last night."

His honesty surprised me almost as much as his vulnerable expression. I didn't know I had that kind of effect on him. My heart beat a little faster in this moment of truth. The urge to turn around within the circle of his embrace and face him was overwhelming. But if I did, where would it lead? Would my heart be free to do what was best for the Pit, not just for me? The stab of jealousy I felt towards Hayley, the humiliation I endured at playing his slave, the outrage that consumed me when I discovered his role in the sterilization program—all those feelings robbed me of my ability to think clearly.

I held his gaze in the mirror. "I missed you too, but maybe if things were different."

"Does that mean we can't even..." He paused mid-sentence, his cheeks turning pink. "Cuddle?"

My next breath came out as a laugh. Did *the* Jack Kenner just ask me to *cuddle*? The soft word was at complete odds with the hard, muscular arms wrapped around me.

A smile lit up my face. "Awwww, Jack. You mean you like it when I snuggle you at night?"

His cheeks flushed red. Oddly, I was enjoying this. "Of course I like it. You're so soft and gorgeous." It was my turn to blush. I opened my mouth to reply—to tell him although I was flattered, it still wasn't a good idea—but he held up his hand to stop me. "Wait a minute. You didn't let me finish. I was also going to say that it wouldn't be a *romantic* thing, it would be more of a *therapeutic* thing."

"Therapeutic?" I asked.

He nodded. "Yeah."

I raised my eyebrows at his reflection, waiting to hear his definition. He looked back at me. "That's it? Just therapeutic?"

"You need more?"

I laughed, relieved to have the tension of a few moments ago replaced with our normal easy banter. Pushing out of the circle of his arms, I took his hand, shut off the light and led him into the bedroom. "Come on. Let's go have a therapeutic cuddle." How did he talk me into this?

I didn't need to see him to know he was smiling. As we approached the bed, he grabbed me around the waist and pulled me down onto the bed with him. "I promise, no romantic stuff."

Snuggling in closer, I savored the feel of his hard chest beneath my hand. "Strictly therapeutic," I said, more for my benefit than his.

For a few moments, the only sounds that mingled with the silence were the beating of our hearts and contented breaths.

"You still think of me as one of them, don't you?" he asked.

I pulled my head back to look at him. He kept his eyes fixed on the ceiling. Despite his stoic expression, the increased beat of his heart told me my answer was important.

Wishing I had an easy answer, I closed my eyes and rested my forehead against his neck. I breathed deeply, hoping to clear my thoughts, and the scent of him filled me. I hated the bourge, but there was no way I hated Jack. What he was doing for the Pit spoke greater volumes than anything he had done as the heir. He was the greatest person I had ever known.

"No. Not anymore." My hand travelled from his chest to touch his lips. The words "I love you" hovered on my tongue...but I wouldn't let them spill out.

Chapter Ten

The sun beamed down on the open-topped jeep. The temperature was significantly warmer than it had been since I had left the Dome. I looked at Gaia out of the corner of my eye. A sheen of sweat glistened on her brow. She didn't really acknowledge my presence. I wondered if that was just her natural disposition or if it was directed at me.

Turning away from my sour companion, I allowed myself the luxury of enjoying the scenery. Today my confidence outweighed my anxiety. I didn't know that a night spent in the arms of someone who truly cared about me was the foundation for inner strength. I was actually looking forward to driving the tractor and seeing Opal and the other ladies. Maybe I would broach the subject of escaping the corral…although I wanted to feel them out a little more first. As I knew only too well, blind trust could get me into trouble.

The corral was bustling with activity as we pulled in through the gates. One truck full of workers left and was quickly replaced by another. A queue formed for the empty vehicle and I got out of the jeep and started toward it.

"Where are you going?" a voice boomed out. I turned to find Hazel and another woman.

"To work," I said, pointing toward the truck.

She shook her head. "Come on back. Today you get to learn how to be a real princess."

I eyed the truck. It was filling up fast. Soon there wouldn't be any room. "I'm sure if you check it out, you'll find that Mr. Kenner has given me permission to work on the farm."

Hazel took a few steps toward me, placing a hand on her side protectively. It was hard not to miss the grimace of pain on her face. It drew attention to the bruise peeking out from under her glasses.

She stopped a few steps away from me. "I have very *strict* orders regarding you."

That she had been disciplined was obvious. My stomach clenched in response to the knowledge. In the Pit, it was an unspoken rule never to comment on someone's bruises. They were just the visible marks. Eyes couldn't see the real scars left behind by being stripped of all pride—the kind of humiliation that came from being defenseless and weak. I wanted to apologize for being the cause, but knew I had to respect her dignity.

"Okay."

Gaia was standing by herself, the jeep gone. Hazel led me back to her and motioned for us to follow. "The general has requested that Sunny be trained in the kitchen. Gaia, you'll be the one training her."

She took us to a building that looked much the same as all the others in this compound, except there was more traffic going in and out of it.

"What is this place?" I asked.

"The services building. The kitchen and cafeteria are on this side," she said as she opened a door for us. Pointing to the other end of the long, narrow building, she said, "And that side is the laundry room. The only food we cook here is for our own consumption, but we do the laundry for the bourge."

She walked us through the busiest section of the kitchen where several workers were prepping food. A wave of familiarity washed over me. How many days had Summer and I spent peeling vegetables in a kitchen almost exactly like this one? The thought of her sent a pang of unhappiness through me. I wished she were with me right now.

"Work on the stove first," Hazel continued. "After they're done with the food prep, they'll need to start cooking lunch. It's important you respect the cooks and stay out of their way." She stopped by a stove. "Any questions?"

Gaia didn't respond. "Nope," I said.

Hazel gave us a satisfied nod and left. As I watched her go, I saw her hand come up to protect her side.

Gaia lifted her glasses and rested them on top of her head. I did the same. "What do you want to learn how to make?"

"I don't know. How about eggs?"

"What kind of eggs?"

"There are different kinds?"

Gaia rolled her eyes. "This is going to be a long day." She went to a refrigerator, took out a few things, and set them on the counter beside the stove. She opened up a box, revealing eggs. "I'll teach you how to make an omelet."

She cracked a few eggs into a bowl and whipped them, just as Jack had done. This part I knew how to do. It was the frying part that had done me in when I tried to make them. I noticed Gaia hadn't heated her frying pan yet.

She took out a wooden board and put a few vegetables on it, opened a drawer and withdrew a knife. Not a little knife—a big, sharp knife. She chopped the vegetables while I stared at the knife, my mouth hanging open.

"We have access to *knives*?"

Gaia stopped chopping and regarded me, a bland look on her face. "Let me guess. You're going to start talking revolt again." She went back to chopping.

I looked around to see if anyone was listening, but the other workers were well out of hearing distance. "It's an obvious weapon. Don't tell me no one has thought of it."

Her efforts at chopping became a little more demanding, escalating to the point of leaving scars on the chopping board. Then she slammed the knife down on the counter.

I instantly regretted bringing it up.

"Look, I'm sorry," I said. "I always seem to be saying the wrong thing around you. I'll just stop talking."

My apology only seemed to inflame her more and she picked up the cutting board and roughly swiped the almost pulverized vegetables into the bowl. Picking up a fork, she began to beat the eggs. Violently. Tears flowed down her cheeks and into the bowl.

I took a step back from the rage rolling off of her. She caught my movement out of the corner of her eye, and then picked up the entire bowl and threw it against the wall. A mangled half-scream escaped her. Everyone in the kitchen stopped to look at her.

Gaia covered her eyes with her hands. I wasn't sure what to do, but I couldn't just stand by and do nothing.

"Everything's fine," I announced, breaking the unnatural silence that followed her outburst. "She just cut her finger, that's all. I've got it."

The kitchen staff looked unsure, but eventually went back to what they were doing. After all, they had to maintain their schedule or suffer the consequences.

"Gaia, what the hell?" I asked. "I told you I wouldn't talk about it anymore and I meant it."

She dropped her hands away from her eyes. They were wet with tears. "Why did you have to come here?"

I was taken aback by her anger since I didn't really feel I deserved it. "You think I had a choice?"

"Of course you didn't have a choice!" she snapped.

"None of us did. The bourge decide for us. *They* decide who lives and who dies." Her breath caught on a sob and she swallowed it down.

"I know, but I don't understand why you're this upset if you don't want to—" I stopped short of saying "rebel" since I promised her I wouldn't speak of it again.

She stepped toward the counter and leaned against it, staring down at the knife. "I've lived my life according to *their* rules. I always showed up for work on time, I always did what I was asked, even when I was sent upstairs to work at their parties. I knew that if I was a good *urchin*, I would live to see thirty-five." Raising her eyes away from the counter, she looked directly at me. Bitterness and pain clouded her features. "And believe it or not, I had a life worth living—a husband I was madly in love with and a son who owned my heart. Saying goodbye to him when I left for the Cull was the *hardest* thing I ever had to do." She squeezed her eyes shut and fresh tears spilled down her cheeks. "But at least I made it to thirty-five, right? Not everyone does. And my husband—Kal—made it too. So when it was time for the Cull, we walked up the stone stairs of the Pit together. I'm not sure I could've walked through those big steel doors into the Dome without his support. I was so scared I could barely walk. But he just kept talking me through every step, telling me we would still be together on the other side."

Her bottom lip trembled and she drew in a long sobbing breath. Hesitantly, I placed a hand on her shoulder, unsure if it was a welcome comfort, but she didn't even seem to notice. She swiped at her wet cheeks.

"Domers escorted all of us through a maze of halls to a big empty room. We were ushered inside and big steel doors closed, locking us in. We all thought we were going to be gassed and some people started screaming. I think I was one of them. But Kal just held me and said he had read about gassing and it wasn't a painful way to go. So we held each other, waiting to die, and all of the sudden another set of doors opened and a blinding light struck us. It was the sun." She looked at me. *"The sun!"* She took a deep breath. "It was scary at first. The thought ran through my head that they would just let the radiation take care of us. I mean we all know that's a horrible way to die. But then armed soldiers came in from outside and told us to line up, gave us glasses, and herded us through the doors out onto a platform. The stairs were steep, and on my shaky legs, I fell a few steps. That's when I saw it—through the space between the steps." Her eyes watered again and her body trembled. "They built that platform over a huge pile of bones, Sunny. *Human bones.* Some of them still with rotting flesh on them." She gasped in a breath.

Bile rose in my throat and I gagged. Had the bourge turned one of the garbage chutes into a gas chamber? Was that how they Culled us? An image of my mother—alone, waiting to be gassed—tortured me. My stomach heaved and I hurried to the sink. Gaia must not have noticed the effect her story had on me. She just kept on talking. Maybe she had forgotten I was there.

"Then we were tagged and stuck in the corral. Kal was the first to speak up and I stood by his side. What they were doing was in direct violation of the treaty. We had more than paid their price and we owed them *nothing!* It didn't take much for Kal to get everyone riled up, because we all knew it was wrong. We weren't just going to accept being forced to stay slaves." Sniffing, she rubbed her nose against her arm. Her lips were drawn into a hard line. "That's when they came up with the idea for the shooting range, and Kal was one of the first sent there. Another corral was constructed and the men and women were separated. And what was my punishment for all of this?" She picked up the knife and drove it into the wooden board. I jumped back, not sure what else she wanted to do with that knife. "The general claimed me for himself. Said I needed taming. *And I let him.*"

Her hand remained wrapped around the hilt, her knuckles white with the effort.

"You didn't have a choice, Gaia," I said, nervously looking down at the knife. "Like you said, none of us do."

"That's right, Sunny, none of us do." She finally removed her hand from the knife and made a sweeping gesture toward the door. "So don't come in here, spouting words like *rebellion* and *war,* as if it were a choice. You're nothing but a naïve little girl who's going to end up getting a lot of people killed."

The silence stretched out between us as I searched for the right response, but I was still struggling to come to terms with what she had told me. Like everyone else in the Pit, I grew up with the knowledge that my life would end at thirty-five. Sometimes at night, when sleep was elusive, it was hard not to think about what the Cull would be like. Would I be shot? Would be I be given an injection? I always thought of the Cull as something that was done to someone. It never occurred to me that I would need to find the inner strength to allow it to happen.

The warmth of a tear travelled down my already-stained cheeks and reminded me I was still crying. Using the heels of my hands, I rubbed away the wetness. "I don't know what to say, Gaia, other than I am really sorry for what you went through."

"I want you to say you'll stop. Stop your campaign to start a war." She took out a clean bowl and started making an omelet all over again. "If General Powell even suspected that I was trying to cause trouble, he'd take it out on Kal. So I don't want to be associated with you in any way. But since I *have* to," she said, "please do me a favor and don't get my husband killed." She put a frying pan on the stove and turned on the element.

I was surprised to hear she thought her husband was still alive. If the man I saw running in terror from the bourge was any indication of life on the range, I doubted anyone sent there lived very long. This wasn't something I wanted to bring up, though. It was probably best if I didn't talk at all. Nothing I could say would make her world right.

And now that I knew how she felt, I would be wise to guard my tongue about my association with Jack. If she found out what we were trying to do, she might just tell the general in order to mitigate any blame.

"Are you paying attention?" she asked, pulling me out of my thoughts. I stepped closer to the stove, so I could see into the frying pan. "The omelet should look like this before you turn it." The eggs were still gooey in the center when she folded it. She looked at me out of the corner of her eye. "I know what you're thinking."

I doubted that very much. "You do?"

"You think I'm a fool for thinking that Kal could still be alive." She flipped the omelet. It was starting to look pretty brown. "It's been almost two years since he was sent there. But he's a smart man. The smartest man I know. And—" She paused, her eyes watering again. "And I'd know if he was gone from this world. My heart would feel it." Her breath caught on a sob. The rage was gone from her face, replaced with a sad, hopeful look. It wasn't an unfamiliar expression. Hope and disappointment were frequent partners in the Pit.

"I'm sure he's still alive." I gave her an encouraging smile, relieved that her rage was spent. "And I promise, I won't talk about it anymore."

Her curt nod was the only acknowledgement of my

promise. Picking up the frying pan, she slid the omelet onto a plate. "And that's all there is to it."

I looked at the omelet. It had a brown crust on it. She gave me a fork and I tasted it. Much better than the eggs I had made. Maybe tears were the secret ingredient.

A few of the kitchen staff were making their presence known and Gaia and I cleared out. "On to drinks," Gaia said, leading me to a quiet area. She set the omelet on the counter and I caught myself worrying if it was going to be eaten or not. Food should never be wasted. "There's no alcohol here, so I'll just show you how to make coffee."

"Ja—" I caught myself. "Mr. Kenner likes coffee. I tried it and don't really like it," I said conversationally.

"So you know how to make it already."

"No," I said, a little confused.

She gave me a curious look. "Captain Kenner makes his own coffee? And you drink it?"

I drew my eyebrows together and shook my head. "No. I mean, yes he makes it because I don't know how. It's one of the things he wants me to learn. I just tasted it when he was...in the shower."

Gaia nodded. "I've been known to sneak a few things when the general isn't looking too."

Silently, I observed how she made coffee, trying to maintain a keen interest. I decided talking was no longer an option for me. It wasn't a question of *if* I was going to get myself into more trouble with Gaia, it was a question of *when*.

The coffee finished percolating through the machine. "That concludes our lesson for today. Did you get it all?

I nodded. "Mr. Kenner will be so pleased when I make him an omelet and coffee tomorrow morning."

She studied me for a moment. "Make sure he is, because if he complains to the general again that you're not trained in the kitchen, it'll be my fault." She walked away, heading toward the door.

"Where are you going?"

"To enjoy what's left of my day in the sunshine."

She went into the cafeteria, grabbed a chair and went outside. I followed suit, even though she hadn't invited me. I set my chair beside hers and we sat in awkward silence. Well, at least it was awkward for me. Gaia seemed to be off in her own world. There was no hint that she ever had an emotional breakdown. She was back to being silent and brooding, with an aura of bitterness.

After a while, it felt like the sun was burning right through the sunscreen I had slathered on that morning. It would be a few hours before the end of the workday, so I got up and walked around. Gaia didn't join me, which was a relief.

There were about a dozen women outside, hanging laundry to dry. A few looked my way and I smiled at them. They didn't return it. They just whispered, giggled and continued with their task. Although I was well aware of how mistresses were viewed, I had never been on the receiving end before. I went in search of a quiet spot to be alone.

The urchin corral wasn't a pretty place. Not at all like the city the bourge had built. There were no flowerbeds, green grass, or picket fences. Only worn dirt paths and long, narrow buildings the color of replicator-grey. Yet with the sun shining down, the clouds chasing each other across the sky and the breeze blowing through my hair, it was still infinitely better than the Pit.

A sad ache plagued me in the aftermath of Gaia's confession. The one thought I had been desperately trying to hold at bay wouldn't go away. My mother walked to her death alone. No one had been there to comfort her.

I sat down on the ground in the shade of a building, away from prying eyes, and let my tears spill.

The sound of voices and the gates opening pulled me back into reality. The sun was lower in the sky and the shadows had grown long. I hadn't heard a horn signaling the end of the workday, but maybe they didn't use one here in the corral. The slaves were already home.

Standing up, I brushed off the dirt and went in search of Gaia. She was in the same place where our driver had dropped us off. She barely acknowledged my presence when I stood next to her. I was relieved when the jeep pulled up, breaking our awkward silence.

As we both walked toward the vehicle, the driver

looked directly at me. "Not you." I faltered, wondering if he was actually talking to me. Gaia looked from the driver to me. I decided there must be a mistake and reached for the jeep door. "Are you deaf? *Not you.*" His voice was loud, catching the attention of anyone close by.

"Me?" I asked.

He nodded.

"There must be a mistake."

Gaia gave me a concerned look but got into the back of the jeep and closed the door.

"No mistake." He pulled away and I watched them go.

It didn't make sense. Why not me?

Maybe Jack was coming for me on the bike.

I had a clear view of the gates, so I remained where I was, waiting for him. Trucks full of farmhands started to roll in, and the workers disembarked. One by one, the trucks came and left. Soon there were no more.

The soldiers closed the gates.

Chapter Eleven

Fear paralyzed me as I stared at the locked gates. If Jack were running late, they would have to open them back up for him, wouldn't they? He was the heir. They would have to do whatever he ordered.

The thought crept into my mind that maybe he *couldn't* come. Maybe the general had found out about him. Was he in custody right now? Being dragged back into the Dome to face President Holt? But if they knew about him, they would know about me. They wouldn't just let me stay here. They would kill me…or drag me back to face Holt, too.

"Looks like you're staying here tonight, princess." At the sound of her voice, I turned to find Hazel standing there with a blanket, pillow, and some toiletries.

"Oh, I don't think I'll be staying the night. I'm sure Mr. Kenner is just running late."

Hazel snorted. "Yeah. Sure he is." She held out the bed linens to me. "While you're waiting you might as well make yourself comfortable. There are bunks available in C Block." She motioned to a building, an exact replica of every building in the compound, except for the big C on the side.

She walked away, leaving me standing there by myself, clutching my bedding.

No one seemed to notice me. They walked by, some in pairs, some in groups. I was the only one on my own. I looked at the big gates one more time and then walked toward the big C.

Where was Jack? Something was wrong.

The interior of C Block consisted of row upon row of bunk beds with only a few small windows. Most of the beds already appeared to be taken. Women stood by their bunks, talking with each other while they gathered their towels and other toiletries. Their chatter faded as my presence became known. I put a smile on my face and walked down the narrow path between bunks looking for an empty bed. I found one a few rows in.

Unfolding the blanket, I made my bed, smoothing every crease and wrinkle in an attempt to look busy. I didn't want them to know I could hear their whispers.

"C'mon, be nice. We should show her where the shower is."

"Pampered little mistresses don't need showers since they don't sweat!"

There was a fit of giggling.

Ignoring it, I left C Block and returned to the cafeteria.

There was already a long queue for dinner and I joined it. Not that I was hungry. But I didn't know what else to do. Besides, if Jack came to the corral looking for me, he wouldn't know to go to C Block. He would probably look for me here first.

It took a long time to make it to where the food was laid out, and still Jack had not appeared. I filled a plate with food I had no desire to eat and went in search of somewhere to sit. The cafeteria was a big open room with tables joined together and running in rows. I scanned the diners looking for a familiar face—Abby, Opal or maybe even my mother—without any luck. I did see a few women with the blank, uninterested stare of having been chemically sterilized, and tried not to make the connection to Jack. My mind still went there.

I sat in the nearest empty seat and set my plate of unappetizing food on the table in front of me. It still niggled that Jack hadn't seen my point of view—that the bourge never included themselves in their own policies. I understood he walked a fine line during his time as heir. He was trying to keep the president happy while staying true to his own convictions. It just rubbed me the wrong way that not one single person in the Dome ever stood up for the Pit.

Picking up my fork, I pushed the food around on my plate. What if I had worked for the president and been given the sterilization program to manage? I'd like to think I would have thrown it right back in Holt's face and told him he should lead by example—that he should be the first in line for that chemical injection. That it was high time a few bourge were rounded up and Culled, too. Yeah. That would go over real well with President Holt. I'd be shot in the head.

Yet, isn't that what I expected someone else to do on the Pit's behalf?

I suddenly realized how naïve I'd been. It was easy to be righteous in the courtroom of my mind, but the real world didn't work that way. It's not that Jack hadn't done enough for the Pit; it was that I expected too much. He didn't exactly know it, but I owed him an apology.

Where was he? Every time the door opened, my heart leapt only to plunge in disappointment. Out of the corner of my eye, I caught sight of a few women gesturing toward me. Jack was right. A seventeen-year-old redhead was hard to miss out here.

"Why so glum?" Opal said, taking the chair next to me. She set her plate in front of her and I noticed her meal was half-eaten. "I'd think you'd be looking forward to a night away from your bourge."

I pasted a smile on my face. "I am. I'm just tired, that's all." The door opened and my eyes shot toward it. No Jack.

"It's the oxygen-rich air out here. It takes some getting used to." As she took a bite, her eyes strayed to someone across the room. She dipped her head in what looked like a nod. Casually, I looked around the room, but no one appeared to be looking in our direction. "Did Hazel put you in C?" she asked.

"Yeah. How did you know?"

"It's the only dorm with beds available."

"Oh. How about you? Which building are you in?"

"I'm in A. Although they all look the same." She took another bite. "Aren't you going to eat?"

I picked up my fork and stabbed a piece of grilled meat. The door opened and my eyes snapped to look at it. Two women came in and joined the queue. A cold sweat broke out on my forehead. At this time of evening, Jack would be expected at the mess with everyone else. Wouldn't he need me there? Unless he wasn't there. Unless they had him in custody.

"Sunny?" Opal said.

"Yes?" I said, maybe a little too quickly. I realized she had been talking to me and I hadn't heard a word.

Opal eyed me suspiciously. "You seem upset about something." She glanced across the room again.

This time, I followed the direction of her gaze to see who she was communicating with. Something was going on. Had Jack been taken into custody and they all knew?

As I searched the faces of women across the room, Opal shifted uncomfortably. I turned in my seat to look directly at her. "What's going on?"

She tried to look surprised. "Nothing. Why?"

I didn't believe her. "Has something happened?"

Her attention snapped to me. "Like what?"

"I don't know. That's why I'm asking you." If something had happened, I deserved to know. She had no right to shut me out of whatever was going on.

She relaxed slightly and shifted in her seat again. "Since you're spending the night in C, there's something you need to know." She looked over at her accomplice again. This time I caught a woman with a distinctive blond streak in her otherwise dark hair giving a curt bow of her head. "A couple of men from the range come every night for food."

For a moment, all I could do was stare at her. It wasn't what I was expecting to hear. I wanted to ask what she knew about Jack, but what if she didn't know anything? All I would accomplish was letting her know something was going on with me.

"Don't look so shocked. We help each other and there's nothing wrong with that," she said, defensively.

"Of course there isn't!" I put my hand on her arm. "You have nothing to worry about. I'm glad you're helping the men in the range." Then I thought about what she said. "Wait a minute—how are they able to leave the range to come here?"

"Not everyone is tagged." She regarded me, her eyes still narrowed in suspicion. "I told them you could be trusted. They can trust you, right?"

I removed my hand from her arm and sat up

straighter. Her question hurt. "Of course they can trust me. What kind of question is that?"

"It's just that…you're with Jack Kenner."

My brows drew together in a scornful look. "If I could free those men myself, I would," I said. "Just because someone owns me doesn't make me untrustworthy. It's not like I had any say in the matter. It's not as if any of us do." I didn't speak for me—I spoke for Summer, Crystal and any other girl who had been claimed by the bourge and scorned by her own people.

Opal looked directly into my eyes. "It wouldn't be the first time a slave fell in love with her master. I've known a few in my time."

My eyes never wavered from her direct stare. Although I wanted to assure her that I was *not* in love with Jack Kenner, I wasn't sure I could pull that off convincingly. My stomach was so knotted worrying about him, I was afraid I would choke on the words. "You can trust me," I said instead.

She made a curt nod of agreement and finished her dinner. The door opened and I looked, but it was only a group of ladies exiting.

"Can you do us a favor?" Opal asked. I returned my attention to her. "It's important you don't tell Gaia about any of this. She might tell the general."

I understood her concerns because I shared them. Though considering Gaia believed her husband to be alive, I doubted she would report them if she knew the men on the range were getting food. "I don't usually spend a lot of time with her anyway."

"Really?" she asked in surprise. "You're the only two out here so I figured you'd spend a lot of time together."

"The only two what?"

"You know…mistresses."

When I thought about it, I realized I hadn't seen anyone other than Gaia. "Why is that?"

Opal shrugged. "General Powell has a strict no fraternizing policy, although, like every other high-ranking bourge, he puts himself above his own laws." She made a face that said, *you know what I mean.* "Of course, that doesn't stop the soldiers from raping us. Parties of them show up here on occasion, threatening to kill us if we talk." She looked at me, eyebrows raised. "Yeah, like we're going to talk. Who the hell would listen?"

I wanted to tell her Jack Kenner would listen. I wanted to say the Alliance was formed and we just needed to get to them. But they barely trusted me enough not to snitch on them for helping the men in the range. It was doubtful they would trust me enough to lead them in a revolt.

"No one, I guess," I replied.

She stood and picked up her empty plate. "Well, I'm off to find a free shower stall."

"Thanks for the company."

She was about to leave, but then turned back toward

me. "By the way, what did you say your mom's name was?"

I perked up, excited. Had she found my mom? "Lilly O'Donnell."

Opal nodded. "If I come across her, I'll let her know you're here."

My heart sank. "Thanks."

I cleared my plate from the table and went back to C Block for my toiletries. After wandering around the compound, I finally found the shower stalls. The sun was just about gone for the day and still no sign of Jack. Something must have happened. He wouldn't just leave me here.

By the time I finished showering, it was dark. My sunburn was still tender, so I gently patted myself dry. Then I dressed, stuck my glasses on my head, and went back to C Block. It was a lot more crowded and noisy as the residents all gathered for bed. As I walked past a group of women talking, I recognized the dark-haired woman with the blonde streak.

I had chosen a bunk with empty beds on either side of it. I liked the feeling of privacy, even though it was false.

"Excuse me." I turned to find the woman with the blonde streak. "Hi, I'm Goldie. You're Sunny, right?"

"That's me," I said, shaking her offered hand.

She had a warm smile. "Opal said that she talked to you about…what happens here at night."

"She did. I'm glad you're helping the men in the range."

"Good, because they'll be here any moment."

Just as Goldie said it, there was a muffled thumping sound. She turned and raced back toward it. Some of the ladies were moving bunks out of the way.

Curious, I walked closer to the action to see what was happening. Goldie removed a few floor panels, exposing a gaping hole. Two men emerged. The taller of the two enveloped Goldie in his arms and kissed her.

"Missed you," he said.

She slapped him on the chest playfully. "It's only been since last night."

"What's on the menu tonight?" the second man asked.

"Roast beef," a woman said, producing two bulging bags.

The man peeked inside, took out a container, and started eating the contents with his hands. "I'm starving."

The tall man hugging Goldie looked at me. "And who is this?"

"That's Sunny O'Donnell. Opal says we can trust her," Goldie said.

"She's awful young. What's she doing out here?" he asked.

"She came out with Jack Kenner," Goldie said, and then immediately placed a hand over the man's mouth. "And I know what you're going to say, but Opal is sure we can trust her. And she's brought news from the Pit—haven't you, Sunny?"

Everyone turned to look at me. I was suddenly on the spot.

The man stepped away from Goldie and held his hand out toward me. "I'm Terran." He pointed to the other man. "And this is Flint." Flint barely acknowledged me—he was too busy eating. "What news do you have?"

Even though my mouth was dry, I swallowed. Opal must have repeated what I told her. I took a moment to organize my thoughts, carefully choosing my words to make sure I didn't give my relationship with Jack away. But as I was about to launch into my story, the door to C Block opened.

It was my mother.

CHAPTER TWELVE

A surge of pure adrenaline went through me, turning my knees to water. *My mother was alive!* Forcing my weakened limbs to move, I rushed into her outstretched arms and she enfolded me in a tight hug.

"Let me look at you," she said, pushing me away. I didn't move far—just enough to let her see my face. She smiled. "You look different. More grown up."

Once, when I was only five years old, my mother was sent upstairs to the Dome to work for what she said would be a week. Back then, I could only watch her go and try to be as brave as she asked me to be. That week stretched into two. It was the first time my father's interest in living began to wane; or maybe it was just the first time I noticed. In any case, I had to get myself ready for school and make my own way to the common room for meals. I would have eaten alone every night too, except my new best friend, Summer, always asked me to sit with her family. Mrs. Nazeem took me in as if I was her own and they became my new family. Soon I began to dread going home every night to a sick father and no one to hug me goodnight. When Mom's absence stretched into three weeks, I began to lose hope that she was ever coming back. I didn't know how to take care of my dad and felt guilty because I didn't want to. And just as the lonely grip of abandonment threatened to consume me, my mother walked through the door. She came home. She put everything right.

I wanted to tell her I wasn't grown up. I was still that five-year-old girl, barely scraping through life without her mom to guide her.

"So much has happened since you left." I bit my bottom lip to stop it from quivering.

She looked different too. The sun had darkened her skin and she wasn't as thin as I remembered. Her hair didn't seem black anymore; there was a shimmer of golden red running through it. She couldn't have looked more beautiful.

"Someone named Opal just told me there was a young red-haired girl here that looked just like me. I couldn't believe it, but it's true!" She hugged me tighter. "What are you doing out here?"

I wanted to tell her everything—about me and Jack and that he was missing and I didn't know where he was—but we had an audience.

"Jack Kenner brought me out with him."

She pulled away to look at me, a frown marring her beautiful face. "I'm sorry, honey. I never wanted that life for you. God knows I tried to protect you from it. Does he at least treat you well?"

I nodded, afraid to speak. For some reason the sight of my mother made me want to bawl my eyes out while she held me tight.

"She was about to tell us some news from the Pit," Terran interrupted. Goldie hit him in the arm. "What?"

"There's news from the Pit?" asked my mother.

"A lot has happened since you left," I said.

"Come and tell me." Taking my hand, she led me to a bunk. I sat down next to her and she pulled me against her side, wrapping her arm around my shoulders. Everyone gathered around us, looking at me expectantly.

Taking a deep breath, I reported the events from Crystal's song and the resulting riot, to what I had overheard General Powell tell Jack. I didn't tell my mother I was married or that Domers had taken Dad away. That would have to wait until we had privacy.

"You're saying that President Holt is *provoking* the Pit into a war so he has a reason to kill everyone?" she asked.

"That's what General Powell said. I heard it myself."

Goldie had a horrified look on her face. "Our daughter is in the Pit with her son and husband."

More voices were raised in alarm, everyone fearful for family members and friends still inside the Dome.

"Holt!" my mother exclaimed. The bitterness lacing her tone made me pull back to look at her. "If only I had killed that man when I had the chance."

I wasn't the only one who looked surprised. Her statement stunned everyone in the room.

"What did you just say?" I asked.

"I meant… er… well, we've all had our thoughts about killing the president, right?"

Flint vigorously nodded his head. "No one's ever gotten close enough, though. That bastard is constantly surrounded by armed guards."

"We *have* to get them out," Goldie said. "What about the doors they brought us out through? Can't we open them?"

"Goldie, first we'd have to get around the tagging system, and then those metal doors weigh a ton," Terran said.

"The Dome is a fortress. No one is getting in," my mother said. That was exactly what Jack had said. But how did *she* know?

"Terran and I have been thinking," Flint announced. "If we can break into the armory, we could get enough explosives to blow a big friggin' hole in the side of the Dome."

"Correction," Terran said. "Flint's been thinking about that plan. I happen to know an explosion of that magnitude would most likely cause a cave-in. Dome engineers stopped using explosive charges in the coal mines years ago because the Pit's on the verge of collapse."

"It might still work," Flint mumbled. He took the lid

off another container of food, scooping the contents up with his fingers.

"Flint and I can keep an eye on the hangar. If they send anyone out, they'll have to open the doors and we can try and sneak back in," Terran said. "What do you think, Hazel?"

Hazel came forward, into the inner circle. How long had she been standing there? I might not have been so forthcoming if I had known she was listening. She had already made it clear that she hated "princesses," especially one that caused her trouble.

"It's a long shot. They haven't sent anyone out in months, except this one and her bourge," Hazel said, looking at me.

"That's not true," I said. "I just met a girl—Abby—who was sent out here when she lost her entire family in the battle after Crystal's execution."

"No," Hazel said, shaking her head. "Other than you and Captain Kenner, we haven't received a group out here since the last Cull."

I tried to remember exactly what Abby had told me. Was she the one who said she had been out for a few days? Or had it been Opal? Abby seemed a little mixed up about things anyway.

"Even if we could open a door, there's an army out here to greet them," my mother said. "Our first step is to shut down the tagging system."

That's exactly what Jack wanted me to prepare

everyone for and my mother was doing it for me. When had she become a rebel leader? I had never seen this side of her before.

"I might be able to help with that," I said. All attention was on me. I didn't want to tell them Jack was part of the plan. I'd lose their confidence. And I wasn't even sure if he was still part of the plan, or if he was in custody. "Captain Kenner is here to fix the comms and I might be able to get access to his computer when he's in the shower or something."

"You know how to use a computer?" Terran asked.

Of course I didn't know how to use a computer. No one from the Pit did. But I didn't think they were ready to hear that Jack was an ally. "Yes."

For just a moment, my mother regarded me with surprise. I wondered if anyone else noticed.

"I haven't seen my daughter in a few months, so if you'll excuse us we have some catching up to do." As my mother stood, she pulled me with her.

"Shouldn't we talk about this a little more?" Goldie asked.

"She already said she's going to try. I'll work out the details with her and let you know. In the meantime, try to come up with a way to get into the Dome." She turned her attention to me. "Where's your bunk?"

My mother always was a take-charge woman, but she was being particularly spectacular tonight. No one questioned her when we walked away. I ducked under the top bunk and crawled onto my bed, my mother right beside me. She leaned back against the wall and I rested my head on her shoulder.

"You've been through a lot lately, haven't you, honey?" she asked. I nodded. Her arm came around me and she stroked my hair. "Tell me everything."

And I did—the whole, pent-up story. A logical voice inside my head warned me that I should be more restrained, but this was my mother. If they did have Jack and I was next, someone out here had to know the truth. But more importantly, I needed to confess about the role I played in her husband—my father's—arrest. I needed to confess because I needed her forgiveness.

She was crying too when I finished my tale and we held each other for a little while. It finally sank into my numb brain that C Block was quiet. Had everyone gone to bed? I had no idea what time it was. And Jack still hadn't come for me.

"It's not your fault," she whispered. "Your father had… *problems* that would be difficult for you to understand. He was never your responsibility. I should've insisted you married that big oaf Reyes before I left the Dome."

"How can you say that about Dad? Of course he was my responsibility. If I had just refused to cooperate with Leisel—"

"—then you and Summer would both have paid the price." She squeezed me tight. "Your father was a grown man capable of making his own decisions. *He* should've been taking care of *you*." She kissed my forehead.

I sniffed away my tears. "He might still be alive though."

She gave me a look—the same one I gave Gaia when she told me her husband was still alive on the range. "You've been through a lot for one so young, and I'm proud of you. You stood up for what you believed in and that takes a lot of guts. I wish I had been more like you when I was your age."

"Why?"

She rested her head atop mine. "Because maybe I could've made a difference, too."

It was an odd thing to say. I mean, it's not as though *I* chose to be part of the wedding; it chose me. Life-changing moments like that were beyond rare in the Pit. "How?"

"Missed opportunities." Was she deliberately being evasive? I wanted to press the matter, but she changed the subject. "You're in love with him, aren't you?" she asked quietly.

My feelings for Jack were private. I hadn't even shared them with him. He and I had grown so close that telling someone else first seemed unfaithful. "Does it matter?"

"Yes, it does. Because no matter how good you think he is, he's still a bourge and you can't trust him."

I shook my head. "You're wrong. Jack Kenner has done more for the Pit than anyone I know." My voice caught on a sob. "And I'm so scared they might have him."

Someone coughed from a few beds away and I was alarmed by how well the sound carried. Could they have overheard my story? So what if they had? I didn't care anymore. If Jack had been arrested, I was next.

Oddly, acknowledging the futility of my situation eased the anxiousness that had gripped me all evening. I allowed myself to relax against my mom, taking a moment to appreciate this second chance with her.

The door flung open, startling everyone. A woman stepped inside. "Soldiers!" she hissed.

Heavy feet hit the floor followed by a "Crap!"

My mom and I scrambled off the bed. Flint was already disappearing into the hole when we got there. Terran grabbed the food and followed him down.

"Help me," Goldie said, trying to rearrange the floorboards. My mom went to her aid while I helped push the bunks back into place. We had just enough time to get everything straightened when two armed soldiers burst into C Block.

"We're looking for Sunny O'Donnell," one said in a loud, clear voice.

My heart pounded. *This was it.* Jack had been arrested and they had come for me.

"No!" my mother cried. The soldiers stepped toward her.

I moved in front of her. "I'm Sunny," I said. She grabbed my hand. "It's okay, Mom." I hoped the encouraging smile I forced hid the fear in my eyes.

"But..." Her panic-stricken eyes strayed toward to the soldiers and back to me.

I needed to reassure her that even if this was the end for me, I was strong enough to face it. "I did what I could, and now I leave it with you, right?" I could face what was coming as long as I knew someone else was ready to take up our cause.

One of the soldiers sighed loudly. "Can we dispense with the drama and go?" He pointed to the door.

Without another word or another look, I left C Block, flanked by my military escorts. I didn't need to turn around to know that everyone was at the door, watching me go. Squaring my shoulders, I held my head high and did my best to walk in spite of my shaking knees.

The soldiers exchanged baffled expressions. "What the hell was that all about?" asked one of them.

"I don't know," said the other.

I climbed into the back seat of the jeep, the driver revved the engine to life, and we drove out through the gates. They went in the direction of town and within minutes we reached the rutted tracks through the forest. I suddenly felt very isolated, alone with two bourge, in the woods. I glanced at them, but the driver was concentrating on navigating and the other one was scanning the forest.

"It gives me the heebie-jeebies driving through here at night," said the one in the passenger seat. "What if the heathens are watching us? They could be right there, in the trees, with arrows pointed at us."

The driver took his eyes off the road momentarily to look at the trees too. "Or the boogieman. He's scary too." He laughed.

Neither one of them showed the animosity I expected of soldiers apprehending a criminal. And not *just* a criminal, but an urchin criminal.

We broke out of the forest and wound our way through the ghost town of empty houses. Finally, they pulled up in front of the house I shared with Jack. The lights were on inside and his security stood at the door.

Jack was home.

Chapter Thirteen

When Jack opened the door, my escorts snapped to attention. "Sir!" they said in unison.

He reached out, grabbed me by the arm, and yanked me inside. He shut the door.

"Where were you?" I demanded.

"Are you okay? Nobody hurt you, did they?" He smoothed the hair back from my face, looking at it closely.

I brushed his hands away. "I thought you had been—" I paused, looked at the door, and lowered my voice. "... *Arrested.*"

"I was kidnapped." He pulled me against him and hugged me tight—almost too tight.

"Jack, you're hurting me." I smelled alcohol on his breath.

"Oh, sorry." He dropped his arms and picked up my hand. "I've been so worried about you."

"Someone kidnapped you and made you drink?" I asked in confusion.

"I didn't want to drink," he said. "Last night they had a surprise party planned for me but I didn't end up going to the mess, so tonight they weren't taking any chances. Alex and some of the other guys showed up at work and dragged me there. And I'd been so close to figuring out the tagging system when they took me."

My heart leaped at the news. "Can you shut it down?"

"I'm pretty sure I can, but we need to get word to everyone once it's shut down so they know to run."

"I kind of prepared them tonight. I found my mom."

Jack looked surprised. "You did? That's incredible! Why didn't you tell me right away?"

"Because this is the first chance I had."

"Okay, start from the beginning." He held up his hand to stop me from talking. "Wait. Let's go to bed and you can tell me all about it. It's been a long night and I could use some therapy."

As I curled up next to him in the big bed we shared, I felt my tension begin to fade away. He was snoring before I even finished telling him about meeting my mother.

It was bright in the room. When had the sun come up? It must have risen during the one hour I was actually asleep. Jack had been restless last night and snored loudly. Stretching, I shifted onto my back, trying to jolt my foggy brain into consciousness.

"I'm sorry about last night," Jack said. He rolled half on top of me and buried his face in my neck. "It was so stupid. I just didn't know how to get out of it."

"It wasn't your fault." I rested my hands on his back. The contact felt good. "I guess if we're going to stay, we have to be prepared for things like that to happen."

He raised his head and looked at me. "Maybe we shouldn't stay, Sunny. Being separated that easily scared the hell out of me."

"It scared me too." He ran his finger along the side of my face and traced the outline of my lips. My breath caught at the pleasure it sent rippling through me. He kissed me lightly on the lips. "Mmmm," I said. "I thought we agreed no romantic stuff." My voice sounded low and husky. I cleared my throat.

He smiled. "I wasn't being romantic. If I was being romantic, I would've done this."

He lowered his lips to mine and kissed me. It started off as a gentle kiss, but grew with such intensity I found myself clinging to him. Winding my hands through his hair, I pulled his head closer. As our breath mingled and our hearts pounded, the world faded away. It was an intoxicating sensation. I never wanted it to end.

When he lifted his head away from mine, a moan of protest escaped me. He held my gaze, his lips curving in a lazy smile. His hair was tousled from my exploring hands and his eyes smoldered. He had never looked more beautiful.

"Did you see the difference?" he asked. He gave me an expectant look. The difference? What was the question? "If you're not sure, I could show you again."

Oh yeah…romantic kiss versus non-romantic kiss. What ever made me come up with that stupid policy? "I think you better show me again." As I pulled his head down to mine, a loud banging on the door jolted us apart.

"What the—" Jack threw back the covers and ran out of the bedroom.

I sucked in a deep breath in an effort to slow my heartbeat.

He came running back into the room and picked up the bedside clock. "We are so *late.* Get up!" He opened the closet door and pulled out his uniform.

Unhappily, I got out of bed and searched for clean work clothes. "I thought the heir could do whatever he wants."

"I have a meeting with Powell and Colonel Anderson in fifteen minutes to go over the plans for the city. I don't want to miss it. I might learn something important."

It looked like Jack was going to strip right there in front of me, so I hurried to the bathroom. I changed, cleaned up and put my hair back in record time. When I came out, he wasn't there.

I went searching for him. "Jack?"

"In here," he called from the kitchen. He handed me a protein shake as I joined him. His was already half gone. "I meant it when I said we should leave. The risk in staying is too much. I'll download as much as I can onto my tablet and then we're out of here."

Relief flooded through me. I didn't want a repeat of last night. "How do we ditch your security?"

He shrugged. "Same way we did before. I'll pick you up at the corral and we'll take off from there. We'll find a safe place to hide until we can figure it out."

I was terrified and elated all at the same time. "Okay. But if you don't come—"

He touched a finger to my lips, cutting off my next words. "I will. No matter what."

Another loud bang on the door reminded us we were late. I took a few gulps of my protein shake, and Jack downed his. Just before he opened the door, he wrapped his arms around me and kissed the top of my head. "Stay safe." I watched him get into the waiting vehicle and drive away.

Across the street, Gaia was already seated in the jeep. Wearing an angry scowl, our driver still stood beside the vehicle, and pointed at me and then to the back seat. Fear tugged at me. If I was in the Pit I knew I would be in for a beating. But I still wasn't quite sure if that happened out here or not.

I hurried into the backseat beside Gaia. She barely acknowledged my presence. Our driver, on the other hand, was still glaring at me from outside the jeep. He looked from me to Gaia and back. My stomach clenched as I waited for a blow.

"Screw it." He sat behind the wheel, slamming the door behind him, revved the engine and threw the jeep into a U-turn. If I hadn't already been bracing myself, I would have been thrown against Gaia.

He raced toward town, in the opposite direction from the corral. I looked at Gaia, silently questioning if she knew what this was about. But she was looking at me with the same confused expression.

We sped through town and took a right turn just before the paved road ended, and drove through a section of town still under construction before turning onto a dirt road that wound its way toward the mountain that hid the Dome. We had to hang on to the roll bar for support as the jeep went off-road. The pitching and rolling was nauseating. I was actually relieved when we came upon a work gang and the jeep came to a halt.

A soldier with more stripes than our driver stomped toward our vehicle. "You're late, Jenkins! And we can't afford that with all these urchins." He motioned toward a group of men digging into the ground. "I need every available gun watching them."

"Sorry, Sarge. It's not my fault," Jenkins replied, getting out of the jeep. "Captain Kenner was late leaving the house and I'm their assigned driver."

"You're only on driving duty until 8 am. After that, you belong to me. Do I make myself clear?"

"Yes sir!" Jenkins snapped to attention.

Sarge turned his attention on us. "Looks like we have two more volunteers. Get 'em a shovel."

Reluctantly, I left the jeep. This was not the way today was supposed to go. I needed to be at the corral by the end of the day for Jack to pick me up. There wasn't any reason for Jenkins to take us to the corral now.

Someone handed Gaia and me each a shovel with a flat edge and pointed to where we should start digging. Most of the diggers were men, although I saw a few women working down the line. Armed soldiers were everywhere, pacing and watching. This had a familiar feel to it. This felt like the Pit.

The dirt was dry and hard, and despite my best efforts, the shovel didn't go in very far. Gaia was having the same problem. She looked at me for suggestions. I shrugged. I didn't know what I was doing either.

Gaia positioned the shovel straight up and jumped on it with both feet. It went into the dirt only slightly farther and she teetered for a moment before it tipped. Unable to get her balance, she went down. I smirked at her failed attempt. A few soldiers were in stitches.

"That worked well," I said, helping her up.

She rubbed her knees, giving me a dirty look. "And once again I have you to thank for a lovely day."

The soldiers laughing at her finally lost interest and wandered away. "How are they allowed to do this to us?" I asked in a low voice. I needed to get to the corral and was still hoping to find a way there.

Gaia drew her eyebrows together. "They can do whatever they want to us."

"But I thought because we're *mistresses* that we're treated differently." There had to be some kind of recourse with Jenkins.

Ignoring me, Gaia struck the ground with her shovel and managed to sink it into the ground by a few inches. She levered it out.

"But if we told them Captain Kenner and the general would be upset with us shoveling, they'd take us to the corral, right?"

She sank her shovel into the ground again, but stopped to give me an angry glare. "You want to get yourself in trouble with Sarge over there, go ahead. But don't you dare bring me into it." The tone of her voice made it clear she was not my ally.

Was there really no way? I wasn't tagged so I could run. The trouble was there were too many armed soldiers. The beginning of panic stirred in the center of my stomach.

Two soldiers were staring at me and I realized I was the only one not working. I struck the earth with my shovel, and after a few attempts, I managed to scratch out some dirt. The soldiers turned their attention elsewhere.

"Are you Sunny O'Donnell?" asked the man working next to me.

I gave him a sidelong glance and noticed a few men appeared to be waiting for my answer.

The man on the other side of him snorted with laughter. "Don't you mean *Mrs. Kenner*."

Fear momentarily gripped me, robbing me of any thought. All I could do was stare at the man, wondering how he knew. Then I remembered how quiet it was in C Block when I told my mother the truth. News travelled fast.

Although Gaia continued to shovel, her attention was on our conversation. I didn't want her to know about Jack. If I couldn't get to the corral by the end of the day, we would need to maintain our cover story.

"I don't know what you're talking about." I struck the ground with my shovel, relieved to hide behind the physical distraction.

The man looked up at the soldiers closest to us. "Terran and Flint came to our corral last night. They said you talked about a war starting in the Pit—that there's already been a bloody battle. That true?" he asked in a low voice.

I nodded. This was information Gaia should know. I just hoped she had missed the "Mrs. Kenner" crack.

"He said he overheard you telling your mom that Jack Kenner is working for our side. That true too?"

All eyes were on me, including Gaia. Sweat broke out on my forehead and I rubbed it away. If I told the truth, Gaia might tell the general, but if I lied to protect Jack's cover, then no one would trust him. We'd all end up working against each other instead of with each other.

I took a deep breath. "Yes, its true. It's all true."

Gaia stopped shoveling, her mouth hanging open. The men also stopped working to stare at me. A few soldiers came closer and ordered us back to work. We all returned to our task. Eventually the soldiers wandered away in search of shade.

"You expect me to believe the heir is on *our* side?" Gaia asked.

"I don't believe it," one of the men said. "Jack Kenner isn't any better than Holt."

"Keep your voice down," I said.

A few soldiers turned in our direction to shoot us annoyed expressions. We stopped talking and concentrated on shoveling. They went back to their conversation. With their attention elsewhere, I quickly gave an abbreviated version of the events in the Pit that led to Jack and me coming out here. Everyone listened intently.

"So what color is the sky in your world, Sunny? Because out here, it's a nice shade of blue and I like it," Gaia said.

"What's that supposed to mean?"

"That I don't believe you're married to Jack Kenner and the two of you are going to free us. Your delusions are going to get us all killed."

I looked at her in shock. "My *delusions* are what's going to get us all killed?" I said, but instead of answering she drew her mouth into a tight line. "You know exactly what President Holt has planned for every last urchin because you heard it straight from the general's lips. Are Jack and I the only ones *deluded* enough to try and stop him?"

The man beside me leaned forward to get a better view of Gaia. "You heard it from General Powell?" Gaia paused for a moment before she nodded her head. I was relieved she decided not to lie. I would've lost all credibility. He turned his attention back on me. "Then what do you and Kenner have planned? How will you stop him?"

"We're trying to get a message to the Alliance, but it doesn't look good," I said, motioning toward the communication cable we were digging up. "In the meantime, he's going to shut down the tagging system. Everyone needs to be ready to go."

Quite a few men had stopped shoveling, too intent on our conversation. A group of soldiers left the shade and strode in our direction. One of them smacked the butt of his rifle against the urchin closest to him. "I'm getting real tired of coming over here," he said.

We all put our heads down and concentrated on shoveling. This time the soldiers didn't leave.

Although the men didn't seem to be having much difficulty shoveling, Gaia and I were struggling. The hot sun beating down on us wasn't helping either. As my arms and legs weakened, the thought of running away to find Jack faded. With my strength sapped and so many armed soldiers, there wasn't a chance I could escape from here alive.

A truck drove by, kicking up dust and rocks.

"Lunch!" someone shouted.

The soldiers ate their lunch in shifts before we were permitted to put down our shovels. We lined up at the lunch truck and soldiers stood close by, ready to deal with any troublemakers. When we collected our rations, they allowed us to sit in the shade to eat. Gaia and I took a seat under a tree. The man who had been working beside me approached us, but a soldier sent him in a different direction. It was then that I noticed the men were segregated from the women during the meal.

"I knew you were trouble the minute I saw you," Gaia said in a low voice.

"Gaia, please don't tell the general. Please. Jack and I will leave as soon as we can."

"Tell the general what, exactly? That the heir's mistress fancies herself married to him? He'd laugh."

I took that to mean she wasn't going to tell Powell, though there really wasn't anything I could do to stop her. It just made our departure that much more urgent.

The midday meal lasted only thirty minutes and then it was back to work. As Gaia and I headed toward our shovels, a soldier stopped us.

"Change of plan. Get in the back of the truck with the others," he ordered.

We looked at the vehicle he motioned toward and only women were getting in. Gaia and I exchanged a worried glance, but we got on the truck. We had no choice.

"I don't know what they're up to—the general doesn't allow soldiers to use women," Gaia whispered. "They wouldn't dare touch *us*."

"I thought you said they could do whatever they wanted."

"Except *that*. If any man laid a hand on me, Powell would kill him."

I hoped she was right.

All told, I counted ten women, four soldiers in the back with us, and two more in the front of the truck. The vehicle made its way up the mountainside. It followed a crude pathway, almost as if a road once existed but was now being reclaimed by the mountain. After ten minutes of driving, the truck came to a stop. We all jumped out, wary.

"Follow me," a soldier ordered, heading toward a wooded area.

The other soldiers motioned for us to get moving. Gaia's hand gripped mine and I held it tight. The soldier we followed stopped and pointed to something.

"This is a cable. Since you're useless with a shovel, your job is to find exposed cable and examine it for any breaks."

Relief flooded through me. Gaia gave my hand a victorious squeeze.

The cable was running along the top of a huge stone outcrop, which explained why it wasn't underground. I had to wonder why they didn't look here first.

"We'll split up into groups. There's a lot of territory to cover."

Gaia and I shuffled closer together in the hopes of not being separated. It worked. Assigned to our group, we headed up the mountain with our armed guards.

Some sections of the cable wound around boulders and skirted thick stands of trees. A nervous excitement began to take root in the pit of my stomach. I might be able to escape after all. If I did manage to run away unnoticed, I knew I couldn't go to the urchin corral. I would head for the slagheap. That's where Jack and I had arranged to meet if we ever got separated.

"No breaks," Gaia announced, interrupting my thoughts.

"I didn't find any either." I wasn't really looking. I was too preoccupied with finding a way out. If I did manage to get away and Jack didn't, would he be blamed for my disappearance? I doubted it. More likely everyone would pity him for losing his mistress.

"It disappears here," Gaia said. I almost asked what she meant but saw she was pointing to the cable. It was partially buried. I examined the ground for any visible signs of having been dug up at some point but couldn't find any. "I think it winds around those boulders."

We were slightly ahead of the rest of the group, but they were catching up. Jack would probably still be at work. If I took off now and word of my escape got back to General Powell, would that prevent Jack from being able to leave? Maybe it was too early to run. Or maybe this was my only chance.

"Let's keep going," I said. My heart was pounding so hard my voice trembled. If we continued, the boulders would block the soldiers' view of us.

"I don't know..."

"It'll be fine," I said. I glanced at the soldiers. They weren't paying attention to us.

We zigzagged through the boulders and ended up in a heavily wooded area. The tree roots were thick on the forest floor, and I doubted a cable could be buried there. Our military escorts would start searching for us once they noticed we were missing, so I didn't have a lot of time. I turned to tell Gaia that I would go and scout up ahead, when I noticed the look on her face. Following her gaze, I saw a small child standing in an open area, dappled in sunlight. He was painted, like the heathens. I peered into the trees and found a few more people standing stock-still. One of them was in a tree, a stick or something in hand.

"We should go," I whispered.

Just as I said it, I heard a soldier right behind us.

"You don't leave my sight!" he said in a threatening voice.

"Sorry, we took a wrong turn. We were just coming back," I said.

Quickly we turned and walked in his direction. I didn't want him to see the people.

"Well, what the hell do we have here?" he said, looking beyond us. "Hey, Rick—get your ass over here. It's a heathen!"

My heart sank when he noticed the child. Even though he was out in the open, I was hoping the bourge still wouldn't be able to see him. Rick rounded the last boulder, escorting the other three members of our group.

"Holy crap, it is!" Rick said gleefully. He took his cap off and wiped the sweat from his forehead with the back of his hand. A smile lit his face. "Hey little dude, where's your mommy and daddy?"

Rick walked toward the child, who remained still except for the quivering of his lower lip. It was obvious Rick couldn't see the others in the trees. He squatted down to bring himself to eye level. "Can't you move?" he asked, laughing. He poked the child in the chest a few times. The quivering lower lip turned into a cry. "Awww... that's right, you cry for your mommy and daddy."

The soldier standing with us laughed and looked around the forest. I didn't see any recognition on his face when his eyes passed over where the people were standing.

"Cry louder. Bring them out in the open. General Powell would be real proud of us if we brought back a couple of heathens," Rick said. He picked up the child and stood, wagging him in the air while he turned in a circle. The child screamed.

It was too horrific to watch. My feet started moving before my brain even ordered them. "Put him down!" I said.

"Get back here!" the soldier behind me ordered.

"I got this," Rick said.

"He's a baby, for God's sake!" I said. The child was absolutely terrified.

"You think you can talk to me like that just because you're some big-wig's whore?" Rick demanded. "Maybe you need to learn you're still nothin' but an urchin."

I had almost reached them when Rick put the child down.

"Run. Now!" I told the kid. I was rewarded by the sight of little feet beating a path into the forest. He stopped screaming, ran past the group standing still, and kept going.

Rick took a step toward me, fist raised, and I cringed in expectation of the blow. But he suddenly stopped and slapped the side of his neck. He gave me a stunned look for a moment before his eyes crossed and he crumpled to the ground. Dumbfounded, I looked at the people in the forest. The one in the tree was in the process of taking the stick away from his—or her?—mouth.

I heard the other soldier running up behind me.

"What the hell did you *do*?"

I consciously kept my gaze from straying to the forest. I was pretty sure he had no idea they were there.

"Nothing. He just fell."

"You did something."

I sighed, knowing I had to accept responsibility. "He was going to hurt me."

An angry glare met my gaze and he punched me in the face. For a split second, stars danced behind my eyes, and then everything went black.

Chapter Fourteen

The truck bounced down the mountain path, and my head boomed with every bump. Rick lay on the floor at our feet, his slack body moving fluidly with the motion. The rise and fall of his chest confirmed he was still alive. As his head lolled to one side, I caught a glimpse of something sticking out of his neck. I stared at the small black protrusion in a vain attempt to identify it. I had never seen anything like it, although I was almost certain it had come from the one in the tree.

Disciplinary action was going to be taken against me, that I knew. If I were still in the Pit, I would die instantly for harming a soldier. Fortunately, things seemed to work a little differently out here, so perhaps I had a chance.

"I'll try to talk to the general," Gaia whispered. "In private, he treats me like his wife. Maybe I can get him to go easy on you."

I was surprised by her offer. All along she had been saying she didn't want to be associated with me. "Thanks, but it's best not to get involved."

Gently I ran my fingers along my cheekbone. It was going to be a decent bruise. At least my sunglasses hadn't been broken.

Jack was going to be upset when he heard I was arrested. I hoped we would be given a private moment together so I could tell him I was okay. We knew all along what we were doing was risky. I'd take whatever consequences I had coming and he could go forward with our plans to free the Pit.

The truck continued straight into town and didn't stop until we reached the medical center. The soldiers wasted no time getting their friend inside. One soldier remained behind as our guard. I dropped my head in my hands and said a silent prayer that Rick was okay. Not that I knew how to pray. But if there was a God, perhaps now was a good time to introduce myself.

When I looked back up, I saw Jack crossing the street with General Powell beside him.

"What happened?" the general demanded. "Who's hurt?"

Our guard snapped to attention. "Sir. This one did something to Private Mayer."

"At ease," Powell said.

"Did what?" Jack asked, never taking his eyes off me.

He clenched his teeth when he saw the bruise on the side of my face. Almost imperceptibly, I shook my head no. He'd have to distance himself from me now. Everything would be lost if he didn't. Out of the corner of my eye, I caught Gaia looking from me to Jack, and I returned my gaze to the truck floor.

"I'm not sure what she did to him, sir. Private Mayer is in bad shape, though."

The general beckoned me. "Come down from the truck."

My legs felt weak but I managed to jump down onto the pavement. Jack moved to my side and as he did, I saw his hand unclip the holster of his pistol. From behind the safety of my dark glasses, I looked at the general and our guard to see if they noticed. They hadn't.

"Who the hell hit her?" Jack yelled at the soldier. "Was it you?"

The soldier remained at attention. "No, sir."

"Calm down, Jack," Powell said. A crowd began to gather across the street. Powell surveyed the street. "Let's talk about this somewhere a little more private."

He headed in the direction of the medical building. Jack seized me by the arm and dragged me along.

"Are you okay?" Jack whispered.

"Don't do it," I begged. But he wasn't paying attention to me. I wasn't even sure my words registered.

As we entered the building, I surveyed the room. Jeffrey sat behind the reception desk and Rick's comrades occupied the chairs in the waiting room.

"Officers in the room," a voice boomed out. All the soldiers stood at attention.

"Who's in charge?" asked General Powell.

A man stepped forward and saluted. "Sir, I am, sir."

"You have one man guarding a truck full of urchins. Get out there!"

"Yes sir!"

The man saluted and led his troops outside. Jeffrey remained at attention behind his desk.

"At ease," Powell said. "How's the victim?"

"He's in with Doc, sir. We haven't had word yet."

"Is there an office I can use?"

"Right this way, sir."

Jeffrey came out from behind the reception desk and led us down a hallway.

"This is the main medical center for the community," Powell said conversationally to Jack, "although it isn't fully staffed yet. A larger hospital is still under construction."

"How many work here now?"

"Just Doc and Jeffrey. Believe it or not, Doc is an urchin and an absolute genius. His work in genetics is unparalleled and we've been able to apply it to crop production. The fact that he's a physician as well made him the perfect choice to bring with us."

Jeffrey stopped and opened a door.

"Aren't you afraid he'll run away?"

"Jeffrey is both his guard and his clerical assistant. Besides, Doc's been out here since the beginning and he's never tried to leave."

General Powell entered the room and switched on a light.

"Will that be all, sir?" Jeffrey asked.

The general nodded. "Thank you."

Jeffrey left us.

There was a single desk in the room and Powell claimed the chair behind it. Jack shut the door.

"Now," Powell said, leaning back in his chair. He regarded me with pursed lips for a moment. "We have a nasty issue to deal with."

Jack stood up tall, squared his shoulders, and looked down on Powell. "No one had the right to strike her. I want whoever did this disciplined."

"Just because she's your property doesn't put her actions above the law," he said, motioning to Jack to sit down. He didn't. "If she hurt a soldier and I don't enforce the rules, I'm sending the wrong message. I have to execute her."

"I was afraid you'd say that."

Jack pulled his gun from the holster and shot the general.

Powell's face twisted into a grimace of horror and confusion. He reached a hand up to the bullet wound and slumped forward onto the desk.

I blinked.

The sound of the gun firing finally caught up with the images captured by my eyes.

Jack was already opening the only window in the office. "*Come on.*"

I rushed past the general, now bleeding out on his desk, and ducked through to the outside. Jack gave me a shove, making me lose my balance and I hit the ground with a thud. He was right behind me, pulling me up by the arm. His gun was still in his hand as we crept along between two buildings. A bike was parked on the street.

"We need that bike," he said. I nodded. Getting to the bike was going to be a problem. The sound of gunfire had soldiers rushing to the medical building. "Now."

Calmly walking out from between the buildings, we made a direct line to the bike. An entire militia was swarming the medical center. As we approached the vehicle, Jack pushed me toward the seat.

Someone yelled, "Stop them!" I didn't need to turn around to know he was pointing at us.

Jack jumped onto the seat behind me and reached around to take control of the vehicle. As we took off in the direction of an alley, I heard shots ring out and craned my neck to look behind us. Men were running, guns drawn. As we disappeared into the alley, the scene was blocked.

Jack drove, weaving between buildings to stay hidden. At one point he stopped the bike and turned it to solar. Silently, we made our way to the edge of town and headed for the woods.

"You okay?" Jack asked against my ear.

I leaned back against him, touching my head to his cheek.

"I didn't hurt that soldier, Jack. I swear."

"What happened?" His voice sounded strained.

I told him about the incident in the woods with the heathens as Jack turned the bike into a shallow stream and followed it.

"So the heathens have weapons," he said. His voice sounded a little off. I noticed that his face was becoming slick with sweat, too.

"Jack, are you okay?" I pulled away from him in order to see his face, which was contorted in pain.

"Fine."

"Stop the bike."

"We have to keep going."

"Jack, where are you hurt? What happened? We need to stop."

"We have to find some place to hide. Somewhere…" His voice trailed off. He shook his head and blinked his eyes a few times. "We need to hide."

His grip on the handlebars slackened. I took control of the bike and pulled it to a stop.

"Maybe I'm not fine," he admitted, giving me a strained smile. "But listen to me. We need to hide. Keep driving."

In the distance I could hear the engines of jeeps and motorbikes—most likely a search party. He was right. We had to keep moving. My panicked brain tried to remember how to drive the bike. Throttle clutch or clutch throttle? The bike lurched forward and a strangled noise came from Jack. I didn't stop though. I turned the bike back out into the stream and drove along the rocky bed. Jack leaned heavily against me, but he was still conscious. I followed the stream for only fifteen minutes before I navigated the bike into the woods to find a place to hide.

The trees were thick and there weren't any visible pathways. That was a good sign. It meant there weren't any humans tracking through here. As I drove deeper into the forest, the distant sound of the search party faded away.

Being in the woods reminded me of our first day outside the Dome, when we discovered vehicle tracks in the earth. Looking in my side mirror, I saw we were leaving the same tracks in our wake.

His eyes met mine in the reflection. "Smart girl." As I continued to drive, Jack pointed to our right. "There's an outcropping over there. Drive on the rocks." He looked frighteningly pale.

I turned the bike toward the rocks, scanning the cliff for any sign of a cave as we went. I found a crevice that looked hopeful.

"We're not far enough away," he said, shaking his head.

"You need to rest." I was firm on that. Jack didn't argue and I hoped that was because he knew I was right and not because he was too weak.

It was a bit of a climb to get to the crevice, but I pulled myself up easily. I wasn't sure if Jack would be able to make it. The crevice was long, but as I sidled in, it opened into a bigger space. The crack in the outcropping continued past the cave and I followed it to make sure it was secure. It led out into a different area of forest, providing us with two escape routes.

When I returned, Jack had both his hands jammed against the seat to keep him upright, sweat glistening on his face from the effort. When he saw me coming, he tried to twist his mouth into a smile.

"Do you think you can make it up there?" I asked.

He dismounted the bike and staggered slightly. I wedged my shoulder under his arm and wrapped mine around his waist. My hand came into contact with something wet—blood.

Panic welled up and I fought to keep it at bay. With every step he took, blood pulsed out. I pressed my hand against the wound, trying to stem the flow.

He leaned against the cliff when we reached it and I took the opportunity to examine his wound. A deep red hole on the back of his left side was weeping slowly and steadily. He had been shot.

"I have to get you help, Jack. This is beyond me. We should go back."

"We can't go back."

"But you're bleeding! And I don't know how to stop it!" My voice sounded hysterical even to me.

"Sunny, listen to me. You'll have to hide the bike and get rid of any tracks that lead here. Do you understand?" I nodded even though I knew Jack was my first priority. "If anything happens to me, promise you won't go back there."

I bit my lip, refusing to make a promise I couldn't keep. Jack turned around and started climbing up the cliff.

"Maybe this isn't the best place for us," I said. If he fell unconscious I wouldn't be able to get him down.

"I need to rest. I think if I can just rest for a while I'll be okay."

He raised his arm to climb and with every pull, his bloodstain grew. I climbed behind him, holding a hand out to catch him in case he fell. The sane part of my mind told me it was an irrational act, but that part of my brain wasn't in control right now.

With an enormous effort, he hoisted himself up onto the crevice. "It's not wide enough."

"You have to keep going. It opens up."

He used the wall of the crevice to steady himself as he walked. I kept my eyes on his stained t-shirt, willing the bullet hole to magically stop bleeding.

"Nice." he said. He sank to the ground and rested his back against the wall of the cave. "Home sweet home."

"I've been in worse places." I squatted down in front of him and wiped the sweat away from his brow.

"I know you have," he said in a sober voice. "And you deserved better." His hand hooked onto my shoulder and pulled me to him.

I resisted. "There's time for that after I get the bleeding stopped."

"You know first aid?"

"No. But I once saw a doctor in the Pit use a belt as a tourniquet."

I fumbled at his belt buckle, trying to undo it, and a weak smile crossed his face.

"I remember another time not too long ago when you had trouble with my belt."

I grinned. "It was the button on your pants, not a belt."

"Oh yeah." He tucked my hair behind my ear as I pulled his belt free. Gently, I tugged on his t-shirt.

"Can you lean forward?" I asked.

He did, but I had to support him. I hadn't realized he was that weak. Shock at the discovery threatened my sanity.

"Mmmm, are you trying to take advantage of me, Mrs. Kenner?"

"Absolutely. After that kiss this morning..." His weak smile grew a little stronger. Tears clouded my eyes. Angrily, I blinked them away. "I really screwed up this time, Jack. I shouldn't have gotten involved. I should have just kept—"

"Sshh." Jack touched the side of my face. "I'm proud of you."

My tears spilled and I cleared my throat in an effort to blast them away.

"I need to see the wound. Can you lie face down?"

Jack did as I asked with help from me. The bullet had entered through his lower left side. A little lower and it would have hit his belt, which might have saved him from injury. The bullet hole was still bleeding, but not as much as it was with the exertion of climbing up here. There was only one wound, which I was pretty sure meant the bullet was still inside him. I didn't know how to get it out. I needed help.

The cave was warm, but he was beginning to shiver. I tore off a section of my t-shirt, folded it, and placed it over the wound. Then carefully, I cinched the belt around his waist.

He groaned in protest. "It's too tight."

"I know, but I have to stop the bleeding."

"How bad is it?"

"Bad enough to need a doctor. I have to get you back to town, Jack."

"They're not going to help us. We're fugitives again."

"But I need help! I can't do this on my own!" Hysteria seized control of me and I covered my eyes trying to blot out the image of injured Jack. I didn't like injured Jack. I wanted my partner back in one piece.

With considerable effort, he sat up and leaned back against the stone wall.

"Come here," he said, tugging my hand away from my face. I allowed him to pull me closer, lightly resting my head on his shoulder. I needed his strength even though he didn't have much left to give. "You can get through this. I know you can. You're the strongest person I've ever known. That's why I'm so madly in love with you."

My lower lip shook with the effort to control my emotions. This wasn't the time for a breakdown.

"I love you, too," I said, choking back a sob. "And I'm going to make everything better. I screwed up, but I'm going to fix it. You just need to hang on. Okay?"

"Look at me," he said. I pulled away from his shoulder to meet his gaze. "No matter what happens to me, you don't go back there. Ever. You can't save the Pit by yourself. Do you understand? Get out of here and save yourself."

His message was clear. He thought he was going to die.

I couldn't let that happen. I rubbed the tears from my cheeks. My wailing wasn't going to save him. I nodded. "Okay," I said. I was pleased my voice was calm and steady. "At least let me go and get water. I need to clean your wound."

"Take this with you," he said, giving me his pistol. "Do you remember where the stream is? It's not far."

"Don't worry. I remember. You should lie down and get some rest." I helped get him settled. Smoothing back his hair, I kissed his lips. "I'll be back soon."

He grabbed my hand and held it tight.

"I really do love you." His voice cracked with emotion. Tears burned my eyes but I refused to let them fall.

"And I love you more than I could ever say."

Freeing my hand from his grip, I left the cave. I had done a lot of stupid things in my life, but letting Jack die wasn't going to be one of them.

The sun was just about to set behind the mountain as I got on the bike and headed back to town.

Chapter Fifteen

Twilight distorted the landscape with long shadows, making already unfamiliar terrain even stranger. I wasn't worried about finding the city. The glowing light was an unmistakable beacon. However, finding my way back might become problematic. Every so often I stopped the bike and overturned a rock or broke a branch and took note of my surroundings. I prayed my marked trail wasn't too noticeable.

Keeping to the stream, I followed the path we took leaving the city until I saw the set of tracks where we entered the waterway earlier. We had left an easy trail to follow. Lining the tires up with our previous tracks, I drove the bike straight across the shallow river and exited on the other side. I continued to drive, ducking low-hanging branches and bumbling over tree roots before I doubled back to town. A few times, I caught a glimpse of distant vehicles' lights. They were still searching for us. Luckily for me, I didn't need headlamps.

Once I reached the edge of the city, I hid the bike in some bushes and went the rest of the way on foot. If they found the tracks and followed them, the worst that would happen is I would lose my ride.

Night had fallen as I approached the residential area of town. Keeping to the forest edge, I observed soldiers performing a door-to-door search of the empty houses. Remaining cloaked in the darkness of the forest, beyond the glow of the electric lights, I made my way closer to the heart of the city.

Eventually I had to leave the safety of the woods and scurry between buildings. There weren't as many soldiers here as I had expected. Perhaps they thought we were long gone and were concentrating their search elsewhere.

I approached the medical center from the back. Staying low behind a hedge, I patiently waited to make sure no one was back there. A dim light illuminated one window. There didn't seem to be any movement in the room. Tentatively, I stepped out from the hedge. I darted to the window and peeked inside. The only occupant was Doc. He was sitting at his microscope.

I hoped I could trust him.

I tried the window but it was locked. Lightly, I tapped on it. Doc looked up from his microscope, but didn't notice me. He went back to his work. I tapped a little louder. This time he looked my way. I waved at him.

He could refuse me, he might even turn me in, but it was still a risk I was willing to take. My skin began to prickle with beads of nervous perspiration. Doc stared at me for a moment, and then came to the window.

"What do you want?"

"Your help."

"Are you hurt?"

"No. Jack Kenner is. He's been shot."

"You've come to the wrong person. I won't save a bourge."

He pulled the window down, but I stuck my arm through the opening to prevent him from closing it.

"Wait! Please! Just give me a chance to explain."

"You're making too much noise!" He peered out the window and looked around the backyard. "I don't want to be caught fraternizing with you."

"Then open the window or I'll scream."

I looked at him defiantly and opened my mouth. He opened the window. I crawled in and he shut it and pulled the blind.

"Stupid little girl! You have no idea what you're jeopardizing."

I drew a ragged breath, frantically searching my brain for the right words to convince him.

"Jack Kenner and I are trying to free the Pit. If he dies, I can't do it alone."

He glared at me. "Your juvenile heroics are putting

my life's work at risk. Get out." He pointed at the window.

"I'm telling you the truth. Why else would he shoot General Powell?"

He crossed his arms over his chest and cocked his head to one side. I took this as an invitation to continue my explanation. Taking a steadying breath, I launched into the story of how Jack and I came together. He regarded me with mixed emotions as I spoke, but when I mentioned Liberty his expression changed. I had his attention.

"I've heard rumors about an organization called Liberty," he said when I finished. He studied me thoughtfully for a moment. "Maybe I can help. But if I do, you have to promise me to tell no one."

"So you'll come with me?"

He raised his eyebrows in surprise at my request. "No. I've already told you I won't jeopardize my life's work for you and your… husband, did you say?"

"But you just said—"

"—I would help. Is that his blood on your hands?"

I looked down at my red-stained hands, unaware of just how much of Jack's blood was on them. He had lost a lot. My hands started to shake and the tremble crept slowly up my arms to spread throughout my entire being. *Jack could die.*

"Yes," I squeaked.

"Don't lose it now. Come here." He held his hand out for mine. I gave it to him and he scraped the blood off into a dish. "You said he was shot?" I nodded. "Where?"

I pointed to the area on my own back. "Right around here."

"There might not be any major organs involved, but I'll go on the assumption there are." He added a solution to the blood. "Did the bullet pass through?"

"I think it's still in there."

"That's unfortunate. You'll have to get it out." He filled a vial with diluted blood and put into some kind of appliance. Next, he turned his computer screen to face him.

"What are you doing?"

"Rendering his DNA."

"Why?" We didn't have time to waste.

He stared down at his computer as various images popped up on the screen. "To help him," he said, absentmindedly.

A hysterical scream was bubbling its way up my throat and I bit it back. Digging my nails into my palms, I tried to maintain a calm voice. "Jack is in real danger of dying. We've already wasted too much time. We need to do something now."

"Please calm down, Miss—" He did something on the computer screen. "There you are. O'Donnell. Some of your DNA is mixed up with his. I need to separate the two of you."

Initially, it was a shock to hear that he had my DNA on record, but then I remembered he'd drawn a vial of my blood the day he was supposed to tag me. What was he up to? I eyed him suspiciously. "Why do you have my DNA stored in your computer?"

He looked away from the screen and studied me with a thoughtful look again. "Nanotechnology—the single most useful piece of science that came into the Dome. I found it in the memory banks after the bourge forced me to work for them. I wanted to concentrate my research in it, but they said no. Said it posed a threat—end of the world kind of stuff." His eyes looked heavenward as he shook his head, and then he turned his attention back to his computer. "Although I know that was just an excuse. The real reason is that the Holt regime didn't want technological advances that would undermine their nuclear control over us. And for that reason alone, we've endured three hundred years of tradition unimpeded by progress."

"What is nanotechnology?"

"Manipulation of matter at the atomic and molecular level. It's pure genius." He gave me a mischievous smile that I didn't return. I had no idea what he was going on about. His smile faded as he saw my blank expression. "They're miniscule robots capable of self-replicating. They'll do whatever I program them to do. I've even taught them to communicate with each other."

"How is that going to help Jack?"

"They can be programmed to repair internal damage."

"Is that safe?"

He shrugged. "It can't hurt. As I've said, it's still in the experimental stage."

Was he serious? "Doc, this is someone's life we're talking about. Someone who means a great deal to me."

He went to a refrigerator and took out packs of liquid and brought them to the table. He wasn't even hurrying. "Do you have a better idea?"

"Yes! Come with me! Fix him!"

"You're trying to save the Pit your way, I'm trying to save it mine. If I were discovered in cahoots with a criminal, they would treat me no better than you. All of my research would be lost, and so would the Pit."

That caught me off guard. I hadn't pegged Doc as the hero type. "How do *you* intend to save the Pit?"

"Bio-warfare is just one possibility." He pointed to the computer screen. "For instance, right now I'm using Kenner's specific DNA in order to make a...*cocktail,* if you will, of nanoparticles capable of self-replicating for cellular repair. In laymen's terms, they can make tissue and skin. I'll combine those particles with nanorobots—the brains behind the operation. This is the first opportunity I've had to try it out and if it's successful, the door opens to a world of possibilities. After all, the Holt regime has gone to incredible lengths to prevent the bloodlines between bourge and urchin from getting mixed. Three hundred years later, there must be a gene or two I can isolate specific to them and design a virus."

I raised both hands as if warding off any evil from the technology. Maybe I had made a big mistake coming to him. "I came here desperate for your help. You have to believe me—Jack is nothing like President Holt. He honestly wants to free the Pit. I'm not going to experiment on him."

"Relax. I didn't say I *had* isolated a gene, I said I was *trying* to isolate one." A message appeared on his computer and he made some adjustments to an appliance as he continued to talk. "I'm also applying the technology to weaponry. Your injury from wearing a bulletproof vest gave me an idea. Using the self-replicating properties—"

"Hey Doc, I heard voices—" Jeffrey said as he walked into the room, but pulled up short at the sight of me. He drew his gun.

My heart banged against my chest as I pulled the pistol from the waistband of my shorts. I suddenly couldn't remember how to use it.

"Drop it," Jeffrey said, inching closer. "Where's the other one?"

"It's just me."

"The other one is hurt," Doc said. "She broke in and threatened to shoot me if I didn't give her medical supplies for him."

My eyes widened at the lie.

"Did she hurt you, Doc?"

"No, I'm fine. You got here just in time."

Jeffrey was standing within arm's reach of me now. He was such a slight man. I almost felt large beside him. He looked at the gun I was holding and my eyes followed his. It shook in my trembling hands.

He laughed. "You don't even know how to use that thing."

He dropped his gun to his side and stepped in closer.

As I watched him reach for my gun, an image of Jack lying on the cave floor bleeding to death flashed through my head. If I was caught, it was the end for him. I couldn't let that happen.

Fuelled by desperation, I swallowed my fear and hit Jeffrey in the head with the pistol as hard as I could. He had been so sure I would just hand over my weapon that he wasn't expecting it. He put a hand to the side of his head and I hit him again. Falling, his own gun still in hand, he staggered toward me. I kneed him with every bit of strength I had and heard a whoosh of breath escape him before he fell. His limp body crumpled at my feet and I used my foot to prod him. He didn't get up. I kicked his gun across the room.

"Stop!" Doc yelled at me. He rushed to the fallen man's side. "Jeffrey? Can you hear me?"

There was no response.

For a moment all I could do was stare at Doc, completely astounded by his behavior. "I didn't threaten to shoot you!"

He ran to the refrigerator and took out a compress. "I *told* you I wouldn't let you jeopardize my research."

At least I understood his desire to protect his secret. Hadn't I been pretending to be someone other than me, all in the name of self-preservation and saving the Pit? Doc's actions weren't so different. Although, I'm not so sure I would sell someone out in order to save my own hide.

He returned to Jeffrey's side, placing the cold compress on his head. Jeffrey moaned and tried to sit up.

"Jeffrey? Are you okay?"

"My head." He moaned again.

I took a step back, ready to run. Doc saw and gestured for me to halt. He went to a cabinet, took out a syringe, and filled it.

"Don't try to get up," he said to Jeffrey. He plunged the syringe into his arm and Jeffrey's body went slack. "That should keep him quiet for the night," he said. "Jeffrey's not much of a soldier, which makes him the perfect assistant. If the bourge ever discovered I was working with contraband technology, I would be killed."

"Maybe I did come to the wrong person for help."

"I'm the only person who can help." He walked past me and returned to his computer. "Look, if I wanted your husband dead I'd simply let him die. Even if the bullet hasn't damaged any organs, blood loss and infection will kill him. What I'm doing right now is putting a surgical team together capable of fixing him. Consider it a gift. I'm rooting for you both to set the Pit free." I was desperate to believe him. He really was my only chance of saving Jack. "With Jeffrey out of the way, you can go to the supply closet and get a bag to carry everything."

I hesitated, not sure if he had any other tricks up his sleeve. He was completely focused on his computer screen. I tried to think of someone else who could help me, but it seemed futile. Even if a medic from the Pit had been spared the Cull, she would be penned inside a corral, unable to leave. Doc really was my only hope.

Slipping out of the room, I stood silently in the hallway straining to hear if anyone else was in the building. It was quiet. Feeling confident we were alone, I went in search of the supply closet.

The closet was full with bed linens, towels, bandage supplies, and other things. I found some survival packs and opened one, removing the things I didn't think I'd need to make room for a blanket, bedroll and Doc's medical supplies.

Doc looked up at me as I came back into his office. "Good, you found it. I'm almost ready." I set the pack on the counter as he walked toward a refrigerator and started taking bags of liquid out of it. "By the way, the soldier they brought in today is fine. I pulled a handmade quill from the side of his neck. I'm still analyzing the substance that was on it, but it's some kind of tranquilizer. I've already told the general that I suspect it was the so-called heathens, not you. Unfortunately you remain on his wanted list. He didn't take kindly to being shot."

"The general is alive?" That was surprising. He had been bleeding all over his desk the last time I saw him.

Doc carried the bags to the counter where I waited with the backpack. "He was shot in a medical facility. I was given no choice but to help him."

He set the bags down and turned to the appliance he had been using and took out a vial.

"Why is it the bourge can't see the heathens?" I asked.

He raised his eyebrows at my question. "Because the

heathens are masters of camouflage. I think what you really want to know is why *we* can see them." I nodded. He filled a syringe with the contents of the vial, and placed it in a hard case. "A funny thing happens to the human body when it's thrown into a cave and deprived of light—eventually, it learns to see differently."

I looked at his face to see if there was any malice in his expression, but his features were emotionless. "I think I understand," I said. "Both meanings."

"Everything is ready," he said. "I'll run through the procedure with you." He showed me how to use the IV and everything else I would need to save Jack's life. It was a lot of information to absorb and I was scared I was going to forget everything in my overwrought state. He picked up the hard case—the one I saw him putting a syringe into—and handed it to me. "The very last thing you'll do is inject this near the site of the wound."

I looked at it warily. "That's the syringe with the surgical team," I said. If Jack responded well with only the IVs, I promised myself I wouldn't use it. It was a last resort.

"Precisely. I'm *very* interested in hearing the results."

He handed me the case and I carefully packed everything into the bag. The IV fluids made it heavy. I shrugged it over my shoulders, secured the front strap and headed toward the window.

"Thank you, Doc," I said as I hoisted my leg through the opening.

"Good luck. And try not to get caught."

I hit the pavement running and ducked behind the hedge. I surveyed the area for soldiers. Nothing. I crept to the next building.

The sound of breaking glass sent a jolt of terror right through me. Looking back, I saw Doc at the window. The sudden shrill alarm hurt my ears. People in the street started shouting and soldiers raced toward the medical center. I realized Doc had created a distraction.

Keeping to the shadows, I crept away into the night.

Chapter Sixteen

I followed the markers I made for myself with ease and it scared me. I knew it would be smart to erase them now, but I had already been gone longer than I anticipated. Jack was my priority.

"Jack," I whispered when I entered the cave. There was no answer. I knelt down beside him. "Jack."

I shook him gently, alarmed by how cold he felt. Holding my breath, I pressed my ear against his chest. My own heart started beating again when I heard the faint drumming of his. But it was weak and his breathing was shallow.

Concentrating on the IV first, I found a solid stick and jammed it into a crack in the stone wall. I hung an IV bag and tested the weight. It held. Now came the hard part: inserting the needle. Putting on the gloves, I sterilized the back of his hand, found a vein and carefully inserted the needle. There was a bit of hesitation, but it easily slid in once the skin was broken. I looked for the flash of blood into the needle that Doc said would happen if it was in the vein. There wasn't. I took it out and tried again. Several tries later, I ran out of veins on the back of his hand and started looking on the inside of his arm. It was frustrating, but I finally got it into a vein and it held. I attached the IV. Doc told me the area would swell if the needle wasn't in right. I waited, but nothing happened. I assumed I had done it right.

Taking a deep breath, I continued to the next step—getting the bullet out. I probed inside the wound for it, trying really hard not to think about what I was actually doing. If I did, I knew I would lose my nerve. My finger finally grazed the bullet. It was in deep. Not wanting to use the scalpel to make the wound any bigger, I attempted to get it with the forceps. Despite several attempts, I couldn't quite get the forceps in far enough to get a grip on the bullet. Reluctantly, I picked up the scalpel.

It wasn't a pretty cut, but it allowed me to get the forceps in deeper. After a few agonizing moments of fumbling for the bullet, I grabbed hold of it. As the bullet came out, so did a lot of blood.

"No no no no no no no!" I tried to stop the bleeding, but the blood kept coming. *"Stop!"*

Flipping the backpack upside down, I emptied the contents onto the cave floor, found a sterile compress and ripped the package open. I put as much pressure on the wound as I could, but the blood kept pumping out. When the bandage was soaked, I threw it down and reached for another one. It soaked through in less time than the first.

"Jack!" I yelled.

He didn't respond. I pressed my ear against his chest again. I couldn't hear his heartbeat.

I couldn't hear it.

I shut my eyes in an attempt to block out the sheer terror and concentrate on Doc's instructions. I cleaned the wound with sterile water, surprised to see the flow of blood slowing down. Something told me that wasn't a good thing. Wrapping my hand around the hardcover case, I opened it and took out the syringe. Doc's little surgeons: my last resort.

Removing the protective cover from the needle, I inserted it close to the wound, just like Doc told me. I prayed for the second time in my life—to a God I only found a few hours ago—that the little surgeons were as smart as Doc said they were. They needed to revive the dead.

Blood and fluid wept from the wound and I covered it with a new bandage. I stopped breathing as I held the bandage there, straining to hear a breath from him. The sound was faint, but it was there.

"Do your job, robots."

I laid my head on his chest, listening for a heartbeat. It was there, but barely. And he was so cold. I affixed the bandage over his wound and spread out the bedroll. Carefully, I rolled his limp body enough to get the bedroll under him and covered him with the blanket.

Nervously I checked the IV. It seemed to be working the way Doc had shown me. I checked the bandage again. There was a bit of blood soaking through, but not much. Resting my head on his chest, I listened to his heartbeat. No change. I rocked back on my heels. Two seconds later, I repeated all of my checks.

Despite the blankets, Jack didn't seem to be warming up. I slipped under the covers and hugged him close.

"As soon as you're warm, I'll go out and erase our tracks like I promised," I said out loud. Irrationally, I waited for him to respond. He didn't. "I know you didn't want me to go back there, but I had no choice. You're hurt and I didn't know how to help you on my own."

He felt so cold. I nestled my face in the crook of his shoulder and neck and placed my hand over his heart. It seemed a little stronger.

The night stretched on, and the need to erase our tracks grew more urgent. There was no doubt in my mind that they would resume their search in daylight. But the IV was close to empty and I remembered Doc said not to let that happen.

Sitting up, I changed his bandage again. The wound was still wet with blood and fluid, but it wasn't actively bleeding anymore. Was that a good sign or a bad one? I recalled that the doctors in the Pit used a needle and thread to close a wound. Should I have done that? Doc hadn't mentioned it. No, he said the nanorobots would make new skin.

Placing a hand on his face, I checked his temperature. He was still cold, but maybe not *as* cold. I listened to his heartbeat. It seemed steady, stronger. How many hours had it been since I gave him Doc's cocktail? Eight hours? More? He was still alive and seemed to be doing marginally better.

I needed to cover our tracks, and soon. Already the first hint of daylight was flooding our small cave. I changed his IV, hooked an empty flask to my belt loop and stuck the pistol into my waistband. For a moment I stood at the cave entrance and listened intently. The night was quiet, with the odd sound from an animal—at least I thought it was an animal.

I climbed down, paused to make sure I was alone, and headed toward the bush where the bike was hidden. Covering up the markers I had made for myself was going to be the easy part. Erasing the tracks from the bike was going to be more difficult. Could I smooth them over with my hand? Or use a leafy branch from a tree?

As I reached the bush, I looked for the tracks of my entry point. There weren't any. I waded into the brambles, their prickles scratching my skin, and searched for the bike. It wasn't there. Maybe I had the wrong bush.

I surveyed the landscape. There were other bushes around, but none of them large enough to hide a bike. Given the proximity to the cave, I was almost certain this was the right bush.

I retraced my path all the way back to the stream, but I couldn't find tracks anywhere. The tree where I had broken a branch to mark my way was still there, but the branch was gone. I examined where it had been snapped off close to the trunk and found a dark substance smeared across the stump, darkening the exposed wood to make it blend with the bark. It was still wet.

The hairs on the back of my neck prickled and a shiver ran down my spine. Was someone watching me? I scanned the tree line for any sign of movement. There was none. I listened intently but only the sound of the stream skipping over rocks reached my ears. The sun still wasn't up and the darkness gave me confidence—the bourge couldn't see in the dark.

Moving deeper into the shadows of the trees, I continued along the stream to the place where it branched and looked for my other markers. Each rock I'd overturned was now back in its place. Each branch I had snapped had been removed and the fresh wood beneath camouflaged. I was pretty sure I could follow my path all the way back to town and find the same thing. Someone had covered my tracks. I wasn't alone out here. I looked around again to see if I was being followed but didn't see anyone.

I filled my empty flask from the stream, took a long drink, and filled it again. Then I began picking my way back to the cave, carefully placing my feet to avoid making noise. The pressure of Jack's pistol in my waistband was reassuring, even if I forgot how to shoot.

At least I could use the threat of it to buy me time to run.

Then I heard a twig snap.

I froze. Only my eyes moved as I searched the area where I'd heard the noise. Holding my breath, I strained to hear any other movements. Then I heard it again. A quick survey of the area told me there was nowhere to hide. I wrapped my hand around the pistol and aimed it at the noise.

"I'm armed," I said.

"Geez, it's a girl." Two men walked out of the forest and approached me. It was Terran and Flint. "Oh, it's *Mrs. Kenner,*" Flint said. Terran guffawed.

I lowered the gun. "Do I have you to thank?"

"For what?"

"Covering our tracks."

Terran shook his head. "We're just coming back from the corrals. Soldiers are tearing the place apart looking for you two."

"Is it true President Kenner shot General Powell?" Flint asked.

Terran rolled his eyes. "He's not the president, you idiot."

I nodded at Flint. "I was in a bad situation and Jack didn't see any other way out."

"So all the stuff you told your mom was true?" Terran asked.

"The entire C Block heard me, didn't they?"

"No, not everyone," Flint said. "The ladies on the far side of the building didn't. I had to fill them in."

Terran closed his eyes for a second, took a deep breath, and looked at me. "The only reason we're partners is because we're not tagged." Ignoring Flint, he kept his gaze on me. "So how come you're out here alone?"

"Jack was shot when we escaped," I said. My lower lip trembled and I bit down on it. "He's not doing so well."

"Hey, I'm sorry to hear that," Terran said softly. Flint opened his mouth to speak, but Terran elbowed him. "If there's anything we can do to help, let us know. In fact, I bet you're hungry." He dug into his bag and pulled out a food container, not so different from the ones we used in the Pit.

"Thank you," I said. "But how did you get the food? I thought you said there were soldiers all over the corrals."

"We hid in the woods until they cleared out. It took them hours, but there are hungry men on the range counting on us."

I held the container out to him. "I don't want to take someone's food."

Terran refused to take it back. "It's okay, you're one of us. And I do mean that literally—you realize the range is a stone's throw that way, right?" He pointed in the same direction as our hideout.

It was alarming news. "No, I didn't know that." There was nothing I could do about it now. Even if I could physically pick Jack up and climb down to the ground with him, I couldn't move him while he was hurt. It would kill him.

"We can pass by here again tomorrow before sunrise if you want to meet us and get more food."

"I'd really appreciate that."

Flint motioned to the rising sun, now peeking over the mountain. "We gotta go."

"See you tomorrow," Terran said.

The first rays of the morning sun streaked the sky as I entered the cave. I dropped down on my knees next to Jack and placed my hand over his heart. It was still beating. He wasn't as cold.

"Jack?" I whispered hopefully. He didn't respond.

I removed his bandage and checked the wound. It looked pinker than it had a few hours ago. I covered it with a new bandage and checked his IV.

"Jack?" I said again. This time I put my ear close to his mouth in case he only had the strength to whisper. All I heard was his breathing. Breathing was a good sign.

Leaning back against the cave wall, I opened the container of pieces of grilled meat and cooked vegetables. As I ate, I watched him. He looked so pale, but the rise and fall of his chest was reassuring.

"You're not going to be happy about this, but I lost the bike," I said, keeping my voice to a whisper. I didn't expect him to respond so I wasn't too disappointed when he didn't. "The good news is someone covered our tracks. I ran into Terran and Flint—did I tell you about you them last night?—and they said it wasn't them." I ate some more. Jack breathed. "Do you have a bourge friend that would help us like that?" I licked my fingers clean and replaced the lid on the container, saving some for him in case he woke up. "Because if it wasn't any of them, I wonder if it was…" I lowered my voice to an almost-inaudible whisper. "The *heathens*?" Not that I liked calling them heathens, but I knew Jack would understand who I meant.

I talked until it was time to change his IV. Maybe he could hear me. Maybe he couldn't. I was going on hope.

Exhausted, I laid down beside him. His body was definitely warmer than it had been last night. I placed my hand over his heart and rested my head close to his, silently listening to him breathe.

The distant sound of voices jolted me from a light slumber. Startled, I looked around the cave. We were still alone. The voices were drifting in from outside. Jack remained on his back, unmoved. He was warm now and his heartbeat was steady.

Putting on my sunglasses, I crept closer to the entrance of our cave to better hear the men's voices below.

"—women out soon because I'm tired of seeing your ugly mugs."

Laughter.

"Like *you* could get a woman!"

More laughter.

Cautiously, I crept through the crevice and lay on my stomach close to the opening. Three soldiers were sitting on the ground using the trees as backrests, and a fourth was in the process of standing up. They weren't far from our cave. I didn't see any bikes with them, so I assumed they were on foot. That made me uneasy. Vehicles were louder and I could at least hear them coming.

The one standing pulled his zipper down and started peeing. "My feet are killing me. I hope they finish that friggin' UAV soon."

One of the men sitting looked up at him. "We have a drone? What the hell are we doing wasting our time out here, then?"

Peeing man turned slightly toward him. "We don't have it yet. Duncan said all the replicators were confiscated to make parts for one. I don't know how long it takes to put it together."

The man closest to the one peeing jumped up. "Jesus Christ, you're pissing all over my pants!"

"Oh crap, sorry," peeing man said.

More laughter.

"It's not funny!" peed-on man said.

"He's right, it's not," said one of the men still sitting. He stood up. "How're we supposed to catch heathens when they can smell us coming?"

More laughter.

"You think it's funny?" peed-on man said, pulling down his zipper. "Let's see how much you like it."

"Put that thing away," said standing man. He was a lot bigger than peed-on man. "One drop of piss hits me and you won't be able to dig my boot out of your ass for a year."

"We should start heading back anyway," the last man sitting said. He stood. "I don't want to get stuck out here at night."

They started walking away.

"Where's the stream? I need to wash this stink off me," peed-on man said.

"You gonna whine all the way home? I said I was sorry."

Their voices were becoming more distant.

"You can both shut up now. We're supposed to be trolling for heathens."

Their voices were fading.

"We're not catching any…" Their voices drifted away.

I didn't know much about drones, other than they were some kind of aircraft that flew by remote. I didn't know how far they could fly or if they had weapons. And I didn't know why they were looking for heathens. I assumed they were looking for us.

Returning to the cave, I opened my flask of water and took a few gulps. A gurgling sound filled the room as the liquid hit my empty stomach. I ate a few more bites.

Jack's IV was still half full, so I estimated I dozed off for about four hours. Removing the bandage, I inspected the wound. I was surprised to see it was almost healed. Did Doc's nanorobots do that? Or was Jack just a fast healer? Either way, I was happy. He just needed to wake up. We were running out of time.

The idea that maybe he wasn't going to wake up crept into my thoughts. Could he be brain-dead? I had watched a movie where one of the characters had been injured to the point where only minimal brain functions were possible. His body kept breathing, but there was nothing else going on in his head. *What if Jack never woke up?*

"Jack!" I whispered as loudly as I dared.

I went nose-to-nose with him, looking for any eye movement or recognition that I had spoken. His eyeballs moved back and forth under his lids; they were the only part of his body that was moving.

Gently, I shook him. "Jack!" Nothing.

Lying back down, I wrapped my arms around him and watched the little spot at the base of his throat beat in time with his heart.

I hung the second-to-last IV. Between this one and the one remaining, it gave him about sixteen hours. Would it be enough? If I remembered correctly, Doc said IVs were for fluids and antibiotics. I tried to remember how long the human body could go without water, just in case I ran out of IVs before he woke up. Three days? Less?

Growls erupted from my stomach, breaking the silence in the small cave. I had finished the food hours ago and my water flask was empty, too. Terran said they usually passed through just before sunrise. I had no idea what time it was, but the sun wasn't up yet.

"I won't be long." I kissed his forehead and studied him for any sign that he felt my kiss. There was none.

Tucking the pistol into the back waistband of my shorts, I left the cave and returned to the spot where I had met the men yesterday. No one was there. A tree with low-hanging branches stood alongside the creek. I climbed it, using its height and foliage as cover, and waited to see if they would show.

My perch gave me a perfect view of the stream and surrounding area. I waited quietly, perking up when I saw movement in a bush. But it was only a small animal wanting a drink from the stream. I wondered what it would be like to hunt. If I couldn't get food from the men, I would have to find it another way or starve. And if I starved, that meant Jack would too.

The animal raised its head, ears standing straight up, and scampered away.

"I'm sure it was right around here," Terran said.

They walked directly under the tree, giving me a birds-eye view.

"I'm telling you, it was back there," Flint said. "Anyway, it doesn't matter. She's not here either."

"Let's give her a minute."

"Why do you like her so much?"

Terran shrugged. "What if she's telling the truth? Don't you want to help free the Pit?"

"Yeah, like President Kenner is actually out here trying to free the Pit. You know how stupid that sounds, right?"

"He's *not* the president!" Terran smacked Flint in the shoulder. "Besides, he shot Powell. The guy can't be all bad."

Flint rubbed his shoulder.

"Thanks for waiting," I said from the tree.

Both men jumped at the sound of my voice and looked up at me. I climbed down.

"You were up there the whole time?" Terran asked.

"Yeah. Sorry. I didn't mean to eavesdrop."

"Sure you didn't," Flint said.

"Sorry," I apologized again. "A group of soldiers passed through here earlier. I didn't want to take any chances, so I hid in the tree."

"Bourge don't usually come into the woods at night, but if they do they always have lights with them. Easy to spot them coming," Terran said.

"Do you ever see the, um, other people who live out here?"

"You mean the heathens?" Terran asked.

I nodded.

"We see them once in a while, but they keep their distance. Rumor has it they tried to make contact with the bourge when they first came out here, but it didn't end well for them…the heathens, that is." He set his backpack on the ground, took out a container and handed it to me.

"By the way, your mom sends her love," Flint said. "And she said she wants you to ditch the bourge and run."

His words felt like a blow. Had my mother really said that?

Terran shot him a dry look. "Did anyone ever tell you

that you have the diplomatic skills of a sledgehammer?"

I understood my mother was worried about me, but I wasn't about to ditch Jack. "You can tell my mother I can take care of myself and not to worry."

"How is Mr. Kenner?" Terran asked.

"No change."

"It's just…you told some men that Kenner planned on turning off the tagging system and a lot of people have their hopes up."

"That *was* the plan." Closing my eyes, I rubbed the heel of my hand across my forehead. I was exhausted and wasn't sure I could handle the weight of everybody counting on us. "Have you tried to get around the fence? You two dug a tunnel into the corral—can't everyone get out that way?"

"We're not stupid," Flint said.

"We have thought of that," Terran said. "But we don't know how far down we'd have to dig to circumvent the tagging system—and even if we tried, who's going to test it? Destroying it is out of the question because it's in armored casing."

Sparkles of light danced off the stream and I looked up to see the sun rising behind the mountain. My sunglasses were on top of my head and I pushed them down onto the bridge of my nose. I hadn't even really noticed that it was getting light out—how quickly I was becoming accustomed to it.

"If something happens and Jack—" I choked on my next words. I couldn't bring myself to say them. "We'll find another way to turn off the tagging system."

Terran put a comforting hand on my shoulder. "We all want him to pull through. But if he doesn't, you should leave here. Your mom is right."

"Come on," Flint said. "The sun's up. There are going to be soldiers all over the place soon." He looked at me. "Seems like the range is the safest place to be these days. Everyone's out looking for you instead of hunting."

"Glad I could help," I said, dryly.

"Meet here tomorrow morning?" Terran asked.

I nodded and held up the container. "Thanks again."

I waited until they were out of view before heading back to the cave. Terran seemed trustworthy, but Flint scared me a little bit.

The hairs on the back of my neck started to prickle, and a shiver went down my spine. I had the sensation that someone was watching me. Keeping my head straight, I scanned my periphery and strained my ears to listen for footsteps. I veered deeper into the forest and headed toward the back entrance to the cave.

Hiding in the bushes, I silently sat and observed the cave entrance. I listened intently for any signs of humans or animals. Silently I sneaked out and made my way through the crevice.

My breath stuck in my throat when I saw the empty bedroll.

Jack was gone.

Chapter Seventeen

The IV bag was still suspended from the makeshift hanger, but the needle lay discarded on the floor. The bedroll, blankets and medical supplies were still all here. The only thing missing was Jack.

I checked every nook and cranny of the small cave, which I knew was irrational. There was nowhere a grown man could hide.

The morning sun was hanging low in the sky when I slipped back out. I searched the ground for tracks and found some boot prints, but the soldiers that passed through yesterday could have easily made them.

The sound of a bird or animal startled me. I wasn't sure what direction the sound came from. I listened intently but didn't hear it again.

Could a hungry bear have climbed in the cave and dragged him out? Did they eat people? Ruby said that wire fences had been put up around the corrals to keep them out. She said they were huge. My fear was quickly turning to panic as I examined the ground for any signs of a bear dragging Jack's body away. I searched as far as the stream and doubled back around the outcropping where the cave was located. I didn't see any signs of Jack having been dragged away.

But he was still missing.

The sun was rising higher in the sky. The bourge had probably already started today's search. They might even be close to our location. What if Jack was out wandering around dazed and confused? He might walk right into them.

Then the thought struck me: what if we really were being watched? Someone took the bike and covered our tracks. Did they take Jack too?

They could be watching me right now.

I didn't think the so-called heathens were hostile, but I didn't know for sure. And Powell had said that there were other people out here—*bad people* he called them.

I heard that sound again—it definitely sounded like a bird cawing. I searched the tree line but couldn't find it. The feeling of being watched crept up my spine and I quietly moved toward denser brush. I strained to hear if anyone was following me. I heard the breeze in the leaves, the distant sound of the stream, the occasional bird and the whisper of my own feet on the spongy forest floor. I walked toward an outcropping, climbed it, and hid behind a scraggly bush on a rocky ledge to get a full view of the ground below.

I saw nothing. No heathens. No bad people. No soldiers. No Jack. *Was he gone?*

Suppressing the panic that wanted to take over me, I climbed back down. I must have missed something. If someone had taken Jack, they might have left a clue.

As I walked, the hairs on the back of my neck stood straight. My eyes roved in either direction as I kept my face pointed straight ahead. I resisted the urge to run. Instead, I calmly walked toward a dense patch of bushes and tried to lose myself in them. I wove around a few boulders and made my way to the back of the cave.

Immediately, I began a search of the small space. There were no visible signs of anyone having been there. The IV hadn't been yanked off the wall. Jack's bedroll was in the same position. I picked up the blankets and looked underneath them. He wasn't there either.

"Are you looking for me?"

I jumped to my feet and spun around, my heart threatening to explode. Jack stood at the entrance of the cave, wearing a mischievous smile.

"Jack!" I ran to him, almost knocking him over. *"Where have you been?"*

"I was—"

"I've been going out of my mind looking for you! Do you know how scared I was?"

"I just wanted—"

"There are bears out there! And soldiers looking for us! Did you even think about that?"

"But I was really—"

I smacked his shoulder. "Don't you *ever* do that to me again! I thought someone—"

"Sunny!" Jack said, holding me at arm's length. "I just went to the stream for a drink. I was thirsty."

"You were?" I asked dumbly.

It never occurred to me that he just woke up and got out of bed. But he looked perfectly fine. I lifted the hem of his t-shirt to check his bandage. No blood was soaking through. I peeled it back to look at the wound. Only a faint scar remained.

"What are you doing?" he asked.

"You're healed." It was incredible.

He brushed two fingers across the scar. "I'm kinda fuzzy on the details, but I thought I was shot? And why is the back of my hand bruised and full of stab wounds?"

I cringed when I looked at the back of his hand. "You were shot. You've been unconscious for a few days. "

He looked at me, wide-eyed. *"Days?"*

"I didn't think you were going to make it." Tears stung my eyes as I admitted my worst fear. I couldn't stop my lips from trembling.

"Don't cry," he said, hugging me against him. I buried my face in his neck, biting back the tears. "I'm still here."

"You don't get it—you almost *died*."

"Thanks to you, I didn't," he said, smoothing my hair. "And I see you got help. Where did you get all this stuff?"

Sniffing away the tears, I raised my head away from his neck and looked at the bedroll and IV. I glanced at him out of the corner of my eye. He tried to make me promise I wouldn't go back. This might cause a problem. I braced myself.

"Doc gave it to me. Sorry about your hand."

His mouth tightened a bit. "You went back to town."

I would have thought that was obvious. "I wasn't about to let you bleed to death."

"Do you know how dangerous that was?"

"Of course I knew it was dangerous, but you were *dying*."

"So you just, what, strolled back into town, knocked on the door, Doc invited you in and gave you a bunch of medical supplies?"

I sighed in exasperation. He wasn't going to be satisfied until I told him everything. "I brought you some food," I said, finding the container and handing it to him.

"Dare I ask where you got food?" He looked at the container suspiciously, but accepted it.

"Terran and Flint—the guys I told you about who are sneaking food to the men in the range."

"The guys you met in the corral."

I nodded. Removing the pistol from my waistband,

I sat down on the bedroll and leaned back against the stone wall. I put my sunglasses on my head and rubbed my tired eyes. Now that Jack was recovered, I suddenly felt exhausted. He sat beside me and I dropped my hand onto his leg. He was warm, breathing and alive.

"There's not much to tell. I followed the stream into town and marked a trail so I could find my way back. I kept to the forest, snuck in the back of the medical building and convinced Doc to help me. He gave me a bunch of IVs, showed me how to use them, and I came back here and did everything he told me to do," I said.

He laughed. "Why do I get the feeling that's the abridged version?" He opened the container, ate a few bites and passed it to me. "You're lucky he didn't turn you in."

"I told you, Doc is from the Pit." I looked into the container—roasted meat and veg. It was good.

"That doesn't necessarily mean he's on our side." Jack shrugged. "Being a doctor is a plum position for someone from the Pit—heck, it's a plum position for someone from the Dome—and I can't see him jeopardizing it by being disloyal."

"Trust me, Doc is *not* loyal to the bourge. He hates them." I passed the food back to him. "He's secretly working on some high-tech stuff that he doesn't want the bourge to know about. He called it nanotechnology. He says it can save the Pit."

Jack stopped eating and stared at me wide-eyed. "Nanotechnology?"

I nodded.

"Are you sure he said *nanotechnology*?"

"Yes, I'm sure. Why? What's the big deal?"

"Because it's not supposed to be real. It's just science fiction. Something about gray goo and machines taking over the world. You know, like little green men visiting Earth."

Uh-oh.

Was he going to be upset that I injected him with it? I hadn't considered that. At the time, he was dying and there was nothing else to save him. I mean it's not as though I had ever heard of it before.

I turned to look at Jack, wanting to emphasize my next words. "Doc said it was the most useful technology to come into the Dome."

He raised his eyebrows at that, and then a look of understanding crossed his features. "You know, he's probably talking about miniaturization—like making a microchip smaller. That kind of thing."

I shook my head, trying to remember how Doc had defined it. "He said it was… manipulating matter at the atomic level, or molecular level, or something like that. He calls them little robots—he has to look in a microscope to see them—and he uses DNA to program them."

Jack turned an indulgent smile on me. "I'm not trying to accuse the Doc of lying, but he does sound like quite a storyteller. Think about, Sunny. Little microscopic *robots*?" He handed me back the container, but I wasn't hungry anymore. My mouth had suddenly gone dry. I reached for the water flask. "If technology that sophisticated really did exist, we'd be a lot more advanced than we are right now."

I seized on that. "Doc said the same thing. He said the bourge didn't want it around because it would challenge the Holts' nuclear control over us. That the only reason we haven't progressed technologically is because the Holt regime didn't want us to."

Jack cocked an eyebrow at me. "*That* I can believe."

I brightened. "So then, it's not so far-fetched to believe nanorobots can actually exist." I unscrewed the flask and took a few gulps.

He shrugged. "I don't know. But if it does exist, it's probably not going to save anyone anytime soon, let alone the entire Pit." I choked on the water I was drinking. "Are you okay?"

I coughed and wiped my mouth with the back of my hand. "I'm good," I said. "It just went down the wrong way." I took another drink to clear my throat and handed the flask to him. "Okay, Jack, I have something to tell you." He gave me a questioning look and took a drink from the flask. I shifted uncomfortably. "First, you have to understand that you were already weak and unconscious before I took the bullet out."

He took the flask away from his mouth and swallowed. "*You* took out the bullet? It was still inside me?"

I nodded. "Then you started bleeding really bad. I couldn't stop the blood. It just kept pumping out and pumping out and pumping—"

"I get it. I was bleeding to death." He motioned for me to get on with the story.

"I wasn't going to use it unless I had to. Honest. But the Doc said they were his little surgeons and they could—"

"Little surgeons?" he interrupted.

He would understand. Doc's technology had saved his life.

"Nanotechnology." The word hung in the air as Jack stared at me and I stared back at him. "Doc said they were capable of making new tissue and could fix you."

He continued to stare at me, his mouth slightly ajar, and the silence stretched out. The occasional blinking of his eyes was the only clue that he wasn't unconscious again. "Just to recap," he finally said. "You went into town to see the genius doctor who's working with banned technology and, you said, hates the bourge, he gives you a syringe full of tiny little robot surgeons, tells you to inject me with it and *you did it?*"

My shoulders sagged. "It sounds bad when you say it like that."

He looked at me, wide-eyed. "It *is* bad, Sunny!"

"It saved your life! There was actually a moment when I thought you *were* dead, Jack. It was a last resort." It hurt that he didn't trust me. I hadn't used Doc's cocktail lightly. "I think you would've done the same for me."

He looked at me in surprise. "I'm not so sure that's true."

My mouth dropped open, and I took a breath. "You'd watch me bleed to death even if you had a syringe full of little surgeons that could fix me?" He closed his mouth and studied me for a moment. I saw a look of doubt cross his features. "Two days ago, your heart was barely beating and you were cold, with a gaping, bleeding bullet hole. Now I can barely tell you were even wounded."

He kept looking at me. I could almost see him weighing the pros and cons. "So what now? Did he tell you if they just biodegrade or something?"

"I don't know. I didn't think to ask."

He snorted and threw his hands in the air.

"You don't know how scared I was! The thought of losing you was more than I could handle." Tears stung my eyes. I stood up and moved away from him.

He stood up too. "*You're* mad at *me*?"

"This isn't how I saw this going at all." Didn't he know how much he meant to me? "Before you were unconscious, you said something to me and..." Maybe he didn't even remember.

The hard line of his mouth softened. "And I remember you said something back."

There wasn't much distance between us because the cave really wasn't that big. I was suddenly feeling awkward and the urge to run away and hide was strong. But I was the one who had brought it up. It was time I accepted my feelings for him; denying them was taking too much of my energy.

I drew in a shaky breath. "I love you more than I could ever possibly say and I couldn't just watch you die. I'm sorry you're upset that I used Doc's cocktail, but I'm not sorry I did it."

The corner of Jack's mouth lifted. He moved to stand in front of me, so close we were touching. My chest tightened. I wasn't sure if it was from his proximity or the honesty of the moment.

"Well, when you put it like that…" His lips brushed mine so lightly it was barely a kiss, yet it stole my breath. "I guess I should be thanking you."

"Or at least not be mad at me?" I asked, putting my hands on his chest.

He wrapped his arms around my waist. "I'm not mad. I'm too crazy in love with you."

Warm happiness made me weak in the knees. I leaned against him. "Crazy?"

He laughed softly. "I must be crazy if I'm not even mad at you for injecting me with tiny little robots."

A cawing sound from outside travelled into the cave. It was the same sound I heard earlier. The first time I heard it I had been close to the stream. The second time, I had been east of the cave. Now it was here.

"What is that?" I pushed away from Jack to go and investigate.

"It's just a bird or something," he said, trying to pull me back.

"I don't know if it is." Staying within the walls of the

crevice, I peered out of the opening and surveyed the ground below. Jack was right behind me, looking over my shoulder.

"I don't see anything," he said.

"We should probably find a better hiding place now that you're able to move." We returned to the cave. "Terran and Flint said we're real close to the range. And a group of soldiers passed by here too. I heard them talking about building a drone."

"A drone?" He made a low whistle. "Somebody's really pissed at us. I wonder who Holt sent out to replace Powell." He walked toward our stuff in the cave.

I trailed behind him. "Powell's not dead. You shot him in the medical center and they forced Doc to save him."

"So I guess we know who's pissed at us." He stooped and picked up the backpack. "We'll take all of this stuff. I don't want any evidence of us being here left behind for anyone to find. Better they think we're long gone."

I gathered the bedroll and blankets. "How far can a drone fly?"

He shrugged. "I don't know for sure."

Jack shoved the pistol into the back of his waistband once we had everything in the backpack. Putting my sunglasses on against the afternoon sun, I perched at the edge of the cave and skimmed the surrounding area for any signs of soldiers. A small animal moved below, running from bush to bush. Birds flew between trees. I caught sight of something in one of the trees. I stared hard for a moment, waiting to see if it moved. The breeze blew through the leaves, making them flash under the bright sun, but there was no other movement.

"What are you waiting for?"

"Do you see anything in that tree?" I motioned with my head.

Jack squinted, taking a good look. "Nope."

"I guess it's just me." I forced my eyes away from the shadow and finished surveying the ground beneath us. Yet my eyes kept snapping back to the tree, hoping to catch the shadow by surprise.

"Let's climb higher and get a better look," Jack suggested.

"Are you sure you should be climbing? What about your injury?"

"What injury?"

He gave me a gentle push in the direction of the cliff face. I shot another look in the tree's direction, but the shadow remained unmoving.

The climb wasn't as steep as it looked and there were plenty of bushes growing on rock ledges that provided excellent cover from below. I hid behind one bush, waiting for Jack to catch up. A bird cawed below and another one answered in the distance.

"What are you doing?" he asked, crouching next to me behind the bush.

I raised myself up enough to peek over the bush and watch the ground below. The shadow I saw in the tree wasn't visible from this angle.

"I get the feeling we're being watched," I confessed.

"Why?"

"Remember I told you I left a trail to find my way back here from town?" I asked. Jack nodded. "Someone covered up my tracks for me and the bike is missing."

"You think maybe this was one of the details you should have told me?" he asked, giving me a wry look. I ignored it and studied the tree again. "Do you see anything? Is it them?"

I knew he was referring to the heathens. "I don't see anyone. I'm probably just being paranoid. Come on," I said, resuming the climb.

Reaching the top of the outcropping, I grabbed a tree root and hauled myself up. Jack had fallen behind.

"Are you okay?" I called down. I hoped his injury wasn't hurting him.

"Were you a monkey in a previous life?"

I smiled. He was fine. I waited patiently and helped him up over the edge.

"It's a good vantage point up here. Let's see if we can put your superhuman vision to work."

"What are we looking—" I stopped mid-sentence when I turned around and saw them.

They looked as if they had been waiting for us.

Chapter Eighteen

I grabbed Jack's arm to prevent him from going any farther.

He stepped in front of me. "I see them."

Within seconds we were surrounded. Some carried spears, pointed directly at us. All had knives tucked into sheaths at their sides and bows slung across their backs. Just like the first time I saw them, they were all dressed similarly and painted.

Jack held up his hands, as if that would stop an assault. "We don't want any trouble." They remained silent. "Do you speak English?" They cast glances at each other but didn't say anything. Jack asked again, more slowly and in a louder voice.

"If they don't speak English, yelling at them isn't going to help. It might even make them angry," I whispered.

"You have a better idea?"

The one standing directly in front of us pulled a face. "We speak English."

"We have no fight with you. There's no need for this," Jack said, pointing to the spears.

"You'll come with us." It wasn't an invitation; it was a command.

"Do you mind telling me why?" asked Jack.

"It's not my place." He turned and walked away.

Someone jabbed a spear at us as incentive to follow. I didn't even see Jack's hand snake out and grab the spear, but suddenly he and the other man were locked in a fight. I scrambled away from the edge of the cliff before I was knocked off, and turned back around to help Jack. But as I did, hands grabbed me from behind and I felt the cold blade of a knife against my throat. Jack looked up, my capture throwing him off guard. The other man knocked him to the ground and the rest surrounded him with spears.

"Dead or alive, you're coming with us," said the one holding a knife to my throat.

"Don't hurt her!" Jack yelled.

They checked Jack for weapons, confiscating his pistol and knife, before they let him up. His eyes never left mine. I knew he wanted me to do something to break my captor's hold. I inconspicuously shook my head. There were too many of them and I saw the speed at which they moved to take him down. We didn't stand a chance.

"A gun. Where did you get this?" the leader asked Jack.

"It was issued," Jack said dryly.

The leader cocked an eyebrow at that and then looked down at pistol in his hand. He tucked it into his belt.

"Keep them separated. I want him up front where I can see him," said the leader.

I watched as Jack was forced to take the lead, two spears pointed at his back. My captor released me and gave me a shove forward.

From my back of the group vantage point, I observed our kidnappers. Even though their hairstyle and clothes were similar, the people themselves were very different. Two of them had extremely dark, almost black skin, while a few of the others were pale-skinned. All of them had long hair twisted into a single plait down their backs, decorated with feathers. Their clothing was made from animal hides, the color of which depended on the wearer; the darker the person, the darker the clothing and the lighter the person, the lighter the clothing. The paint on their faces and arms extended over their dress, visually blending wearer and garment into one. The markings seemed random at first glance, but as we walked through the forest and the sunlight dappled through swaying branches, I understood how they could disappear into their surroundings.

The outcropping we were on gradually sloped downward, back to the valley floor. They seemed to be constantly alert, reacting with suspicion to every sound.

Although they walked quickly, each step they took landed on a rock or a tree root. With feet wrapped in thick skins, they barely left a trace.

Silently we walked for what seemed like hours, keeping to the dense cover of the forest, until we came to the edge of the valley. The only place we had left to go was up. The pathway was steep and the higher we went, the thinner the forest became. Soon the path became so steep that we were forced to climb.

"Follow me. Put your hands and feet where I put mine. Got it?"

As my captor spoke, I noted the fine bone structure and full lower lip. She was female. With my eyes hidden behind my dark glasses, I looked over the faces of the rest of the group, but it was too difficult to tell their gender with only a quick glance.

It was a short climb and the rest of the group was waiting for us when we reached the top. Jack moved toward me when I pulled myself up, but he was held back. I shot him a reassuring look to let him know I was okay.

The terrain at the peak was rocky, interrupted by stands of trees sharing infrequent patches of soil. One by one, people began to emerge from crevices and caves. They watched us pass with silent curiosity. We were led through a narrow opening between two huge boulders, which opened into a clearing that looked like a naturally formed courtyard.

Many people were gathered here, busily performing various tasks. A few fires were lit around the courtyard and the smell of food wafted up to greet us. On my left, two people seemed to be scraping an animal skin stretched out on the ground. Children chased each other, getting in the way of the adults. As our presence became known, everyone stopped to stare.

We were led to an area where six old people were squatting around a low-burning fire. A pot was set on the coals. I wondered why they were gathered near a heat source on such a hot day. They all stood as we neared.

"We've been waiting for you," said the shortest of the six. "My name is Amini. Welcome to my barangay." Her white hair contrasted sharply with her dark skin.

"Not much of a welcome," Jack said, motioning to the spears. The leader of our group cuffed him on the side of his head.

"Diego!" exclaimed one of the grey-haired men. He leaned heavily on a stick that had been worn to a polish. "You *will* control yourself."

"I beg you to forgive Diego. He's very upset," Amini said.

"And rightly so," said a female voice. A tall woman walked to Diego, placed a hand on his shoulder and whispered something to him. He stomped away. She turned an accusing glare on Amini. "I wonder who approved him to go on the mission in the first place."

Amini scowled. "His brother was taken captive. He had every right to go."

The taller woman crossed her arms over her chest. "I disagree. And it was *my* place to coordinate the mission, not yours."

It wasn't just Diego who was upset. It felt as if the entire community was anxious. Something had happened and I wondered what we had to do with it. I looked over at Jack to get his reaction, but his attention was on the group of old people who were staring at us.

With a sniff, Amini turned away from the taller woman and focused on us. "This situation has us all on edge."

"What situation?" asked Jack.

The tall woman, who looked like the youngest member of the group, motioned for us to join them. Jack took the opportunity to move beside me and no one stopped him. We sat down on the ground, cross-legged.

"I'm Dena," the tall woman said. "This is Seru, Li, Ghica, and Carlos. We each represent our own barangay, and together we lead our nation. Now, perhaps we can have the honor of your names."

Jack and I looked at each other, silently communicating. He was the diplomat, not me. I didn't want to do the talking. He nodded.

"I'm Jack Kenner and this is Sunny O'Donnell."

"It's nice to finally make your acquaintance. We know so little about your people. We did attempt in the past to make friends, but our advances weren't very well received."

"That's an understatement," Seru murmured.

"I've only recently learned about that incident," said Jack. "It was horrible and inexcusable. I'm sorry it happened."

At first I wondered what they were talking about, but then I remembered General Powell's story about the trade the heathens tried to make. It ended with the bourge killing two of their people.

Seru nodded. "I appreciate your recognition of the tragedy of that event. Our entire nation went into mourning." A murmur of agreement went around the circle.

"And we're very relieved you feel that way," Amini said. "It gives us hope in resolving the current situation peacefully."

Jack gave me a quick sideways glance, his expression wary. "Current situation?"

"Some of our children were captured by your people yesterday," Amini said.

"I'm sorry," he said. He drew his eyebrows together. "How were they captured? Your people seem to be very good at hiding."

"A group of foolhardy teenagers who should've known better than to expose themselves out in the open," Amini said. "Your people took four of them and the rest were allowed to return here to give us a message—they want the two of you handed over to them, or the four children will be killed."

My stomach clenched and nausea rose up. This wasn't good. Not for the hostages. Not for us.

"I think you better tell us what this is about," Dena said.

"I'm sorry they involved you. This isn't your fight," Jack said.

"I think I know why the bourge involved them," I said to Jack, and then spoke to the circle of people. "A soldier was picking on a child—one of yours—and I told him to stop. Maybe they think we have a friendship with you."

"Friendship is considered a crime?" Amini asked.

"When one of your people shot the soldier with something, the bourge thought I'd done it. There was a good chance I was going to be executed. We escaped and now they're looking for us. They probably think you're hiding us."

"Why would they kill you? The soldier wasn't hurt. He was darted with a mild sedative. If anything, *he* should be held accountable for *his* actions," Dena said.

"I'm a slave. I sealed my fate the minute I challenged that soldier's authority."

The crowd surrounding our circle bristled at the information. "It's true! They are slavers!" someone shouted.

A nervous chatter among the crowd rose up.

"They're going to keep killing us!" a shout rang out.

"We need to take action against them!" a voice yelled.

"No! We need to leave the valley!" someone yelled back.

"It's time to fight back!"

Dena stood. "Enough!" she called in a booming voice. Looking at the guards surrounding us, she flicked her head toward the crowd. Several of them moved toward the crowd, directing them to leave. "Everyone, go back to what you were doing. We'll report later."

Amini turned an angry glare on us. "It's time you told us exactly who you are and where you came from." Jack opened his mouth, but Amini put up a hand to stop him. "No. From her," she said impatiently. "I'm beginning to distrust anyone wearing that uniform."

Jack and I both looked at his military fatigues. He regarded me with an uneasy expression.

I looked back at the group of old people, now staring at me expectantly. How did I even begin to tell them that the mountain they thought gave them protection was really a custom-built refuge for the important people considered worth saving? And how did I do that while the man I was in love with sat here wearing their uniform?

I decided that it was in our best interests to stick to the facts and keep my emotions out of it. It was doubtful anything I said would change their minds about handing us over to Powell—trading two strangers to get their loved ones back was a small price to pay.

When I finished my story, Ghica was the first to speak. "She's lying."

Carlos nodded. "I think they're Ryder's people."

Amini shook her head. "I thought we've been in agreement for some time that they aren't Ryder's people. Look at their technology—Ryder isn't that advanced."

"He's been gathering technology for years," Carlos said. "We have no idea how advanced he's become."

Dena looked at him. "Why would they lie?"

Carlos looked uncomfortable with her directness. "To scare us," he said with uncertainty. "By lying about how many more people are in the mountain. There's probably no one. It's just them."

"Yet if it is true, it explains much of the mystery surrounding the mountain," Amini said.

"And even as the legend protected our nation all these years, now the truth threatens to destroy us," Li said.

"Perhaps this will convince *everyone* that it's time to move our nation," Amini said, pointedly looking at Dena. "This valley is no longer a safe haven."

"We still have the issue of retrieving our children," Li pointed out. "General Powell gave his word that no harm would come to them if we did as he asked."

"You can't trust him," Jack said. "If you hand us over, he'll assume you were hiding us all along and seek retribution. You'll play right into his game."

"And if we don't hand you over, he'll kill four children," Amini said. She pointed an accusing finger at Jack and appealed to the other Elders. "That is nothing more than a plea for mercy. If he shot a leader, then I don't blame their people for wanting to hold him responsible for his actions!"

"I agree with Amini," Li said. "This is not our fight. We should retrieve our children and leave this valley. I don't know if these people are Ryder's men or the *bourge* as this young lady says, but I do know they're dangerous."

Dena wasn't as quick to concur. "We can't forget how we were treated when we made an offer of peace."

"I thought we had agreed that was an unfortunate misunderstanding," Amini said.

"Our ruling in that matter never sat well with me, as I'm sure you all know. I understand that they think we *stole* the animals, but killing two people for it was hardly justified," Dena said.

"Yet the matter was concluded. They've never come looking to extract any more payment from us," Amini said.

"Until now," Dena reminded her. "It seems to me that what Jack is saying fits with their behavior."

"So what is the alternative?" Li asked. "We can't just abandon four of our own people when we've been given the opportunity to save them."

"I understand that," Dena said. "However, it would be wise to send a group of Protectors to oversee the trade."

"I have no problem with that," Amini said.

"We're all in agreement then," Li said.

Amini addressed one of our guards. "Send a team with a message. We'll make the trade tomorrow at noon. Until then, keep these two separated and under constant guard. I don't doubt they'll run if they have the chance."

Chapter Nineteen

As Jack and I stood, my guard put a hand on my arm. "This way."

Jack's guard gripped his arm as well, and he yanked it away.

"Get off me!"

Two more guards came to assist.

"Jack, don't," I pleaded. We couldn't fight them—there were too many. He would only end up getting hurt.

Three guards were trying to control him. One of them did something to his neck that appeared to send a jolt through him. He stopped fighting. My captor prodded me to get going, but I pushed back. I needed to make sure he was okay.

"Don't worry. They won't hurt him," my captor said.

"It looks like they already did."

"They'll let him go once he calms down. Come on."

Without much choice, I followed. I kept Jack in sight as long as I could.

"I'm Jin-Sook and this is Maria," she said, motioning toward the woman on my other side. I noticed she was carrying a lit torch.

The sound of running feet came from behind me, slowing their pace as they neared.

"What are you doing here, Willow?" Maria asked the newcomer.

"My name is *Will* and I'm here to help with the prisoner," she replied.

"This is not a job for little girls," Jin-Sook said.

"Grandma gave me permission," Will said, her chin tilted in defiance.

Maria groaned. "You mean we have to put up with you all night?"

They led me through an entrance in the rock wall into a manmade grotto. A staircase led us down into an open cavern. I was surprised to find wooden homes strung together along one side of the cave. They weren't unlike our apartments in the Pit.

The torch seemed to burn brighter in the confined space even with my sunglasses on. Averting my eyes from the direct light, I kept my head down as we walked. My guards chatted. People passed us, shooting curious glances at me. I put my head down.

Jin-Sook stopped at one of the apartments and opened the door. "You'll stay here for the night."

The room was quite spacious and held comfortable-looking furniture. A big bed was pushed against one wall with a brightly patterned blanket draped over it. On the other side of the room were a table and chairs. A dresser and mirror separated the two living areas. To my immediate left hung a curtain.

"What's behind the curtain?" I asked.

"The bathroom," Jin-Sook said. She lit several candles that were scattered about the room. "Maria and Willow, can you get some food?"

"It's *Will!*"

"Do I have to take *her*?" Maria whined.

"Yes," Jin-Sook said firmly.

"I can stay and guard the prisoner while you two go," Will suggested.

"Go!"

They left, squabbling the whole way down the hall. Jin-Sook gave me an apologetic look.

"I think they actually like to argue," she joked.

My expression remained blank. I didn't care.

An awkward silence hung between us as she finished lighting the candles. "I'll be right outside the door," she said.

Shutting the door behind her, I was left alone in my comfortable prison. The silence of the room contrasted sharply with the clamor of my thoughts. Jack and I had come so far only to arrive here—locked up and ready to be dragged back to the bourge.

It was bright in the room with all the candles lit. I lifted my glasses and tried to look at the glow of the flame, but it burned my retinas. I extinguished some of them.

Behind the curtain, I was surprised to find a toilet and sink not unlike the kind we had in the Dome. The words *American Standard* were inscribed on them. Warm water flowed from the faucet when I turned it on, only adding to the mystique of the place. Splashing my face with water, I thought of Jack. I hoped his accommodations were as comfortable.

There was a knock on the door and I heard someone come into the room.

"You're in luck. There was still some bear meat stew left," Will said. "Why is it so dark in here?"

I came out from behind the curtain. "I'm sensitive to light."

"But I can barely see." She set the food down on a table.

The other two women came into the room, carrying the torch. They wedged it into a holder on the wall, where it continued to burn brightly. I dropped my sunglasses back onto my nose.

"What's going on?" Jin-Sook asked.

"She likes being blind," Will replied.

"I'm not blind."

I retreated to the bed, away from the torch and my captors. They made themselves at home around the small table.

"Do you always wear those glasses?" Jin-Sook asked.

"The flame is a little bright," I said.

"Bright?" she asked in disbelief, but relocated the torch to the hallway. "Is that better?"

"Yes. Thank you." I tried not to look stunned by the gesture. I removed my sunglasses again.

"Why do you hate light so much?" Will asked.

"I don't hate light. I'm just not used to bright light."

"How can you not be used to light?" Maria asked.

"You won't believe this," Jin-Sook said, and repeated the story I told the Elders. The look of complete horror and astonishment on Will's face was almost comical. I bit my lip not to laugh at her.

Will looked at me, her mouth still agape. "You grew up in a mountain without any light?"

"We have a type of light called fluorescent. It's dimmer and more…diffused. It's not like a flame."

"You mean you have light bulbs," Maria said dryly.

Her answer gave me pause. I had just assumed they wouldn't know what a light bulb was.

"My barangay—well, not *my* barangay, but the one I'm from—has some lights in the main areas. The rest of the barangays don't have electricity yet," Jin-Sook explained.

"There's nothing to making it," Will said. "We learned as kids in school to make electricity with a potato and light a filament."

"Do you know how stupid that sounds, Will?" Maria said. She looked over at me. "Honest, we don't use potatoes to power our lights. We use geothermal."

A giggle erupted from me at the thought of a potato power plant and I bit my lip to stop it. These women were my guards and sharing a joke with them seemed unnatural.

"So it's really true? You lived *inside* that mountain all your life?" Will asked in awe. Maria punched her in the arm. Will drew a fist to punch her back, but Jin-Sook put up a hand to stop her.

"That's enough, you two!" Jin-Sook said. "I apologize for their rudeness. Please, come and have something to eat."

I didn't know what to make of them. With the bourge, I always knew where I stood. The food did smell good, though. Hesitantly, I got off the bed and sat at the table.

"Your eyes are so black!" Maria exclaimed.

I looked down at the bowl in front of me, feeling self-conscious. After a lifetime of trying to cover up my red hair so I could blend in, I had escaped the Dome only to remain an oddity.

I took a bite of the bear meat stew. It had a strong flavor and was chewy. I took another bite. Food was food and I was hungry.

"I love her eyes. They make her look dangerous and beautiful all at the same time," Will said dramatically. "I wish I looked that dangerous. It would make me the best Protector ever."

I stole a look at Will. Her skin was dark and her large round eyes were an unusual shade of green. It was difficult to see her as being dangerous.

Maria snorted. "You? A Protector?"

"I'll be as good as Jin. Maybe even better."

"You need to have self-control to be a Protector, Will," Jin-Sook said.

"I have self-control," she said. "When I want to," she added under her breath.

"Which isn't very often," Maria said.

"How about we give Sunny a chance to speak," Jin-Sook suggested.

All three looked at me. "I don't have anything to talk about."

"Your husband's kind of cute, in a foreign way," Maria said. She leaned a little closer, looking conspiratorial. "Is he really a slaver?"

Jin-Sook almost choked on her food. "Maria!"

"Oh c'mon Jin. You think he's cute too," Maria smiled.

I could tell Jin-Sook was trying not to smile, but her lips curved despite her efforts.

Will rolled her eyes. "Talk about self-control," she said sarcastically. "Don't mind them. They're boy-crazy. I have no idea why. I'm never getting married."

"He's not a slaver though, is he?" Jin-Sook asked.

"No he's not. In fact we're trying to free the slaves."

Will's head snapped toward me when I said that. "Really?" A look of respect came into her eyes. "You must be very brave."

"How do you plan to do it?" Jin-Sook asked.

"We need to get a message to the Alliance, inside

the Dome. If my people know the Earth is fine, they can fight their way out."

"What is the Alliance?" Jin-Sook asked.

That wasn't an easy question to answer. Part of me felt I should keep that information secret from my captors, yet another part of me wondered if they would be sympathetic. Once Jack and I were handed over to General Powell, there would be no one to shut down the tagging system. No one to knock on the Dome's door and let the Pit know their enslavement was over.

Taking a deep breath, I retold how Jack and I came to be married for what seemed like the hundredth time. As I spoke, they set down their spoons and listened intently. Tears sprung to their eyes when I told them about life in the Pit… about how they dragged my father away… about Crystal's sacrifice. I ended my story by admitting Jack and I ended up falling in love. Jin-Sook and Maria sighed. I didn't tell them about Summer, though. I knew how ashamed she felt at being forced to be the president's mistress. Her secret was safe with me.

"Even though you two are all dreamy and in love and stuff now, you're still going to free the slaves, right?" Will asked.

I shook my head. "Tomorrow we'll be handed over to General Powell. We failed."

The girls exchanged silent glances, guilt and sympathy clouding their features.

"Maybe the Elders will change their minds," Maria

said. Her hand reached out to cover one of mine.

"I doubt it," I said. "I understand why they're doing it. They want the hostages back safe and sound."

"I wish there was another way," Jin-Sook said.

"There is," I said. "I heard the shouts from the crowd wanting justice. So fight them. *Take* your children from them. But play by their rules and they're only going to betray you."

Maria's hand retreated from mine and Jin-Sook sat up straighter.

"We always seek a peaceful resolution to any conflict we encounter. Fighting is only a last resort and always in self-defense," Jin-Sook explained.

"Yeah, and I don't get it, either," Will chipped in. "We spend our entire lives learning how to fight just to be told we shouldn't."

"We are not taught to fight, we are taught to defend. If you want to be selected as a Protector one day, you need to know this, Will," Jin-Sook said.

"I'm just saying, when I'm a Protector and hunters or recruiters come around I'll give them a reason to run," Will said.

"Hunters and recruiters?" I asked.

Jin-Sook nodded and scooped up a mouthful of stew. I raised my eyebrows, looking from one to the next.

"You don't know who they are?" Maria asked.

I pointed to myself. "Just came out of a mountain fully believing that humans had been wiped off the face of the Earth."

"Right," Jin-Sook said. "Hunters are people who want to kill us and recruiters are people who want to enslave us."

"Oh," I said. It explained nothing. I understood the whole enslavement thing—I was born into that life. But hunted? "Why do hunters want to kill you?"

"Because we're Asian," Maria said. "Well, our original ancestors were anyway. The story goes that after the bombs, gangs seeking revenge on the enemy that bombed us targeted anyone who looked even remotely Asian. Eventually, the victims grouped together for their own protection and set out to find a place to live in peace. They ended up here."

Maybe her story made sense to her, but it didn't to me. "Why would Asians be targeted as the enemy?"

Jin-Sook gave me a crooked smile. "You really don't know, do you?" I shook my head. She put her elbows on the table, crossing her arms, and leaned toward me. "Korea started the war that almost ended the Earth and there are people who still want revenge."

My mouth dropped open in surprise before I thought to control my reaction. I closed it quickly. It never occurred to me that anyone would still be held responsible for the war. I had always accepted that what was done was done. There was no one left on Earth to blame. That is, until Jack had told me about the Holts' original sin. But in my world, the Holts were to blame for a lot.

"You look surprised," Maria said.

All three were staring at me, waiting for me to say

something. I decided it was in my best interest not to divulge that Jack had told me General Holt had tricked President Taylor into launching the warheads three hundred years ago. It wasn't Korea that started the war. They probably wouldn't believe me anyway. "I guess I am. If your ancestors were living here when war broke out, doesn't that mean they were Americans?"

Jin-Sook nodded. "Yes, they were." She shrugged. "Emotions run high when you watch your loved ones—everyone and everything you've ever known—be destroyed. It's human nature to want to place blame and seek justice."

I knew the feeling. How many times had I watched my loved ones get hurt or killed in the Pit? "Your ancestors were hunted and killed—did *they* not want to place blame and seek justice?"

Jin-Sook leveled a sober look at me. "Our nation was built on the belief that peace will never be achieved through hatred. When hatred enters our hearts, we meditate to find the root cause and open our minds to another alternative."

It wasn't that I disagreed with her. It was a lovely concept. But clearly she hadn't grown up in the Pit, being beaten for the slightest infraction.

I regarded them with a sheepish expression. "Not everyone in your nation looks Asian." *With the exception of Jin-Sook,* I thought to myself. Her delicately shaped amber eyes and fair complexion were reminiscent of people I had seen in movies. Maria had soft brown hair and large brown eyes with an olive skin tone. And then there was Will—one of the most stunning people I had ever seen. Her dark smooth skin framed her green eyes.

"Anyone who embraces our peaceful philosophy is welcome to join our nation," Jin-Sook said.

"Like my great-grandparents," Maria said. "They found the nation by accident, because they didn't know well enough to stay away from the mountain. Not everyone knows about the legends."

"The legends?" I asked. Then I remembered what General Powell had said—the mountain was haunted and gave them protection from the bad men.

Will made her eyes even bigger as she nodded. "But only one legend has really stuck—Yugo. He's a monster from the scorched lands."

My thoughts turned to President Holt and I couldn't help but think that particular legend really wasn't too far-fetched.

"So the scary mountain keeps the hunters away?" I asked.

Maria nodded. "Sometimes the recruiters pass through here—they aren't afraid of anything—but usually we live undisturbed. When they do come, we know the best defense is to not be there." She ran her fingers along her painted arm.

"Is that why you paint yourselves?"

"It's not paint, it's dye," Will said.

"We learned from the animals how to blend in with our surroundings and we're taught from a young age how to stand very still," Jin-Sook said.

"I can stand still the longest in training," Will said. "No one ever finds me in the woods."

"Nobody wants to find you," Maria said. Will stuck out her tongue.

I remembered on the trek here how they walked on rocks and tree roots, leaving barely a trail behind them. In fact, their entire barangay was built in rock, hidden away from the outside world. They had learned to live in secret.

"Is that why you all dress alike—to blend in and hide?"

Maria looked at me, tilting her head to one side. "Can I ask you a personal question, Sunny?"

I nodded.

"Why do you dress that way?"

I looked down at my t-shirt, shorts and work boots. They were dirty and needed a good laundering.

"I guess I am kind of filthy. Jack and I have been on the run for a while."

"No, I mean they show your…um…lady curves. People can tell you're a woman," Maria said in almost a whisper.

"I am a woman," I said.

"You shouldn't let people know you are, though," Will said. "The recruiters do bad things to women."

"What are recruiters?"

"Gangs sent out by Ryder to recruit men into his armies," Jin-Sook said. "The only use they have for women is to rape them or take them as camp wives."

General Powell had talked to Jack about men he called warlords. I wondered if Ryder was one of them.

"So that's why you all dress alike," I mused. All three looked at me and I realized I had said that out loud. "I'm sorry, but I can only tell the women apart from the men up close."

"That's the way we want it," Maria said.

Will's mouth dropped open as she stared at Maria. "During the spring tournament you were doing everything you could to show off *your* lady curves in front of Dre." Will clasped her hands together and hugged them close to her cheek. "Oh Dre, look at me! Aren't I beautiful!"

Maria gave Will a look of disgust. "I did *not* look like that!"

"Yes you did," Jin-Sook chimed in. "You were shameless."

Their easy banter about boys made me think of Summer again and how we always passed the time at work talking about boys. A pang of sorrow hit me. I would probably never see her again.

"Sorry, Sunny. We didn't mean to upset you," Jin-Sook said.

It took me a moment to register that a tear had run down my cheek. I wiped it away.

"We're being really thoughtless—you're probably worried about your husband. Hey, why don't you two go and check on him and let her know how he's doing."

Will was the first to jump out of her chair. "I can do it by myself."

"You go with Maria or not at all," Jin-Sook said firmly. Willow sucked air through flared nostrils and blew it out in a dramatic sigh, but she followed Maria out of the room. "Sorry, I guess we get caught up in our own lives. I do realize your life isn't so great right now." I smiled weakly and pushed my bowl away. "You must miss all your family and friends in the Dome."

I did miss my family and friends… that is, if I had any family left in the Dome. I didn't know whether my father was alive or not. And it looked like I would never get the chance to find out. Tomorrow I would be given back to the bourge and my life would be over. Everyone I loved would die because I failed. If I thought too long about it, remorse would eat up what little sanity I had left.

"What's a Protector?" I asked.

She looked as if she was about to say something but decided against it. Instead, she put a smile on her face, although it looked a little sad to me. I breathed around the lump constricting my throat.

"Protectors are those chosen to defend our nation. Every spring, the barangays gather for the annual tournament where warriors are tested for their strength, agility, fighting technique and intelligence. Only the best of the best are chosen as Protectors."

"You're a Protector?"

"Yes. I've been one for several years."

I studied her face, trying to discern her age. Twenty-five maybe? It was hard to tell. "Do you like it?"

"I do. It takes a lot of discipline, but the reward is great."

"And what about family? Do you have children?" I asked. Jin-Sook appeared a little uncomfortable with my question. "I'm sorry. I didn't mean to pry."

"No, it's fine," she said. Her features suddenly looked fragile. Perhaps I had touched on a subject I shouldn't have. "I was promised to someone I thought was an honest man." She tried to smile, but a tear slipped down her cheek. Angrily, she rubbed it away. I scolded myself for my stupidity for bringing up a touchy subject. "But there's always next year's tournament, right?"

"Um, right," I said. I had no idea what she was talking about.

"I talk as if you know us," she said apologetically. "Getting permission to marry isn't easy. We're encouraged to marry outside of our barangay because it strengthens ties between our villages. So the spring tournament is very important to us. It's not only a chance to become a Protector, but it's the time to find a mate. Once two people decide to marry, their family history is charted to ensure genetic diversity and then they must wait for the approval of the council. Diego and I went through all of that and later I discovered he was in love with someone else. Someone from his own barangay."

"Diego?" I asked. "He was the man that led Jack and me here?"

Jin-Sook nodded. "His little brother was one of the ones taken by the bourge."

"That explains why he was so upset."

"They shouldn't have allowed him to go." She rubbed the moisture from her cheeks. "And I didn't need to see him again."

I didn't know why I felt so bad for this woman who was my guard, but I did.

"I think you're a good person. You didn't deserve that."

She tried to smile, but her lips curved down instead. "So are you, Sunny. I really wish there was something I could do to help you."

"Maybe you can. When I'm gone, convince your nation to free my people. If I know they stand a chance, I won't feel as bad when I'm executed."

"Will the slavers hunt us too?"

I looked thoughtfully at Jin-Sook, wondering how she would take the news. President Holt would annihilate them all for the same reason he was planning to kill everyone from the Pit: to keep the bloodlines clean.

I nodded. "Yes. They think of you as heathens."

So many truths had been laid bare between us, but this one truth seemed to have the most impact on Jin-Sook. She dropped her face into her hands. I understood how she felt. I was well acquainted with the heaviness of the load I had just given her.

She raised a tear-stained face to look at me. "I swear I'll do whatever I can."

Maria and Will came back into the room, their bickering interrupting the somber mood that had settled on us. Jin-Sook and I both wiped the tears away from our eyes.

"Your husband's okay. He's… um…" Will hesitated.

"Sleeping. He's sleeping," Maria interjected.

I eyed them suspiciously. "You mean he was darted."

Maria shrugged. "It's just a mild sedative. He'll be all rested up for the hike tomorrow."

I bit my tongue against the angry comment I wanted to spit out. *How dare they touch Jack!*

"Speaking of tomorrow, you better get some rest," Jin-Sook said. "We'll stay with you tonight."

"I'll take first watch," Will said.

"Willow!" Jin-Sook admonished.

My lip twitched with the urge to curl into a sneer. "It's okay. I'm a prisoner."

They all looked a little guilty as I got up from the table. I returned to the dark corner where the bed was located and lay flat on my back. Staring at the wooden ceiling, I started counting the number of knots in each plank… anything to keep my mind off tomorrow. But thoughts of failing the Pit crashed through the emotional barriers I had erected and I was consumed with hopelessness.

"Good night, Sunny," Jin-Sook said.

Rolling over onto my side, I turned my back on the trio. Perhaps I should have fought them instead of making friends. Maybe they would have darted me, too.

Chapter Twenty

The smell of food brought me back to the present. I hadn't really slept, but at some point I had become mesmerized by the wall in front of me. I rolled onto my back. Maria was the only other occupant in the room.

"I was about to wake you. They're waiting." She held a bowl out to me.

I got off the bed and accepted the bowl, knowing it was probably my last meal. It didn't taste bad, but the food dropped into my stomach like a stone and set it roiling with nausea.

"I'm not hungry," I said, setting the bowl down.

Maria nodded. "We should go, then."

Jack was already in the courtyard flanked on either side by guards. It was all I could do to restrain myself from running to him. The scowl on his face melted into an apology when his eyes came to rest on me. I suspected he felt bad because he couldn't fight our way out of this one.

"Are you okay?" he asked.

I nodded. "Just worried about you."

A lot of people had gathered to watch us leave. Many of them were armed with bow and arrows, spears and knives sheathed in their belts. I assumed they were the Protectors Dena had ordered to oversee the trade.

As the Elders emerged from a cave, the throng parted to let them through. Jin-Sook walked beside Dena but broke away from the troop to stand beside me. She gave me an encouraging smile.

Dena stepped forward, a look of respect in her eyes.

"Jin-Sook has told me much about you and your people. Please believe me when I say I wish there was another way."

I gave a curt nod of acknowledgement. Her sentiments were not going to save the Pit any more than they were going to save Jack or me.

"General Powell doesn't really care about her," Jack said. "It's me he wants. I'm the one who shot him. Please, let her stay here with you."

I appreciated what Jack was trying to do. Really I did. But if he actually thought I was going to stay behind even if his request was granted, he didn't know me very well.

"The general asked for both of you. I'm sorry," Amini said.

"At least let me say goodbye to him," I said.

Amini turned to the other Elders. They gave a nod of approval. The guards let go of Jack.

I ran and threw my arms around his neck. He hugged me so close my feet left the ground.

"We're going to find a way out of this. We always do," Jack whispered.

A shaky laugh escaped my lips. "You mean you don't have a plan?"

"They drugged me last night. I didn't have time to come up with one."

"It's looking pretty bad, though."

"Keep your eyes on me today. If I see an opportunity to break free, be ready to follow my lead." I nodded against his shoulder.

"Time to go," someone said, pulling Jack's arm.

Reluctantly, I dropped my arms and took a step back. Two guards urged him forward. Jin-Sook came up beside me, laying a comforting hand on my shoulder. Even though she was my guard, I was relieved to have a familiar presence escort me to my end.

We all filed out of the courtyard and descended the rocky path to the ground below. Jack was forced to maintain his frontline position and I followed a short distance behind. Glancing back, I was amazed by the steady flow of armed Protectors still coming out of the barangay. As they reached the ground they spread out around us and vanished into the woodland.

For the better part of our hike, we stayed in dense forest. Walking was treacherous—tree roots and rocks jutting up everywhere—yet our captors glided through the forest effortlessly. More than once I stumbled, and every time I did, Jack stopped to look back at me. They always urged him to keep moving.

"He's concerned for you," Jin-Sook said in a whisper.

"I'm concerned for him too," I whispered back.

"Naoki won't hurt him."

I assumed Jin-Sook was referring to the man beside Jack. He wasn't as tall as Jack, but he was wiry and looked mean. A bow was slung across his back and knives were sheathed on either side of his legs. I stole a look at Jin-Sook's pants and saw she carried knives too.

As we neared our final destination, our captors slowed. They seemed to hug the trees, stopping every so often to stand stock-still and listen to the sounds around them. Birds chirped, a nearby stream babbled and somewhere in the distance came a caw. A member of our group paused and repeated the call. This was the sound I had heard when Jack and I ventured out of the cave, just before we were caught.

Silently, we continued to move through the forest. Naoki gave a signal and we all moved to hug the trees again. Standing still we listened—only this time there were no birds chirping. Jin-Sook and Naoki pushed Jack and me into a thick bush, while the rest of our group blended into the trees.

Within moments we heard the sound of feet crunching across the forest floor. The sound wasn't far away and it was getting closer. Jack looked worried. He moved to get a better view and Naoki shot him a warning look. Jack pointed two fingers at his eyes and then turned the fingers toward the sound. Naoki nodded.

From my vantage point, it was hard to see the intruder, but whoever he was, he was oblivious to our presence. We waited until he was long gone before Naoki chanced a whispered conversation.

"That was one of your soldiers," he said to Jack.

"Do we need to go over this again, Naoki? I am *not* one of them," Jack said angrily. "That was a sharpshooter. He'll go to high ground where he has an open view and train a rifle on us during the trade. My guess is there's more than one shooter. You should find them and put them out of commission before the trade."

Naoki's expression was hard. I remembered Jin-Sook said they only used violence in self-defense.

"At least have someone watch them," Jin-Sook said to Naoki.

"I don't like this," Naoki said. "Maybe we should go back."

"The Elders won't be pleased if we return with these two instead of our own people," Jin-Sook said.

"I don't trust them," Naoki said.

"That's the smartest thing I've heard you say," Jack said.

"You don't get a vote in this," Naoki snapped at him.

"I know how they think," Jack replied.

"Please listen to him," I said. "He can help."

"I'm not taking orders from the prisoners!" Naoki said.

He shifted uncomfortably, obviously agitated. Ignoring us, he looked directly at Jin-Sook. "We'll do it your way, Jin. I'll send someone to keep an eye on the shooters."

We left the bushes, and Naoki sent someone to relay his message to the unseen army of Protectors.

"How far are we from the meeting place?" asked Jack.

"The other side of that ridge," he said. He motioned for us to keep moving.

Jack looked around. I knew him well enough to know that he was sizing up our situation to see if there was a way out. There wasn't. Ten guards walked with us and at least forty more were soundlessly gliding through the forest armed with arrows, knives and darts.

As we approached the forest edge, I could see three jeeps parked in a clearing. There were at least a dozen heavily armed soldiers. Two officers stood by one of the vehicles while the other soldiers patrolled the area, rifles at the ready.

"There are more somewhere," Jack whispered. "There's no way only twelve would come to this show."

"Where are the hostages?" Naoki asked.

"There," Jack said, pointing to two people sitting in the back of a jeep.

"That's only two," Jin-Sook said.

"I don't like this," Jack said. "Let me go down there on my own and negotiate the trade."

"No!" I almost screamed. "You are *not* going down there alone."

"Sunny, they're not going to kill me. I'm betting they

already sent someone into the Dome to tell Holt that I shot Powell, so by now they know I'm a traitor. The president will want me alive to face the tribunal. He needs to indict me in order to charge my family with being sympathizers. I'm a crucial piece of his plan to influence the other families to take action against the Pit."

"You don't know that for sure."

"No, I'm not one hundred percent sure, but I am ninety-nine percent sure." I shook my head and Jack grabbed me by my shoulders. "You're not important to them, Sunny. They won't hesitate to kill you. You can't go down there." He turned to Naoki. "Don't let this happen."

"I'll keep her with me," Jin-Sook told Naoki. "There are only two of our people visible. We should only give them half of the promised trade, too."

Naoki flexed his hands into fists, turning his knuckles white. A sheen of sweat glistened on his forehead. Biting his lower lip, he looked from me to Jack thoughtfully, and then turned his attention on Jin-Sook.

"I'll take only Jack and you stay with her. I don't know where the other two are, but I'll negotiate for them. When they bring them out, you come with Sunny."

I shook my head again. "No, it's not happening that way. I stay with Jack."

"It's not your decision to make," Naoki said in a hard voice.

"If you think I'll just sit here, you are—"

"Can I have a minute with her?" Jack asked Naoki.

Reluctantly, he gave his consent.

Jack led me a few steps away from the group, but one of the guards gave us a warning with his spear and we went no farther. Jack put his hands on my shoulders and rested his forehead against mine. "It's not me I'm worried about," he said in a hushed voice. "They won't hesitate to kill you, Naoki or Jin. But I know they'll take me into custody and turn me over to Holt. Let them take me. It might even be the opportunity we need to get back inside the Dome."

I wasn't ready to admit defeat. I couldn't sit here and watch him risk his life alone. I didn't want to be in this world without him.

"Holt wants me, too. I heard Leisel tell her boyfriend she wants to give her father the matching set. They'll hand us both over and then we can both go back inside." I shifted so I could look into his eyes. "We're partners—we stay together."

His weak smile told me he understood. "This time I have to do it on my own."

That wasn't what I expected to hear. "Jack, no," I said. "I can do this too. The most important thing is for us to stay together. If we get separated—"

"We need to go," Naoki interrupted. He was standing right next to us.

"I'll come back to you as soon as I can," Jack promised. He hugged me close.

"No!" I cried.

Without giving me a chance to say anything else,

Jack turned and left the safety of the forest. Naoki was right behind him and the other Protectors in our group scrambled to get into position with their bows.

The soldiers saw them as soon as they stepped into the clearing. They stopped their pacing and trained their weapons on the two approaching figures. My heart migrated to my throat. The whole scene was too surreal to comprehend. Fear urged me to take action, but my brain still wasn't sure what action to take. I eyed Jin-Sook's bow, even though I didn't know how to use it.

"Be ready. They'll double-cross us. They always do," I said.

"If anything happens, stay with me. We picked this location because we have an escape route."

"I'm not going anywhere without Jack." I ran behind a boulder at the forest edge.

Jin ran after me. "It's not safe here," she said, crouching down beside me.

"Safer than where they are." I motioned to Jack and Naoki.

Two armed soldiers walked out to meet the pair while the rest of the small army surveyed the forest edge through the scopes on their rifles. I tucked in tighter behind the boulder. Jack's voice called out to one of them and I peeked at what was happening. The two soldiers marched Jack and Naoki to stand in front of the officers. The negotiations had begun.

Jack seemed to be doing a lot of the talking and I

wished I were close enough to hear what he was saying. The officers seemed upset. The tallest one of the two vigorously shook his head *no* and motioned one of the soldiers over to the two hostages. The soldier took out a pistol and pointed it at the captives.

"I'm going down there."

"Sunny!" Jin-Sook grabbed my hand. "They haven't given a signal."

"I'd say that soldier pulling a gun on the hostages is a pretty big signal."

Jin chewed her lower lip, looking from me to the scene playing out before us.

"You know I'm right."

She nodded. "Okay."

As I approached them, the scowl on Jack's face told me exactly what he thought of my heroics. The two hostages were let out of the back of the jeep and brought forward. They stood, hands tied behind their backs, looking terrified. The other two were nowhere to be seen.

"That's a good little urchin. You know who's boss," the tallest officer said. "It's a lesson the heathens need to learn."

"Leave them alone, Anderson," Jack said. "They weren't hiding us. They just did your work for you after you captured four of their *children*. You owe them."

"That's where you're wrong, Jack. They're in our valley seeking protection from our mountain. The way I see it, they owe us, but do they understand that?" Anderson cocked an eyebrow at Naoki.

"We've done nothing to you," Naoki said.

"I disagree. We've given you protection and you repay us by stealing our cattle and hiding traitors."

"We didn't steal your cattle. We traded. Your people were sick with influenza and the satchel of herbs we left behind held the cure."

"We don't need your damn heathen concoctions. Look around you, boy. Don't you recognize power when you see it?" Anderson demanded.

Naoki drew his lip back in a sneer.

"They have no idea how powerful we are, so let them go," Jack said. "You have me and the girl. Make the trade."

Anderson looked at one of the soldiers and gave a curt nod. As the two hostages were pushed toward our group, a few soldiers went to the back of a jeep and heaved cloth sacks over their shoulders. Without ceremony, they dumped the sacks on the ground by our feet.

"General Powell sends his regards," Anderson said, kicking the bags. "This is your last warning."

The sacks were damp with blood. In horror I realized these were the other two hostages. A twisted scream erupted from Naoki. Before I even saw his hand move, a knife lodged itself in Anderson's chest.

"Run!" Jack yelled as he grabbed the gun from the stunned officer standing next to Anderson.

An arrow whistled through the air and hit one of the soldiers standing beside the hostages. The other soldier ran for cover. A bullet from an unseen shooter ricocheted off the hard, dry ground close to my feet, sending up a spray of dust.

The hostages were out in the open, hands bound behind their backs, not knowing which way to turn for cover.

"Go for the trees!" I told them, pointing.

A swarm of arrows came flying out the forest, arced in mid-air, and then raced toward the ground. Soldiers scattered, taking cover under the jeeps.

Pushing the hostages into action, I urged them out of the range of the arrows. Crouching behind a boulder, I undid their binds. A bullet whipped past us, too close for comfort. I scanned the horizon, looking for the shooter, but I didn't see anyone. As I searched, a spray of bullets tore into the jeep closest to Jack. A soldier jumped him from behind and they both went down on the ground. My breath stopped as I watched, hoping he hadn't been hit by a bullet or arrow. But Jack was still moving and getting the upper hand.

Two soldiers were on Naoki. As one seized him from behind, Naoki used him as leverage to drive both his feet into the chest of the other soldier. When his feet touched the ground, he bent and flipped the soldier holding him over his head. He unsheathed his knife. I turned away.

Despite the chaos going on all around me, the sound of more vehicles registered.

"More are coming," I told the hostages.

"Come on," said one of them.

But he didn't head for the trees. Instead, he crossed the battlefield. I followed, yelling for Jack to come with us.

The soldier he had engaged was lying motionless on the ground. Two more soldiers were working their way out from under the jeep. Naoki did something to the soldier he was battling and the man just dropped.

Jack ran toward me, grabbing my hand. "Naoki!" he yelled as we went.

The two hostages were moving fast and we ran hard to catch up. My lungs screamed for more oxygen, but the sound of gunfire and Jack's grip kept me going. Ahead of us I saw the meadow come to an abrupt end. With a sinking feeling, I realized we were trapped. I didn't need to look back to know we were being chased. We didn't have time to climb down a mountain.

The hostages kept running at full speed, despite the fact they were running out of land. Maybe they had a hiding place up ahead. As a bullet whipped past us, Jack sped up, pulling me along with him.

Then the hostages disappeared… right off the edge.

Jack didn't slow down. I tried to pull back, but his grip tightened.

"NO!" I screamed as we raced to the edge.

And then we were airborne.

Jack tried to maintain his grip on my hand, but we were torn apart the minute our feet left the safety of the ground. Below me water rushed down the mountain, sending up a spray as it curled around rocks. One thought popped into my head: I didn't know how to swim.

I hit the water feet first and was completely submerged into the cold, murky depths. Panic told me to start clawing my way back to the surface. I kicked my legs wildly and raised my arms toward the light and pulled harder. The river didn't stop for me, continuing its race down the mountain, dragging me along with it.

When I broke the surface, I gulped for air. Despite the sun glaring down at my unprotected eyes, I saw a rock jutting out of the water ahead of me. I used my feet to propel me away from it.

Water washed over my face, choking me. Desperately, I rolled onto my stomach in an attempt to keep afloat. I tried to find Jack, but all I could see was the river ending.

How could it just end?

As I was hurled over the edge, my body dropped like a stone. Water rained down on me as I went. I screamed, but the roar of the waterfall overpowered any sound I could make. Then I was plunged back into the cold, silent, watery world.

I assumed I would bob to the surface, as I did the first time I hit the water, but the current swirled around me, holding me down. I opened my eyes and searched the murky depths for a ray of light to tell me the direction of the surface. I wasn't sure which way was up, but it must be above me. That would make sense. Kicking my legs and moving my arms, I tried to get to the surface.

The urge to breathe was overwhelming. Too late, I realized that my screaming on the way down had pushed most of the air out of my lungs.

I raised my arms and flapped again, propelling myself forward. What little oxygen was left in my lungs escaped. I pulled through the water again. My arms felt like they had weights attached. I kicked my legs.

Reflexively, I breathed in.

Instead of the oxygen my body was desperately seeking, water burned its way down my throat and into my lungs. My brain told my legs to move, to keep heading toward the surface, but all of my muscles felt weak. Relaxed. They didn't want to move. I didn't have control over my body anymore. With a jolt, I realized I was dying.

Regret pressed in on me heavier than the water filling my lungs. I wasn't ready to go yet. The Pit still needed me… and I still needed Jack. An image of his face popped into my head. I willed my limbs to move, to find the surface, but they wouldn't budge.

I felt strangely peaceful as I floated in my weightless world, the image of Jack becoming a happy memory.

I closed my eyes.

CHAPTER TWENTY-ONE

Something heavy on my chest dragged me back into the real world. Water travelled up my throat, preventing me from taking the breath my body so badly craved. Hands turned my head as it poured from my mouth. I tried to gasp for air, but all I could do was choke.

"Breathe!" someone yelled at me. More water escaped my body. Finally, I drew a long, deep breath. "Oh, thank God!" Jack said.

He cradled my head against his chest as I learned how to breathe again. We were in a cave—the roar of water loud in the enclosed space. A curtain of water covering the entrance beat down into a shallow pool.

"I don't know how to swim," I said. My voice sounded hoarse.

Jack tried to smile but failed. "I know that now." He

pressed his lips against my forehead. "I lost my grip when we jumped. I tried to get back to you, but the current was too strong."

"It's not your fault."

"Naoki was right behind us. He pulled you out." Jack gave the man a nod of appreciation.

I followed his gaze. Naoki and the two hostages were staring at me.

"Thank you," I said.

"I'm the one who should be thanking you. Those soldiers would've killed them if you hadn't given yourself up," Naoki said.

"Are they okay?" I asked.

"They're just scared, right?" Naoki asked the pair. They nodded, their eyes wide and round. They couldn't have been more than twelve or thirteen years old.

A head surfacing in the shallow pool caught everyone's attention. It was Jin-Sook. She paused for a moment, looking at our ragged group. As her eyes fell upon the two hostages, her bottom lip quivered. I remembered she said Diego's brother was one of the ones taken and I guessed he wasn't here.

She waded out of the pool. "Sunny, are you okay?"

"She doesn't know how to swim," Naoki said.

Great. I was the only one who almost drowned during our spectacular getaway from the bourge. Embarrassment speeded my recovery. I pushed out of

Jack's arms and stood on wobbling legs.

"I'm fine," I said. Jack drew himself up beside me, putting his arm around me. I appreciated the support.

Jack looked at Jin-Sook. "How far away are they?"

"Not far. We should stay here until they clear out of the area," Jin said.

"And where exactly is 'here'?" asked Jack. He pointed to the waterfall curtain. "Is that the only way out?"

"Without a torch it is," Naoki said. "There's an entrance to the caverns over there." He pointed to the back of the cave.

My interest was piqued. "Caverns?" I left the steadying comfort of Jack's arm to make my way toward the back.

"Where are you going?" Jack asked me.

It was a good-sized entrance and the faintest ray of light shone through. "This is a way out."

"No it's not," Jin said. "There are several kilometers—maybe even hundreds—of caverns."

"If we follow the light, we'll find a way out," I said.

Jack came up behind me, peering at the hole over my shoulder. "What light?"

I turned my head to look at him, a smirk playing about my lips. "I forgot. You're blind in the dark."

The rest of the group joined us and we all stared at the dark hole.

"I'm with Jack—I don't see any light," Naoki said.

I surveyed the group, taking in their squinty eyes and dubious expressions. I had always assumed it was just the bourge who were blind.

"Well, I'm not going back into the river, so for me this is the only way out. Are you coming?"

"Um...You sure about this?" he whispered.

"Yep."

"Sunny, I know you can see well in the dark, but it's a maze in there. You'll never find your way out," Jin-Sook pleaded.

"I think we're safer down here than up there with soldiers looking for us," I said, and entered the cavern. I reached for Jack's hand and he held mine tight. "It's not that dark in here."

"I disagree," Jack said, peering into the darkness.

"Wait!" Jin-Sook called.

We stopped and looked back.

"If she can find her way through there, it is safer," Jin-Sook said, to Naoki.

"No one can find their way through there without a torch," Naoki said.

"I know she can see in the dark, I'm just worried about getting lost in the maze," Jin said.

"I'll mark a path back to here," I said.

Naoki paused, looking at the trembling teenagers, and then back at Jin-Sook. "We'll go a little way with them, but if she stumbles even once, we turn back."

While we waited for the group to join us, I squatted

and rummaged through the stones on the cave floor until I found a drawing rock. As kids, we always used stones to write on the walls of the Pit. I must have written my name down there at least a hundred times—most often alongside Reyes's.

When I finished, I took Jack by the hand and instructed the group to hang on tight to each other. One of the young hostages took Jack's other hand, and on down the line it went, with Naoki taking the end position. As we set out into the cavern, I was painfully aware that I was the only one who could see. When we came to a fork in the path, I carved another marker and scanned the line to make sure everyone was present before I continued.

"This way," I said, keeping left.

"Are you sure?" Jack whispered.

"Trust me."

"We no longer have a choice," Naoki called from the back.

A faint sound echoed through the cave, bringing us all to a halt.

"What was *that*?" I asked.

Naoki and Jin drew their knives.

"Bears den in the caverns," said one of the hostages.

"That didn't sound like a bear," Jin-Sook said. "Besides, it's too early for them to den. Winter is still months away."

"It wasn't a bear," Jack said. "It was familiar and I don't know what bears sound like."

"You're right, it was familiar," I said, although I

couldn't actually identify it. I lowered my voice to a whisper. "Do you think the bourge are down here?"

"Maybe," Jack said. "If they are, they'll need lights and you'll see them coming. Whatever that was, it sounded a long way off."

"Let's keep moving," I said.

"I'm scared," the other hostage whimpered.

"There's nothing to be afraid of—" I paused, realizing I didn't know her name. In all the confusion, there hadn't been time. "My name is Sunny and this is Jack. I don't know your names."

"I'm Chesa," she said. Her voice wobbled. I prayed she wasn't about to become hysterical.

"Jae-Son," the other said.

"I think you guys have been extremely brave. You're safe down here, away from those bad men," I said, trying to reassure them.

"The bad men?" Jae-Son repeated sarcastically. "You think we're two?"

I almost gave myself a head smack. He was only a few years younger than I was. "Sorry. I was just trying to calm everyone down."

"Personally, I'd rather be taking my chances up top with the bad men. I can't see them coming down here," Naoki said.

"I'm having second thoughts too," Jin chimed in.

The confined hallway we travelled eventually grew

into a larger cavern. Stalactites cascaded into tapered points from the high domed ceiling and a shaft of light turned a small pool into a shimmering turquoise.

"It's beautiful," I breathed.

"What's beautiful?" asked Jack.

"The view."

"I can't see the view."

"Are you kidding? Daylight is pouring in."

"You mean that tiny little hole way up there?" Jin asked. "Is that the light you saw a few kilometers back?" There was a note of disbelief in her tone, edged with panic.

"Yeah, I think it is," I said.

"It's too small and too high up." Naoki said, exasperated. "We need to go back."

"But there's more light coming from over there." I pointed before I realized they couldn't see where I was pointing. I dropped my hand. "Come on."

As I led the group toward the next ray of light, my foot hit something. It rolled ahead of me a few feet, making noise as it went.

"What was that?" asked Jack.

I stooped to pick it up. "It's an apple," I said, confused. I scanned every corner of the cave. I didn't see anyone.

"It probably washed down here in a storm," Jin said. "The valley is old farmland. There are lots of apple trees around."

I dropped the fruit and it rolled to rest against the

cavern wall. Maybe some of the little rodents I had seen scurrying around would appreciate the meal. I continued toward the light.

The path became steep, but luckily it was dry and walking was easy. "Where are we going to go once we're out of here?" I asked Jack.

"Maybe back to the cave if no one has found it yet. I want a place to hide for a few hours to dry out this pistol and my tablet."

"What's a tablet?" Naoki asked.

"A computer," Jack said.

"You have a *computer*? And it works?" Naoki exclaimed.

"Well, it was working before I went for a swim."

"Do we need it?" I asked. The cave was getting a lot brighter. I was sure this would lead to a way out.

"I downloaded a bunch of stuff from the main computer before we had to run. The schematics for the tagging system, communications, the power grid, everything."

"Hey, I can see a little bit," Jin said.

"Me too," Chesa said with relief.

"Finally. I'm wishing I had my sunglasses. It's going to be bright out there," I said.

"Mine are in my pocket," Jack said.

The way out was a narrow tunnel that we had to crawl through. We emerged into a rocky area. I put on Jack's glasses, glad to have some protection.

Naoki was already climbing up a nearby outcrop and

the rest of us followed. At the top, we lay on our stomachs, staying low and out of sight. From our position, we had a fairly good view of the surrounding area.

"That high peak over there," Jack said, pointing, "is the Dome. The cave we holed up in and the range are east of it."

"The cave really is close to the range. Do you think it's a good idea to go back there?" I asked.

"I'd like to find those two men who aren't tagged. Maybe we can team up with them," he said.

"Terran and Flint?" I asked. He nodded.

We heard a cawing noise in the distance. Naoki and Jin perked up, listening for the direction of the sound. It came again, and Naoki cupped his hands around his mouth and cawed back.

"Do you always communicate like that?" asked Jack.

"It's effective," Jin said. "You two never caught on, and we were watching you for days."

Jack gave me a questioning look. He hadn't even been conscious, so it was just me who had never caught on—until right before they captured us.

A bright flash of light caught our attention. Half a kilometer away, a jeep came into view and the sun glinted off the windshield. It disappeared behind some rocks. Staying low, we all climbed down.

Jack looked worried. "They're close, and who knows how many more vehicles are combing for us out here?"

"We should go underground again. I can probably

find my way east," I said.

"Probably?" Jack raised his eyebrows and looked at me. "I'm not going back into the big, dark, scary cave, Sunny."

"Neither am I," Naoki said. "Our barangay is south, not east."

"I think you two should come back with us," Jin said.

"Why? So we can give the senior citizens another crack at us? I don't think so," Jack said.

It wasn't really a noise that caught our attention, more like awareness that another presence had joined us. We all looked in the same direction at the same time. Two Protectors stood, and then Dena emerged from behind some boulders. A few more Protectors came behind her.

"Dena!" Jin exclaimed.

Chesa ran and threw her arms around the woman's waist.

Jack sidled closer to me, sliding his hand around mine.

Dena wrapped her arms around the girl and hugged her close. She surveyed us with concern.

Naoki stood taller and squared his shoulders. Beads of sweat broke out on his forehead. "I take full responsibility for my actions, Elder."

Dena gave the young girl a final squeeze and set her aside. She walked toward Naoki and placed a gentle hand on his shoulder. "I decided to oversee this mission myself, so I witnessed the entire exchange. I'm not so sure I wouldn't have reacted the same way in your place." She cast a thoughtful look at Jack and me as she said it, then turned her attention back to Naoki and Jin. "We've been looking for you. You had us all very concerned. Where did you disappear to?"

"Sunny led us through the caverns," Jin said.

Dena raised her eyebrows. "Indeed?"

"And we were just on our way back down," Jack said. He gave my hand a tug.

"I owe you two an apology," Dena said. "You were right about the bourge. They behaved exactly as you predicted." Jack gave a curt nod. "I also owe you for helping get these two out safely." Dena motioned toward Chesa and Jae-Son. "Please consider coming back to my barangay. There's a storm building, and we can offer you food and a dry bed."

I looked in the direction of her nod and saw dark clouds in the distance. I had never experienced a storm before and I felt the nervous flutter of anticipation.

"How many guards will be assigned to watch us this time?" asked Jack sarcastically.

She shook her head. "No guards. I'm asking you to come as our guests and, hopefully, allies."

"Allies?" asked Jack. "That's an interesting word to use."

"I don't always agree with Amini."

"So you're saying that if you were calling the shots, you would've done things differently?"

"No. I still would've attempted the trade. It's the after-effects I take issue with. You see, Amini has swayed a majority of Elders in favor of moving our nation to safer territory if peace with the bourge couldn't be reached. I think it's safe to say we didn't achieve peace. However, unlike Amini I prefer to stand my ground. Our people have done enough running."

I understood what Dena was suggesting. Hadn't I asked the same of Jack myself? He had inside knowledge of how the bourge worked. He would be an asset if the bourge moved against Dena's people—and maybe we could bargain for their help in freeing the Pit.

"It's a good partnership," I said to Jack.

"It's only good if they agree to help us too."

I was relieved to hear we were thinking the same thing.

Dena nodded. "Jin told me about your mission to free the slaves. I think we can be of assistance."

I was surprised by her easy acceptance. By the look on Jack's face, so was he.

"Sunny and I would like a moment to discuss it."

Dena nodded.

We moved as far as we could away from the group while still remaining hidden behind the outcrop.

"What do you think?" he whispered.

"I think we should trust them."

"Why?"

I had to stop and work through that for a moment. "I kind of got to know Jin and a couple of others during my captivity. I trust them."

Jack's expression remained impassive. "You trusted Leisel too."

I rolled my eyes. "So did you."

He grinned. "Touché."

"They can't trade us again—that door is closed. Other than helping them figure out the bourge, we're of no use to them."

Jack was quiet for a moment. "True," he said. "But they were quick to take Powell up on his offer of a trade."

"If someone kidnapped your loved ones—a son, a daughter…a wife—wouldn't you trade two strangers to save them?"

He rubbed a hand across his eyes. "Is that my only option in your scenario?"

"Look, all I'm saying is that I understand why they attempted to make the trade. But when it was obvious we were being double-crossed, they didn't abandon us. They fought to save us, too. Now they're offering us a trade—information on the bourge in exchange for helping to free the slaves. My mom's there, penned in an urchin corral. So yeah, I'm willing to make the trade."

He sighed heavily.

"And even if it turns out they can't help us, we can at least help them. They don't know what they're up against."

He bit his lower lip and studied me for a moment. "And she did say food and a bed."

I smiled. "She did."

"Okay."

We returned to the group and Dena broke away from the hostages to come and meet us. "Have you decided?"

"Like Sunny said—it's a good partnership."

Chapter Twenty-Two

The trip to the barangay was made in silence, save for the occasional cawing of the Protectors. Dena, Jin, Naoki, Jack, the hostages and I all stayed together in one group, while the others fanned out on either side of us. I was beginning to notice a pattern to their caws, although I still didn't know what they meant.

I tried to move as they did—walking from rock to tree root without leaving a trace. It took a lot of focus to constantly search the ground for a place to step that wouldn't leave a mark, yet they made it look effortless.

"Don't worry too much about leaving a trail," Jin-Sook whispered from behind me. "The storm will be here in a few hours and will wash away any footprints."

It was a relief to hear. Instead of worrying about leaving a trail, I concentrated on keeping up and staying quiet.

After a few hours of trekking through the woods, we started our ascent up the mountain. It looked like we were climbing a concrete staircase that had fallen into disrepair. The angled blocks were distinctly manmade. And as we neared the top, the stairs disintegrated completely, requiring us to climb the last few feet. I glimpsed archers from time to time, peering down at us from above. The height of their village gave them an excellent defensive advantage. I understood why they made their home there.

I wasn't worried about Jack's injury anymore. If it hadn't reopened when he jumped into the river and went over a waterfall, it wouldn't reopen on this short climb. I pulled myself up over the edge with Jack right behind me. Dena was next and Jack held out a hand to help her up. She waved it away and stood up on her own.

Wiping the sweat away from her forehead with the back of her hand, she smiled slyly. "Not bad for a senior citizen, eh Jack?"

Pink stained his cheeks, but he managed a smile. "Not bad at all."

As soon as we reached the top, people came running toward us. Someone scooped up Chesa and hugged Jae-Son close. More came and gathered around the young people. It was a bittersweet homecoming, since instead of four there were only two.

I noticed this barangay was different from the last one. The entire courtyard floor was tiled in stone, although the tiles were crumbling and heaved in some areas. An arched entranceway surrounded a door that led into the mountain. It reminded me of the pictures of ancient ruins I had often seen in books.

"What is this place?" I asked.

"An old hotel. It was a popular tourist destination before the war. It started out as simple tours of the caverns, but after a geothermal plant was built here, they invested in a hotel that would draw more tourists and money to the area. We've reclaimed it and expanded the living space by building dwellings inside the caverns. All the infrastructure was already here—an energy source, heat, staircases to navigate the uneven caverns—everything."

People were emerging from seemingly nowhere to watch our arrival. Oddly, they all looked to be mostly older people and children. Their attention made me uncomfortable. I edged closer to Jack and slipped my hand into his.

He squeezed my hand. "How do you know such detailed history about this place?" he asked.

Dena shrugged. "Hotel flyers and information booklets mostly. We've found old pocket computers too. Most of them are beyond repair, but we can get the odd one working again."

Jack's interest was captured. *"Really?* You have *that* kind of historical documentation? I'd love to see them—especially the old computers."

"Some of us collect them," Naoki said. "Whenever I have the chance, I go to the old city and look for them."

"This place is a lot bigger than Amini's barangay," I said.

"It is," Dena said. "This is where our ancestors originally settled, because of the old hotel. But as our population grew and the threat of recruiters became more persistent, we broke up into smaller groups. This way if one barangay is attacked, the others can come to their assistance."

A gray-haired person emerged from the throng, walked up to Dena, and kissed her. "I'm glad you're home safe and sound. I missed you."

If I wasn't mistaken, she was a woman. I was still finding it difficult to differentiate gender.

"This is Sunny and Jack," Dena said to the newcomer. "This is my wife, Yean-Kuan." She settled an arm around Yean-Kuan's shoulders and squeezed her close.

Did she say *wife*? My brows knitted together in confusion. Maybe she meant sister, because that kind of marriage was against the law. Or at least it was against the law in the Dome. Then again, my marriage was against the law, too.

Jack was staring at them with a weird smile on his face and confusion in his eyes. I nudged him with my elbow.

"Pleased to meet to you," I said, extending my hand. Jack followed my lead.

Dena turned her attention to Jin, Naoki and the rest of our group and instructed them to join the others for meditation.

Yean-Kuan's eyes were bright with excitement. "The entire barangay is talking about it. You've been living *inside* that mountain?"

I smiled and nodded.

She gawked with the kind of keen interest of one seeing a freak for the first time. I looked down. After a few seconds, I peeked back up at her. She was still looking at us. It was getting awkward.

When the Protectors had left, Dena returned her attention to us. She gave her wife's shoulder a tap. "Honey, you're making them feel uncomfortable. Stop staring."

Yean-Kuan put a hand to her cheek. "Oh, I'm sorry! It's just...they're pale, aren't they?" I wondered if she was aware that we could hear her.

Dena laughed. "I apologize for my wife," she said. "When your people first made camp in our valley, we assumed they arrived through a hidden passage in the mountain. We all wondered how they came through unscathed by Yugo. But it quickly became obvious Yugo wasn't something they would fear considering the technology they possessed. It still didn't dawn on us that you came out of the mountain."

"Yugo," I repeated. "He's a monster from the scorched lands." Jack cocked an eyebrow at me. "Jin told me about him."

"What are the scorched lands?" Jack asked.

"An area that was hit directly by a bomb," Dena said. She turned toward the center of the courtyard and gestured for us to follow her. "Those sites are high in radiation."

"Why would anyone *want* to live on a bombed site?" I asked.

Dena shrugged. "Some say they're descendants of

survivors who never left the area, and others say people ran to the scorched lands to escape a world gone lawless. Whichever is right, and maybe they both are, the scorched lands aren't for the weak. The people who live there have evolved to tolerate the radiation and—if the rumors are true—most don't even look human anymore."

We entered the middle of the courtyard, and children ran toward us. With our arrival, excited chatter erupted. Jack seemed oblivious to the commotion we were creating.

"And Yugo is a mutant from the scorched lands?" he asked.

Dena nodded. "A lot of different stories surround your mountain, but the most believable is Yugo. The story goes that he loved to eat all day and night and was so well nourished on radioactive plants and animals that he grew into a giant. His village could no longer support his huge appetite, so they sent him away." Dena grinned. "Hence the name You-Go." She snickered. "For years, rumors circulated of a mountain with an old military base hidden inside. Yugo went in search of the old base to make it his new home. He found it in that mountain." She pointed toward the Dome. "But the winter here is long and food is scarce, so Yugo began to eat humans to satisfy his enormous appetite, casting their bones into a pile. Anyone who strays too close to the mountain never returns."

Jack shot a wide-eyed look at me. The myth of Yugo was riddled with truth. How could anyone have possibly known about a military base inside the mountain? And people going missing if they came too close to the mountain tied in with Powell's claim that a number of heathens had been captured for interrogation. How would these people react when they learned the real story? Maybe coming here wasn't such a good idea after all.

We came to a wooden table and Dena motioned toward a bench, inviting us to sit. Yean-Kuan muttered something about getting food and excused herself. Several children and a few adults approached the table to join us, but Dena waved them away.

"It seemed believable enough since there's a big pile of bones up on the mountain," she said once we were seated. She leaned forward, her gaze unwavering. "Until a few years ago, when one of our people saw the mountain giving birth to the dead. He said a hole suddenly appeared in the side of the mountain, dead bodies were spit out, and the hole disappeared again. That made me question the existence of Yugo, because I don't think he would waste perfectly good food."

She raised her eyebrows in question, obviously expecting a response to her story, but I was too focused on trying to rid my mind of the image of *the mountain giving birth to the dead.* Gaia's description of the Cull and the pile of human remains she saw was still vivid enough without hearing Dena's version. I had personal experience with the way the garbage chute worked, so it was easy enough for me to work through the mechanics of it all. Victims of the Cull would be herded into a garbage room and the big, heavy steel door would seal them in. I didn't know how long it took for gas to kill, but I knew that the garbage ventilation system worked on a twelve-hour cycle, so if garbage had been dumped right before the Cull, there would be plenty of time to make sure everyone was good and dead. At the end of the twelve-hour cycle, the doors to the outer chamber would open and the conveyer belt would transport the pile of lifeless bodies into the next room. Another set of steel doors would close behind them before the doors to the outside world opened up. The high-powered ventilator would come on to expunge the stench of death from the Dome, and the conveyer belt would advance to dump the dead unceremoniously into the outside world.

Bile rose in my throat. An image of my people—*my mother*—being herded into a garbage chute that doubled as a gas chamber played out like a horror movie in my head.

"Sunny?" Dena said.

I hadn't realized that I was actually gagging. Choking back the bile, I faked a cough to conceal my nausea. Jack's hand sought mine under the table and I reached for him, finding strength in the contact.

I'm not sure why I felt a twinge of shame. It's not as if the Cull was my fault. My people were the victims of an unjust treaty. But still, I didn't know how to explain that to Dena. I didn't know how to tell her that we were consenting participants.

Jack gave my hand a gentle squeeze. "I can see how a pile of bones gives credibility to the legend of Yugo, the giant cannibal."

"Only now we know it's not a giant cannibal from the scorched lands living in the mountain."

"No, it isn't." The corners of Jack's mouth turned down for an instant. "The real monster living inside that mountain is a whole lot scarier."

"How scary?"

Jack looked down at our clasped hands and bit his lower lip. "Nuclear-weapons kind of scary."

Dena blew out a long breath, as if she had been holding it.

"They would never use the warheads as a first line of defense," Jack said quickly. "Their first strike will be with conventional weapons."

"Conventional weapons?"

"Guns, maybe grenades…a drone."

"What's a drone?"

"A remotely operated aircraft equipped with surveillance and weapons."

Dena let out a short, sarcastic laugh. "Lucky for us they won't be using the nuclear weapons." She sobered. "We've had some clashes with recruiters and a few run-ins with hunters, but never an enemy this strong."

"Recruiters?" asked Jack. I remembered Jin mentioning recruiters and hunters.

"Ryder's men," she said. She stared back at our blank expressions. "Forgive me. I forget that even though you're from around here, you're not from around here. Thomas

Ryder is the self-proclaimed leader of the biggest settlement in the south. He's power hungry and wants to control the territory. He demands rent payments from anyone setting up a home or a farm on what he's declared to be his lands. Payment must be made in the form of food, fuel, pieces of technology, or whatever they happen to have—although most have nothing. Our nation has grown a lot in the past few years because of him."

"Why does he need recruits?" Jack asked.

"About fifteen years ago, northerners came south during the winter months in search of food. Some of the farmers that pay Ryder rent complained, so Ryder sent his men to chase them back north. It caused bad blood and they've been fighting ever since."

"Let me guess," Jack said. "He's not exactly *asking* people to join his army."

"No. He recruits by force," Dena said.

"What about the north? Do they recruit too?" I asked.

"Daemon leads the north and from what we hear, he's worse than Ryder. It's rumored he sends children into battle—that he hides behind them."

Every word she spoke was like a boulder being dropped on to my childhood fantasies, smashing them to little bits. Summer and I had always imagined that once we were released from the bonds of the treaty, we would live a peaceful, free life on a sun-drenched Earth. The world Dena was describing was anything but peaceful. It was more like the war was still being fought.

"Three hundred years later, and we're still fighting," I said.

"We were always taught that, with the exception of us, humanity had been wiped from the planet," Jack said. "It's hard for me to comprehend that the population is already large enough to be fighting over territory."

"It's not about territory," Dena said. "Thousands of kilometers of uninhabited land separate the south from the north. Their fight is over dominance and it's fuelled by hatred."

She paused when Yean-Kuan returned with a tray of steaming bowls and a basket of bread. My stomach growled in anticipation. I couldn't remember the last time I ate. I plucked a piece of bread from the offered basket with my thanks.

"Thank you, Yean," Dena said with affection. Yean gave her a warm smile and sat next to her. "The war did almost wipe out humanity. We've found diaries describing the years right after the bombs and it gives a grim picture. Those lucky enough to survive the immediate fallout had the nuclear winter to face, and that lasted over two years. Without sunlight, nothing grew. Attempts to make greenhouses out of salvaged technology were somewhat successful, but ultimately it was the death of some who served as bread for others that allowed humanity to survive."

It took a moment for her meaning to penetrate. The bread I was chewing suddenly dried up into a hard, gummy knot in my mouth. I wasn't sure I could swallow. Yean must have noticed my distress because she poured me a cup of water. Gratefully, I drank. When I took the cup away from my mouth, Jack took it and finished it off. He handed me back the empty cup.

Our discomfort wasn't lost on Dena. "Their deaths could have been meaningless. Instead, the memory of their sacrifice lives on."

Suddenly, I had a better understanding of the choice that had faced Benjamin Reyes and the group he led into the Dome.

Dena picked up her spoon and dipped into her soup. I looked down at my own bowl. It looked like vegetables in some kind of broth. Even though my appetite had waned, I forced myself to take a mouthful. By the third bite, my hunger had returned.

Yean was looking at us again.

"It's delicious," I said of the soup. "Thank you."

Her eyes brightened with curiosity. "It's probably not like your food, is it?"

I thought of the stew, made from bourge leftovers, that was served three times a day in the Pit. "It's much better," I assured her.

"Much better," Jack agreed.

Yean looked pleased.

"The Elders will be arriving this evening and I expect a long debate. At my request, our army has already started gathering in the tournament field to prepare for confrontation. Amini won't like it. She'll see it as an aggressive act instead of a defensive one. I'm hoping both of you can help convince her otherwise."

Jack put his spoon in his empty bowl. "The problem is I'm not sure I disagree with Amini."

Surprised by his change of heart, I snapped around to look at him. "Jack!" What was he thinking? We had already discussed that they were our only hope of freeing my people.

He put a hand on my leg. "I'm not comfortable being the one to convince a group of people armed with only arrows to go up against automatic weapons. It's suicide."

Dena sat back in her chair, crossing her arms. "To the south of us is Ryder's territory; to the north is Daemon; and the east coast is nothing but scorched lands. A lot of our ancestors arrived from the far west, so if that were a good place to settle they would've stayed. So where do we go, Jack? And how far do we have to go to outrun nuclear warheads and drones?"

Jack closed his eyes and pinched the skin at the bridge of his nose. "You can't outrun the warheads or the drones." He opened his eyes and dragged his hand through his hair. "But if you leave now, it would buy you time to get better prepared to go up against Holt's forces."

Abruptly, Dena pushed away from the table and stood up. "Perhaps I can get your opinion on something." She bent and kissed the top of her wife's head. "The soup was delicious."

"I'm glad you enjoyed it," Yean said. "I'd best get back to making the arrangements for the Elders. They'll be here soon."

Jack and I stood as well, offering our own thanks for the soup.

The dark clouds that had been so distant earlier were now almost on top of the barangay. As we left the courtyard and made our way down a rocky path, I felt humidity pressing in on me. Beads of perspiration broke out on my forchead.

"My ancestors came to this valley seeking refuge from persecution. Our nation grew out of the need to protect ourselves from hatred. For us, defense isn't an exercise. It's a way of life," she explained as we walked.

We crested a peak and she swept an arm toward the view below. In a large clearing, surrounded by dense forest, was an army of a few hundred.

They were training for battle.

CHAPTER TWENTY-THREE

"It's an army of Protectors," I said.

"Not just Protectors," Dena responded. "We all learn from a young age how to defend ourselves. Protectors are those who demonstrate remarkable ability. In times of need we all pull together."

"You're a Protector, aren't you?" asked Jack.

Dena smiled. "Since I was eighteen." She began to make her way down the cliff side. It was steep and the number of small, round pebbles made it treacherous, but Dena navigated it expertly. Jack and I were a bit slower. "In order to become an Elder, one must possess a specialty that is of benefit to the nation. Mine is defense. I lead the army."

The farther down the path we went, the more it smoothed out. From this distance I could clearly see that the army was separated into four groups. Each group was practicing something different. The archers were the most imposing. They moved together in rows, as if performing a choreographed dance. As the first row loosed their arrows, they crouched low to the ground and the second row let fly their arrows, and they crouched and the next row sent theirs flying. Wave after wave of arrows flew high, arced, and raced toward the ground.

As I stopped to admire their skill, Jack pressed close behind me. "That's impressive," he said against my ear.

"Do you think they stand a chance?" I asked.

"Nope."

"I heard that," Dena called out as she continued down the path. Without stopping to look back, she made a *come on* motion with her arm.

Jack and I shared a look of surprise. "She's not only spry, she's got superhuman hearing," he whispered.

There was an electric feeling on the field, as if the anticipation of battle had coalesced into something solid. Keeping a good distance away from the archers, Dena led us toward a small squadron sparring with long poles.

"Hapkido is a Korean art," she said.

"I'm familiar with it," Jack said.

Dena cocked an eyebrow. "Really? Have you practiced it?"

"A mix of martial arts is taught at our military academy," he said.

Dena looked delighted by his answer. "Then perhaps you wouldn't mind demonstrating your abilities for us."

Jack attempted to decline, but she put her fingers to

her mouth and whistled hard. The participants stopped sparring and moved to the sidelines.

"Ryan," Dena called out. A young man about the same size as Jack stepped from the sidelines and moved to the center of the field.

Jack looked confused. "You want me to fight?"

"Of course. How else can I gauge your skill?"

"But…" He turned to me, pleading with his eyes for me to help him.

I took a step back. "Don't look at me. I suck at fighting, remember?" He gave me an eye roll. Ignoring it, I smiled. "I'm rooting for you, Jack!"

Someone cheered him on and a few more voices chimed in. Hesitantly he moved into the clearing to face Ryan. Dena dropped her arm. Ryan sprinted at him, jumped, and landed a foot squarely on Jack's chest. I heard a whoosh of air leave him as he hit the ground.

"What was *that*?!" Jack demanded.

Ryan shrugged. "A kick to the chest."

Jack picked himself up, rubbing a hand across his chest. "I wasn't ready."

"I know," he said.

Ryan came at him again, jumping high into a spin, one leg out. Jack's eyes widened and he ducked, just barely escaping a foot to his head. As Ryan's feet touched ground, he dropped into a crouch and, spinning on his heel, picked up a long, thick stick from the ground and used it to sweep Jack's legs out from under him. Jack went down again.

This time Ryan didn't give Jack a chance to get up. He came at him with the pole and Jack rolled to avoid it. In one fluid movement, Jack pushed himself up off the ground onto his feet. Someone threw him a stick and he grabbed it just in time to block Ryan's next assault. A loud *crack* reverberated through the air and I cringed, thinking that had almost made contact with Jack's head. Jack had told me the first rule in sparring is to not actually hurt your partner. They weren't playing by the rules.

Jack became more aggressive, trying to push Ryan back with each contact their poles made. Ryan used it to his advantage by levering his pole against Jack, flipped in the air, landed behind him and used the stick to put Jack in a chokehold.

Jack dropped his pole and grabbed at the one pressed against his throat. He was turning a little red in the face. I bit my lip. It wasn't looking good for Jack. Dena wouldn't let Ryan kill him, would she? I looked at her, waiting for her to call off Ryan. She didn't. My heart pounded harder.

What if they fought to the death here? I took a step toward the men, not really sure what I was going to do. But then Jack dropped a hand away from the pole and did something that made Ryan scream and drop his hold.

Dena laughed and called a halt to the fight. "A pinch to the thigh! Well done," she said.

Ryan walked back to the sidelines, massaging his thigh, and Jack came to stand beside me, gently rubbing his throat. His face was red and I knew it wasn't just from the chokehold.

Ryan had kicked his butt. For someone like Jack, the darling of his Academy, his pride must be hurting. Not that I would ever say anything. In the Pit, it was just good manners to ignore a beating if the victim was capable of walking away.

"So am I right in assuming all of Powell's soldiers have the same training as you?" she asked.

I knew the answer to her question. Jack had admitted himself that he and his brother were the best the Academy had ever produced. It stood to reason that the rest of Powell's soldiers weren't as good.

I looked at Jack to see how he would respond. A mix of emotions played across his face. "Yes," he said, sullenly. "But with all due respect Dena, a battle with Holt's army won't be fought hand-to-hand. It'll be waged with automatic weapons, some of them long-range. All they have to do is find you."

Dena nodded. "So you've said."

A drop of water hit my nose, startling me. Another one hit my shoulder, soaking through my t-shirt. Jack held out his hands and looked skyward. "The storm's here?"

"Almost," Dena said. "Come on. I'll show you the rest of the army."

We followed her to a group engaged in throwing knives. The blades whistled as they sailed through the air, making a dull thump as they hit the target. Throwers moved in quick succession, one after the other, sending a barrage of knives at the wooden stump with deadly accuracy. One thrower barely had time to step out of the way before another was aiming for the target. That required a lot of trust in the skill of the person behind.

The big fat drops of water falling from the sky became more frequent, plopping onto my head and rolling across my scalp in thin rivulets.

Dena moved on to the last two squadrons. She stopped at each one to critique their skills and seek Jack's input. With every question he answered, she learned more about the bourge and their fighting techniques. I know she did, because I learned too. And it seemed to me the bourge relied heavily on their weapons, whereas Dena's soldiers were skilled in the art of defense.

The drops soon gathered speed and turned into a downpour, as if someone had turned on a showerhead. It made a drumming noise against the hard-packed earth, which came as a surprise. I had no idea rain made a sound.

Everyone on the training field carried on as though there wasn't a storm in progress. Dena continued with her tour. It wasn't until a flash of light lit up the sky that Dena said it was time to go inside. The unexpected flash was blinding, but it was the booming noise that followed that sent me careening into Jack's side. For just an instant I wondered if it was an attack.

Jack's shoulders shook with barely concealed laughter. I shot him a look. "As if you've ever been in a storm," I said.

The trek back up to the courtyard was a little trickier on wet ground. As we went, the lightning became brighter and the thunder louder. Jack's sunglasses weren't much protection. I never thought I'd be relieved to go back inside a mountain again, but I was.

Pausing inside the entranceway to shake the water off, I took in the big empty room—what was once the lobby of the hotel. The grotto was made entirely of stone tile with high arched ceilings. The ghostly outlines of bygone furniture hinted that the hotel was once quite grand, but now crumbling tiles and dark stains ground into the stone had robbed it of its beauty. I rubbed the toe of my boot against one of the dark stains, wondering what it was.

"Human misery is a stubborn stain," Dena said. "A lot of skeletons were found here, the floor darkened by their decay."

A shiver went down my spine when her meaning registered. How many people had sought refuge here after the war, only to die a slow horrible death? Were they from the valley? Were they the same people who had been turned away from the Dome by the bourge? The stains of decay were everywhere. For a moment I closed my eyes against the mental image of what they must have had to clear out of here in order to reclaim this building.

Behind me the door opened and a few people entered the lobby. They glanced in our direction and continued to the far side of the room.

"The entire hotel is built inside the mountain, hidden to the outside world," Dena said.

I watched the small group open the bags they carried and spread out blankets on the floor.

Jack pointed to the artificial lighting. "You've made your own light?"

Dena smiled. "It's not nuclear science. It's just a filament."

Jack looked a little embarrassed by his question. I had thought the same thing until Jin-Sook had corrected me. As much as I professed that these people weren't heathens, I still made assumptions about them, as though they wouldn't be as smart as we were. But as we walked through the reclaimed ruins, I was reminded of the ingenuity of the human spirit. As someone who came from the Pit, this was not something I should've forgotten.

"Amini's barangay didn't have electric light," I said. Even though Jin-Sook had already explained why it didn't have electricity, I wanted to come to Jack's rescue.

"Amini's is one of the newest outposts and we're still in the process of extending power there. All the plumbing is in place though, so they have heat and hot water," Dena said. "And we don't generate a lot of voltage with the plant. Only enough to power a few lights in the common areas, run the air exchanger and other necessities. It's still a work in progress."

"Where's the geothermal plant located? Doesn't it draw attention to your settlement?" asked Jack.

Dena shook her head. "It was all built inside the mountain as part of the tourist attraction. Even the wind turbines that run the pump were camouflaged, although we were only able to get a few turbines working again."

"Where do you get all of your supplies?" asked Jack.

"From the old city. Luckily for us pipe and wire were made to be pretty indestructible. We salvage whatever we can. Come on, I'll give you a tour."

The lobby was getting crowded as Dena led us through an arched doorway. The ceiling in the hallway was rounded and much lower. It had a deliberate cave-like feel. Dena went into the history of the hotel and how it was a novelty for tourists to live in a "cave" powered entirely by the earth's own heating system. Hotel guests had a private entrance into the caverns, which back then were lit with electricity. All the elements were here to convert the caverns into living spaces.

At the end of the tour, she allowed us to read the hotel flyers they had preserved. Among all the advertising pamphlets there was a map of the cavern system. It was a series of caves joined together by manmade tunnels. The map was only of the immediate tourist area, but Dena explained the valley floor was riddled with caves.

We returned to the lobby, now crowded with people staking out bed space on the floor. There was an air of excitement to the chatter filling the room. I recognized a few faces from the training field.

"As the place of our original settlement, the barangays gather here for the annual spring tournament and the winter solstice celebrations," Dena said. Her lips tightened. "This is the first time we've gathered under the threat of war. I'll admit, it makes me nervous to have our forces all in the same location."

Jack nodded his agreement. "Whatever action you decide to take, you'd best do it soon."

"That will depend on how the Elders vote. After all you've seen today, I'm hoping you both agree with me and will help sway them."

"We'll meet with your council, but we're going to be honest," Jack said.

"That's all I ask," Dena said. "Speaking of which, I should be preparing for the meeting. I'll show you to your room."

Dena took us to one of the private rooms in the hotel and we immediately protested. We'd watched the army making beds on the floor in the lobby—we shouldn't be shown special treatment. But she wouldn't hear of it. We were guests and would be treated well.

"You'll probably want to get out of your wet clothes," she said. She lit a lantern in the bathroom and showed us a hidden cord above the tub. "Hang them here tonight and hope they're dry for morning."

As she turned to leave, Jack stopped her. "Dena, there's one more thing you should know before you meet with your council." She gave him an expectant look, but he hesitated. "President Holt isn't mentally stable. He intends to repopulate the earth with his own 'master race' and I believe he intends to wipe out everyone who doesn't fit. I'll admit, Sunny and I need your help freeing her people, but I stand by what I said earlier. If you run now, it buys you time to prepare to go up against him later."

Dena gave him an appreciative nod. "Thanks for your honesty, Jack."

The door clicked behind her, leaving us alone in the quiet room. Oddly, I felt momentarily awkward. It had been a while since we were alone…since we declared our feelings for each other. Now here we were in a room, dominated by a big bed, and nothing to put on once we shed our wet clothes. I was suddenly conscious that my shirt was soaked through and clinging to me. I crossed my arms.

If Jack noticed my embarrassment, he didn't mention it. Instead, he unsnapped the cargo pocket on his pants and took out his tablet. He tried to power it up. It didn't switch on. Next he took out his pistol and laid both on the table. "Hopefully they'll dry out." He looked around the room. "This place is amazing. I wonder what it was like before the war."

I wasn't sure if he was actually appreciating the room or the fact that the hotel still stood as a testimony to another civilization. His eyesight was poor in the dark, so it was doubtful he could see beyond the glow of the lantern. Unfortunately I could, and the blemish of suffering and decay was in this room too, mixed with centuries-old grime pulverized into the crumbling tiles.

He moved toward the bathroom and I followed, not wanting to be alone with the ghosts in this room. "I can't believe they got a geothermal plant running again." He turned on the faucet and smiled. "It's hot. I'm looking forward to a shower."

For the first time, I wished I were as blind in the dark as Jack. If only I couldn't see the grunge of suffering maybe the ghosts in the room would vanish. I shivered and wrapped my arms tighter around me.

"You should to get out of those wet clothes," he said. "You can have the shower first."

He went to squeeze past me in the narrow doorway, but I wrapped my hand around his arm, preventing him. "Wait." He stopped, our shoulders pressed together in the confined space. I didn't want him to go. And it wasn't just because I was a little creeped out by this place. "I don't want to be alone."

He laughed softly, but my expression remained serious. "I'll be right out here."

I loosened my grip on his arm and let my hand trail down to lace my fingers through his. My stomach began fluttering. I took a deep breath and held it, hoping he hadn't changed his mind about me.

His laughter faded and his expression sobered. "Life's been quite a ride lately." He raised his free hand and smoothed my wet hair away from my face. "When Naoki pulled you out of the water and you weren't breathing…it scared the hell out of me. I thought you were dead."

I think I actually had been—at least for a few minutes. And it would've been a peaceful escape from this violent world if not for one thing: regret. There was just too much unfinished business with Jack for me to leave happy. Too much to say. Too much left to live for.

"I almost lost you too, so I think I know how you felt," I said. Maybe now he could understand why I used a syringe full of nano-surgeons to save him. His mouth curved into a crooked smile, as if he knew exactly what I was thinking. I pressed my cheek against his cupped hand. "But we're here, still very much alive." I tugged on his wet t-shirt, trying to pull him closer, but he resisted.

"What about your no-romance policy?" He avoided looking me in the eyes when he asked, concentrating instead on putting a strand of hair behind my ear.

"I thought we both knew that stupid policy was just an overreaction on my part."

"Yeah?" he asked. "An overreaction to what?"

He wasn't going to make this easy on me. I couldn't blame him. One day I was begging him to make love to me, the next I was clinging to the side of our bed trying to avoid contact. He deserved an explanation. The trouble was that I wasn't sure I understood it all, myself. Somewhere between saying "I do" and uniting the Pit for a rebellion, I learned to trust Jack.

"Seeing you as a…bourge again," I said truthfully.

He drew his eyebrows together in a pained expression. "Sunny, I am from the Dome, but it doesn't make me a bourge. After all this time—"

I put my hand over his mouth to stop his next words.

"I know what you're going to say. But trusting you doesn't come easy for me, Jack." My breath caught on a sob. It wasn't something I ever wanted to admit to him. But he deserved honesty. He took a step away from me, and I dropped my hand away from his mouth. "You might think you know what life is like in the Pit after being down there with me, but you didn't grow up there. I did. I had a lifetime to form an opinion about the bourge."

I knew I could never explain the depth of that opinion to him. There were no words to describe how I felt when I watched my father beaten by guards to within an inch of his life. I was only eight years old the first time it happened, and it stole my voice for an entire week. But I was young and naïve. Maturity and experience taught me that a fear of the bourge was healthy and would help keep me out of trouble.

The one thing I never did learn was how to deal with the sense of helplessness I felt when I watched someone I loved being hurt—until I met Jack. He showed me that I didn't have to be helpless.

"Nobody's ever believed in me before," I said. Tentatively, I brushed my fingers against his, hoping he wouldn't snatch his hand away. He didn't. "You were the first and it made me a stronger person." I wound my fingers through his. "You've done more for the Pit than anyone else in the history of the Dome. And I'm really sorry that it's taken my head a lot longer to figure out what my heart has known for a while. I didn't marry the enemy. I married the hero."

Jack didn't say anything. He just looked at me so intently with his crystal blue eyes that I found myself holding my breath. Slowly, his lips lifted in a smile and his hand trailed down my arm, coming to rest at the hem of my shirt.

I exhaled the breath I was holding only to suck it back in again when his fingertips burned a path along my bare sides. I raised my arms above my head, felt the cold wet shirt as he pulled it off me, and heard the wet slap it made on the tiled floor. He felt warm against my cool skin as he pressed in close. His head moved toward mine.

His kiss never tasted sweeter.

Chapter Twenty-Four

I didn't think it was possible to love Jack any more than I already did. But that was before I discovered it wasn't just my heart that could hold love; my entire being could be filled with it too. I felt it in my toes as they made a lazy trail along his bare leg. My fingertips tingled with it as they traced his lower lip. It wasn't just our lives that were entangled anymore. I really felt like he was a part of my soul.

His eyes fluttered open sleepily. "Good morning, Mrs. Kenner," he said, his lips moving against my fingers.

"Is it morning already?" I asked. "It's hard to tell without windows." My internal clock had already synced itself with the rising and setting sun.

"I think so. Did you sleep well?"

I smiled instantly while the heat of a blush rushed to my cheeks. He knew exactly how little sleep I'd had. "Best night of my life."

He rolled over, pushing me off the elbow I was perched on, and pinned me to the bed. "Liar," he said, kissing my neck. It had been a while since he'd shaved, and the growth of his beard tickled. He propped himself up on his elbows and looked at me. "I'm sorry I hurt you. I thought…you were ready."

The memory of just how ready I was made me close my eyes in a moment of embarrassment. I had no idea I was capable of feeling such exquisite pleasure, so the sharp pain of our first union caught me by surprise. It shouldn't have—experienced friends had forewarned me that the first time hurt. Still, I couldn't help the scream that escaped me. "I was ready…and it only hurt the first time." I opened my eyes to find him at me. I smiled through my awkwardness. "The third time was the best, though."

His eyes smoldered at the memory. "It was, wasn't it?" He kissed me and I wound my arms around his neck, hoping we were headed for a fourth time. He pulled back to look at me again with those incredible blue eyes. "Do you have any idea how much I'm in love with you?"

"No. I think you better show me." I pulled his mouth back to mine.

A sharp rap on the door startled us both. Jack's head snapped up, looking in the direction of the intrusion. "Who is it?" he asked.

"Dena sent me," a male voice yelled from the other side of the door. "She asked if you could meet with the Elders in an hour."

"Tell her we'll be there," Jack said.

Reality dispersed the happy fog that had settled around me. In a vain attempt to keep it, I buried my face in the crook of Jack's neck and breathed in the scent of him. If I couldn't freeze time, I could at least sharpen the memory.

"I guess our honeymoon's over," he said.

"Have you thought about what you're going to say to them?"

He rolled onto his back and flopped down on the pillow beside me. "Nope. I was a little distracted last night," he said with a smile. "We need to figure out what we're going to say, though. I'm still torn. I feel guilty as hell telling a group of people armed with bows and arrows to go up against an elite army."

I propped myself up on my elbow, resting my head on my hand. I knew Jack wasn't being condescending. The fact was that Dena's army was not as well armed as Holt's, yet they had something Holt's army didn't have: strong unity.

"Their world is so different from ours," I said, looking around the time-ravaged room. "It was born out of the ashes of destruction."

"Wow, that's really poetic, Sunny."

"You know what I mean, though."

He tucked his arm under his head and turned toward me. "Their world is primitive and our world is advanced."

"No," I said, tracing a finger along his stubbly jaw line. "I mean our worlds evolved differently." I laid my head on his shoulder and snuggled in. "At least inside the Dome, we were sheltered from all the nuclear destruction. They weren't. Think of the kind of strength it would take to not only survive on a devastated Earth, but manage to build a nation too."

Lazily, he stroked my hair. "I can't imagine. All I can say is the human will to survive is strong."

"Its like Dena said—defense isn't just something they practice, it's their way of life. They've built their entire culture on protecting themselves. You saw their skill on the training field."

Jack shot me a droll look. "Thanks for the reminder."

Too late I remembered he got his butt kicked. "I didn't mean *that*," I said. "I meant they all moved together, like parts of the same machine. If the bourge didn't have automatic weapons, I think Dena's army would have the advantage."

"But they do have automatic weapons."

As I thought about it, a plan started working itself out. Flint had mentioned an armory. "Aren't weapons kept in an armory?"

"Ye-es…" Jack said.

"Are *all* weapons kept there?"

"Inventory is kept there…are you thinking what I think you're thinking?"

"What do you think I'm thinking?"

"About blowing up the armory."

"Actually, I was thinking about breaking into it and arming the heathens. But your idea's better."

He opened his eyes wide and raised his eyebrows. "*My* idea?"

"It's brilliant! If our two worlds are going to collide, then the least we can do is level the battlefield."

He studied me for a moment. "Every soldier carries at *least* one sidearm, and there's going to be some ammo around the base…" He paused again. "If we take them by surprise, we might cripple them temporarily. Of course, that's assuming they're not in contact with Holt yet. If they are, reinforcements would be sent out from the Dome."

"But if Holt is trying to keep the city a secret, would he really send an army out and take the chance of being exposed?"

"Huh," Jack said, giving me an appreciative look. "Maybe not…although if he thought he was about to lose the city, he might risk it."

I allowed myself to feel the tiniest glimmer of hope. This plan might work. "Do you think the Elders will go for it?"

He shrugged. "It depends on Dena persuading them to stay and fight."

"Maybe our plan will help convince them. We can lay it all out at the meeting."

"We still have a few points to work out, Sunny. Like how we're going to get into the city and blow up the armory."

I smiled mischievously. "I don't know Jack. It was your idea." His eyes widened and he made a growling noise, but before he could pin me to the bed again, I pinned him. He let me.

My hair fell around us as I held his wrists above his head. My eyes strayed from his blue eyes to his full lips. I lowered my mouth to his, closed my eyes, and let myself get lost in him.

Chapter Twenty-Five

As it turned out, the Elders had already made their decision by the time we got to the meeting. Amini was in the minority; she was the only one who wanted to leave behind the nation they had built. The others had come to the conclusion that they would have to face Holt and his weapons whether they ran or not. Nuclear war had already devastated the planet and a few, like Dena, felt they were the first line of defense against the bourge wreaking havoc again. I was undecided about whether that was noble or a little crazy, considering how the rest of the world had treated them.

The Elders left the strategy of the attack to Dena, the head of their military. She invited Naoki, Jin-Sook, and a few other Protectors to help her coordinate the plan.

Jack brought his computer tablet, vainly hoping it would work since he had the entire map of the city downloaded on it. It didn't. Naoki found the computer interesting. From his pocket, he took out two miniature versions of Jack's tablet. "Not so different from these," he said.

Jack picked up one of the small screens, examining it. "It's almost the same," he said, his tone a mix of curiosity and disbelief. Somewhere in the recesses of my mind I heard Doc. *Three hundred years of tradition unimpeded by progress.*

Someone produced a piece of paper and a coal lead. Jack drew a map of the city from memory. From what I remembered of the city, it looked accurate, but the only places I knew for certain were the farms and the urchin corrals. Jack was better acquainted with the military base.

"These structures are empty?" asked Dena, pointing to a residential area.

"Yes," Jack said.

"And here," Dena pointed. "What are these?"

Jack hesitated. He looked from his map to Dena, and back to the map. He bit down on his bottom lip.

Suddenly it hit me. Those buildings were the officers' barracks where his friends Alex and Hayley lived.

"We should concentrate here," I said, pointing to the corral. "Our goal is to set the slaves free. We don't have to destroy the city."

Jack drew his eyebrows together. "No. That's not right. If we do this, we have to cripple them."

I narrowed my eyes, wanting to catch his, but he refused to look at me.

"We do this with minimal bloodshed," Dena said. I was glad to hear her say that. "Tonight our goal is to set the slaves free and let the soldiers know we're not easily intimidated. After that, we come back here and remuster."

Jack dragged a hand through his hair. "Okay," he breathed. "Naoki and I break into this building." He pointed to the map. "It'll be guarded, but it's the only way to turn off the tagging system, so we have to get in. We do this first, before we blow the armory." Jack looked at me.

"I know," I said. We had already planned it out before we came here, even though I was still bristling at the fact that he had the dangerous job. Once the tagging system was shut down, I was supposed to lead everyone out. Jack made the excuse that he couldn't do it because it would be night, and he would be blind. But I think it was just a reason to try to keep me out of harm's way. "Jin-Sook and I wait in the corral until you give the signal and I lead everyone to the caverns."

We still had the obstacle of getting into the corrals undetected. I was going on the hope of finding Terran and Flint while they were out for their nightly food run. Jin-Sook told me they were well aware of the men's routine and knew where to intercept them. If that didn't work, then with any luck we could find the entrance to their tunnel. It was a worry, but it was the least of them. For now, I had the day stretching out ahead of me and I wasn't sure how I was going to get through it with this bubble of anxiety threatening to devour me.

Dena invited us to the training field. I was relieved to be given a distraction and by the look on Jack's face, so was he. Jin-Sook was excited to have me with her, and she grabbed me by the hand and almost ran all the way to the field. Jack stayed with Naoki. I looked behind me from time to time to see them both engrossed in conversation, slowly making their way down to the field.

Jin's weapon of choice was the bow, and that was the first division she took me to. The archers lined up ten across and at least twenty deep. Each front line aimed and let fly, and bowed for the line behind. The second line became the front, time and again in rapid succession, creating an undulating rain of arrows. When they finished, the younger ones standing on the sidelines ran to collect the arrows. Another group formed to take their turn.

"Want to try it this time?" Jin-Sook asked.

I shook my head. "I've never used a bow in my life," I said.

"Come on—I'll show you," she said.

She led me away from the skilled archers to a quiet area, choosing a fallen tree as the target.

"I'll aim for that stump," she said. It was a small target, yet after watching the other archers, I knew she could do it. She did. "You want to try?"

I nodded. Other than worry about tonight, I had nothing else to do. I accepted the weapon from her. "It's heavy," I said, a little surprised.

"It's exactly the right weight for me, so you might find it a little awkward. If you like shooting, you can make your own."

"Make my own?"

"Of course. Who is else is going to make it?" she asked.

"A replicator," I said.

"A what?"

"A machine that makes it for me."

She raised her eyebrows. "I wouldn't mind having a machine like that."

She tied a piece of leather around my left arm down to my wrist and then showed me how to stand, cock a bow, pull back and let go. My first attempts were laughable failures, but the longer I tried, the closer I came to the log. After only about twenty minutes, my fingers started to bleed and it was obvious I wasn't going to become a master archer by nightfall.

My favorite weapon turned out to be the dart gun. It was light to carry, easy to load and since it was only used for close range, it was easy to aim. The fact that it didn't have the capacity to kill gave me greater confidence in using it.

Eventually we made our way to what she referred to as the dojo area, where they practiced martial arts. There were several pairs engaged in sparring and I wasn't surprised to see Jack among them. He and Naoki were partnered and it appeared they weren't showing each other any mercy.

"You don't fight to the death here, do you?" I asked Jin.

She laughed. "No."

"Good." I relaxed a little and watched Jack fend off Naoki.

I hated to think it, but Jack's movements seemed slow compared to theirs. When he made a strike against Naoki, he backed up for a split second, giving the other man a chance to recover. Naoki didn't fight that way. There was no hesitation, no pausing. It was relentless. And anything was fair game as a weapon. Jack was routinely caught off guard. Dena's army fought for survival, but Jack was taught to fight in a controlled environment with no visible enemies. Before he met me, his survival had never been threatened.

Someone called out and all sparring stopped. The partners split up and moved off the field.

"The time is getting closer," Jin said. I hadn't realized how low the sun was sitting in the sky. It would be dark in a few hours. My stomach lurched with anxiety. "It's time to meditate and prepare for battle."

"Meditate?" I asked. She nodded. "Why do you do that?" The way I was feeling I couldn't imagine sitting still long enough to meditate. This was it—the first stage of freeing my people. It's what Jack and I had been working for since the day we were married. If we failed, we might never get another chance. And if we didn't free them, who else would? The panic I had worked so hard to keep at bay all day now stole every drop of moisture from my mouth.

Jin-Sook examined my face. "You know that feeling you're feeling right now?" Was it written all over my face? Or maybe it was my shaking hands that gave me away. "That's why we meditate."

"How do you do it?"

"I start with relaxation exercises to ease tension and clear my mind. Then I visualize my body going through the motions of archery. If I were preparing for hand-to-hand combat, I would concentrate on my body moving through the steps of martial arts. Through this meditation technique, we memorize the movements and strengthen our confidence. We always end meditation with thanks to the spirits and ask for their blessing."

Absentmindedly, I tilted my head to the side as I looked at Jin. It never once occurred to me that they prayed. In the Pit, there were people who prayed to a God I was never really convinced existed.

"I take it you don't meditate," Jin said.

"No. And I don't pray either. I don't know how."

"So what do you believe in?"

I had to think about that question. What did I believe in? Once I believed in salvation—that our treaty of bondage would be fulfilled and we would all leave the Pit free. But the discovery that my people had spent the last three hundred years clinging to an elaborate lie showed me how naïve we really were. I wasn't so sure believing in something you couldn't see was as fulfilling as Jin-Sook thought it was.

"Me," I said. "I believe in me. And Jack. I know we'll do what we can to save my people, even if we die trying."

Jin put her hand on my shoulder. "You can believe in us too, Sunny."

I hoped so.

Jack was suddenly beside me. "How'd your day go?" he asked.

He was half-naked and dripping with sweat. "Not as tough as your day." I swiped a finger across his sweaty chest to emphasize my point and left a bloody trail.

He picked up my hand and examined it. "I'm not so sure," he said, and kissed my cut-up fingers.

We followed the long trail of people back to the courtyard. A light meal and pitchers of water were available. As people finished their meal, they disappeared into the hotel. Dena approached us just as Jack and I finished our broth.

"You're welcome to join us in meditation," Dena said.

Jack raised his eyebrows at me in question. "Jin explained they always meditate before battle," I said.

"Not just before battle," Dena corrected me. "It's a daily ritual."

"I appreciate the offer," Jack said. "But Sunny and I have a ritual too. We'll go back to our room and prepare there."

I smiled and nodded, even though I had no idea what Jack was talking about.

There were quite a few people already deep in meditation in the hotel lobby, although I had also seen many outside under the setting sun. Quietly, we made our way through the lobby and back to our room.

It didn't seem as creepy now that it held the memory of our lovemaking. I lit the lantern for Jack, closing my eyes against the bright flash of flame. "We have a ritual?" I asked.

He pushed the table and chairs against the wall. "You mean you've forgotten?" It finally dawned on me. We were going to train.

"It's been a while," I said.

He went into a crouch and I copied his movements. I'd forgotten how soothing this was.

"I saw you trying your hand at archery," Jack said.

"Hence the mashed-up fingers," I replied, flashing them at him. "Guess I suck at just about everything."

He laughed softly. "Hardly." He raised a leg, arced it in the air, and placed his foot behind him, stretching his body forward. I followed, feeling my muscles begin to relax and the blood flow into my head. His expression sobered. "I want you to take the pistol tonight."

"No, Jack. Then you won't have a weapon."

"I still have my knife." He breathed in deeply and shifted his weight to his other foot and repeated the movements. "Naoki found a full magazine in the bike they took from us. It's not a huge ammo supply, but better than nothing. You remember how to change it?"

"I'll be at the corral far from any fighting. Once you blow the armory you'll be in the thick of it. I'm not taking the pistol, Jack."

He came to a standstill and turned to face me. "You'll take the pistol or I'll call this whole damn thing off."

My mouth dropped open. Jack had never spoken to me like that before. "What did you just say to me?"

He drew his lips into a hard line. "I'm not backing down, Sunny."

And he thought *I* was the one who should back down? With the bourge armed to the teeth, the only hope we had of succeeding was that they underestimated Dena's army—that they wouldn't expect an offensive attack. The risk of one or both of us not living through the night was real, but Jack was at greater risk than me.

"When you blow the armory, every soldier in that city is going to run toward it. A knife isn't going to help you—you need a gun." I let out an exasperated sigh. "Why are you being so stubborn?"

His expression was full of reproach. "I was thinking the same about you."

"Maybe I am better off meditating." I turned toward the door.

"Stop!" he said in a loud voice. I kept going, stopping only when I felt his hand on my arm. It was a surprisingly tender hold considering the tension in his face. "I'm sorry. Please don't go. I didn't mean to yell." I let go of the breath that up until now I hadn't realized I was holding. "I'm scared as hell and I'm just barely holding it together."

I couldn't blame him there. I relaxed ever so slightly. "Me too."

He tugged me toward him and I gave in, wrapping my arms around his waist. He pressed me harder against him, as if I might change my mind and try to leave again. I wasn't going to. This wasn't the time to fight. I needed his strength too much.

He pushed away from me a little and took my face in both his hands and rested his forehead against mine. "You take the gun." I opened my mouth to protest. "Just listen for a second, *please*. I have my knife and the minute I can get my hands on a gun, I'll grab one."

"Jack..."

"Sunny, I can't do this unless I know you're protected. Okay? Just this one thing for me. Please."

His blue eyes watered, dampening his lashes and he bit down hard on his lip. He took a deep, unsteady breath, his pleading eyes never leaving mine.

Never, in my entire worthless life, had anyone ever looked at me with that much love.

I tried to breathe around the lump lodged in my throat, but it was getting increasingly difficult. Taking his face in my hands, I nodded. Pressing closer, I kissed him, tasting the salt of our tears. I didn't want to think about what was facing us, or why I might need a gun.

If I closed my eyes, and felt the heat of his lips and his hands trying to hold me closer, I could really imagine that the only future I cared about was right here in this room.

Chapter Twenty-Six

I never thought I would be loath to leave our creepy hotel room. It's funny how making memories could give an old room new life. I figured if I did die tonight, my spirit actually could live on...*in that room.* If there were other ghosts living there, they would just have to make way for me. My claim was stronger.

Before we left the barangay, Jack hugged me close and tucked the pistol into my waistband. I didn't protest. That was our agreement. And his end of the bargain was to grab a gun as soon as he could, and stay alive.

For now, we were in the forest trying to stand as still as Naoki, Jin-Sook and twenty others while we lay in wait for Terran and Flint. It was a lot harder than it looked. As the breeze moved my hair, sending it tickling across my cheek, I understood why they tied their hair back. I was dying to scratch.

"Stop moving," Jack whispered.

"I'm trying," I whispered back.

Naoki eyeballed us. We stopped talking.

At least we didn't have long to wait before Terran and Flint made an appearance. Jack and I stepped forward, startling them.

Flint was the first to recover. "Geez, it's President Kenner!"

Jack gave me a questioning look. I shrugged.

"He's not the—" I started, but decided against correcting him. "We need your help getting into the corrals."

Terran looked at Jack warily. "Sunny said something before about you shutting off the tagging system."

Jack nodded. "That's right. Once it's off, you need to get everyone out as fast as you can."

"How do we know when it's shut down?"

Jack motioned toward Naoki and Jin-Sook and everyone came out of hiding. "Because they'll send a volley of flaming arrows at the armory. You see arrows lighting up the sky, the system is off."

"What the hell!" Terran said, backing up a few steps.

"It's okay," I said. "They're on our side. The bourge haven't been very nice to them either."

Flint didn't seem to mind their presence. His eyes gleamed with excitement. "You're going to blow the armory, sir?" he asked excitedly. "Because I know about blowing things up. I can help."

Jack looked to me again. I widened my eyes and shrugged. Flint was an odd soul. "You do? What have you blown up?" asked Jack.

"Well, nothing yet, sir. I've been planning to blow a big hole in the side of the Dome to let everyone out," he said.

Jack raised his eyebrows. "Good to know. I think for tonight, though, I'll ask you to go tell the men in the range to be ready to go. Are you okay doing that?"

Flint nodded his head vigorously. "Yes, sir."

"Are there many men there?" I asked.

"Too many," Terran said in disgust. "Some aren't in great shape. Two men have infected gunshot wounds."

Naoki motioned to two of his men. "Ryan and Lito will go with you. They can take the injured to our doctors."

Doc was probably a better choice, but Amini's barangay wasn't far from the range. I thought of the sedative they used on their darts and knew the injured men would at least appreciate that relief. If I was able to bring Doc to them later, I would.

The three men left for the range. It was time to put our plan in motion.

A slight touch of our hands was the only acknowledgement that it was time to part ways. We had already said our goodbyes and there was nothing to be gained in dragging it out. I resisted the urge to look back and watch him walk out of sight, concentrating instead on putting one foot in front of the other.

With Jack's group gone in the other direction, we were down to just Jin-Sook, Terran, five other Protectors, and me. Dena's army was hidden in the forest, ready to move if they were needed. I hoped it wouldn't come to that. I hoped it went according to plan—shut off the tagging system, set the armory on fire, and sneak everyone out of the corrals while the bourge were distracted. It was a good plan. It should work.

Terran led us around the back of the corral, and we stayed low, under the cover of trees and brush. Floodlights lit up both compounds, making it hard to see.

"I don't remember these being lit the night I stayed," I said to Terran.

"They've been turning them on every night since you disappeared. They stepped up the number of guards and do routine sweeps around the pen too." He grinned mischievously. "Just makes it a little more interesting getting in and out, but not impossible. Stay low and follow me."

He took us right up to the edge of the forest and started moving a pile of deadwood, revealing a hole in the ground.

"Last one in pulls a few logs back over the hole," he said.

"Wait. We need to split up to warn the men in the other pen," Jin-Sook said. She pointed to the Protectors. "You two go with Terran, you two hide in the forest and watch for Naoki's signal, and come and get us when you see it." The last Protector stayed with us.

Terran shook his head. "My wife is in that corral. I want to make sure she gets out safe."

"I can't sneak into the men's corral. I'll stand out," I said. He wavered. "I promise I'll get Goldie out."

Finally, he lifted himself back out. "Okay." He waved for the two Protectors to follow him, and went in the direction of the other corral.

"I'll go first," I said.

I looked from the entrance of the tunnel to C Block and tried to judge the distance. It was going to be a fair crawl to get there. I knew that for a couple of miners, digging a trench this long wasn't difficult. But still, it must've taken them months, and they did it without getting caught. They must have been desperate for food and news from their loved ones.

I dropped down into the entrance. The smell of damp earth hit me full in the face and I coughed. Slapping a hand over my mouth, I looked up at Jin-Sook. She stood stock-still over the hole, looking in the direction of the corral. She stayed that way for at least five minutes before she motioned for the next person to join me. I began my crawl to C Block.

It was tight, even for me, and I wondered how two men like Terran and Flint managed it. As I expected, the tunnel seemed to go on forever. Even if I wanted to turn back, I couldn't—I had two more people crawling behind me. What if the end of the tunnel was barred? Or collapsed? Could we all back up synchronously? I bit the inside of my cheeks and told myself to stop thinking like that. There was an end to this tunnel.

And when I reached it, I banged with both fists.

Above me, I heard rapid footsteps and the scraping of furniture. *Patience,* I told myself. They needed time to move everything out of the way. Finally, the trap door opened.

Goldie peered down at me, a look of alarm crossing her features. "Where's Terran?"

I pulled myself through the trap door and into C Block. My sudden appearance had everyone on edge, but when the next person turned out to be a heathen, the spectators turned and ran.

"Where's Terran!" she demanded again.

"He's fine," I said quickly. "He's helping us tonight."

Jin-Sook emerged from the hole.

"What the hell is going on?" someone said a little too loudly.

"Keep it down!" I whispered loudly.

"What *is* going on?" Goldie asked.

"If everything goes according to plan, the tagging system will be shut down soon. You all need to be ready to move," I said.

There was resistance. It wasn't every day someone strolled into their prison and said she was unlocking the door. And when that someone was the mistress of the next president, accompanied by people they only knew as "heathens," there was bound to be mistrust.

Goldie's expression was skeptical. "I want to know where Terran is."

"He's next door getting the men ready to go. Please,"

I begged, "we don't have a lot of time to get organized. Once we get the signal, we need to move fast, before the bourge have a chance to figure out what's happening."

By now, everyone had gathered back around us. Jin-Sook remained silent, her eyes alert and one hand on her knife. The tension in the room was palpable, and it was up to me to defuse it. I knew gaining everyone's trust was going to be impossible. After all, I was asking them to trust me enough to step across an invisible fence that could kill them. I wasn't sure I'd be so easily persuaded, either. But I didn't need to convince the entire room—I just needed to convince the one person everyone here already trusted.

"Goldie, you overheard everything I told my mom the night I stayed here. Why would I lie about that? What purpose would it serve?"

The door opened and my mother came in. Someone must have rushed to get her when they saw me.

"Is Jack Kenner in on this?" my mother asked.

I nodded. "We've aligned with the—" I almost said *the heathens*. It wasn't that I thought of them as heathens; it's just that I didn't know what else to call them. "The Nation," I said, motioning toward Jin-Sook. "They've had a run-in with the bourge too."

My mom silently took in the two people standing with me. "You trust them?" she asked me.

"I do."

"What's your plan?" Goldie asked.

"My plan is to get everyone out through that tunnel

once the system is shut off, but with so many soldiers around tonight it's going to be difficult to sneak everyone from the other two buildings in here."

"The army has been using the cafeteria as a center of operations for their search of you and Kenner," my mom said. "They make us keep the kitchen open around the clock. Though I think something big must've happened recently. There are a lot more soldiers coming and going and tensions are running high. Do you know why?"

"I guess they're a little mad that we killed a few soldiers," I said. I went on to explain about how the trade went awry. I knew the bourge would be really mad about having their men killed, but it never occurred to us that they would use the corrals as the center for the search. Liberating kitchen staff was going to be more complicated—they'd be missed right away.

We were running out of time. Jack and Naoki would have reached the city long before we arrived here, which gave them a head start on shutting things down.

My mother, Goldie and I went to B Block and started getting everyone into C. There wasn't as much resistance there since I had the help of two of their own. We broke them up into groups of varying sizes—sometimes in threes, or in pairs, and the odd person on their own—seemingly leaving B Block to go to the shower room or other common places, but then backtracking to C.

"When is curfew?" I asked my mom.

"In about thirty minutes."

"Obviously, kitchen staff isn't bound to the curfew?"

"No, but they have to stay inside the building until the shift change at midnight."

Once B Block was cleared out, we made our way back to C. The place was packed and there was a disagreement in progress. Elbowing my way through the crowd, I went looking for the cause of the commotion. The Protector who had been left to watch for the signal was standing in the entrance of the tunnel.

"Anna says she saw the first arrows fly. It's time," Jin-Sook said.

I turned toward the group gathered around the hole. "We need to move! What's the problem?"

One woman was pushed forward but immediately stepped back, shaking her head.

"They're afraid," Jin-Sook said.

"What if it's not shut off?" someone asked.

My mother stepped up. "I'll go first."

My mother sat down on the edge of the hole. A scream bubbled up inside me and I swallowed it. *What if it's not turned off? Why did my mother have to go first?*

"Mom," I said. But I didn't know what else to say without losing the trust of everyone in the room. Why had I been so confident about sending someone I didn't know down the hole first?

She gave me a reassuring look. "You get ready to send the rest."

I dug my nails into my palms. "Okay."

She disappeared into the hole. It was going to take a few minutes for her to crawl to the other side…to get past the tagging fence. I bowed down over the hole, waiting to hear a scream. The entire room was silent. They were all waiting, too. None came. I waited. Four minutes passed, and still no screams. *Maybe the chip in her neck prevented her from screaming.* I banished the thought. If she had died, Anna would come back to tell us…if she could get past the body.

"I'm going to check," I said, dropping back into the hole. I crawled more than halfway.

"Mom," I whispered. No reply. Then I remembered I was underground and it was unlikely the bourge would hear me. "Mom," I said louder. "Mom!"

"I made it," her voice replied from a distance.

I breathed.

Unable to turn around, I backed up out of the hole.

"It's off," I said.

Jin-Sook stayed to organize the evacuation while Goldie and I went to A Block and started to clear it out. From outside, the sound of jeep engines roared into the corral.

A voice boomed from outside. "The armory's on fire!"

The cafeteria doors banged open and the urgent sound of boots pounding on the ground and soldiers being called into action urged us to move faster. We were running out of time and we still had to get the kitchen staff.

The women in A Block were beginning to show signs of panic. A few of them pushed their way to the front of the line to get out the door first and broke into a run straight for C Block. Wildly, I looked around to see if they were noticed. More women pushed their way out.

"Stop!" I said as loud as I dared.

"I'm not going to be left behind," someone yelled. "I'm getting out!"

Mad chaos ensued. They tripped over each other trying to get out the door. There was no way either Goldie or I could control them. Opal lived in this Block, and she tried to come to our rescue, but the panic-stricken women were beyond listening to reason.

A gunshot rang out and a soldier barked orders. "Get back in your bunks or the next one's aimed at your heads!"

I pulled the pistol from my waistband and looked at Goldie and Opal. "You two get to C Block and get out of here."

"We're not leaving you alone," Goldie said.

"Terran's waiting to meet you and he'll have my head if you don't show up," I said.

"No one's waiting for me," Opal said.

"You're unarmed. Get to the tunnel."

I fought my way out the door and crept along in the shadow of A Block, heading for a large garbage bin at the end of the unit. As I made my way toward it, the first shots were fired. Screaming erupted from the women still left out in the open. Peeking around the bin, I saw the unmistakable glow of fire lighting up the night sky—the armory.

Three soldiers within shooting range were firing their semi-automatic rifles. I took aim at a floodlight, shot at it and missed. I hugged close to the bin, waiting to see if my failed effort was going to give my position away. It didn't. There was too much gunfire for mine to stand out. I aimed at the floodlight again, steadying my hands, and shot it out. Then I aimed at one of the soldiers, fired, and ducked back behind the bin. I breathed in and out, in and out. My heart pounded. I looked again. The soldier I shot was on the ground and another soldier was hunched over him. I took aim and pulled the trigger again, and then stepped back behind the bin. I sucked air into my lungs.

More shots were fired—this time, at the bin I was hiding behind.

I pulled myself into a ball as bullets pounded the only protection I had, and just as suddenly, they stopped. I looked around the bin and saw a soldier with an arrow sticking out of his chest lying on the ground.

Jin-Sook.

I wildly scanned the area for her, and finally found her when she stepped out from behind B Block to loose another arrow.

"We're under attack!" a soldier yelled.

Right after he announced it, a boom in the distance shook the ground.

The cafeteria doors slammed open and dozens of soldiers came pouring out, drawing their weapons.

I pressed against the bin I was hiding behind,

wishing I could mold myself into it and disappear. They were going to find me.

Jin-Sook pointed toward C Block. She wanted me to run.

The rest of the women, including Goldie and Opal, left A Block and took off at a run toward C. Soldiers opened fire. As if in slow motion, several women stopped running, their bodies jerking one way and then the other. They fell to the ground. It took a moment for it to register that the women had been shot. Repeatedly.

Opal was on the ground.

My feet were moving before my brain could tell them. A stinging pain slammed into my arm. I ducked lower, hoping to make myself a smaller target.

Jin-Sook walked out from behind B Block and fired arrows in rapid succession. I got to Opal, but she was dead. I found Goldie still alive.

"Can you make it to C?" I asked. She nodded.

As she got up and ran, I fired at the soldiers creeping toward us. Between Jin-Sook's deadly accuracy and my bullets, they backed off a little. I didn't know how many shots were left in the magazine. The other one Jack gave me was still in my waistband.

I looked for more survivors as Jin-Sook ran toward me. That's when the first rain of arrows hit the compound.

"Dena's here," Jin yelled. "Take cover!"

We headed straight for C Block amid the sound of men screaming as arrows tore into them. I tried to remind myself they were reaping what they sowed. They deserved it.

"Where the hell are they coming from?" a soldier shrieked over the sound of rapid gunfire.

There were still at least twenty women still in C Block. Goldie was among them, bleeding from a wound in her leg. Jin-Sook and I stood guard at the door, watching the pandemonium outside. The soldiers were scattered, seeking cover from the relentless torrent of arrows. A jeep started up and tore out of the compound. Three more followed, all of them packed with armed soldiers.

That's when it happened: an explosion so powerful it knocked us off our feet. The entire building shook, toppling a few bunks. A cloud of dust rose up from the tunnel entrance.

"Oh my God!" I screamed and ran toward the entrance. "How long has it been since the last person got in?"

Goldie's eyes were open wide. "I don't know. Three, maybe four minutes."

"Was it three or four?" I demanded. *"Think!"*

"We have the chance to go *now,*" Jin-Sook hissed from the doorway. "We head toward the back fence, away from the battle area."

I didn't want to leave. I wanted to find a shovel and dig my way to anyone trapped in the tunnel. But the other women were already heading for the door and Jin was urging me to hurry up. We had to go.

I ran through the door, out into the open and headed for the kitchen.

"Where are you going?" Jin-Sook said. "This way!"

"I'm not leaving them."

Between the blast from the armory and arrows still spitting down, the compound was almost empty. That meant the soldiers had taken cover in the buildings. I made my way to the backdoor of the cafeteria building—the direct entrance to the kitchen. Jin and the other ladies followed close behind.

I slammed open the door and aimed my gun inside. Six kitchen staff, crouched behind the counter, snapped terrified looks in our direction. The door separating the kitchen and cafeteria was closed. I didn't know if there were any soldiers still in the building, but I was willing to guess there were. I motioned for the small group to come with us.

When everyone was out, we headed toward the back fence. No one gave chase. The bourge were too preoccupied defending themselves against the people they thought of as heathens. I prayed Dena kept the upper hand.

Jin-Sook used her knife to loosen enough of the wire fence to bend back out of the way. As we slipped under the fence and went toward the forest, the sounds of fighting faded. The night sky glowed orange from the burning armory. And yet even in the midst of all the death and destruction, one undeniably happy thought crept into my mind: *we were free.*

For my own mental stability, I tried to refrain from tallying the cost.

Chapter Twenty-Seven

As we headed toward the designated meeting spot, we met some of the men going toward the corrals.

"Terran!" Goldie called.

I was helping her walk, but when Terran heard her calling him, he came running toward his wife. "I've been worried sick," he said, wrapping his arms around her. He eased her down to the ground. "Where are you hurt?"

"My leg," she said.

Terran pulled his shirt over his head and tied it around the wound on her leg.

I surveyed the group of men, some armed with rifles. "Where are you going?"

"We were coming for you, but now that you're safe, we'll go join the battle," Terran said.

"The fighting is just about over and we're supposed to get everyone into the caverns," I said. This was not part of the plan. But then again, the bourge showing up and opening fire wasn't part of the plan either.

Terran finished tying off the tourniquet. "You do that. We're joining the fight. Take care of her for me." He kissed his wife and led his troop away.

Everything was going wrong. It was supposed to be a simple plan of sneaking everyone out of the corrals, disabling the bourge by taking away their weapons, and going back to Dena's barangay to remuster. Instead, the dead lay scattered all over the compounds, bourge and urchin alike. Why did it have to come to this?

Between those who had died and the group of men who left to fight, the number of people waiting for us in the forest was considerably smaller than I had originally anticipated. Some were wounded and moaning in pain.

"Sunny!" my mother exclaimed. She ran toward me. "There was so much gunfire. I was terrified you wouldn't make it out."

"I'm fine," I assured her. I had fared a lot better than most. "We need to get everyone to safety. There's a cave close by."

My mother shook her head. "I'm not hiding in a cave. The men had the right of it—this is our fight."

Those who were still able-bodied were bristling at being left behind by the men. They wanted to fight too. It was obvious none of them were going to be led into a cavern to sit and wait it out.

"What do we do?" Jin whispered to me.

I was divided between honoring my duty in our plan

and joining the fight myself. How many years had we put up with the bourge beating us? Killing us? We were finally fighting back. I didn't blame them for not wanting to run and hide while someone else fought their battle.

"Nothing," I said. "They're free. Free to make their own decisions."

The wounded were our biggest concern and we decided to send them to Dena's barangay for help. A small group was put together to get everyone there safely. The rest of us went in the direction of the corrals.

Crouching low in the brush, we observed the women's compound. The dead littered the ground. Movement caught my eye—someone was moving among the dead soldiers, collecting rifles. I pointed to him and Jin-Sook nodded. He was one of us. We all crept down to the corral, under the fence, and started collecting weapons, too.

One of the men approached us. "We got here right at the tail end of the fight. Any bourge left alive got into a jeep and took off. Both places are empty," he said, pointing to the men's corral. "The fighting's moved to the city."

"The city?" I echoed. I thought our plan was to free everyone, blow the armory and get out.

He motioned toward Jin-Sook. "Their army has the bourge pinned."

That was news. Big news. "Do you know where Jack Kenner is? Is he in the city?"

He nodded. "Last I heard he was."

We finished collecting as many weapons as we could.

With the rising sun, someone was thoughtful enough to grab a bag and collect sunglasses from each bunk. When we had everything we needed, we set out in the direction of the city. There were about eighty of us, mostly women. Terran and the other men had already made their way to the front lines. We skirted the residential area, where the houses stood empty and untouched by conflict.

We passed a group of archers standing motionless along the tree line before we found Jack, Dena, and Naoki in the forest, deep in conversation, with only the archers to protect them if the bourge opened fire. They were so close to the city.

I wasn't expecting my knees to go weak when I saw Jack. Irrationally, tears sprung to my eyes and my hands started shaking. I noticed the side of his pant-leg was stained with blood.

"Jack!" I called.

At the sound of my voice, he spun around. I ran to him, threw my arms around his neck, and felt my feet lift off the ground as he squeezed me tight. I buried my face in his shoulder.

"Are you okay?" he whispered in my ear. "Your arm's bleeding."

"I'm fine." He pulled away to look at my injury. I had felt the searing pain during the battle, but forgotten about it. "A bullet grazed me, that's all. You're hurt too," I said, motioning toward his leg. I bent down to examine it, concerned by all the blood.

"It's nothing," he said, pulling me back up. "I'm fine now that I know you're okay. I was scared to death when I heard all the gunfire at the corrals."

"The corral was full of soldiers. They were using it as the center of operations for the search for us. The armory blowing drew them away. That was quite a bang."

He nodded. "It turned out that's where they were building the drone. They had the gasifiers in there for the replicators." He hugged me close. "Someone told me the tunnel collapsed. God, I'm happy you're okay."

I pushed away so I could see him. "What happened to the plan? Free everyone and go back to the barangay to remuster?"

He hesitated before answering. "My people are creatures of habit. They'd never miss cocktail hour, which lasts most of the night. So I knew the mess would be packed and, when the armory blew, they'd come running out."

"Oh my God, Jack." I didn't know what to say. I couldn't even imagine what kind of emotional struggle went into making that decision.

"It's okay," he said quickly. "They behaved exactly the way I thought they would. As soon as they ran out and discovered they were under attack, they ran back inside. The mess is still full. Some of the other buildings have soldiers in them too, and they're firing at us if we get too close. Dena's army has taken up strategic positions around the city. No one's moving."

"So we're in a standoff with them."

He held up a communicator. "I've been talking with Powell about a ceasefire. I've asked him to come out and meet with me personally."

"Tell him to bring Gaia."

He looked out of the corner of his eye. "Sunny—there's a woman staring at us. Do you know her?"

I looked in the direction of his gaze. My mom was trying to appear as though she hadn't been watching us. "That's my mom."

His eyes widened and he loosened his arms. "You could've told me she was there before I started making out with you."

"Do you want to meet her?"

"Now?"

I stepped back, taking his hand in mine, fully prepared to get this awkward introduction out of the way. My mom had always been very vocal about how much she hated the bourge. Having a daughter in love with one probably wasn't going to sit well with her. But before we could reach my mother, Jack's communicator came to life. He looked relieved. Stepping away from me, he answered.

Dena and Naoki both started toward Jack when they heard his communicator. His conversation lasted less than a minute. He clicked off the device and looked at us.

"Powell's agreed to meet with me."

It was more than a little intense walking onto the

city streets. We both knew there were snipers in the buildings with weapons trained on us. Dena's archers took up strategic positions around the meeting area. If anybody got trigger-happy, bullets and arrows would start to fly with us caught right in the middle.

There had been a lively discussion about who should be the one to go with Jack. Dena felt it should be her, but Jack was right when he said her presence could complicate things. Better to let us go and smooth things over with Powell before they met for the first time.

Powell and Gaia came out of the mess at the same time we emerged onto the street from between two buildings. He was holding his arm where an arrow was sticking out of it. He paused on the step of the building as two soldiers came out and set up a table and two chairs in the middle of the street.

"Guns on the ground!" Jack called out. The soldiers stopped what they were doing, showed us that they were unarmed, and completed setting up the table. The four of us walked toward it at the same time.

Jack gave the man a curt nod. "General Powell, sir."

"*Sir*, is it?" The general smiled. "Always the diplomat."

Jack motioned to the table and chairs. "What's all this?"

"No need to be uncivilized, Jack. Have a seat." Powell sat down heavily. His forehead was slick with perspiration. He looked to be in a lot of pain.

"I think you're missing a couple of chairs for Sunny and Gaia," Jack said.

Powell raised his eyebrows. "Two more chairs," he called out. "And a bottle of scotch!"

Jack refused to sit down until Gaia and I were seated. I tried to gauge how she was reacting to all of this, but she was wearing glasses and her eyes were hidden. The only thing I had to go by was the thin set of her lips.

A bottle of scotch and four glasses were put on the table. "Do you mind doing the honors, Jack? I'm not feeling so good." He indicated the arrow sticking out of his arm. The first few buttons of his shirt were undone, revealing a bandage underneath. I wondered if it was for the bullet wound Jack had given him.

Jack poured the general a glass of scotch and set the bottle down.

"I hate to drink alone, Jack."

"But you will."

Powell picked up the glass and tossed it back. "Gotta get some pain relief somehow. Unless you're willing to let Doc come here and take this damn arrow out of my arm."

"I don't have a problem with that."

"Gaia," Powell barked.

I curled my lip. It irked me that he thought he was still in control. "You ask her nicely or that arrow can stay right where it is," I said.

His head snapped toward me in a flash of anger. I returned his scowl. After all I'd been through, it was no longer in me to cower from a bourge. He looked at Jack, perhaps waiting for him to correct me. He didn't.

Powell rolled his eyes. "Gaia," he said in an overly sweet voice. "Would you please get Doc for me?"

Gaia didn't even look at him. "No."

"Great," he muttered. Turning slightly in his chair, he yelled toward the mess, *"Someone get Doc!"* A soldier ran out and headed toward the medical center. Powell leaned forward and slopped another drink into his glass. "So Jack..." he drawled, leaning back in his chair. "We seem to have a situation."

"It would appear so, General. I'm hoping you'll see reason and lay down your weapons."

"Just one question." He stared down at his drink, twirling the glass, then looked at Jack. "Why? Why all this fighting, Jack? Because you fell in love with your urchin, and you're pissed at me for wanting to hold her accountable for her actions?"

Jack looked confused. "I assumed you'd been in touch with President Holt by now."

Powell shook his head. "No. Communications are still out."

"Huh," Jack said, drawing his eyebrows together. "Has he been silent for this long before?"

"Routinely. We only speak about six times a year. You know Damien. He's so damn paranoid someone's going to find out about this city and expose his plan that he doesn't risk opening a channel very often." Powell shifted his injured arm and grimaced. "I really wasn't concerned about communications shutting down this time until you showed up. I figured Damien sent you out here to spy on me. Or maybe your wedding went better than planned, there was a full-on war being waged in the Dome, and you were here to get things ready. Now I don't know what the hell is going on. Why are you here, Jack?"

Jack frowned. "I thought you knew."

Powell shook his head, looking at a loss.

"If you didn't know, then why were you so determined to find me? Why did you capture *children* and *kill* two of them in an attempt to get to me? Why did you start this damn war if you didn't know?"

Powell looked incredulous. "*I* started this? *You* shot *me* and took off with her!" he said, glaring across the table at Jack. "Jesus, I'm not going to fault you for falling in love with your urchin—it's not the first time in the history of the Dome that's happened. But you're the goddamn president's son-in-law! Damien would flay me alive if he discovered I let you take off to live out some teenage wet dream. I needed to get you back, get rid of the girl, and sweep this all under the carpet before he found out about any of it." Powell sighed heavily, looking around at the empty street. "But it looks like we might've passed the point of no return. He's gonna find out about *this*."

Jack laughed. Not a funny kind of laugh, but the kind you do when you realize the irony of something. "You killed children just to save your own ass?"

"I killed *heathens* to save not just my ass, but yours too! And don't look so damn surprised. You and I both know that once Damien comes out of the Dome, their days are numbered."

"Oh, that's right—Holt's plans for his master race." Jack leaned across the table, leveling a hard stare at Powell. "And you support him."

A disgusted snort erupted from Powell. "Look who's accusing. You knew about his master race and you *still* married Leisel. I have to say, Jack, given that you're a Kenner, I was real surprised you went through with the marriage, knowing it. You gave Damien exactly what he wanted."

"What the hell does marrying Leisel have to do with Holt's master race?"

I was confused too. I thought Leisel was the one who had orchestrated the marriage—conned her father into accepting a Kenner as a son-in-law, then framed him for treason.

It was Powell's turn to look puzzled. "You don't know?"

Jack slammed his open palm down onto the table, making the rest of us jump. *"What the hell was he up to!"*

Powell nervously looked around. They weren't visible to the eye, but we all knew there were weapons trained on us. "I'll tell you everything. Just calm down." Powell scanned the area one more time before he continued. "We *all* have family heirlooms, Jack. Priceless mementos passed down through the generations. I know the Kenners do." He directed a conspiratorial smile at Jack. I wondered if he was referring to the videotapes the Kenners protected—the tapes that exposed Edward Holt. "One of my family heirlooms is a bunch of scrapbooks.

My ancestors were into breeding dogs—a certain kind called golden retrievers. Retrievers come in all different colors—from light to dark—and if you want the offspring to be a light color, then you choose a bitch and sire with light colored ears. If you want a dark coat, then you look for dark-colored ears. So you see, Jack, in order to achieve the right color, you need to breed the dogs according to their ears. Of course, both dogs need to have the right pedigree as well, which was a bit of a problem."

Jack's hand was still open, facedown on the table, but with Powell's anecdote his fingers drew into a fist. "What does *that* have to do with *me*?" he asked, his eyes never leaving Powell.

"Because when it came to eligible bachelors in the Dome, you were the fairest of them all. A perfect match for the blonde-haired, blue-eyed Leisel Holt," Powell said. His lips curved into a satisfied smile.

Jack sneered. "Are you telling me that the *master race* is the *Aryan race*? That Holt is some kind of Nazi?"

Jack looked about ready to jump across the table and grab Powell by the throat. I put my hand over his fist and squeezed, hoping it might calm him down. There were too many weapons around to start a fistfight. And the revelation that Holt might be a Nazi didn't really change anything. It just explained that his insanity wasn't random—there was actually a reason behind it.

Powell nodded. "Now you're getting it, Jack." He

downed his scotch and wiped his mouth with the back of his hand. "Although the Holts don't call themselves Nazis, they do claim to be direct descendants of Hitler." Gritting his teeth, he shifted his injured arm. A new sheen of moisture broke out on his forehead. "The story goes that Adolf Hitler had an affair with his niece, and she ended up pregnant. It happened during his campaign to become Chancellor of Germany, and incest wasn't a stain he wanted on his reputation. So the girl was locked up, she had the baby, and it was taken from her. It was public knowledge that his niece lived with him and there was already speculation about an affair, but when she committed suicide, it got tongues wagging and almost ended Hitler's political career. He knew he had to get rid of the evidence but couldn't bring himself to kill the baby—a son—so he had the child smuggled out of Germany and into the United States. They changed the child's last name to Holt to protect his identity. But everyone close to the Fuhrer knew about the child and when Germany lost the war, hundreds of war criminals immigrated to America incognito, in search of Hitler's legacy." He paused to study Jack's reaction. "Or so the story goes. Could be it's all just an elaborate lie made up by someone who was delusional. Point is, the Holts believed it and so did the Nazi Party."

Jack seemed to be in a mild state of shock. He was staring at Powell, his mouth slightly agape. After a few moments, he sat back in his chair and studied the general thoughtfully. "You know about the videotapes my family protects, don't you?"

Powell nodded. "I'm aware of their rumored existence."

"They exist. I've watched them. And I've read Theodore Kenner's diaries. He uncovered evidence that Edward Holt convinced President Taylor that North Korea had already launched so she would input her codes to retaliate with nuclear warheads."

"Are you asking me if Edward Holt started the war three hundred years ago? Yes, Jack!" he yelled. "World War Three wasn't an accident. General Edward Holt was privy to a lot of information, including the existence of the Dome. The planet was in dire straits from climate change, people all over were suffering, and every leader in the world had their fingers on the button. The timing was perfect to annihilate humanity—to get rid of the vermin and repopulate the Earth with a worthy race. We just didn't expect anyone would survive the holocaust."

"And killing everyone in the Pit figures into the plan how? What if some of them turn out to be blonde?"

I thought of Goldie—her dark hair with a blonde streak. Would that make her eligible for Holt's race?

"Once a slave always a slave, Jack. That's their heritage. You can't take it out of them."

Jack snorted his disgust and looked away from Powell. His eyes came to rest on my hand, still clutching his fist and, picking it up with both of his, he kissed it. He gave me an apologetic look. I appreciated how he felt, but in my mind there was no need for him to apologize. He's the only one from the Dome who ever did anything for us—who risked his own neck to free the Pit.

He turned his attention back to the general. "And the Powells, the Wests and the Forbes—you're all Nazis aren't you?"

Powell shook his head. "Just because my lineage is Nazi doesn't mean I am. I was honest when I said I wanted to change Damien's mind about killing all the urchins. There's no sense in it. We need them just as much out here as we do in the Dome."

Jack almost did jump across the table at him, but I pulled him back. This was getting out of hand.

He jabbed a finger at the general. "You see, Powell, this is where you and I don't see eye to eye. We should be goddamn ashamed of ourselves for treating human beings worse than garbage! Making them *live* in the same goddamn hole we forced them to dig while they served our every need!"

"Jack!" I burst out. He turned a wild look on me. I knew without a doubt he was going to lose it if we didn't get back on track. "This isn't why we're here," I said in a calm voice. "There are a lot of lives at stake if we don't agree to a ceasefire."

He just stared at me and I wondered if anything I said had registered. Then he took a deep breath and let it out. He turned back to Powell. "Are you prepared to surrender?"

General Powell didn't say anything. He just reached for the scotch. Jack pulled the bottle away from him. "You've had enough pain relief. I need you to have a clear head."

Powell leaned back in his chair. "You still haven't told me why, Jack. What the hell is all this for?" He swept his arm toward the unseen guns and arrows aimed us.

Jack smiled. "Because I didn't marry Leisel. I married this lovely lady," he said, picking up my hand and kissing it. I almost laughed at the look of horror on Powell's face. Jack's smile broadened. "Now you're getting it, General! I'm not the heir—I'm a goddamn traitor."

Powell's mouth dropped open and fresh beads of sweat made his forehead slick. He ran a hand over his face and sucked in a breath. "Jesus."

The sound of a door creaking open drew our attention. Doc emerged from the medical center.

"Terms of surrender are simple," Jack said. "You lay down your weapons and everyone goes peacefully to the corrals."

Powell raised his eyebrows, a tight smile playing around his mouth. "The corrals? I take it they must be empty."

"Everyone's been set free. They could've run, but they decided to stay. Most of them have rifles trained on you right now."

The general's expression sobered. "So the heathens and urchins have allied?"

Jack nodded. "You're outnumbered."

Doc reached our table and stood quietly, medical bag in hand.

"And if we don't agree to your terms?"

"Then these negotiations have failed and we return to fighting. Dena, head of the so-called 'heathen' army, is prepared to send a volley of flaming arrows at the mess. I'm praying it won't come to that, General. I have friends in there."

Powell shifted uncomfortably in his chair. He hissed in pain when he moved his injured arm. He was sweating profusely now, although I wasn't sure whether it was from the pain of his wound or his situation. Maybe both.

He looked at Doc. "Can you help me out here?"

Doc looked at me. "Nice to see you again, Miss O'Donnell. I take it you were successful in that plan you were discussing with me?" I nodded. "Everyone is free?"

"Everyone out here," I said. "The Pit is next."

He pointed to Powell. "There's no one left out here *he* can hurt anymore?"

"Those still alive are safe."

He turned back toward the general. "No. I can't help you."

Powell slammed a fist down on the table. Jack kicked me under the table and covertly motioned toward Doc. I guess we needed Doc's help if we were going to be successful in getting Powell to agree to our terms.

"Although if you help the general it might show him

that it's not war we want," I said. "We're looking for a peaceful resolution."

Doc gave me a sarcastic smile. "You mean a show of good faith? Take the high road?" He shook his head and turned his focus on Powell. "How about this, General. You agree to their terms and I'll treat your injury. You don't, I won't."

"Of course I'm going to agree to their damn terms! I don't have any choice!" he snapped.

It was almost anticlimactic. I tried to remain calm and keep the look of shock off my face.

We'd won.

CHAPTER TWENTY-EIGHT

Getting Powell to agree to surrender turned out to be a lot easier than the actual process of surrendering. After he waved the white flag, our side advanced into the city to oversee the process. There was a lot of distrust on both sides, so most of the bourge were reluctant to part with their weapons, although some threw down their guns immediately and declared themselves to Jack as Liberty members.

I knew this was hardest on Jack. It visibly pained him to have to deny anyone claiming to be on his side, especially Alex and Hayley. But at this point, he couldn't trust anyone. He could only explain that no harm would come to them and they would be free to go once we liberated the Pit.

Powell was among the last to leave. Doc worked on his arm, right there in the middle of the street, while his army was stripped of their weapons. There was a lot of hollering and screaming from him since Doc decided not to give him a shot of pain relief until after he removed the arrow and cleaned the wound with disinfectant. Since he was in no condition to walk, Jack put him on a bike and drove him to the corral. I promised to meet him there.

Gaia remained stoic throughout the negotiations, but after Powell was driven away, she turned on me. "What have you done!" she screamed.

"Gaia, the men on the range—" I began, but she grabbed me by the shirtfront and cut off my words.

"—are probably all dead because of *you*! Did you even stop to consider them?!"

I tried to pry her hands off me. "The tagging system is off. They're free too!" I appealed to Doc with my eyes, willing him to help me.

"But there were soldiers up there! Hunting them! You could have set them off, made them kill all the men!"

I was taken off guard by her anger. "They're free, Gaia! You can finally find out if he's—" I stopped mid-sentence because it hit me. She had spent the last two years convincing herself that he was still alive. Now the moment of truth lay before her and she was scared. What if the truth was he was dead?

Doc pulled out a syringe and gave her a shot in the arm. A few seconds later, her yelling calmed and she collapsed. I helped him get her to the medical center. I prayed she found her husband alive, but I wasn't holding out much hope.

"I'm happy to see that Jack Kenner is alive, in more ways than one," Doc said, after we settled Gaia on a bed. "Did you use my cocktail on him?"

He went to a cupboard and took out some disinfectant and sterilized pads. He motioned for me to sit down.

"I didn't really want to, but he started bleeding to death after I took the bullet out. I guess it was the nanosurgeons that saved him. Thank you for all your help."

"I'm sure it was the technology," he said confidently. He soaked a pad and dabbed at the injury on my arm. I sucked in a breath at the sting. "Perhaps you can mention to him I'd like to draw a sample of his blood."

"I don't think now is the time, Doc. He's a little busy." He finished cleaning the wound and dressed it.

"You'll live," he declared. "May I ask what your plan is?"

I stood up. "My plan?"

"Yes. Once you've liberated the Pit, what's your plan?" He put the disinfectant back in the cupboard and discarded the pads.

I searched my brain for the right answer, but I was suddenly exhausted. "I don't know, Doc. Once everyone is out of the Dome, they're free to do whatever they want."

He headed out the door and I followed him back to the waiting area.

"Well, that's not exactly true."

"What do you mean?"

"Radiation still plagues the Earth and we have no defenses against it."

"What are you talking about? The Earth is fine."

He shook his head. "It's fine for someone who was born into this environment, like your heathen friends. Over the past three hundred years their physiology has evolved to adapt to the high amount of radiation found in water and plants. We don't have their tolerance."

It's not that I didn't believe Doc, but something didn't add up. "How do you know about the physiology of the heathens?"

My question appeared to have caught him off guard. He looked contrite. "I was *forced* to perform tests on some of the subjects that were captured and brought into the Dome. It's not something I'm proud of."

"I don't get it. Then how does this city function? Why aren't you, Powell, and everyone already dead?"

"Our water is treated and our plants are grown in a special soil concentration I designed to trap radioactive isotopes. So our food and water are virtually free of radiation. Our only threat is when the seasons change, and the wind blows from the wrong direction, but each house is capable of being sealed against radiation storms. They don't usually last long."

If what Doc was saying was true, none of us could leave the Dome. We were all still tethered to our life-giving Arc.

"Jack and I drank the water from the river. And Dena's barangay shared food with us. We're not sick," I pointed out.

"It would take at least a year of drinking non-filtered water and eating off the land before there was enough radiation built up in your system to poison you. Maybe less time, if you were subjected to radiation storms. But you now have radiation in your system and it's permanent. I can run some tests on your blood and see how much, if you'd like."

I tried to ignore the sense of futility bubbling up inside me. It was bad enough that ever since the fighting had started, I was struggling with regret. Constantly questioning if all the deaths were worth it in the end. Now I had to wonder what we were even fighting for—an Earth we couldn't survive on?

"Then what's this all for, Doc? Why the hell are we killing each other over a sick planet?"

"*We* didn't start the killing, *they* did. Every time a worker didn't perform. Every time we had the gall to stand up for ourselves. Every Cull for three hundred years. Please keep that in mind when you begin your fight to free the Pit—to free the thousands of people Holt is planning on mass murdering. Because if you can keep that in mind, Miss O'Donnell, your conscience won't bother you about a few dead bourge."

Doc did have a way of getting to the point. And he was partially right. My conscience did still bother me, just not as much. I didn't like all the bloodshed, but I wasn't about to abandon the Pit. They had to be freed.

"Thanks Doc. I guess I needed to hear that." I headed toward the door, prepared to get away from him. My brain was already on overload and I couldn't process any more information.

"One more thing," Doc said. I almost moaned. "I'm going to set up a clinic to remove tags. Please send everyone here."

I nodded and left the medical center.

I always wondered what that old saying meant, *sight for sore eyes.* But as I stood here with sore, tired eyes and took in the sight of Jack, I thought I knew. His was the only face that could actually make me happy. Maybe the word *happy* was too strong. "Grateful to be alive" was more apt.

He was inside what used to be the women's corral—the big gates shut, preventing anyone from coming or going. All around the wire fence, archers and urchins with rifles stood attentively, ready for any bourge foolhardy enough to try to escape.

The smell of food drifted on the wind as people emerged from the cafeteria carrying big steaming pots. As they approached the gates, Jack went forward to give the word to open them. His eyes found me and his face broke into a smile. He looked exhausted. As soon as the gates were open, he came out and caught me in a tight embrace.

"I was beginning to wonder what happened to you," he said.

"Doc kept me talking. He's an interesting guy," I said.

Jack touched my bandage. "I see he took care of you. Good."

"You should probably go and see him too," I said, bending down to look at his leg. He tried to pull me up, seemingly uncomfortable with what I was doing.

"I'm fine," he said.

I caught a glimpse of new skin peeking out from the torn fabric on his pants. "It's gone!"

Jack pulled me back up. "Ssshhh," he said, looking around. "Maybe those stupid robots are still working. Don't tell anyone."

"Excuse me, Mr. Kenner," a voice interrupted.

A woman I didn't recognize stood holding two bowls of stew. We gratefully accepted the offered stew and found a good-sized boulder not far from the corral and to use as a seat. We ate in silence. I was hungry, exhausted, and just content to be next to Jack, touching shoulders. When we finished eating, he set aside our bowls and drew me against him.

"Maybe later we can find a quiet bed and I'll let you snuggle me while I sleep," he said.

I smiled. "That's awful nice of you."

"Well, I know how much you like to snuggle." He kissed me lightly on the lips. "Powell's still out of it from the meds Doc gave him, but once he comes around I'll try to find out how to get into the Dome. Dena said she doesn't mind keeping things together out here, but she doesn't want to send her army inside the Dome. I don't blame her. They don't know what to expect in there."

"Do you have a plan yet?"

"It's hard to come up with one when I'm exhausted and still trying to sort out all of this," he said, motioning toward the corral. "What were you and Doc talking about?"

I relayed all of Doc's messages, including the one about the world still being a radioactive mess. Jack was just as surprised by the information as I was.

"So even once the doors are open, we're all stuck here together," he said.

"Looks that way." I rested my head on his shoulder. "I guess we're all going to have to learn to get along."

"Or kill each other trying," he added. "I forgot to tell you, I overheard your mom asking if anyone had seen you lately."

My mom. Once I'd known she was safe, I hadn't thought about her much. Not because I wasn't happy to find her alive and have her back in my life, but because there was just too much going on and I knew she was strong enough to look after herself.

"I should find her and let her know I'm alright," I said.

Jack slid down off the boulder, but I was reluctant to let go of his hand. He pulled me down as well and planted another kiss on my lips. "Come on, Mrs. Kenner. You go find your mom and I'll go see if Powell is awake. Then we'll meet back here and find a quiet place to get some sleep. Deal?"

I kissed him back. "Sounds like heaven."

I walked as far as the gate with Jack and then went in search of my mom. I didn't have far to look. In fact, she was in direct view of the boulder we had just vacated. I wondered how she was taking my relationship with a bourge.

"Sunset," she said, smiling. "I was worried about you."

She folded me into her embrace and I remembered how much I missed her when she was gone.

"I'm doing okay. How are you? Did you get some food?"

"I just had something to eat. I was going to come and join you, but I saw you already had company."

There it was—my moment to talk about Jack.

"He's nice, Mom. I think you'd really like him."

"As much as I hate the bourge, he's done right by us so far."

Done right? I thought. It seemed like such a shallow remark considering all Jack had done for us. He put his own life and the lives of people he grew up with at risk in order to do *right by us.* I swallowed back a biting retort. Her remark wasn't an insult; it was just an understatement. And I was tired and irritable. "Yes he has," was all I said.

My mom was about to say something else when a frantic girl came running toward us.

"Sunny! Sunny! Please help!" she cried.

As she came closer, I recognized Abby. My relief at finding her alive turned to alarm when I realized she was hysterical. Her hands were dirty and bloody, her clothes torn and filthy.

I ran to her. "Abby, what happened?"

"There was a cave-in! I've been trying to get back home, and I can't!" she sobbed. "I need to get home, Sunny. My brother's going to be so worried."

"Her brother?" my mother repeated. "Isn't she one of us?"

I nodded. "I think she lost her family during that

battle I told you about in the Pit. She's a little…distraught about it."

"Please come and help me," Abby sobbed.

"Well, if she's from the Pit, she can't have a brother."

"Mom, that's not the point," I whispered. I don't know why I whispered. It's not like Abby couldn't hear us. She was standing right there. The conversation was getting awkward.

"What can we do to help, dear?" my mother asked.

"I told you! There's been a cave-in and I can't get back."

"How about we get your hands cleaned up, Abby," I said. I gave her a little tug in the direction of the corral, hoping she would follow me.

"No!" she screamed. "I'm not going *there*! I'm going home!"

"Hey, calm down," my mother said. "You'll be okay."

"Please help me. There's just a few rocks to move, but they're too heavy to move by myself."

Mom looked at me. "What do you think? Go help her move a few rocks?"

"Mom," I whispered again. "You know she's a little…" I left it hanging.

"Upset," she finished for me. "And maybe moving a few rocks will help calm her down. Then she'll let us clean up her hands—right, Abby?"

She nodded her head vigorously.

"Okay…" I said uncertainly. "I should let Jack know I'm going."

"Is he your keeper now?" my mother asked sharply.

"No. He's my—" I almost said husband, but realized that might upset her more. "Partner. We keep tabs on each other."

My mother shouted to a woman not too far from us. "Hey Reesa, can you get a message to Jack Kenner?"

Reesa nodded.

"Tell him Sunny O'Donnell has gone to move a couple of rocks. She'll be back in fifteen minutes."

Mom glared at me when she said it. I realized maybe I was being a little ridiculous. We really weren't going that far or for that long.

"Come on," I said.

Abby led us away from the corrals, in the direction of the mountain that housed the Dome. We walked a lot farther than I had anticipated and I was about to suggest we turn back when she pointed toward a small opening in an outcrop. We had to get on our hands and knees to crawl down through the opening, and then navigate a steep incline to the floor of the cavern.

"Okay Abby, far enough. Where are those rocks you want us to move?" I asked.

"Back here. Not much farther," she said, and took off quickly. We walked at least another ten minutes, in a straight line, and came to a dead end.

"This is as far as we can go," I said. I just wanted to get this over with, take her back, clean up her hands, and find that quiet spot to sleep with Jack.

"This is it. These are the rocks." She pointed to two

rocks almost the size of boulders, with smaller rocks on top of them.

My mom rubbed her hands together. "Let's get to work."

I rolled my eyes, exhausted, but I put my back into it. The rock budged. All three of us pushed at the same time and it rolled. The smaller rocks on top clattered to the cavern floor.

"That's one rock," my mom said.

We attacked the next one. It was wedged in a little tighter, but we worked it loose. More rocks clattered to the cavern floor.

"How's that Abby?" my mother asked, wiping sweat off her forehead.

"I don't know how to thank you!" She hugged us both.

Then she crouched down and crawled through the space.

That was unexpected.

A jolt of panic shot through me. "Abby! Get back here!" There was no answer. Oh God, what had we done? "Abby!"

"Where did she go?"

"Through that hole!" I said, stating the obvious. "Abby!" I yelled.

Her head finally poked back out. "Stop yelling," she said. "The guards will hear you."

A creepy feeling came over me, raising gooseflesh on my arms. "Did you say guards?"

"Yes. They're mostly nice now because of you and Mr. Kenner. But there are still some bad ones. You need to be quiet."

My mother looked at me wide-eyed. "Is she talking about what I think she's talking about?"

"There's only one way to find out."

I crawled through the hole, close on Abby's heels. It was a short, narrow tunnel that emptied out into a bigger area. But this place didn't look like the natural cavern we just came from. This was a manmade room, with the cloying scent of coal. It was an intimately familiar scent. It permeated every crevice in the Pit and clung to the clothes of every miner. I was pretty sure it was even in our blood.

We were home.

Chapter Twenty-Nine

My mind flashed back to when I was leading everyone through the caverns. That manmade noise we heard was the distant sound of *bong bongs*.

I didn't know my way around the mines very well. I had only ever visited a few times, back when Reyes and I first started seeing each other. They were foolhardy rendezvous made all the more exciting by being forbidden. But we were young and thought we would live forever, or at least until the ripe old age of thirty-five.

"This way," Abby said.

I hesitated, thinking that I should go and get Jack. But the tunnel we came through wasn't that stable. What if we left and it collapsed? I'd never get back in. This might be my only chance.

I heard my mother breathe in deeply. "Smells like

home." She spoke my thoughts aloud. "I hate to say it, but I missed this place."

"Me too," I echoed. Hard to believe I spent a lifetime dreaming of leaving here only to find out I was emotionally bound to it.

"I wonder what time it is here?"

"I don't know. I remember when Jack and I left we discovered the Dome was out of sync with the natural world. Maybe it's night here."

"It's not lights out yet," Abby said.

This was unfamiliar territory for me, but Abby seemed to know her way. Most of the lights were out, only the odd one illuminating the shaft. I wondered if it was an area of the mine that had been abandoned. Maybe they had stopped mining here because they had come too close to breaking through the mountain wall. That would make sense.

Abby opened a door that squeaked loudly on its hinges. We walked through into a hallway. Homes were strung along the side of the stone wall and a few people came and went from them.

"What level are we on?" I asked.

"The second level," Abby said.

"We should go home to six. There's bound to be someone we know in the common room," my mom said.

Summer might be in the sixth level common room, too. This could be my chance to save her. Catch her before she went upstairs to Holt. I could smuggle her out of the Dome.

"Okay," I said.

"But the Alliance meeting is on the fourth level," Abby said.

"We'll come back to it," I promised. As soon as I had Summer safe beside me.

The stone steps were just as I remembered them—narrow and worn smooth enough to be a little bit slippery. There was traffic on the stairs, including guards patrolling the area, but no one stopped us. Either they were Alliance guards or it was that most special hour in the Pit—evening. That was when work stopped, dinner was served and we had some time to socialize. Moving between common rooms was technically against the rules, but as long as we did it peacefully, the rule was never enforced. And now that the Alliance ruled down here, it was doubtful we would be stopped.

People were staring at us though—me in particular. I was still wearing shorts. No one in the Pit wore shorts. Jack's pistol was still in my waistband. Sunglasses were sitting on top of my head. Then I realized my hair wasn't covered. It was full-on red. No coal, no hat. I smoothed it down, gathered the ends in my hands and hoped that sufficiently hid it. *Yeah, I blend right in now.*

Two more levels to go before we hit the sixth, my old home.

Summer. God, what was I going to tell her? How many nights had we spent watching movies and fantasizing about life outside the Dome? I could hardly wait to be the one to take her by the hand and lead her out into the sun. Watch her face as she discovered that the wind made a sound when it blew through the leaves. That a babbling brook really did babble. And that the sun did rise and set, only it was more beautiful than the textbooks ever taught us. But mostly I wanted to see her face when she filled her lungs with her first deep breath of *fresh* air. The thought gave me renewed energy and I quickened my pace.

As we approached the common room, the guards came to full attention. They were watching us. The look on their faces wasn't good. I slowed down. Their eyes zeroed in on me.

One of the guards opened his mouth. *"Sunny O'Donnell?"*

Did my red hair give it away? Or did he recognize me from when I lived on six? Either way, I was hoping to deny the charge. If they were Alliance guards, they'd spread the word pretty fast that I was back in the Pit. If they weren't, they'd arrest me and take me to Holt. Neither one of those scenarios was ideal at the moment.

"Um..." I said stupidly. "Distant relative?"

"Of course it's Sunny," Abby said. She brushed past them and opened the doors to the common room.

I pushed my mom ahead of me. "Tell me if you see Summer," I said. I didn't want to go in and cause pandemonium. By now the entire Pit probably knew Jack and I had left to find out if the Earth was habitable or not. My return was bound to create excitement.

My mom didn't hesitate. She stepped into the common room with Abby and the door closed behind them, leaving me alone with the guards staring at me.

"Did you really make it outside?" asked one of them.

Wasn't that obvious? My skin was pink and I was pretty sure my freckles had multiplied. Of course my glowing skin could be mistaken as a side effect of radiation poisoning…which would scare everyone into *not* going outside. I was still debating on how to answer his question when my mom burst out of the common room, Abby right behind her.

"I didn't see her, Sunny," my mom said. "I saw that fat ol' Giza though. I swear she's bigger than when I left. She's gotta be eating her husband's rations too—he's thinner than paper."

"Did anyone recognize you?" I should've thought about that before I sent her in. People might get a little nervous when they saw Lilly O'Donnell resurrected from the dead.

"No one noticed us. Someone's singing at the front of the room and all eyes were on him. He had a good voice."

"If they're into the entertainment part of the evening, we don't have a lot of time left before lights out."

Before we turned to go back to the stairs, I put a finger to my lips and gave the guards the *ssshhh* sign. I didn't need them spreading the news just yet. I had no idea what impact my return was going to have. What was I going to say? *Hey everyone, I've been outside to the promised land*

and there are a few thorns. Oh, and by the way, the Earth's still a little toxic so don't stray too far. That probably wouldn't go over well. It might even cause a riot, considering everyone in the Pit suspected Holt planned to annihilate them. If they thought going outside wasn't an option, they might feel trapped. Maybe I could say, *the world isn't perfect, but it's still better than being killed by Holt.* That was at least more positive. It showed that outside the Dome was the better option.

Here we were. Fourth level.

The thought of Jack filled me.

I had never spent much time on the fourth level until our accidental marriage. If I turned right instead of left I would find our old apartment—the place where I started a new life. The place where we hatched the idea for a revolution. The birthplace of the Alliance. It was on this level that I met Crystal. Her beautiful song united the Pit and her horrible execution propelled them to violence—the real start of the war.

My steps drew me ever closer to the fourth floor common room. Would the Alliance still be meeting here? Two guards stood sentry on either side of the closed doors. There were a few people traversing the hall, casting odd looks our way. The guards did a double take when they looked in our direction.

Abby reached the door first and pulled it open. Voices raised in argument drifted out. There was no singing coming from this room. I recognized David

Chavez's voice. Then I heard Bron. This was an Alliance meeting in progress.

A guard stopped us. He took in my odd appearance and cast a glance at my mom. Her skin was dark from the summer sun, her hair chestnut brown, and her sunglasses rested on her head. But at least she was wearing pants. "Excuse me. Are you sure you're on the right level?"

"I'm part of the Alliance," I said.

"She's Sunset O'Donnell," Abby said from the open door. At the mention of my name, the arguing that drifted out from the common room lowered to a murmur. The guard looked at me suspiciously but stepped aside. "Come on, Sunny. Everybody's here," Abby said.

The guard backed up a step, allowing us to pass. I caught the door just before it closed and pushed it open.

All eyes turned to me.

I hesitated, my mouth suddenly dry. I still didn't know what I was going to say.

I recognized David, Bron, Raine and Micah. Reyes was there, now on his feet with a girl clinging to his hand. We all just stared at each other, none of us knowing where to begin.

Then my mom pushed me in the rest of the way.

"Mom!" I hissed.

"Well don't just stand there. Go in," she said.

I clearly heard the door close behind us because there was no other sound in the room to drown it out. I took a few steps closer to the stunned group.

"Hi," I said, giving a little wave. "I'm back."

David's chair made a loud scraping sound as he came to his feet. "Sunny!" He strode toward me. "Did you make it outside?"

Excited chatter began to fill the room.

"Has anyone seen my brother?" Abby yelled above the voices. No one paid attention to her.

"Where's Jack Kenner?" someone shouted.

I held up my hands in a plea for the crowd to calm down. Bron stood and whistled. Abby was beside me, becoming agitated.

"I'll tell you everything, just please calm down," I said in a loud voice. "Can someone help me find Abby's mom or dad?"

"Someone get Angel," Bron's voice called out. "We found his sister."

His sister? A memory niggled at the back of my mind—the story of a set of twins. In a rare act of kindness, the bourge doctors allowed them both to live since one was expected to die within weeks of birth. I couldn't remember whether the child lived or died…I had always thought the story was just an urban legend.

My mother stepped out from behind me and Bron stopped in mid-stride. "Lilly?" she asked in disbelief.

She walked up to Bron and gave her a hug. "It's good to see you again."

At the sight of her, Reyes' eyes widened and his mouth gaped open. "*Mrs. O'Donnell?* You're alive?"

"Excellent observation, Reyes," my mother quipped. "You always were quick."

My mother never did care for Reyes. *Good-looking but dumber than a replicated plank,* she used to say. I wondered if throwing insults at him just came naturally to her. How else could the snipe just roll off her tongue in the middle of all this commotion?

Reyes extricated himself from the girl clinging to him and strode toward me. My stomach tightened. This was not a conversation I wanted to have right now. He stopped a few steps away because he couldn't really get any closer. David made it to me before him, Abby was still at my side, and more people were flocking around me.

"I didn't think I'd ever see you again," Reyes said.

It was hard to tell if he was sad about that or if he'd actually never *wanted* to see me again. By the look of the girl eyeballing us, I'd say he had moved on. Good. I was happy for him.

"There were times I wasn't sure myself," I said. The anxious chatter in the room grew louder. My ears started to buzz with it. I turned my attention to David. "This is getting out of control. We're going to attract Domers."

David shook his head and cast a glance over at Reyes. "Too many Domers went missing so they don't send them anymore." Reyes smiled broadly. "They send armed soldiers for frequent, random checks instead."

"An armed militia is worse than Domers," I said.

"I won't argue there. They've been brutal. But we're

armed now and ready to start fighting back."

"Things have really progressed since I left."

David nodded. "Tensions are high between us and the Dome. Something's going to break soon, so I'm hoping you have some good news for us."

I realized that everyone had been listening to our conversation and now all eyes were on me again, waiting for my reply.

"First the bad news," I said. I figured if they had the bad news first, it would make the good news seem not as bad. "Radiation is still a problem outside." A collective groan rippled through the group. "But! The Earth is habitable."

Confusion.

"Well, is it safe outside or not?" someone asked.

"It is, but we're still dependent on the Dome for drinking water and food," I said.

Reyes narrowed his eyes and looked at me. It wasn't an unfamiliar expression. He always looked at me like that when I had done something to make him mad. "Are you telling us we're still stuck being slaves to the bourge?"

My mom came to stand beside me. "Not anymore. Sunny and Mr. Kenner allied with the heathens and took the city. The bourge no longer control the outside."

The room went from orderly to chaotic in seconds.

"There's a city outside?" someone cried.

"There are *heathens*? Where did *they* come from?!"

"That really wasn't helpful, Mom." I climbed up on a

table and tried to get everyone's attention. "Stop!" I yelled. It had no effect. "Please, everyone! Quiet down!"

David climbed up beside me and let out a loud whistle. The room turned to look at him. "Please let her finish," he told them.

I nodded my thanks. "What my mom was trying to say is that Holt is in the process of building a city, preparing to leave the Dome and…we're not invited. Crystal's song was true. He intends to shut off the ventilation system and leave us for dead." More anxious chatter and I had to raise my voice. "That can't happen now! We found a way out and we have control of the city. But we're going to have to be smart about getting out of here. Holt still controls the Dome with nuclear warheads. I have it on good authority that he'd rather blow us all up, himself included, than give up his power."

"Then let's get the hell out of here, *now*," Reyes said. Murmurs of agreement rose up.

"I agree," I said. "But we need to be organized. We're going to need some mining equipment and a crew to stabilize the tunnel. Once that's done, we can start evacuating level by level."

Reyes held up his hand. "I'll go." More men raised their hands and stepped forward.

"I'll organize a security detail to watch over the miners in case the militia shows up," Bron said.

"Are they in the habit of showing up during the night?" I asked.

"Not usually, because of the curfew," Bron said. "But it's better to be prepared."

I looked to David. "How long do you think it will take to brace the tunnel?"

"I haven't seen it yet," he said. "But if it's only a few feet deep and we have enough miners, a couple of hours."

"You mean, we can start evacuating the Pit in just a few hours?" I asked.

"It's possible."

"Where's the tunnel?" Reyes asked.

There were a lot of expectant faces waiting for me to answer. It made me nervous. This group could easily turn into a mob and start a stampede. "One of us will show the miners."

Bron gave me a curious look and I let my eyes skim the group. She looked around too, turned back to me and nodded her understanding.

"I think for now, we need to keep the tunnel a secret," Bron said in a loud voice.

"You mean I can't report back to my own level?" someone asked.

An argument broke out and I learned that there were two representatives from each level present at every Alliance meeting. It had become much better organized than when Jack and I were here. I'm not sure what I expected to find when I returned, but I was surprised by how far the revolt had progressed.

A young man entered the room and Abby ran toward

him. I figured he must be her brother, Angel. I recalled the first time I met Abby on the farm—filling her pockets with apples, telling everyone she had to go home. Why didn't I realize then? Why did I just assume she was crazy? Yet, I saw the value in finding out later rather than sooner. Until earlier today, I had no idea we were still bound to the Dome for water and food. I would've made the mistake of telling everyone to run—run away from the bourge, away from the Dome and find a new life. They would've been dead of radiation poisoning within a few years.

The arguing finally subsided and a crew was put together. Since Angel was a miner, Abby volunteered to lead them to the tunnel. Bron turned to go with the other guards, but I jumped down from the table and stopped her.

"Can I have a word?" I asked. We went to a quiet corner. "Do you know where Summer is? Is she still upstairs?"

Bron nodded. "He has her."

"Do you mind helping me find her in the morning? Once she's back here, she shouldn't go back up." Bron chewed her lower lip. It was a nervous reaction and one I didn't miss. It scared me. "What are you not telling me?"

"She doesn't come back here anymore," she said. A flash of something—guilt?—crossed her features. "She's with him all the time now. It's rumored he's sick and bedridden."

"Then how are we supposed to get to her?" I demanded. That wasn't part of the plan. She had to be evacuated with everyone else.

"I don't know, Sunny."

"We're *not* leaving her," I said. I just had to think. Think of a way to get to her.

She was on the presidential level, which was heavily guarded. But I had been to that level before, smuggled there by Jack and Leisel. How had they gotten me up there without being noticed? Then I remembered—Leisel was having an affair with the head guard and they had cleared all security from that level to let me pass. Jack had jammed the cameras. So I knew it was possible to get onto that floor…I just needed Leisel's help.

She really hated me. Wanted me dead. But she did want me. She wanted Jack too. Maybe I could use that.

"How do I get in touch with Leisel?"

Bron's mouth dropped open. "*What?* Leisel Holt?!"

My mother wandered over and stood beside us.

"Yes, Bron, Leisel Holt. I'm going to ask to meet with her."

"Are you crazy?" my mother demanded.

"Just listen to my plan. Leisel has no idea that Jack isn't inside the Dome. I'll tell her I'm insane with worry for my best friend Summer and I want her back. I'll ask for a trade—Jack's location for Summer. I'll arrange to meet her at her apartment."

Bron shook her head. "She's not going to give up Summer that easily. She'll just take you into custody and torture Jack's location out of you."

"I expect her to double-cross me," I said. "I also expect her to clear the way for me—cameras will be jammed and security will be cleared in order to let me get to her apartment undetected by her father. *Voila.* I'm on the presidential floor and can get to the president's suites."

"That's the most insane idea I've ever heard," Bron said.

"It worked to get me into her apartment on her wedding day. It could work again."

"But you still have to break into the president's suites. You'll need to get past Leisel's apartment and she'll probably have a couple of Domers in there waiting for you," Bron pointed out.

"Then hopefully I can talk you into coming with me. I could use the help."

"You're not leaving me behind," my mother said.

"Oh, good Lord, I can't believe I'm going to do this," Bron said. "But I think I can help get you into the president's suites. I owe Summer. Let's go get her back."

Chapter Thirty

Bron came up with the idea that we could dress as guards to get into the Dome. Their regular shift change happened after lights out, so we didn't have much time. A few of the guards accompanying the miners gave my mom and me their uniforms.

Bron, my mom and I were the only ones left in the common room. The crew of miners and their security escort had left twenty minutes ago. Everyone else had gone home. At least the evening curfew would prevent tongues from wagging tonight. Once the news spread, it was going to be impossible to contain everyone. I prayed it wouldn't take them long to stabilize the tunnel. They planned to start the evacuation as soon as it was possible—maybe even tonight.

The lights went out.

"That's our cue," Bron said. We left the common room

and headed for the stairs. "Almost every guard down here is Alliance now. I think you'd be surprised by the number of people who hate President Holt."

"I wonder why it took us all this long to find out we had so much in common," I said.

"Social inequality," my mother said. "We've been so focused on our differences that we didn't notice we're really all the same."

"Some of us, anyway," Bron added. She and my mom exchanged a knowing look.

"What does that mean?" I asked.

We reached the stairs and stopped.

"It means you weren't the first one to think of starting a revolt. You were just the most successful," Bron said.

"Who was the first?" I asked.

"There's been a lot of people and a lot of failed attempts," Bron said.

"And this attempt isn't over yet," my mother added.

Why did I get the feeling something was going on between these two?

Guards were coming down the stairs, some of them exiting onto the fourth floor. No one left their post until the new shift was there to replace them. Finally, it was our turn to go up. There were others on the stairs with us so I refrained from asking more questions in case we were overheard.

We left the Pit and entered the lobby area. Some

guards took off their helmets, but most left them on. That was good for us, because we *couldn't* take ours off.

There was a lineup of white uniforms at the far end of Reception. Bron headed toward it.

"We have to return our weapons before we can go through the doors," Bron whispered.

A nervous flutter started in the pit of my stomach. I still had the new chip Jack had created for me in the back of my hand. I remembered my first name was Crystal but couldn't remember my last name—although that was the least of our worries. Mom still had her old chip.

It didn't take us long to hand in our weapons, and we started toward the big steel doors that protected the Dome. One by one people scanned through and then it was our turn. Bron went first. Then me. It crossed my mind that Leisel may have tracked down the identity of my new chip. The night Jack and I escaped from her apartment, we ditched the identities we had been using and registered new ones. If Leisel were watching the registry she would easily pick up on the coincidence.

I waved my hand over the scanner. It beeped and the green light came on. I moved through the doors. My mother was right behind me. Without turning around, I heard the scanner buzz. I knew it was a red light.

"What's the problem?" my mom demanded in a gruff tone.

Bron stopped and turned back toward me. "So what are your plans tonight?" she asked conversationally. She was stalling.

I heard a man growl behind me. "I wish they'd replicate us a new scanner," he grumbled.

"Not much. How about you?" I said back to her.

She looked over my shoulder at my mom and I stole a glance too. A man was checking the scanner, punching buttons.

He gave a hearty laugh. "Says here you're Lilly O'Donnell, *deceased*."

"Get that thing fixed," my mother said and started to walk away.

"Come here. Try it one more time," he said.

My mother hesitated but only for a second. She moved her hand over the scanner again. The man looked at the scanner and scratched his head. He motioned to the next guard standing in line. "You try it."

I felt beads of sweat break out on my upper lip.

The guard stepped up. The scanner worked.

"It's not the scanner," he said to my mom. "It's your chip. I'll let you go this time, but you need to get it fixed. It's gotten crossed in the system somehow."

My mom waved her thanks and walked away. I breathed.

Bron led us down a few different hallways before she stopped at a particular room. It was a crowded stock room. A desk with a computer sitting on top was wedged into a corner. Bron sat down and typed on the keyboard.

"Somewhere in all the Alliance communications is Leisel's personal address. While I'm finding it, think of what you're going to say to her," Bron said.

"Can't she trace the message back to us here?" Mom asked.

"Yes she can. So we need to keep it short and to the point," Bron said. "Found it."

"Are we ready?" I asked. Bron nodded. I dictated as Bron typed.

Sunny: *I have information on Jack Kenner's whereabouts. I'd like to make a trade.*

We waited. It took less than a minute.

Leisel: *Who is this?*

Sunny: *Sunny O'Donnell.*

Leisel: *I thought it might be you. I was just alerted that Crystal Malloy entered the Dome.*

Malloy. Now I remembered.

Sunny: *Are you interested in a trade or not?*

Leisel: *What did you have in mind?*

Sunny: *Summer for Jack Kenner's location.*

Leisel: *Tempting. How would we go about this trade?*

Sunny: *You can meet me in the Pit.*

Leisel: *Not likely.*

Sunny: *I can't stay in the Dome long. Someone will recognize me. I need to get back to the Pit.*

Leisel: *Lucky for you Summer is here with me right now. Why don't you come and see her?*

Sunny: *I don't trust you.*

Leisel: *I don't trust you.*

Sunny: *Then I guess we're at an impasse. Too bad.*

There was a pause.

Leisel: *You're nothing Sunny. It's Jack I want. Come get your little friend.*

Sunny: *I'll be arrested as soon as I walk onto the presidential floor. No.*

Leisel: *I give you my word no one will arrest you.*

Sunny: *You've given me your word before.*

Leisel: *Summer has become a thorn in my side. I'll be happy to see her go.*

Sunny: *Still not buying it.*

Leisel: *My father is gravely ill and I'm running out of time. I need Jack Kenner. Come to my apartment in thirty minutes.*

Sunny: *Okay. But if I don't see Summer, I don't tell you where Jack is.*

Leisel: *Fair enough.*

Bron shut off the computer. "And we're out of here, now."

The three of us vacated the stockroom and joined the general traffic in the halls. Bron took us to her apartment. I was surprised to find out she had a husband. Not that I thought she shouldn't be married; it's just that I never thought of her as having a personal life. She was always in the Pit.

"Cam, we need some military uniforms," she told him.

He jumped up off the sofa at the sight of us. "Who are they?"

"Friends. You going to help us or not?"

"I can't just lend out my uniform. It's illegal."

"It's a matter of national security. Trust me."

"I only have one uniform here."

"Does your boyfriend have one?"

Boyfriend? I thought he was her husband.

"I can ask him."

"Don't tell him it's for me. Just tell him you need an extra one because…you ripped yours or something."

"What's this all about?"

"I told you—national security."

"Right."

He didn't question her any further. He left the apartment, I assumed to go find another uniform from his boyfriend. It was all a little confusing.

I took off my helmet. "That's your husband?" I asked.

"Officially, yes," Bron said. She disappeared into the bedroom.

"What's going on between you and Bron?" I asked my mother.

She took off her helmet. "What are you talking about?"

"That whole thing about I'm not the first to start a revolt."

Bron came back into the room. "We'll talk about it later," she said.

She handed my mom Cam's military uniform and told her to get changed. I was getting anxious. We were running out of time. Cam finally returned with another uniform. Bron ducked into the bedroom and changed. Cam didn't ask any questions. He just sprawled on the sofa and picked up his tablet.

Bron emerged from the other room, dressed in military gear. "If I don't come back tonight, you didn't know anything about this," she said to Cam.

He just waved a hand in the air.

There were two ways to get to the presidential floor—stairs or elevator—and we planned to use both. I was taking the stairs where Desmond and his buddies would inevitably be ready to grab me and take me to Leisel. Bron and my mom would take the elevator and use their military disguise to declare that intelligence reports indicated Sunset O'Donnell was there and they had been ordered to take me into custody.

I hated to be separated from them and go on my own, but I had done this kind of thing before. The nervousness I was experiencing now was nothing compared to what I went through pretending to be Leisel on her wedding day. Still, my steps became a little slower and my legs a little wobblier as I approached the tenth floor.

As I suspected, Domers were waiting for me. Desmond whipped off my helmet. "Sunny O'Donnell," he sneered.

"I *knew* I couldn't trust her!" I ground out between clenched teeth.

He grinned. "Oh, she's still interested in your trade."

He grabbed me roughly by my upper arm. I put up

a fight. A Domer grabbed my other arm while a third Domer opened the door. They dragged me through while I kicked and tried to twist out of their grasp.

Leisel was in the hallway, nervously watching the door to her father's suites. "Hurry up!"

They dragged me down the hallway and I continued to struggle. I waited to hear the ding of the elevator.

We got closer to Leisel's apartment.

Now I really started to struggle. If they were successful in getting me into her apartment, there was no guarantee I was coming back out. My plan was about to fail. I tried to kick at Desmond, but I wasn't far enough away from him to gain any momentum. I bowed my head and bit his hand as hard as I could. He let go.

"You little bi—"

As soon as my arm was free, I punched the other Domer. He was ready for me and grabbed me by both my arms.

I heard the ding of the elevator.

Stiffening my legs, I dug both feet into the plush carpet in an attempt to hold my ground. He tried to twist my arm behind me.

"What's going on here?" Bron sounded brisk and official. "Where's the president's security team?"

Desmond came to attention. Leisel swore. The Domer holding me let go.

"We intercepted a message indicating Sunset

O'Donnell is on this floor," Bron said. She drew her gun and looked directly at me. "We have instructions to take her to President Holt."

"On whose authority?" Leisel demanded.

"With all due respect, ma'am, she's a wanted criminal," Bron said. She stepped forward, grabbed my arm, and yanked me out of the grasp of the Domer. She marched me in the direction of Holt's suites, my mother right behind us.

"What the hell are you doing?" Leisel called after us.

"Our duty, ma'am," Bron answered.

We were almost to the door. All we had to do was get in.

"Wait a minute," Leisel said. "You're not officers. You're not allowed on this floor."

Bron quickened her pace, reached the door and banged on it.

I looked back. Desmond and the other two Domers reached for their weapons.

The door opened and one of the president's security officers stood there.

"I've been instructed to deliver Sunset O'Donnell to the president," Bron said, giving me a shove.

"What the—" he said, looking at us. "Is that really Sunny O'Donnell?"

"You can verify it," Bron said.

He pulled a tablet out from his pocket, manipulated the screen, looked at me, and looked back at the screen.

"Holy...! Bring her in." He looked past us to the armed Domers in the hallway. "Thanks for your assistance."

I knew it wasn't yet time to celebrate, but our plan was going so well. If there was one thing Jack taught me about outsmarting the bourge, it was that the bourge weren't very smart. They were creatures of habit. And right now that was working in our favor.

"Wait!" Leisel called out. I heard her walk down the hall and slip inside the door behind us. *Great.* "Daddy will need me."

We stood in an antechamber with still another door to get through before we were in Holt's suites. They scanned me for weapons. I didn't have any. Mom and Bron weren't scanned. They obviously carried a sidearm and, as Dome soldiers, had every right to carry one. When the scan was finished, the locks on the outer door were secured.

We were led through the second door and ushered to a sofa in what looked to be a receiving area. I was made to sit on the sofa, with Bron and my mother flanking me and two burly security men, arms folded in front of them, staring at me. Leisel occupied a big, overstuffed chair, with one leg crossed over the other. The only indication of her impatience was the rapid swing of her leg.

It seemed like an eternity, but finally a door opened and the president emerged. He was in a wheelchair. He looked gaunt. Sickly.

Summer pushed the chair.

It was all I could do not to run to her. How long had it been? I wished I could say she looked good, but she was thinner than the last time I'd seen her. And Summer had always been too skinny.

Her big round eyes turned the size of saucers when they fell on me. I was dying to assure her that this wasn't what it looked like—that I was here to rescue her. But I couldn't take the chance of giving myself away to anyone else in the room.

"Daddy!" Leisel exclaimed, jumping up to kiss her father. He patted her kindly on the shoulder. "I have the best news for you! I caught Sunny O'Donnell." She stood up straight and proudly presented me to him.

President Holt looked in my direction with tired, uninterested eyes. I had only ever seen the president up close once, at my infamous wedding. We posed together for pictures and even though it only took a few minutes, I remembered how intimidated I was by his powerful presence. This sickly creature sitting in a wheelchair didn't look anything like that Holt.

"Indeed?" he asked in a hoarse voice. He looked at my mom and Bron. "Well, what are you waiting for? Execute her."

My heart leaped into my throat. That was it? No negotiations about Jack's whereabouts? No trying to get information out of me? I could tell her father's response took Leisel by surprise too because the smug expression she had been wearing transformed into one of shocked disbelief.

"What about Jack Kenner?" I blurted.

"What about him?" Holt asked.

"Don't you want to know where he is?"

He sighed heavily. "Yes. Are you going to tell me?"

That was direct. I expected more of an interrogation process. "Maybe."

He tilted his head to one side and gave me a weary look. "There's no maybe. Either you're going to tell me or you're not. In the meantime, he's serving a greater purpose."

I opened my mouth to argue and then closed it. That was a point of view I hadn't considered. As far as Holt knew, Jack was doing his part to provoke the Pit into war. Holt's purposes were better served by keeping him alive. I had no leverage with this man, nothing to bargain with.

We were in trouble.

Holt waited a moment for my answer. None came. "Kill her," he said.

My mother stepped forward, took off her helmet, and glared at him. "Kill her and I'll tell Leisel everything."

The president's men drew their guns. Bron did too. I didn't know what game my mother thought she was playing, but she was going to get herself killed. No one suspected she was anything but a soldier, here to escort a criminal. There was no need to blow that cover. She could still get out of here alive.

"What's it going to be, *Mr.* President?" my mother asked.

He narrowed his eyes at her. *"You!"* he sneered.

"Leisel, I can tell you the real history of your birth," my mother said, her eyes never leaving Holt.

Leisel looked from my mother to her father. Holt's sickly lips were drawn into a tight line. "You wouldn't dare," he said.

My mother glared back at him. "I wasn't quite fourteen when I was sent up to the Dome the first time, and the president hand-picked me for himself." My mother now had my full attention. I had already suspected that she had been a mistress, but she belonged to *President Holt*? "That's when I met your father, Sunny," she said with deliberate intent.

"You shut your mouth," Holt said in a threatening tone.

"Because it isn't just the men who are looking for *companionship*," she scoffed. "The women in the Dome are every bit as bad."

Holt looked at his security team. "Take this urchin out of here. Kill her."

"I want to hear what she has to say," Leisel said.

"Leisel, my darling, she's deranged."

"I'm deranged?" my mother echoed. "I was the one who watched *you* go insane when your wife—"

"—you shut your goddamn mouth!"

"—gave birth—"

"—I'm warning you for the last time!"

"—to an *urchin*!" she yelled.

All eyes in the room went to my mother.

CHAPTER THIRTY-ONE

"*Kill her,*" President Holt shrieked.

Everything happened so fast. Out of the corner of my eye I saw Bron shoot one of the president's men. My mother had a gun in her hand. She pulled the trigger. Twice. Summer dove out of the way. Gunfire came from my left, where the security team was standing. My mother was falling to the floor. And I still wasn't on my feet.

The one security man still standing was moving toward my mother, gun pointed. I threw myself on top of her. He stood over us, pistol ready.

"We don't have to do this," Bron said. She had a gun pointed at him.

Leisel was crouched in a corner, a hand over her mouth.

"She killed the president!" he said.

"And there doesn't need to be any more killing,"

Bron said.

"That's right, there won't be," he said in a threatening tone. "There'll be a small army outside that door in about one minute."

"What are you talking about?"

"An alarm was triggered on the first shot. Every guard on this floor is on his way here."

Wide-eyed with terror, Leisel frantically shook her head. "I sent them all away! Oh God, what have I done?"

"Then we have a few minutes to get out of here before the militia shows up," Bron said.

He kept his gun pointed at me. "Nobody is going anywhere."

My mother moaned underneath me.

Bron cocked her head to one side. "How much trouble do you think you're going to be in for failing to protect the president?" She shifted her gun and trained it on Leisel. "How much more for not protecting his daughter?"

"What are you doing?" Leisel screamed. She looked at the security guard. "Kill her! Kill all of them!"

"Wait!" I held up my hand as if that would stop him from carrying out Leisel's plea. I looked at Bron. "Maybe we should tell him the truth."

"Tell me the truth about what?" he demanded.

I saw the look of indecision on Bron's face. We didn't have much time left before armed soldiers would fill the hallway—certainly not enough time to escape, especially with my mother injured. If we were going to get out of here, we'd need this security guard on our side.

Another thought also struck me. If we were able to keep the militia focused on us tonight, they would leave the Pit alone. No random searches.

"That President Holt's been lying to everyone," I said.

He gave me an *oh come on* look. "You'll have to do better than that."

I picked up my mother's right hand. "Scan her chip. Her name is Lilly O'Donnell, she's thirty-five years old and she was Culled last spring."

"What's that supposed to prove?" he asked.

"That no one was killed in the Cull. They're being used as slaves to build Holt's city outside the Dome."

The room was silent.

"You're lying," Leisel said. "Daddy would've told me about a city."

"Oh, I think your daddy keeps lots of secrets from you, Leisel," I said. She had no idea he was the one who'd manipulated her into getting engaged to Jack. She had no idea she was just another pawn in his political games. "How is your plan to become the next president working out for you?" I asked. "I mean, weren't you a little surprised when your father didn't care if I knew where Jack was?" A look of doubt crossed her face. "He wants Jack loose in the Pit so he can lead the revolution against the bourge, giving your father the reason he needs to shut off our ventilation system."

"That doesn't make sense," the security guard said.

"We need the Pit."

"You only need the Pit for as long as you live in the Dome," I said.

"The president wouldn't kill everyone in the Pit. That's insane," he said.

"He wants to repopulate the earth with his master race," I said, looking at Leisel. "With a blonde-haired, blue-eyed race to be exact."

Leisel sneered at me. "Is that some vicious rumor the Kenners are starting?"

"No. I heard it from *General Powell*. He's overseeing the construction of the city." I felt a small, victorious sense of satisfaction when I saw her eyes widen. She started a retort, but there was a scuffling noise in the hallway outside. The militia was here. We were running out of time.

"I know where to find the proof about the master race," Summer said. She was behind me somewhere. I hadn't even looked at her, unable to take my eyes off the guard holding a gun at me. "I saw him write something about it in his journal one night."

Holt's computer! Why hadn't I thought of it before? If Jack was right, communications with the city outside were hardwired into that computer.

I looked at the man holding the gun on me. "She can prove Holt's plan, and I might be able to prove the existence of the city. Just take us to Holt's computer."

Sound from his communicator filled the silence

following my request.

"That's them," he said. "They'll want to know what's going on in here. If I don't answer them, they'll bust their way in."

"Then you better answer them," Bron said, cocking her gun at Leisel. "And be ready to explain why the entire presidential family is dead and you're still alive."

His eyes shifted to Bron then quickly back at me. Sweat had broken out on his upper lip and he wiped it away with the back of his free hand.

"Wouldn't you rather live to see the sun?" I asked.

"I swear if you're lying to me, I'll put a bullet in both your heads." In one move, he unclipped his communicator and held it to his mouth. "Evans," he said into it.

"What is the situation in there?" asked a disembodied voice.

"I have it under control," he said.

Silence. The voice came back on. "Several gunshots were registered and I have an eyewitness who says Sunny O'Donnell is in there."

A look of panic came over Evans's face.

"Tell them President Holt and Leisel are alive and we're holding them hostage. We won't hesitate to kill them. They have to back off until we're ready to negotiate," Bron said.

He repeated it into the communicator.

"How many are wounded?" the voice asked.

"Just one security guard," he said.

"What do they want?"

He looked at Bron. She shrugged.

"Clemency," I said. "Tell them I came here looking for all charges to be dropped against Jack Kenner."

Evans repeated it. They finally granted us an hour, although I wasn't sure they'd stick to it. The only thing deterring them from breaking down the door was the threat of the president being killed.

"Summer, can you turn on the television?" Bron asked.

I looked at Summer for the first time since the shooting started. I remembered seeing her dive to the floor when the gunshots rang out, but now she stood at the far side of the room, well away from Holt's lifeless body. She looked a little rattled, but she did as Bron asked.

"What channel?" Bron asked Evans.

"Twenty-three."

Summer set the monitor to that channel and we were given a view of the hallway outside. There were six armed soldiers, Desmond and the two Domers.

"That's just the frontline. There'll be more in the stairwell and out by the elevator," Evans said.

Leisel stood up from her crouched position in the corner. She glared at Evans. "You're not actually going along with this?"

He ignored her.

"Can you help me get Mom on the sofa?" I asked Summer.

"We should check and see how badly she's bleeding first," Summer said.

Summer was right, of course. It was basic first aid in the Pit. You never moved a victim after a beating because you never knew if something was broken. Gently, I rolled her onto her back. There wasn't a lot of blood. Her eyelids fluttered for a moment before she opened them.

"Sunny?" she asked.

Leisel stepped out of her corner. "*Do* something!" she screamed at Evans.

"It's okay, Mom. You're not bleeding a lot. Try not to move," I said. Instead of relocating her to the sofa, Summer took a cushion from the chair and put it under her head. "We need to go into the computer room, but I'll keep a close eye on you."

"We should tie Leisel up," Bron suggested.

"*What?* You don't touch me!"

Bron looked at Evans. "If I have to shoot her, I will. She's safer tied up."

Evans waved his gun at Summer. "Tie her up."

Summer left the room, and we all waited in silence. It gave me an opportunity to check my mother's bullet wound. It looked to be lodged in her shoulder. I recalled how much Jack bled when I took the bullet out of his wound. It was better off staying in her shoulder for now.

"Sunny," Mom whispered. She motioned for me to come closer. "Don't kill Leisel."

"I'm hoping we won't have to," I said.

Mom grabbed my hand. "There are things you don't know," she whispered. It was a complete understatement, after her brief exchange with Holt before she shot him dead.

Summer returned with a bunch of neckties.

"Don't you dare come near me with those!" Leisel said.

"She might be your sister," my mother said. "And if she is and you kill her, you'll feel bad about it later. I know you."

It took a few moments to realize I had stopped breathing.

"Did you hit your head when you fell on the floor?" I whispered. "Because I thought you just said Leisel might be my sister."

I heard them struggling behind me to tie Leisel up.

"I thought about telling you before I left for the Cull. I hated leaving you with your father the way he was, because I *knew* you were going to stay with him and not marry Reyes. Even though I never cared for Reyes, he was still the better option for you over your father."

"What do you mean 'might'? Wouldn't you remember giving birth to two babies?"

"Not me, Sunny—your father. He was only thirteen when Amelia Holt took him as her lover. But your father is a romantic and he fancied she was actually in love with him. He fell hard for her, stupid fool," she said, shaking her head. "It was during the time she was using him that she became pregnant. Holt knew she had a lover and didn't really care. They married each other only because they were both from the right breeding stock. So when Leisel was born with eyes as black as an urchin, he went insane. It was a bad night. I thought he was going to thrash your father to death."

"Leisel's eyes aren't black," I said.

"She wears contacts to make them blue."

I looked over at Leisel, now almost secured to a chair. She was fighting so hard it took all three of them to get her tied up. I didn't see a family resemblance. But we were the same height. And I was able to convince the entire Dome I was Leisel at the wedding.

Oh my God. She was *my sister*?

"Was Dad her only lover from the Pit? Maybe she had more," I said hopefully.

"I don't know for sure. I know Holt took out his anger on your father. You don't need to know the details, but there's a reason why your father suffered from depression. Holt turned on me, too. I'm surprised your dad and I both lived through it. We stayed together after that."

Leisel was tied up now and Summer was suggesting they tape her mouth shut.

"Maybe she's not my sister," I said.

My mom gave me that smile. The indulgent whatever-you-want-to-think-Sunny smile that meant she didn't want to have an argument with me. "Maybe not."

Whether or not the spoiled brat yelling profanities at us was my sister couldn't be my main concern right at this moment. We had an army in the hallway waiting for us.

"Are you okay here on the floor for now?" I asked.

"I'm fine," my mother said.

"Okay." I stood and looked at the others. Leisel was secured to the chair with grey-and-black patterned neckties, another tied around her mouth, gagging her. "We should bring her into the computer room with us. I don't want her out here with my mom."

Evans shot me an exasperated look, but he and Bron picked up Leisel's chair and carried her into the room.

Bron didn't waste any time. She sat down at Holt's computer.

"We should try to connect with the city first. Jack thinks it's hardwired to this computer," I said.

"I have no idea where to start looking for it," Bron said.

"Try Powell, or General Powell, or city, or…"

"Those sound like files, not channels. It wouldn't be named like that. It would have an address—wait a minute!" Bron peered at the screen. She ran her finger down a list. She clicked on one item. Nothing. She tried another. Her fourth try, something happened. "I think it's trying to connect to something."

We waited. Nothing. She tried again. Waited. It connected.

General Powell's face came into view. He was sitting up in bed, his hair smoothed down, and dark circles under his eyes. "Mr. President," he said.

"You did it," I said to Bron.

"Is that General Powell?" Evans asked. "I thought he was in quarantine."

I peered into the computer screen. "General Powell. You're looking better," I said.

"What the—" he started. "How the hell did you get

in there?"

A hand holding a gun flashed into view for just a second and then a familiar face peered into the screen. "Is that *Sunny*? Is she in the Dome?"

"It's me, Terran, and yes I'm in the Dome."

"Good Lord, we thought it was Holt calling. The last thing we need right now is for the president to suspect something's up and send out reinforcements."

"I don't think the president will be bothering you…I do need to speak to Jack though. It's urgent."

"Jack?" he repeated, a little discombobulated. "Mr. Kenner? He's um…" He moved out of the view. "Somebody get Jack Kenner!"

By the look of the background, Powell was in a bed in the urchin corral.

"How did you get into the Dome?" the general asked.

"A little girl led me here," I said honestly. "Where's Jack?"

"Putting a search party together for you, last time I heard."

"We're a bit pressed for time. I'd appreciate it if you could let everyone know it's urgent that we find him."

"What the hell is going on?"

"I'll wait to tell that to Jack."

An awkward silence followed. He peered into the screen and we peered back. I noticed the background scenery had piqued the interest of Summer, Bron and Evans. Late afternoon sun poured in from an open door, casting a type of shadow never seen inside the Dome.

There was a commotion on his end—a blurred screen—then Jack's face came into view.

He peered into the screen. "Sunny?" he said in a tight voice.

Bron moved aside and I sat in the chair. "It's me."

He covered his eyes with his hand for a moment before he pulled it through his hair—a clear indication he was frustrated. "I thought we had a date."

It was a statement. In fact, it almost sounded like an accusation.

"We did. I mean we do. I mean—" I rubbed my eyes.

"I went to look for you, and I couldn't find you. Someone I've never met before told me you left a message—you were going to move a couple of rocks. Rocks, Sunny. That's all I had to go on."

"I thought that's all it was going to be, Jack, but it turned out to be a way back into the Pit. I had no idea."

"Why didn't you come back and get me?"

"I wasn't sure the tunnel we came through would hold. It was my chance."

He nodded. "And I'm going to assume you're in Holt's office?"

"We are," I confirmed. I cleared my throat. "Summer's been stuck here. He hasn't let her go."

"I see."

"And President Holt is dead."

He opened his mouth slightly and then closed it.

"Are you sure?"

I nodded. "Very."

A variety of different expressions flitted across his face, finally ending with a triumphant grin. "We won. If the codes to the warheads died with him, we won."

I was glad Jack was happy. However, I had an army outside the door waiting to kill all of us.

"Jack, I have someone here with me. His name is Evans. I was wondering if you could show him a bit of the outside."

Jack's expression sobered. "Why?"

"We could just use him on our side right now, that's all."

Evans moved to peer over my shoulder, intent on the screen. Jack squinted back.

"No problem," Jack said. He started walking. "So Evans, are you one of the president's men?"

"Yes I am."

"Are you the only security guard in there with Sunny?" he asked.

He left the building and walked into the sunlight. I noted the surprise on their faces as they drew closer to the monitor. This wasn't a movie. This was Jack Kenner, live from outside the Dome. He held up the tablet and gave a panoramic view of the area. Mostly, it was the corral in the foreground, but in the distance I could see the wire fence and some of the people beyond it—including Dena's warriors. The mountains, blue sky and white fluffy clouds completed the picture.

"Yes I am," said Evans absentmindedly, mesmerized

by the images he was seeing.

Jack's face came back into view. "And what's the situation in there?"

Evans licked his dry lips, staring into the computer screen. "Armed forces are outside the door. They don't know the president is dead. We've told them Sunny O'Donnell is holding him captive in an attempt to extort clemency for you. They're waiting to negotiate."

"Good," Jack said. "Because I'm coming in there. And if Sunny so much as breaks a fingernail, I'm holding you responsible, Evans. Do I make myself clear?"

Evans straightened. "Yes, sir."

"Where's the entrance, Sunny." It wasn't really a question. More like an urgent demand.

As he walked, the background scenery continually changed. My companions were riveted to the screen. Summer put her hand on my shoulder and squeezed.

"North, behind the corrals. We walked toward to the Dome for about…twenty minutes? There's an outcrop with an entrance into the caverns. The tunnel to the Pit is at the back. There's a mining crew working on the tunnel, so you might be able to hear them. They're going to start evacuating the Pit as soon as it's stable."

He gave me a nod of approval, which would have seemed impersonal except for the fond grin. "Are you all armed?"

"Bron and Evans are," I said.

The sound of a jeep coming closer drifted through the computer. "If the army tries to bust their way in, don't hesitate to start shooting. Threaten to kill both Damien and Leisel. Make them believe it. Don't take any crap from them, Sunny."

"Jack, can't we do this without shooting? I mean, look how Evans and Bron are reacting to seeing this. Everyone in the Dome wants to get outside just as much as the Pit. Can't we put this on television?"

He stopped walking and stared into the screen. People ran around behind him, there were shouts. A jeep drove by. But Jack was still.

"Did I ever tell you you're a genius?" he asked.

I smiled. "Once or twice."

"Bron, can you link me into the mainframe? It's time to get in touch with my family."

I started to rise out of the chair to give the computer back to Bron. "I'm going to go check on my mom."

"What's wrong with your mom?" he asked.

"She was shot. I think she's okay, but she needs a doctor soon."

"Hang tight. I'll be there as soon as I can." I stood the rest of the way. "Sunny?" he called me back. "We're still partners, right?"

Maybe I should have been surprised by that question, but I wasn't. Even though I knew it might be my only chance to get into the Dome, I felt the weight of guilt the moment I decided to come in here without even telling him. As though I was breaking an unspoken rule between us.

"Always," I said.

Chapter Thirty-Two

My mom had managed to get herself up onto the sofa by the time I returned to the reception room. She was in a lot of pain but seemed to be holding up.

"We might want to get rid of them before they start to smell," she said, pointing at Holt and the dead security guard.

Summer, Bron and Evans were still in the computer room, so I did it myself. Holt was easy to move since he was in a wheelchair. I saw the look of horror in Leisel's eyes as I wheeled him past the open office door. A pang of sympathy hit me. She was strapped to a chair, a necktie gagging her, and her father was killed in front of her. I shouldn't feel sorry for her—she wasn't the type to show mercy to a fellow human being. The problem was, I wasn't like her.

The security guard was more of a challenge. He was a heavy, dead weight and the thick carpet only added to the drag. With great difficulty, I managed to get him into the same room where I stashed Holt and closed the door on both corpses. I didn't mind doing the cleanup. It kept me busy.

I found a blanket for my mom and made sure she was comfortable before I returned to Holt's office. Summer was leaning over Bron's shoulder, directing her to different areas on screen, and Evans watched with interest.

"How's your mom?" Summer asked.

"She needs a doctor, but she's doing pretty well right now. Is Jack still on?"

Bron shook her head. "We lost reception with him so he's probably out of range. Before we were cut off, I was pretty sure I recognized the guard who gave you his uniform."

"Did you see anyone else familiar?" I asked. "Maybe they've started the evacuation."

She shook her head.

I wondered if the guard gave up his uniform with the full intention of never needing it again—went to the tunnel, said goodbye, and left. How many more would be just like him?

"Our hour is almost up," Evans said. "We're going to have to contact them soon. What do you want to say?"

"How about we demand retribution?" Summer jeered. "Payment for a lifetime of abuse!"

Bron was caught up with whatever she was doing on the computer, but Evans and I turned a startled look on her.

"We're trying to stall them, not provoke them," I said.

Summer pointed to something on the monitor. "There and there."

Bron peered at the screen. "Unbelievable."

"What is it?" I asked.

"Holt's formula for a master race. He made it mandatory for every baby born in the Dome to be genetically tested." Her eyes searched the monitor, bringing up different files. "And it doesn't stop there. He has a list called 'Deviants,' which appears to be people with undesirable traits…like homosexuality." She typed something on the keyboard. "Look at that—I made his list. So did Cam. How did he know? I thought we kept it secret." I walked around the desk to have a look at the list. It was long.

"So it wasn't just everyone in the Pit he was going to kill."

"He was planning to get rid of anyone that didn't fit in," Bron said. Her face was red with anger, her eyes alert and focused on the screen.

Evans' communicator came to life. "What are you going to tell them?"

I thought about it. "Tell them the truth—we're waiting for Jack Kenner. The president has granted clemency and Jack is coming to claim it." Evans raised the communicator to his mouth. "Oh, one more thing. They should clear the way for him or Holt will die."

"Don't you think you're pushing it a little bit?" asked Evans.

"I don't want them to think we're wimpy. We need to let them know we mean business."

Summer straightened. "Anyone want a drink?" she asked.

I followed her out into the other room. She went over to a hutch and opened it to expose a small bar. She poured herself a big glass of something and took a gulp. When did she start drinking?

"Is there any food?" I asked.

She motioned toward a door. "In the kitchen."

"Do you want to help me?"

"Sure."

She topped up her drink and led me through a door into Holt's private rooms. I had never felt uncomfortable with Summer before, but there was an obvious tension between us. Maybe she was angry with me for not paying enough attention to her. But in my own defense, we had a lot going on.

Holt's living quarters were a lot bigger than even Leisel's apartment and much plusher. He even had his own kitchen. Summer opened up the fridge door for me and then hoisted herself up onto the counter.

"Aren't you having anything?" I asked.

She raised her glass. "I'm good."

Was that why she was so thin? She had traded food for alcohol? This went beyond being mad at me; she was different.

"I can make you some eggs," I said optimistically. "I know how."

She ignored the offer. "So, that's really something about his city. I didn't see that one coming."

I closed the fridge door, turning my full attention on her. "It's better than we ever dreamed about, Summer. The way the wind feels blowing across your skin. And the sun's so warm! Hot, really. I can't wait to take you outside!"

Summer smiled at me. Not her usual silver-lining grin that I was accustomed to. This one had a hint of something foreign in it. "And will Jack Kenner be joining us?"

The way she said it was like a slap in the face. Not that I had planned to bring Jack with us. I had envisioned taking Summer by the hand, telling her to close her eyes, lead her outside, and then tell her to open them. I wanted to see the look on her face as we realized our lifelong dream together.

But I didn't like her tone when she spoke about Jack.

I shook my head. "It's our special time, Summer. Just you and me."

"It's a special time for the entire Pit, Sunny. We're finally free!" she said, her words slurred ever so slightly. She looked around the kitchen. "As long as we can get out of here in one piece, that is."

"I just meant you and I have dreamed about this since we were kids. Don't you remember that movie we watched all the time—the one with the girl running around the mountains with the guy and the goats?"

"Heidi?"

"Yeah! That one. That's when we started fantasizing about life outside the Pit. Making up stories about what life would be like and acting them out. Don't you remember?"

"I remember. I also remember there were no bourge in our made-up world." The words weren't spoken as a reminder; they were meant to be a challenge. "Last time we saw each other, you said that you and Jack weren't together *like that*."

So that's what was making her angry. She searched my face for an answer. I wasn't sure how to respond. I didn't want to lie to her, but I didn't want to upset her any more either.

"I *knew* it!" she burst out. My silence must have confirmed it. "The way he practically pounded his chest and threatened Evans if anyone hurt you. And you were all *always Jack*." Her expression was sour as she tried to mimic me. "Ach!"

"Once you get to know him, I know you'll like him."

She leaned forward and stared directly into my eyes. "He's a *bourge*! I'll never like him. I can't even imagine how you let him touch you."

I wasn't shocked by the fact that she hated the bourge. It was the depth of her hatred that surprised me. She was so passionate about it and I just wanted to shrink away.

"I don't want to talk about my personal life right now," I said.

"Good. Because the thought alone makes me want

to heave." She jumped down from the counter. "You getting something to eat or not?"

Turning away from her, I rummaged through the fridge and found some vegetables and thinly sliced meat. I filled a couple of plates. Mom was still awake on the sofa and I offered the plate to her.

"I'm not sure I can eat," she said. That worried me.

Evans came into the room.

"What's Bron doing in there?" I asked him.

"She put together a message exposing Holt and now she's sending it to everyone she knows. She promised I could go next," he said. He sat down in a chair. "It's incredible. The whole thing. He's been lying to everyone."

He looked like he was in shock. I offered him some food, which he declined. Instead he got up and went to the bar. Summer sneered at him and moved next to me.

"Your turn, Evans," Bron announced as she came into the room. He practically ran. "It's going through the system like wildfire. Before I even finished sending out all the messages, I was getting responses back. I sent the original files straight off Holt's computer."

I examined Mom's wound. It was starting to look red and swollen. She needed treatment. "Summer, are any drugs or meds kept here?"

I looked up just in time to see Summer turn an alarmed face toward Bron. Bron shook her head in response.

"What do you mean?" Summer asked me.

Something was going on. "I mean a topical antibiotic or

some pain relief for my mom. What did you think I meant?"

Her face went blank. "That's what I thought you meant. I'll go see."

I watched her leave, wondering what secret she and Bron could possibly have. I decided not to pursue it. We had enough to deal with.

Mom's hair was plastered to her forehead and Bron got her a cool, wet cloth. I was hoping infection hadn't set in yet. Summer came back with a tube of topical antibiotic and bandages.

"Sorry, Mom, but this might hurt."

She nodded and gritted her teeth while I treated and dressed her wound.

I went into the kitchen in search of a glass of water for her. That's when I spied the coffeemaker. We were in for a long night, so it couldn't hurt.

Summer declined coffee, preferring the drink she already held in her hand. I helped my mom drink the water and then took the tray of coffee into the office to offer some to Bron and Evans. I looked at Leisel on my way by, her eyes spitting venom at me. Her hatred helped ease my conscience on leaving her in such an uncomfortable state.

Evans was sitting at the computer, Bron peering over his shoulder.

"How long have we been here?" I asked.

"It's been almost four hours," Evans said.

"Should we make contact again?"

"Already did about half an hour ago," Evans said. "I told them we were still waiting on Jack Kenner."

"What are you doing now?" I asked.

"Going through Holt's computer. He has links to every system in the Dome, including the genetics department," Bron said. She raised her eyes to look at me. "He killed babies. Any child born with what Holt considered an abnormality was euthanized. *Euthanized!* But officially, it's recorded as a stillbirth."

Bron shook her head in disbelief, her expression outraged. I wasn't shocked by the news. The Holt regime had been killing us for years. It wasn't so unbelievable that he would kill his own people, too. What was truly unbelievable was that he had convinced so many others to do the killing for him.

I thought of Abby and realized just what a true miracle she was. Not only was she of urchin stock, but she would also fall into the category of "abnormal." Was she alive because the doctor on duty the day she was born couldn't stomach any more killing? What a twist of fate for her to be the one to escape death and grow up to point the way out of the Pit.

"Something's happening!" Evans burst out.

He ran into the room with Bron close on his heels. He picked up the remote and changed the channel on the television.

Blurred images came to life on the screen. A horde of terrified, screaming people dropping dead as automatic weapons sprayed bullets at them. Some diving behind vehicles parked on the tarmac, but most forging head-on into the bullets. This was the video Jack told me about on our wedding day. Tears had run down his face when he tried to describe it. And now I understood why. Words couldn't describe this. It defied logic. It was incomprehensible. What would make mothers carrying babies run *toward* the men shooting at them? And how could they shoot?

"What is that?" Evans asked.

I swallowed down the nausea rising in my throat. "It's our initiation into the Pit. The day we entered the Dome."

Evans's eyes widened in horror. "This is *real*?"

"Is this playing all over the Dome?" I asked. Evans nodded. "It's really late though. Probably not many people are seeing it."

"They're seeing it," Evans said. "And news this big is going to spread fast."

As we watched, the gunfire ceased. People came out of hiding and ran toward the hangar doors. There was a sea of people surging toward a hangar already full with helicopters, jeeps and other vehicles. A man entered the hangar, shouting commands. The camera zoomed in on him.

"Everyone in the Dome is going to recognize that face," Bron said.

"Who is it?" I asked.

"Edward Holt," Evans said. "The Dome's first president. His picture is everywhere."

"It's not in the Pit," I said.

Then the hangar doors began closing. Voices were raised in terrifying screams. People were still trying to squeeze through the opening even as it narrowed and finally closed. Bile rose up and I snapped my head away from the gruesome sight.

As soon as the video ended it, it began to replay.

"This is going to start a riot in the Dome," Bron said.

Summer made a guttural sound. "Why?" she asked. "It's just bourge shooting urchins. Everyone in the Dome will probably think that's just good sport!"

And she wouldn't be far off in that assumption, I thought. The first place I stumbled upon in the great outdoors was the shooting range. But out of respect for Bron and the newly aligned Evans, I kept that information to myself.

"Not everyone in the Dome supported Holt," Bron shot back. "And you of all people should know that."

Summer pouted. "I'm just saying that video won't change anyone's mind. If they hated us before, they still will."

"Can we change the channel?" I asked. I couldn't stomach seeing that video again.

Evans still had the remote and he changed it back to the security camera. The hallway was cluttered with even more soldiers now and they appeared to be having an intense conversation.

I sat on the edge of the sofa beside my mom. Her eyes were closed and it alarmed me. I checked her pulse—

still strong. She was just asleep.

"Is there sound?" I asked.

"No," Evans said. "They're probably reacting to the video and messages we sent out."

As I watched the screen, I was sure I saw the slightest movement of the door at the end of the hallway. The soldiers didn't seem to notice anything, too engrossed in whatever they were discussing. I stared at the door. It opened slightly and the barrel of a rifle poked out. I saw the jolt of the barrel a split second after I heard the sound of gunfire drift in from the hallway.

The men in the hallway had nowhere to hide. They drew their weapons and backed up toward Holt's apartment. They were practically standing under the camera.

The door at the end of the hallway opened wider. The full rifle and the hands holding it were visible. The stairwell door opened and someone stepped halfway into the hallway, a rifle pointed at the cowering soldiers.

I heard shouting out in the hallway, although on the television screen no one appeared to be moving. The voices drifting into the apartment were too muffled to make out. The person at the door at the end of the hallway stepped forward. Two more men carrying guns were right behind him.

Narrowing my eyes, I leaned forward and peered at the screen to get better look at one of the men. "That's Jack," I announced to the room.

"Are you sure? You can't really see his face," Bron said.

I didn't need to see his face. I could tell by the way he stood and how he moved. "I'd know him anywhere."

The man at the stairwell door stepped out into the hall. He wore the white uniform of a guard from the Pit. "It looks like he has the Alliance with him," Bron said.

The militia was backed into a corner with the Alliance advancing. Jack walked forward, pointing the barrel of his rifle at the ceiling and holding up his other hand in a *stop* position. More Alliance members poured into the hall. I was pretty sure I recognized Reyes.

Jack talked for what seemed like an eternity. He was the front man—the person who was going to get shot if any of the soldiers decided to raise a gun. I wanted to run out of the door, distract the soldiers, and do anything to take their mind off Jack. But I knew bursting out during an intense situation wasn't a smart thing to do. All I could do was watch and wait.

Finally, there was movement. The soldiers were setting their guns on the floor. The Alliance moved swiftly down the hallway.

Bron and Evans cheered. Our imprisonment was over.

CHAPTER THIRTY-THREE

I jumped up from the sofa, the sudden movement waking my mother. "What's going on?" she asked.

"Jack's here," I said.

Evans was already at the door, opening the locks. Within seconds Jack walked through the door. Reyes and Micah were right behind him with a few other Alliance members.

Jack's eyes found me right away, concern, frustration and relief all crossing his face. I took a step toward him, but a familiar tug pulled me back and made me hesitate. I hadn't felt that pull in a very long time—that latent urge to hide myself, to be small and insignificant. I wasn't sure of the last time I felt that way. At some point during my life with Jack, I forgot I was supposed to be inconsequential. But now, with so many witnesses in the room, I wished I had a piece of coal to make myself anonymous again.

I knew the moment I stepped into Jack's waiting embrace that I would offend people. My mother and Summer, who hated the bourge. Reyes, who might be hurt and definitely wouldn't understand. Anyone in the room who believed an urchin and bourge were not meant to be together. It really wasn't that long ago that those pressures would have had me running for cover. But something deep within me rose to challenge those old feelings. It told me the only person I was most afraid of offending was Jack.

I held my head up a little higher, defying the urge to be inconsequential. What I had with Jack was nothing less than beautiful. It was not small. It was not insignificant.

I ran and threw my arms around him, hoping he didn't notice my split second of hesitation. He buried his face in my shoulder and held me there so tight I could barely breathe.

"You came for me," I whispered.

He pulled back to look at me, a smile lighting up his face. "I don't like being stood up."

"Then I guess I have some making up to do."

He nodded. "And I'm going to hold you to that." He dipped his head toward mine and kissed me quickly. "How's your mom?" he asked.

"She's in a lot of pain." I looked over at her and was surprised to find someone attending her. "Who's that?"

"I messaged an old friend. He's still a med student, but he can patch her up until we get her to the hospital."

I suddenly flashed back to when he first met my father. He was considerate then, too. "Thank you."

"Are you okay with leaving her in his hands? You and I have something to do."

For some reason I didn't like the sound of that. Hadn't we done enough? Wasn't it time to escape the Dome with the rest of the Pit? "Should I ask what?"

"There was a camera crew covering the hostage situation when we came up, although they took off when they saw us coming. I think you and I should find them and make a statement."

"What? You mean a *public* statement?"

My outburst caught the attention of everyone in the room. All eyes turned to look at us.

"It's time to come out of hiding, Sunny. If we don't go out there and own this—the president's death, the city outside, everything—we'll live like fugitives for the rest of our lives. We need to be the ones to expose all of Holt's secrets."

"It could work," Bron said. "Based on the replies Evans and I have received from our messages, people are quickly turning against the president. There's a lot of evidence on his computer that babies and children were *euthanized* because they weren't genetically perfect," she added for the benefit of the newcomers.

The young doctor attending my mom looked up. "A colleague sent me a message about a lynch mob outside the hospital, but she had no idea why. Do you mind sending her those messages?"

"Give me her address," Evans said. He looked at Jack and me. "And if you need me to back you on your statement, I'd be honored."

My hands started shaking at the very thought. No one would want to hear from me. I was just an urchin. "You make the statement."

"No. The Pit needs to be represented and you're the most recognizable face. And Sunny, you've earned the right to have your say."

"But Jack, I don't—"

"I'll be right beside you."

I scanned the room, my eyes stopping at Reyes. His face was covered in dirt and dust after a night of working on the tunnel. But he didn't run with everyone else. He was here. Staying to fight. Micah looked just as exhausted. Summer was back in her corner, hiding away. And my mother lay on the sofa, a bullet in her shoulder and a tag in her neck.

Freedom as we always dreamed about it wasn't going to happen. The lands weren't safe for us. We were all going to be stuck together in this valley—urchin and bourge alike—dependent on technology for clean water and food. The abuse, the killing and the oppression had to stop. We wouldn't leave the Pit only to be tagged, kept in a corral, and used as slaves. We were no longer bound by the treaty and someone needed to make that perfectly clear.

Jack was right—I did need to make a public statement. But not for me. For them.

"Okay," I said.

I caught the twinkle of fondness in his eyes, a look that had become intimately familiar. He kissed my cheek. "Thank you," he whispered. He stepped away from me and addressed the room. "We split up into groups. I need a team to take the stairwell and a few armed men in the elevator with us."

"I'm staying here to guard that computer," Bron announced. "I wouldn't put it past Holt's cronies to come in here and destroy evidence."

"I'll stay with her," Evans said.

Summer stepped out of her corner. "I'll stay with your mom and make sure she's okay."

I looked at Reyes and Micah. It was difficult to tell what Reyes was thinking since his features were often clouded with anger. "I'll go with the team taking the stairs," he said and stomped out of the room.

I ignored the impulse to stop him, to try to explain everything, conscious that Jack's eyes were on me. It was no longer my place to worry why Reyes might be upset, but it was hard not to feel guilty for possibly being the cause.

As we put our plan into action, my hands began to shake. I knew from experience that once we were in the elevator, it wouldn't take long to reach our destination—the second level. Although the last time I took this trip, I was shrouded in white and unrecognizable. This time I would arrive as me—Sunset O'Donnell, a known traitor and fugitive. At least I had my criminal husband beside me, giving me support.

With a hallway full of armed Alliance, the president's militia was nowhere to be seen—at least not on this level. Most likely, they had retreated elsewhere to regroup and make a new plan of attack. It was doubtful they expected us to come down via the elevator and ask to be interviewed.

The elevator doors opened and four of us—two armed escorts and Jack and I—got on. The doors closed. It was quiet. The memory of struggling to control the rhythm of my breathing when dressed as the bride came back to haunt me. It was happening again, now.

Jack reached out and smoothed either side of my hair, tucking it behind my ear.

"What are you doing?" I asked.

"Fixing your hair for the cameras," he said. He pulled back his lips. "Anything in my teeth?"

The two Alliance members tried to keep a straight face.

I looked at his teeth. "No, Jack. There's nothing in your teeth."

"I always used to check my teeth before an interview because you never know."

I couldn't stop the smile that spread across my face. I wasn't sure if he was being honest or just trying to take my mind off things. Either way, my breathing returned to normal.

"You're going to be great. Don't worry," he said.

The elevator stopped and the doors opened. Our armed escorts poked the ends of their rifles through the opening, cautiously stepping into the foyer. No one was there. But a commotion from the main reception level drifted up to us. We walked to the balcony at the top of the grand staircase that I once descended as a bride. There were at least a hundred people gathered in the lobby, voices vying to be heard over one another. On the big screen dominating the room, the Kenners' video—the fateful day we entered the Dome—still played.

"Is it a riot?" I asked.

"If it isn't yet, it soon will be," Jack said.

I wondered if this was a mistake. When Jack presented the idea of making a public statement, I had pictured us up here on the second floor with a camera crew and no one else. This was a big crowd and they were upset.

"Maybe this wasn't—" I started, but someone in the crowd turned and pointed at us.

"It's Jack Kenner!" someone shouted.

Another voice raised the alarm. "And the urchin girl—O'Donnell! She was the one holding the president hostage."

The crowd surged forward, toward the stairs. I backed up a step, but Jack held me firmly beside him. Our escorts raised their rifles, but he motioned for them to stand down. There were only a few soldiers here, and none of them had drawn a weapon.

A camera crew pushed their way to the bottom of the staircase.

"This is it," Jack said. He took a communicator out of his pocket and held it up to his mouth. "Now." I gave him a questioning look and he pointed at the big screen dominating the room. A picture of the two of us flashed up on it.

Holding my hand more tightly, he gave me an encouraging look and we descended a few steps. The mob started to quiet. A member of the camera crew ascended a few steps, holding a microphone toward us while keeping a safe distance.

"I guess I have some explaining to do to the good people of the Dome," he began. All chatter ceased with the sound of his voice. His shoulders squared, his eyes unafraid to return the stares of every single person in the room, he exuded power and strength. I felt a stab of fierce pride. "First, I'd like to formally apologize for the events on my wedding day. Although it was not my intention to marry the beautiful lady standing beside me, it was the best thing that ever happened to me—that ever happened to all of *you*—because it gave me the opportunity to see our government from a different perspective." He took two steps down, moving closer toward the transfixed crowd. The camera crew didn't back away. "And it gave us the opportunity to expose the Holt regime for the corrupt organization it is. By now you've at least heard of, or maybe even read, the messages containing files on President Holt's plans for a master race. Those files were taken directly from his personal computer. They are all true. My sincerest condolences go out to anyone who may have lost a child due to our president's insanity. My thoughts are with you." He paused and held out his hand to me. Reluctantly, I reached for it and moved to stand beside him. I loathed being in the spotlight. Jack was doing such a good job of captivating everyone I wasn't sure why he needed me. I squeezed his hand to stop the shaking of my own. "And my thoughts are with our neighbors in the Pit—the true victims of the Holt regime."

Jack turned an expectant look toward me. I guessed that was my cue to start talking. I didn't know what to say. Jack's intro of an apology threw me off. It never occurred to me to plead for forgiveness from the bourge. To apologize for causing *them* any undue concern.

"I'm not the diplomat my...husband is, but I'll try my best." There was murmuring from the throng at my use of the word "husband." Jack gave me an encouraging nod. "I'm not blaming any one of you for the conditions in the Pit. If there's one thing I learned from Jack, it's that most people in the Dome take it for granted that we're doing okay down there. So I'm here to clear up a misunderstanding. We are human beings, just like you. We're not invisible machines with the sole purpose of ensuring *your* every need is taken care of in the Dome." Jack squeezed my hand harder, a clear indication that I was going in the wrong direction. I cleared my throat and continued in a calmer voice. "We are people. We feel pain when we're beaten. We feel horror when we watch a loved one be thrashed to death. We feel grief when our parents are killed in the Cull." My voice rose in anger again. "We feel humiliation when we're forced to perform sexual favors. But mostly, we feel outrage because we are *not* machines. We. Are. People." Jack was inflicting considerable pain on my hand and I gritted my teeth against it. "But I know these things are not *your* fault, because you didn't know about the conditions in the Pit." He relaxed his grip. I took a moment to pause, perusing the faces of those staring up at me so intently, wanting my next words to count. "Now you do."

A sea of faces looked back at me, some shocked, most disbelieving. A part of me hated to excuse them from blame, but if our two races were ever to get along, forgiveness needed to start somewhere. And Jack was the inspiration. He had been every bit as naïve as the people standing in front of me when he first entered the Pit. Now he was the champion for change. The optimistic part of me wanted to believe there were more like him.

"It's important that we clear up this misunderstanding so that relations between the Pit and the Dome can begin to heal. Today is historic. The treaty no longer binds us." An anxious ripple went through the crowd. Somewhere in the distance I heard excited shouts. I had to raise my voice. "Today will see us leave the Dome to begin a new life outside."

The crowd went into a frenzy. I couldn't have been

heard above the din even if I screamed. Cheers went up as they embraced each other.

"That was quite a speech, Mrs. Kenner," Jack said.

"We didn't even tell them the president is dead."

"Probably best to take it one step at a time. The doors are going to be opened—nothing can compete with that right now."

I looked at the ecstatic mob. "Do you think there'll be a stampede to get out?"

"I'll send a message for the Alliance to get to the hangar and keep the exodus orderly." His expression sobered and he took one of my hands in both of his. "You and I are free. We're not fugitives anymore."

I caught his meaning—we didn't *need* to be partners. The Alliance had won, the Pit was liberated, and we were no longer running from execution. If we stayed together, it would be because we wanted to.

"No, we're not." I stepped in closer, leaning against him. "Do you think that means we'll sleep better at night?"

He smiled. "Not if you keep looking at me with those eyes. I can't imagine we'll sleep at all."

He caught me in the circle of his arms, pulling me even closer. I put my hands on his chest, feeling the hard muscle beneath my fingertips. I opened my mouth to give him a flirty retort, but my words were cut off when his lips pressed against mine. He took me by surprise. We were on the grand staircase with a camera crew and at least a hundred people watching us. But as the heat of his breath mingled with mine and I felt the gentle pressure of his embrace holding me to him, my arms slid around his neck. *This* was the moment I was finally free. Free to love the man I was labeled a traitor for marrying.

And standing there locked in his embrace with the entire Dome watching, I was happy to let freedom reign.

CHAPTER THIRTY-FOUR

We left the grand staircase and the exultant crowd to make our way back upstairs—Jack to the eighth floor to liberate his family and me to the tenth floor to get my mom and take her out to Doc. We promised to meet at the house we shared in the city, assuming the lock was still set for Jack's code and no one else had moved in.

There were armed Alliance all over the tenth floor. Bron and Evans were still searching Holt's hard drive. My mother looked more comfortable, so I assumed the young doctor had given her some pain relief. And Leisel was still tied to a chair. How long had she been there like that? I couldn't remember.

I stood in front of her and she barely looked at me. The fight seemed to have left her, leaving her looking exhausted and broken. Sympathy crept into my heart and I gave it an eye roll. I shouldn't feel anything but disdain for this woman. But she looked so pathetic now, stripped of her father's power. I breathed out a heavy sigh and began the task of untying her restraints, starting with her legs. She gave me a wary look.

As I worked, I stole quick glances at her. Her nose was slightly hooked. It definitely wasn't her most flattering feature and, if anything, was a testimony that she was Damien Holt's daughter. Her sapphire blue eyes *were* her best feature and I tried to imagine them black like my own. Black eyes would look out of place with her fair hair… although now that I peered into her eyes, I could definitely see the ring of contact lenses.

Was Leisel my sister? Yeah, we were the same height, but I was pretty sure the resemblance stopped there. Almost positive.

Summer came alongside of me. "What are you doing?"

"She's not a threat anymore," I explained.

Summer gave an exaggerated snort. "Are you serious?"

I undid the last of the knots, and then finally removed the gag. Leisel barely moved her limbs, but by the look of consternation on her face, she was trying. Her bluish-white hands told me her circulation had cut out. I felt a little ashamed of having left her tied up for so long. Picking up one of her hands, I tried to rub the circulation back into it.

"Leave me alone," she said, her voice thick.

I dropped her hand. "Okay."

I walked away, even though my conscience screamed at me not to. I yelled back, telling it my mother was still hurt. It was my duty to get her to a doctor. Leisel could look after herself.

The young med student was still keeping a vigil over my mom. "Thank you for looking after her."

"No problem. She's probably going to need surgery on her shoulder, but she's stable for now." He picked up his medical bag. "Are the doors to the outside really open?"

"If they aren't already, they soon will be."

"Well then, thank *you*. I need to go find my girlfriend." He headed toward the door, but stopped midway. "Your mom's fine to move. I gave her a shot of painkiller, so she'll be a little woozy." Then he left.

"How are you doing, Mom?" I asked, leaning over her.

She smiled. "I feel fine. Don't worry about me." I wondered if it was the drugs talking.

"Summer, can you give me a hand getting my mom to Doc?" I helped my mom into a sitting position.

"Who's Doc?" Summer asked. She positioned herself on the other side of my mom and we hoisted her off the sofa.

"Our doctor on the outside. He's from the Pit."

"We're going outside?" She gave me a fearful look.

"It's amazing." I smiled. "You're going to love it."

The only people milling around on the presidential floor were Alliance guards. I wondered where everyone was. The Forbes, Powells and Wests all lived on this floor. They must have heard the news by the now. The doors were opening—everyone was free.

It took the elevator a long time to come to the tenth

floor. I thought about using the stairs but knew it would be too difficult for Summer and me to navigate my mom down so many flights. Finally, the elevator arrived, empty. We stepped on, the doors closed, and on the next level we filled up to full capacity. It continued to stop on every floor, although no one else could fit in.

A mob of excited people greeted us on the main floor. It was difficult to even get out of the elevator. The steels doors that had always been used to separate bourge from urchins were now flung wide open. The sea of people in the lobby poured through, not even bothering to scan out. Alliance guards, Domers and military soldiers all worked together for crowd control.

It was going to take a long time to reach the hangar doors.

Above the din of excited voices, I heard my name being shouted. I searched the sea of faces until I found him—Jack. He was on the grand staircase, caught in the throng, waving at me. A man who looked an awful lot like him was at his side.

The mob on the stairs was so thick it took forever for him to descend even a few steps. Then he hopped over the railing and dropped down onto the floor, people pushing to get out of his way. His doppelganger went next. The two pushed their way through the crowd toward us.

"How's your mom?" asked Jack when he reached us.

"She's holding up so far, but we have to get her out of here." Her hair was plastered to her forehead and although she didn't seem to be in pain, she could barely stand on her own.

Jack motioned toward the other man with him. "This is Ted, my brother. Ted, this is Sunny—your sister-in-law."

Ted smiled and nodded at me.

"Hi," I said a little awkwardly. "This is my friend, Summer."

Jack smiled. "I've heard a lot about you, Summer. My wife thinks very highly of you."

Summer didn't say anything. She just gave him a curt smile and looked away.

"Maybe we should go through the tunnel—the Pit was half cleared out when I came through hours ago," Jack suggested.

It was a good suggestion, except that as we got closer to the entrance, we saw that the door to the Pit had been barricaded. Someone didn't want the urchins to go free. I wondered how surprised they were going to be to find everyone from the Pit was already outside.

Jack took out his communicator and asked the Alliance for help. It took a while, but finally several guards found us and helped clear a path to the hangar. Jack carried my mom and I grabbed onto Summer and held tight, not wanting to lose her in the crowd.

The hangar was already bright with sunlight and Summer put a hand up to shield her eyes.

"It gets brighter," I told her. "But Doc has glasses for us."

As we exited the Dome, Summer put her arm over her eyes. Even at this time of evening, the sun was brilliant. I cursed myself for leaving my glasses—the ones Jack had given me—in the Pit with my clothes.

I kept my eyelids half closed, looking around to see as much as I could. People were climbing trees, picking flowers and turning their faces toward the early evening sun. Goosebumps rose up along my arms and down my back. I wasn't sure if it was from the breeze or a side effect of the elation I was feeling at seeing everyone outside under the sun.

I looked behind us, watching the mass exodus from the Dome, but the sight made me think of another image I had recently seen—the Kenners' video. I tried to shake off the image of so many people running toward those very doors only to be gunned down. I tried not to think about how many bodies littered the road I was walking on. I needed to ban those images so the memory of today—the liberation of both the Pit and the Dome—wouldn't be marred forever.

The sound of a vehicle coming up the old road distracted me. I wondered who could be driving. Only the bourge knew how to operate a vehicle, and they were locked up in the corrals. I gave Jack a questioning look.

"Powell, Dena and I had a conference call after you and I made our announcement," Jack said. "The Dome is free, so everyone in the corral is, too, although they're not getting their weapons back. Anyway, I asked them to send Alex so we could get your mom to Doc."

When the jeep came, we piled everyone in.

Jack sat in the front seat beside Alex. "So what was that, putting *me* in a corral?" Alex demanded.

"Sorry. I didn't know who to trust," Jack said.

"We've known each other since we were kids. We were best friends at the Academy. My family has supported Liberty since...*forever*."

Alex was angry with Jack and complained all the way to the medical center. It looked like Jack was going to have to do some damage control with his friends.

The medical center was busy. A lot of people had been injured in the conflict and this was the only medical facility available to them. But upon seeing my mom, Doc took her right away. While we waited, I found survival packs for all of us in the supply closet. About thirty minutes later, Doc came out and led me to a hospital room.

My mom was asleep, her shoulder heavily bandaged.

"She's fine. Leaving the bullet in was a good call—there was little blood loss. Her shoulder joint needs to be reconstructed, but I'm confident I can replace it."

"Let me guess—nanorobots."

He nodded. "By the way, well done, Miss O'Donnell. Honestly, when you told me you were going to free the Pit, I thought it was laughable."

"Thanks, Doc," I said. The sarcasm was evident. "And thank God it's over. I'm not sure I could take any more fighting." I looked at my mom.

"Oh, it's not over yet," Doc said. "We may have won this battle, but the revolution is only getting started."

I stared at him for a moment, tempted to ask what he meant. But I was exhausted. And I still had one more important thing left to do before I could join my husband on that date I promised him.

"So, when are you going to do the surgery?"

Doc shrugged. "I can't answer that right now. The hospital is overflowing and I'm hoping the Dome will send assistance. Check with me tomorrow. Oh, and bring Jack Kenner with you—I'd love to get a blood sample."

I thanked him and left.

On my way back to the waiting room, the sound of voices carried out from behind a door slightly ajar. I peered in as I walked by, surprised to see Gaia sitting beside a man lying in a bed. I stopped and backed up to get a better look.

Doc left my mom's room and came up behind me.

"Who's Gaia with?" I whispered to Doc.

"Her husband," he whispered back.

My mouth dropped open. "How can he still be alive? He was sent to the range almost two years ago."

"The range is a fairly large area—five square kilometers, with lots of dark caves to hide in. At least the bourge gave them a sporting chance." He continued down the hall and motioned for me to follow. I realized I was intruding on their privacy. "A few of the first group sent to the range made it out alive, but unfortunately their life expectancy isn't good. They had to live off the land and they're suffering from radiation poisoning."

"A couple of men were taking food to them from the corrals," I said.

"If their diet was supplemented, that explains why they're not dead yet."

"It's still a miracle, though."

He cocked an eyebrow at me. "If you believe in those."

I motioned for Summer to get on the back of the bike. She looked at it dubiously. "*You* know how to drive?"

Jack and Ted had already claimed another bike parked along the street. Jack revved the engine, more for effect than anything, and raced away from the curb. He was on his way back to the house we shared, hoping squatters hadn't taken up residence yet. I'd promised to meet him later.

"Yes, I know how to drive. And if you're nice to me, I'll teach you tomorrow," I lied. It didn't matter if she was nice to me or not—I'd teach her anyway.

She climbed on the back and I slid onto the front seat. I turned it to gas. It was faster that way.

I drove along the road for a little while, and then turned the bike toward the open countryside. We didn't have much time before the sun went down behind the mountain. I stopped as soon as I found a good boulder for us to sit on. I parked the bike and we both climbed off.

"So what are we doing?" Summer asked.

"Watching the sunset."

I sat down on the boulder and patted the rock next to me. She sat down too, although she was a little stiff about it.

The sun was a bright orange, the bottom of the sphere already disappearing behind the mountain. As it sank lower, the orange began turning to red, streaking out on either side and filling the horizon with a fiery glow. I looked at Summer out of the corner of my eye. I was surprised to see a tear run out from under her glasses. I moved my hand to cover hers. The sun disappeared with a final flash.

"Is he really gone?" Summer asked. "Is that monster really dead?"

My heart grew heavy and a lump formed in my throat. I put my arm around her shoulders. "He's gone. He won't ever hurt you again."

Her shoulders began to shake with sobs and as her tears spilled, I held her. My own tears fell silently.

Chapter Thirty-Five

...Ten Months Later

The buzz of the alarm clock interrupted what was a perfectly good sleep. Jack rolled over and curled in behind me, threw an arm around my waist, and pulled me closer. I snuggled in.

"Turn it off," I suggested.

"No. We'll go back to sleep," he mumbled against my ear.

"That's the point."

"Mmmmm...not today. It's going to be fun." Fun? I wasn't sure how much fun going to an old, crumbling city looking for books, tablets and communication devices was going to be. But my husband, the avid historian, was excited to go. "If we go early enough, we can stop by your dad's headstone."

It had been a few weeks since I went out there. My mom and I had found the perfect rock—it faced the sunset. And at night when the sun went down, the rock looked like it turned pink. Not that my dad was actually buried there. I had no idea where his body went...and I looked and asked everyone I could think of where someone who was tortured to death might find a resting place in the Dome. No one could answer me. In fact, according to the records, he wasn't listed as deceased. The only reason I let my mother talk me into carving a headstone was in case he was alive and found his name there. It would be like a beacon, telling him his family was looking for him, and maybe he might stay by the rock waiting to be found. At first I checked every day... then every other day... and ten months later it stretched into weeks. So far, he was a no-show.

My mother had already accepted he was gone. Apparently, their marriage hadn't been a love match. Not that I should be surprised. There were few marriages in the Pit forged from love—most were out of necessity. But believing my parents were actually in love was like having an anchor in life. Love was a hard bond to break—it meant committing to each other forever. I just didn't know that desperation and necessity could accomplish the same goal.

Jack was softly snoring against my ear. I thought about giving him a nudge but decided not to. Even though the worst of winter was over, the spring mornings were still freezing and our bed was warm and cozy. I slid my hand over the back of his and pulled it closer to my chest. There was no place on the entire planet I would rather be.

The movement stirred him. He drew in a deep breath and let it out while his strong arm pulled me even closer. "You're trying to get out of this, aren't you?" he asked drowsily.

"I'm not the one still asleep."

I felt his lips curve into a smile. "You shouldn't have kept me up so late."

It was my turn to smile. He didn't complain last night. And I didn't make love to him in the hopes of tiring him out for today—last night was all for me. It was just a bonus if he was too tired to get up and brave the freezing temperatures this morning.

"Just five more minutes," I said.

He sighed dramatically to let me know he was disappointed, but rolled over, hit the button, and curled back around me. I shimmied closer.

Maybe he still didn't know that I would do anything he asked of me. And after all the nights he stayed up studying with me, I was happy to share in his passion for history. It had been a long school year. There were times I regretted letting him talk me into going to the Academy. I hadn't had the educational background for it at first. In the Pit, we only received education to grade six, and once we turned twelve we entered the workforce. In the Dome, education went to grade twelve, and the kids from elite families were allowed an additional two years of finishing studies. The only reason I was able to get accepted into the Academy was because Jack spent night after night after night helping me prepare for the entry test. I passed. But then came the hard part—not flunking out. If not for my attentive, supportive, and extremely sexy husband staying up most nights to help me study, I probably would have.

But all those nights of pulling my hair out in frustration, wanting to throw my books against the wall and yell *what's it all for?* had been worth it, because today, the day after my final exam of my first year at the Academy, I could answer that question: I was gaining insight. I always envied Jack's ability to forecast what the bourge were going to do next. And although I wasn't quite the expert at it that he was, I was getting there.

In the weeks following our liberation from the Dome, chaos had ruled. The bourge insisted that the city—all the homes and commercial buildings—belonged to them exclusively. They rationalized that the president used *their* taxes to build the city, and claimed ownership. The urchins disagreed. They rationalized that it was urchin labor that built the city, and since they were outside of the Dome the treaty wasn't in effect. The bourge owed them. As tension between the two groups increased, fighting started to break out on the streets. People began to carry guns at all times. But the worst of the violence occurred when a couple from the Pit were barricaded in the home they had claimed and it was set on fire. They died. The very next night, the Pit retaliated and burned a bourge family to death.

It was out of control.

With the threat of more violence looming large, Jack was finally able to convince General Powell that negotiations were the best way to ease tensions. The Pit could no longer be controlled by the military. The urchins were free to take up arms to not only defend themselves, but also possibly defeat the bourge and take control of the city. After all, they had the backing of the Alliance and *that* had General Powell's attention.

Since the president died with no visible heir to claim the title, the head of the military was next in line. Powell claimed temporary leadership, with the backing of his cronies Forbes and West, until a new government could be elected with equal representation from both sides. To say no one from the Pit was happy with the temporary leader would be an understatement. More than once, Molotov cocktails were thrown through the windows of his home, setting fire to more than just the curtains; it inflamed the ire of every supporter of the old regime. Fistfights breaking out in the street became common and within weeks the entire city pulsed with hostility. The election process was expedited.

Nominations were taken from both sides and I was surprised that the Pit nominated Jack Kenner. Jack was surprised that they had not nominated me. I wasn't. Not only had I just turned eighteen—although middle-aged by Pit standards—but a female leader was unheard of. That's when Jack insisted I attend the Academy.

Jack wasn't a popular candidate among his own people. They distrusted him after seeing him as the president-in-training-turned-traitor. They questioned his role in President Holt's death. Even though Holt had been in ill health, the people of the Dome wanted retribution for his assassination. When the Pit countered, looking for retribution for the suffering they endured under Holt's control, the Dome dropped the subject. The ownership of a city was at stake and they weren't about to waste their bargaining power on a dead president who had betrayed them. This came as quite a relief since it wasn't just Jack I was worried about. I found out Summer was the reason for Holt's illness.

I knew something had been going on between Summer and Bron…and between Bron and my mother. Getting the truth out of them hadn't been easy. They made me promise not to tell anyone—Jack included—that Bron had given Summer poison to put in President Holt's drinks. Even if my mother hadn't shot Holt, eventually he would have died anyway. Not that my mother felt bad about shooting a dying man. She said her only regret in life was refusing to give the poison to Holt herself when Bron approached her with the idea years ago. Like Bron told me—I wasn't the first person to think of a revolt, I was just the most successful. I put it down to good timing.

Voting Day was perhaps the most glorious day in our history. I'll always remember it as the day we were truly liberated—urchin and bourge alike—from life under a brutal dictator. Long before the poll station opened, before the sun even rose, the line started. By the time the polls opened, the queue stretched for at least a kilometer. At the end of the day, Jack, Doc and David Chavez were elected to represent the Pit; General Powell, Malcolm West and Martin Kenner, Jack's father, were elected to represent the Dome. Jack said the election results demonstrated how divided the bourge were, with the majority still supporting the old establishment.

In the aftermath of the new government being formed, a cautious truce developed between the two factions. Although peace didn't exactly reign, there was at least hope of resolving the issues.

Doc was perhaps the most questionable elected representative. I was the one who nominated him and campaigned for others to back him too, even though he made it clear he didn't want any part of the new government. But aside from Jack, he was the smartest person I had ever met, even if he was a little eccentric. He accepted my nomination on the condition I help him put together a militia—a covert underground (literally; Doc located his lab in the caverns) organization trained to carry out strategic strikes against an enemy in case our differences with the bourge came to war. Although I wasn't supposed to discuss it with my bourge husband, I did of course. Jack called it "special ops" with a whiff of "terrorism" and we both agreed that if Doc was going to organize a militia, I should be there to keep it honest. I accepted the role.

Uncurling my legs, I stretched them out, feeling the tightness in my calves. Doc had really put us through our paces with the new suits. A product of nanotechnology, Doc designed the suits to protect the wearer from an assault, including bullets. He said my injury from wearing a bulletproof vest coupled with my determination to free the Pit was the inspiration. In testing the suits, he wanted us to run, jump and do everything a human body was meant to do, while he analyzed the response from the nanorobots. It had gone on for hours, and I was still sore today.

Reyes was part of this elite army, as were Raine, Micah, David, and Summer. Although Summer rarely showed up. It was difficult to get her sober and Doc was adamant about his army being clear-headed. He pointed to how easily the bourge had been defeated because they loved cocktail hour.

The stupid alarm started buzzing and Jack's body jerked at the sound. He had been asleep again.

"That wasn't five minutes," I said.

"I have it set for a three minute snooze."

"Then you owe me two minutes."

He laughed softly. "Not a chance. Get up."

"You're not up."

"I'll get up when you get up."

"Okay." I smiled to myself and wedged closer to his warm body. I was good with staying here all day.

"Nice try, Mrs. Kenner. Get up."

"Oooohhhh," I moaned. "It's so warm and you feel so nice. I don't want to get up."

"It's your turn to make coffee."

I couldn't argue with that. He had made coffee for the past fourteen mornings, even after he had stayed up with me most nights studying for final exams. The man was a saint.

"Okay," I said in defeat.

I pushed out of his arms, reaching for the side of our enormous bed. He grabbed me back against him. "Wait a minute," he said.

"What?"

"Where are you going?"

"To make coffee."

He nuzzled the soft spot between my shoulder and neck. "But we always say good morning before coffee."

I laughed softly and turned back around toward him. Twining my arms around his neck, I said, "Yes we do."

It was still dark in the house when I padded into the kitchen to make coffee. Jack was in the shower and the other occupants of the house were still asleep, so I was quiet. There were a few dirty dishes left on the counter and one of the glasses smelled like rum. Summer. I tried not to get angry. I did my best not to throw the glass against the wall. I concentrated instead on making coffee.

Even though I was frustrated with her, I was glad Summer was living with us. After her parents ventured into the great outdoors for all of twenty minutes, they decided it wasn't for them—too much risk of radiation poisoning. The sun was too bright and the wind too foreign. They weren't the only ones who felt that way. There were many urchins and bourge who decided not to leave the safety of the Dome.

Summer was more than happy to leave. In fact, she never wanted to go back inside. So even though I had taken up residence with Jack—one of the hated bourge—I still managed to persuade her to live with us. I guess we were the lesser of two evils. Now if I could just get her sober.

Surprisingly, Jack's parents also decided to remain in the Dome. Jack hypothesized a lot of reasons why they chose to do that—everything from his mom being scared, to his mom not wanting to give up control of the Dome. Personally I think it was because when the lottery was drawn for homes, their names were selected for an apartment. She was livid when the verdict was read. And her embarrassment over having an urchin for a daughter-in-law was obvious. She was pressuring

Jack to take legal steps to have our fraud of a marriage dissolved. He just ignored her.

Jack and I were exempted from the draw in recognition of our efforts in exposing Holt's secret and opening the doors to the Pit. But it was such a big home, we both wanted to share it with the ones we loved. So my mom, Summer and Ted all moved in with us. Summer and my mom had the upstairs rooms and Ted occupied the lower level. We kept our room on the main floor.

Jack came into the kitchen, his damp hair curling slightly and his cheeks pink from his hot shower. "Your turn," he said. I handed him a cup of hot coffee and he gave me a long, appreciative kiss. "Make it a quick shower. We're running late."

I knew what today meant to him and I wouldn't make him late. I got ready in record time. When I returned to the kitchen, dressed in three layers of warm clothes including thick socks, I was surprised to find Ted up and ready to go.

"Ted wants to go too," Jack said.

Ted acknowledged me with an early morning grunt.

I liked Ted. He was quiet, usually preferring to play games on his tablet to socializing, but he was nice enough. And at least he liked me, or I think he did. He didn't act like his parents, who were so painfully uncomfortable around me they tended not to acknowledge my presence. Ted talked to me.

"So am I the only girl going?" I asked. I should've thought to ask Jin-Sook to come with us.

"What about Summer?" asked Jack.

"Um…she's still asleep," I said, shooting him a look that said *you know why.*

Jack came close and whispered in my ear. "Maybe you could ask your sister," he said with a laugh. My expression must have said it all, because the smile dropped off his face and he took a few steps back. I knew he was just trying to be funny—make light of the situation so I wouldn't take it so seriously.

I had put Jack, along with everyone else who had been in the president's suite, under a strict gag order about the *possibility* of Leisel being my sister. Although I did confide in Doc and he offered to do a blood test to confirm it, but I said no. If it turned out we were sisters, I wouldn't know what to do with that information. And I doubted Leisel wanted to know either. She preferred to maintain her superior role as the president's orphaned daughter, which she would lose if it were discovered she was half urchin. And considering she had moved in with the West family—the Holts' closest friends—being labeled an urchin might mean she would be out of a place to live.

My stomach growled and I looked in the fridge for something to eat. Well, not just *something.* I really wanted a tomato. I was pretty sure I ate the last one yesterday, but I looked just in case I was wrong. My mouth watered in anticipation of finding one. I didn't.

"I have a protein shake here for you," Jack said, handing me a glass of the vile stuff.

"Oh." I shut the fridge door and took it from him—a poor consolation for the food I was really craving. "I was hoping there were tomatoes left. Anyone see any?" I asked hopefully.

Jack regarded me with a weird look. "You ate the entire box in three days. And I thought you hated tomatoes."

I shrugged. "I like them now." In fact I loved them. They were the best food on the planet. Biting back my extreme disappointment, and, yes, anger, at not having any more tomatoes in the house, I drank my shake. We were going to have to start buying two boxes per week. Period.

"Naoki's probably waiting. We should get going," Jack said.

Ted put his tablet away as I downed my shake and tried not to gag. It was better than going hungry.

There was still an hour before the sun came up. The air was cold and crisp. My breath fogged in front of me as I straddled the seat of the bike. Jack climbed on in front of me. He liked to do the driving, even though I could see better in the dark. I didn't mind, though, especially when I was still tired. I was content to wrap my arms around his waist, lean my head on his shoulder, and try to get some more sleep. He also made an excellent windbreak.

Ted got on his bike, snapped the kickstand out of the way, and revved the bike to life. Jack shot him a dirty look. He was going to wake Summer and my mom. He switched to solar.

This was the first time we were going to the old city, which Jack pinpointed on a map as possibly being Front Royal, although he wasn't positive. There were lots of settlements scattered throughout the valley before the war, most being homesteads and farms. The bigger, major cities were farther east, along the Atlantic Ocean. Those were also the areas the Nation referred to as the scorched lands.

That's what I had decided to call the barangays—the Nation. And everyone who resided there: the People. I asked Jin-Sook how they referred to themselves and she said they didn't. They believed part of the problem that led to a world war was that labels differentiated groups from each other, which led to segregation, which ultimately led to hate. The Nation's philosophy was that people were essentially all the same. So they shunned labels. My way of thinking wasn't nearly as advanced, as I found I needed to refer to them as something...a name that differentiated them from us. So, the Nation stuck.

The wind was cold as we raced across the valley and I tucked in more tightly behind Jack. It had been a long winter, but not entirely unwelcomed. The novelty of the first snowfall had everyone outside, playing in the foreign stuff. Someone even fashioned a sled and soon the entire town was searching for good sliding hills. It was a great day. It was a day when everyone forgot to hate. But soon enough, the novelty of snow wore off and they remembered their animosity. At least the bitterly cold winter kept most indoors for the season, so the fighting was kept to a minimum.

Naoki was already waiting on the outskirts of town with Ryan and someone he introduced as Talon.

Jack greeted Naoki with a brief man-hug. They had become good friends over the course of the last ten months. Jack and I spent as much time in Dena's barangay as we could. It was the only place where we were accepted. No one saw us as bourge and urchin. We were just people. And thanks to water-filtering flasks and freeze-dried food packs that Doc invented, the creepy hotel room—the place where we first made love—had become our second home.

We parked the bikes amongst some bushes and hiked the rest of the way. Ted hung back with me, maybe feeling as out of place as I did. He had visited the Nation a few times with Jack but hadn't really made any friends. I think he still felt like they were exotic foreigners... or maybe even heathens. I hoped the latter wasn't true.

Melting snow and early morning ice combined to make for a treacherous hike, yet our companions from the mountains left no visible sign of their passing. Jack, Ted and I didn't even bother to try. It was enough to walk without slipping.

The old city was everything Naoki had described and less. Most buildings were collapsed ruins. Bricks, pulverized mortar, and rusted-out steel frames littered either side of a road reclaimed by trees and roots. The trees were still leafless and I thought the city probably wouldn't look as desolate in the summer with greenery and wild flowers adding a touch of life. But at this time of year, it had a ghostly feel, as if the few cement buildings still standing had eyes peering out at us from the glassless windows. I never understood my husband's fascination with the old. I found it just plain eerie.

Jack was ahead of me, walking alongside Naoki, so I sidled closer to Ted. He gave me an understanding look. For a moment I wondered why Naoki and the others weren't using their usual caution in trying to stay hidden, but realized the ghostly city didn't provide much camouflage.

"That was the town library." Naoki motioned toward what was probably once a cement basement, but was now filled-in with debris. "Or at least we're pretty sure it was. We found a few books that had been wrapped in plastic, so they were still preserved. Nothing left there now, though."

"Where did you find the old tablets?" asked Jack.

"Mostly in homes and apartment buildings," Naoki said. "There's a building farther up that we haven't fully explored. We got lucky there a few times."

As we walked along the deserted street, the hairs on the back of my neck stood up. I remembered feeling that way before—when the People were watching us after our escape from the bourge. I had been right then. I prayed I wasn't right this time. Using only my peripheral vision, I scanned either side of the road along the crumbling buildings, but didn't see any movement. I rested my hand on the grip of my pistol just in case.

Naoki and Jack were deep in conversation, but Talon's head snapped up and he was suddenly alert. That had my heart racing. Now I knew it wasn't just me. Talon and I made eye contact for a split second before we both turned around to look behind us.

There was a group of men coming up behind us, arrows pointed at our backs.

"Recruiters!" Talon yelled, just as the first arrow flew.

We all dove out of the way of the deadly missile, splitting our group in half. I pushed myself off the ground and someone grabbed my arm to pull me toward cover. I ran but stopped when I realized it wasn't Jack I was running with—it was Ted. I wrenched my arm away from him.

"Where's Jack?" I looked around wildly for him.

Two more arrows flew toward us. *"Come on!"*

He grabbed me again just as I felt a hot stabbing in my side and I faltered. Ted stopped to yank me with him, looked at my side, cursed, and picked me up. The feel of his hands on my side was excruciating.

"Put me down!" I yelled. But he didn't listen. He kept running toward the crumbling building.

Cramps gripped my abdomen, pushing me beyond the limits of my pain threshold. The world went black.

I floated along on a hazy dream, the world spinning ever so slightly. The cramps in my abdomen were still there but less intense. The burning pain in my side was gone. My mouth felt dry, as if someone had deliberately sopped up my spit with a cloth. I smacked my tongue against the roof of my mouth and my eyes fluttered open.

I was in a hospital room. Mom was sitting in a chair to my left, reading a tablet. Ted was sitting in a chair to my right, bent over his lap with his head resting in his hands. I searched the room for Jack, but we were the only three.

"Mom?" I asked.

She dropped her tablet on the bedside table and stood, smoothing the hair away from my forehead. Ted's face shot up from his hands, his mouth slightly open.

A smile lit my mother's tired face. "You're finally awake."

"Was I asleep for long?" I asked. "Where's Jack?"

My mother's lips turned down for a split second before she pulled them into a tight line. "You just concentrate on getting better. Doc says you're pregnant. You need your rest."

Pregnant? I wasn't pregnant. I turned away from her. "Ted? Where's Jack?"

Ted frowned, his eyes red and swollen. A cold shiver gripped me. "Where's Jack?" I demanded again.

"Sunny…" he said.

I looked at my mother and grabbed her hand. *"Where's my husband?"*

"Sunny, don't get upset. The baby…"

I dug my fingers into her hand. "Tell me!"

"He's gone," Ted said, his voice cracking. "They have him."

My entire body went numb. Time seemed suspended. I heard the silence of the room, Ted's intake of breath after his confession, my mother's hands shifting to cover mine.

I'm not sure how long I stayed that way. I think they talked to me, but my brain was still processing the information. They couldn't just tell me something like that and expect me to believe it. Start having a conversation about it as if it were really true. As if Jack were actually gone.

"Who has him?" I asked Ted.

"The heathens called them recruiters." He rubbed the heels of his hands against his eyes. "I think I saw them kill him. I think my brother's dead."

I leapt off the bed and pulled his hands away from his eyes. "You *think* you saw, or you really did see it? Which is it?"

"I don't know, Sunny!" Tears streamed down his face. "I went back to look for him, but I couldn't find him. Not even his body."

The cramping in my abdomen was getting worse. "That must mean he's still alive. Why aren't you out looking for him?"

"We *have* been!" Ted snapped.

"Sunny, Doc says you can't get up."

I brushed her away, ignoring the pain. "I'll get dressed and go with you." I looked around the room for clothes. My cramps were getting really severe.

"Sunny, you're bleeding again," Mom said.

I looked down at the patch of blood on my hospital gown. It wasn't that much. Certainly not enough to stop me. I started toward the closet to look for clothes when something trickled down my leg and splattered on the floor. Blood. The room started tilting at an odd angle. I heard my mother's distant scream. I reached out for something to steady myself, but there was nothing to grab on to. My head hit the floor.

The next thing I knew, the sun was warming my face. The hospital bed I was lying in was parked beside a window. It was a beautiful day outside—the sky was blue with only a few white fluffy. From my vantage point, I could see people walking down the street, sweaters tied around their waists. It was a warm spring day.

Someone cleared her throat.

"Summer?" I asked. I looked around the room. She was sitting in a chair by my bed.

"I'm here," she said. She stood and reached over the bed to hug me. "I'm glad you're awake."

"I was never asleep."

"Sunny... it's been a few days since they told you that Jack..."

"That the recruiters have him."

"That he's dead," she said, thinking she was correcting me.

But she wasn't, because I knew better. I knew Jack was strong, a good fighter, and smart enough to get himself out of trouble. I knew he wasn't alone—Naoki, Ryan and Talon had been taken as well. They would look after each other. And I remembered after the battle with the bourge how quickly his wound had healed.

Most of all I knew Jack wasn't dead because I'd *know* if he wasn't in this world anymore.

My heart would feel it.

End of Book Two

A note from the author, S.M. McEachern:

If you enjoyed reading *Worlds Collide,* you may be interested in reading the Satellite Stories I've written to go along with the series. Satellites are short stories designed to give the reader greater insight into areas of the story that the main character, Sunny, cannot see. They are an accompaniment to the series, but not a necessity. They're just for fun!

For updates on the the *Sunset Rising* series you can visit my website and sign up for my newsletter.

smmceachern.com

Photo by G.R. Martin

S.M. McEachern (also known as Susan) has had first hand experience in international affairs and policies through her career in international development and resource management, as well as being the wife of a military officer. She attributes Elizabeth Mann Borgese—daughter of Nobel prize winner, Thomas Mann—as one of the greatest influences on her view of world politics. Susan had the privilege to work and study under Mann Borgese, an author, teacher, political activist for world peace, and Nobel nominee. The Sunset Rising series combines Susan's knowledge of politics and resource management with her love for action, adventure and romance.

Made in the USA
Las Vegas, NV
10 February 2022